Double Wedding Ring

Double Wedding Ring

by

Patricia Wendorf

HAMISH HAMILTON

London

HAMISH HAMILTON LTD
Published by the Penguin Group
27 Wrights Lane, London w8 5tz, England
Viking Penguin Inc., 40 West 23rd Street, New York, New York 10010, USA
Penguin Books Australia Ltd, Ringwood, Victoria, Australia
Penguin Books Canada Ltd, 2801 John Street, Markham, Ontario, Canada l3r 1b4
Penguin Books (NZ) Ltd, 182–190 Wairau Road, Auckland 10, New Zealand

Penguin Books Ltd, Registered Offices: Harmondsworth, Middlesex, England

First published in Great Britain by Hamish Hamilton Ltd 1989

Filmset in Monophoto Bembo
Printed in Great Britain by Richard Clay Ltd, Bungay, Suffolk

A CIP catalogue record for this book is available from the British Library

ISBN 0-241-127424

Contents

Dedication

In the years of depression in Victorian England more than two million British men and women sailed from Liverpool Docks to the land they called the New World.

They have been called by historians 'the invisible immigrants who merged easily into the landscape'. They were the quiet pioneers who brought to America their particular qualities of steadfastness and honour.

The legacy to the country of their adoption has rarely been recorded or evaluated.

This book is dedicated to them.

Acknowledgements

I am deeply indebted to all my American cousins for their interest, enthusiasm, and great help in the preparation of this book.

My especial gratitude is owed to:

Esther Salter Watson
Edith Vickery of Suamico
Patricia and Donald Salter
Margaret Gillingham Dubinski
Rhoda Salter Woodstock
Esther Salter Roberts

PART ONE

Chapter One

The snow had come with the first light, sifting from a yellow sky; he watched it drift and gather in the corners of the windows, heard a shift in the great beams of the kitchen, felt a tremor beneath his feet as the old house braced itself to face the storm. He prowled through the rooms, stroking the thick lintels of the doorways, seeking reassurance from old oak and polished elm. It seemed to William, who was sensitive to the vagaries of stonework and timber, that in times of stress the very fabric of the house took on his own unease.

The announcement, made at breakfast that morning, of his intention to remarry, had been received without comment by all his children, save Susanna. It was the foster-child, the orphaned niece, taken in as a baby and reared as his own daughter, who had dared to say:

'And what about us? This Mrs Dening has three daughters of her own. When you marry her – why, there'll be nine females in your household. Have you considered that, Uncle?'

His progression through the house brought William to stand at last beside an upper window. From distant fields his older sons, James and Mark, were bringing home the sheep and cattle before the weather worsened. Down below, in the yard, his youngest son, William, made fast the shed doors, and ensured that all implements and waggons were safe within the barn. From the kitchen came the clatter of dishes, as his last child, Ann, prepared the usual Sunday repast of bread and cold meats.

The nature of the storm seemed to change and deepen. Already, at noon, the daylight was fading. The path that led down to the house was steep and winding, bordered by tall trees and falling away at its edges into dark coombes. Even as he watched, four slight figures appeared on the pathway. Footfalls which had been shallow on their way up to church were ice-filled now, and treacherous, obliging them to cling together. Elizabeth walked with an arm tight about the waist of her sister, Joan. Susanna and Rhoda, arms linked and skirts hoisted to clear the powdery whiteness, trod cautiously behind them.

They came into the house bringing with them a flurry of snow and cold air. He heard the stamping of their caked boots, imagined the shaking out of cloaks, their swift gathering about the inglenook fire. He lingered beside the upper window, admired its proportions, the thickness of its broad sill, and took vague comfort from it.

The Tithing of Dommett lay within the Parish of Buckland St Mary and under the north ridge of the Blackdown Hills. It was an isolated hamlet, said to be a favourite haunt of fairies and hob-goblins.

William Greypaull had come to Dommett as a young man, barely twenty years old, newly married and soon to be a father. The house called Patchwood, built of golden stone with a pillared entrance and mullioned windows, had at first seemed too large for his and Sarah's occupation. In his marriage-lines William had been described as a Wheelwright, the occupation of his father that of Yeoman Farmer. He had been conscious even then of the curious spread of fortune that marked his ancient family. A titled ancestor who once served at King Henry's Court had been a poet of distinction. The architect who built several local churches had been another kind of craftsman; and then there was always the solitary rogue-male thrown up by each God-fearing generation. William thought his own blood kinship lay closest to that of the architect forbear; wood was his passion, sanding and polishing, going with the grain, working with his hands, building for eternity.

He and Sarah had done their best to carry on the name of Greypaull. She had died, leaving him an inheritance of three sons and five daughters, all of them healthy and strong save Ann, who had been blinded in an accident in childhood. Sarah

4

had been the sweet love of his youth and he had mourned her for three years and a day. But he was not by nature a celibate man, and the widow of his choice was a comely woman who would bring land and money with her. He took for granted his children's acceptance that he would, one day, remarry. He had made no secret of his growing regard for Mrs Grace Dening.

The meal of cold meats and bread had been consumed in silence. It was Ann, unhampered by vision, and keenly aware of the least of constraints within her family, who said at last:

'Something's wrong here! I can feel it.'

Rhoda said: 'There's nothing wrong, dear. We got frozen to the bone up in church this morning.' She laid down her knife and fork and gazed meaningfully towards Susanna. 'The light of day is nearly gone. 'Tis your turn and mine to do the milking and feeding. Best we get started.'

Their church-going dresses were exchanged for older garments, hessian aprons tied about their waists, and thick black shawls hugged about their shoulders. Susanna assembled wooden pails and forked hay from the loft, while Rhoda wiped udders with a cloth wrung out in warm water. They worked with the economy of effort that comes from practice. They still used the tiny elmwood milking-stools made for them by Father when they were small girls. Rhoda picked up the stool that had the letter R branded on it; she sat down beside the cow, and pressed her forehead into the warm flank.

'You spoke up well this morning.'

Susanna smiled. 'Easier for me. I'm a niece, not a daughter.'

'It won't make any difference. The first Banns are to be called next Sunday.'

Susanna said: 'We don't have to bide beneath the same roof as the Denings.' She paused. 'I shall be twenty-five years old on next January eighth. That's when I come into the money left me by my parents. I have a plan, Rhoda, but I can't manage by myself. I shall need to have you with me.'

A lull in the storm brought back familiar sounds: the rhythmic swish of milk against the pail's side; the rustle of straw beneath the cow's hooves. Rhoda thought of all those times when she,

5

four years younger than Susanna, had followed faithfully this beloved cousin. The affinity between them extended into the smallest of matters. Even now, the movements of fingers ceased on the selfsame instant; the fair head was raised towards the dark one, and grey eyes gazed into green.

'So tell me,' she said gently, 'tell me 'bout your plan.'

The scandal, said William, would kill him. The shame would destroy his very life's work. Whatever would Parson Soames have to say about it? (William had hoped, secretly, to fill the shoes of Parish Clerk, in the death of the present incumbent.) Then there was the Family! He had sought but could not find a single precedence among the Greypaulls for a departure so outrageous as that just proposed by Susanna and Rhoda. Tears filled his eyes. He gazed at them across the dusty dimness of the parlour. He blew his nose on a snow-white handkerchief. He asked with a break in his voice, how this would look to the people of the Parish? What was more, how ever could he explain to dear Mrs Dening the mass exodus of his daughters from their father's house on the eve of his marriage to that lady? The compliance of Rhoda with Susanna's plan he took for granted. It had ever been so between the cousins. That Joan, who was sensible and practical, should fall in with such a scheme was beyond his comprehension. The inclusion by the three of Elizabeth, who was barely seventeen years old, was, said William a matter of criminal folly, and not to be thought of. The Lord had seen fit to try him sorely in the past few years. There had been the blindness of little Ann, and the death of his poor Sarah! William blew his nose again, hunched his shoulders, and summoned visibly all the power of his usually mellifluous voice.

'Grocers!' he bellowed. 'There has never been a single grocer in the family down the generations; no unmarried female Grey-paull has ever thought to leave her father's rooftree. You have no experience of business matters. What sort of living do you hope to make from the selling of a farthing's worth of bulls'-eyes, a poke of sugar, a knob of blue, a half-ounce of tea?'

'Old Mr Rowsell,' Rhoda pointed out, 'has made a good enough living to retire to a tidy little cottage out in Bishopswood. The shop has been allowed to run down. We thought to bring in fresh stock, to take on new lines. People need not be so dependent then on pedlars and hawkers.'

Her tone grew eager.

'We've taken a look at the living quarters; only from the outside, of course. We reckon there must be at least three bedrooms. There's a big living room behind the shop, and a scullery and dairy. Us c'ud keep our own milch-cow and a pig and a few hens. Oh t'would be so lovely, Father!'

The proper speech approved by William tended to desert her in times of high excitement. She went on in a more careful style.

'We should keep strict accounts. Every farthing would have to be a matter of record.'

Rhoda paused.

'Like we've all been saying, that seems such a shame that we four maidens can't ever put to use the good education what cost you so much money. All that reading and writing, all the reckoning, adding and subtracting! All gone to waste and never used.'

William said: 'You would be unchaperoned. Four young females prey to any evil, with no man to aid you!'

'We can chaperone each other,' said Joan, 'or perhaps,' she offered slyly, 'you could spare James or Mark, or young William to stay with us?'

'Never! I need my sons at Patchwood!'

The tears came back into William's eyes. 'I never dreamed that my girls would want to leave me . . .'

It was Susanna who went towards him, who linked her arm in his and laid her fair head on his shoulder.

'I'm sorry for the shock, Uncle. Mrs Dening is a good woman and she'll make you a fine wife. But just you think about it. She'll be bringing her three daughters with her. There'll be nine women in your household. Patchwood is a big house, but with all the goodwill in the world, there's bound to be friction.' She stroked his hand and gazed up into his face. 'We want you to be happy in your new life, and we shan't be all that far away. The shop is right beside the church, and you're always up there on some business or other. We shall,' she said firmly, 'need all the advice and help you can give us. It'll seem to outsiders as if 'tis really your shop – and so it will be if you'll only give your blessing to us.'

William sighed. 'I shall have to pray about it. Words will have to be said with Parson Soames. Without his good offices we can do nothing. I shall also need to speak to Mrs Dening on this subject. I can't have her taking offence at this stage of our courtship.'

The lease of the grocer's shop in Buckland St Mary was assigned to Susanna Greypaull on March 21, 1850. She was to be accompanied in the venture by her cousins Rhoda and Joan. Should the business prove successful, their sister Elizabeth might be allowed to join them later.

It was decided by William that Susanna should be the head of the household, responsible for all matters of business, the pricing of stock and the moral welfare of the others. Joan, he said, was to have the care of livestock. Her tasks would be to milk the cow, feed the chickens, cultivate the vegetable garden.

To Rhoda he gave a Ledger. Profit and Loss was to be recorded, and figures submitted to him, monthly. They were, he reminded them, speculating with capital left to Susanna by her dear departed parents. For the sake of their memory it behoved them to use that money wisely.

★

The Grocery. Buckland St Mary. County of Somerset.
April 1, 1850.

Father gives to me this Ledger of loose-leaf pages, covered with green leather and having a clasp I may lock with a little brass key. I am to keep note of all Transacshuns and show them to Father. He does not trust us. Paper is costly and I must

8

write without blots. If rekords are spoiled because of my own fault I must buy extra leaves at my own expense. Am already reckless with my inheritance and using up paper for my own pleashur. Must remember to unhook this bit of private notes what is made only for my own eyes – the temptashun of the blank page being too much for me – before showing my book-keeping to Father.

We go from Dommett on a Monday morning. The snow lies deep and the waggon gets stuck in a steep place with all our goods on it. James and Mark urje the horses on, while young William pushes from the rear with the help of we three maidens. It is good to have our brothers with us. Elizabeth and Ann shed tears on our departure.

Father allows us to take our pine bedsteads, carved by his own hand when we was infants. Likewise our linen bedding, wool blankets and feather mattresses, with clothes-robes and dressing-tables. He finds for us one hardwood table (damaged), four chairs, and a bureau for to keep safe all bills and things private. For the kitchen he gives a much scratched oak dresser, three cups, three plates, several forks with bent prongs, and knives too blunt to cut butter. It looks like a poor start to our adventure, but Father gives way in the very minute of our leaving, cannot hold his grudge against us, and piles up the waggon with his own hands. He strips the parlour of things treasured by our mother. Now we have lamps, ornaments and cushions. I don't know what the Widow Dening will have to say about all this, but as the New Wife she will doubtless bring her own stuff with her to Patchwood (not to menshun her three daughters).

Young William bides here with us until all made straight. He mends the table, sands and repolishes the dresser, shifts heavy things for us, and sets to rights the outbuildings, what will hold cow and hens. He puts up new shelves in the shop and makes the counter longer.

Our first stock brought up this day by carrier from Taunton and set out upon the new shelves. A very moving moment for we three. Susanna weeps. Joan laughs. I chew the nails on my left-hand fingers, what is my habit in times of high feeling. Oh dear. This first leaf of Father's Ledger quite took up with my private writing, and no list yet made of our *stock*. Shall turn to a fresh page and do my *duty*.

April 1, 1850
Purchased wholesale this day from Merriman's of Taunton

	L	S	D
1 sack of Sugar	1	12	0
1 pound crate of Indian tea		12	0
2 ounces cocoa		1	0
4 ounces coffee		3	6
1 drum of salt		15	0
assorted spices (nutmeg, cinnamon, pepper, ginger, mustard)	1	0	0
5 pounds of candles		4	0
1 sack of rice		3	0
1 sack of washing soda		1	2
1 drum of starch		1	0
12 bags of Blue			3
Half-gallon vinegar		1	2
1 small sack of Lentils		1	3
1 small sack of currants		4	0
A few Sweeties for the children		1	0
8 dozen Soap Bars	3	4	0
Assorted Paper Bags		2	0

From the Miller

	L	S	D
1 sack of coarse-ground Flour		1	2
1 sack of fine flour		1	3

From the Tobacconist

	L	S	D
1 dozen packets tobacco 'Best Bird's Eye'			
1 dozen packets tobacco 'Bishop's Blaze'			
Assorted clay pipes			
1 small box of Cigars, all together		6	0

	L	S	D
Total	£8	14	9

I take up my pen to make my second monthly Ledger entry, but cannot seem to deny myself the wicked pleasure of setting down my own thoughts. This is a day for throwing bonnets over windmills!

We have made a *profit* of £2.1.6¼ on our first month's trading! Joan says people come to gawp at us, then stay to buy. Father not much interested in this acheevment. He now married to Mrs Dening. We are tired but content. All goods sold out and shelves empty. Go down to Taunton last Friday with James and Mark. Ride with them on the cart, pigs netted-fast behind us. Snow still lying up here in the Hills, a bad spring and many sheep lost. All is green in the lowland fields, and we sing as we rattle down the road to Taunton. James comes with me to Merriman's Warehouse. My brother, being used to business matters, tells me what to look for as to qwality and freshness, and not to be fobbed-off with stale goods. Brother Mark also helpful. All signs of pigs cleaned from the cart by him, and fresh straw laid down for the journey home. Our order from Merriman's loaded this time on to our own cart, thus saving the carter's fee, what is *extorshunate*. A day of excitements, this being only my second trip to Taunton in all my twenty years.

Was introduced to friends of my brothers as we left the Market. Shook hands with a Mr George Salter, son of a Dorchester farmer. Mr Salter has a proud look, but black waving hair and a most sensitive face. Cannot seem to see him as a slaughterman, but that is his proffeshun, so says James.

We are a peepshow in the village. The people of the Parish walk for miles just to gape at the Lady Grocers, and have a laugh at our expense. They give us six months, so I hear, before we go bankrupt, and crawling back to Father in Dommett. But that will never happen. Susanna is full of plans, and I keep a keen eye on prices and profits. We all help with the milking and butter making. Joan digs and plants the garden. We have pear and apple trees, and fruit bushes. If, by the end of this month, we are again sold-out, I might see Mr Salter once more in the cattle market.

Our stock renewed and shelves filled. New paper bags hang from a string behind the counter. Father displeased by bought-in paper bags, says they will mop-up all our profits. Susanna reminds him of the old story of a Parish Clerk who was also a grocer, and who used valuable Church Records to wrap up lumps of cheese and bits of bacon. Proper bags, says Susanna, show refinement, and like I pointed out to Father, the cost is added on to the selling price of goods – so nothing lost! Dreamed last night that Mr Salter came into our shop to ask for bootlaces, and I too tongue-tied to confess that we do not stock them.

Now to my Ledger entries.

James and Mark busy with Haysel, so am obliged this time to go down to Taunton with Father. All my pleasure at Merriman's quite spoiled with *him* looking over my shoulder. Bootlaces, he says, will never sell in Buckland St Mary, twine being cheaper and most men wearing laced-up boots only on a Sunday. Order one dozen mixed brown and black pairs anyway!

Do not go into the Cattle Market but keep to Father's orders that I must bide outside the railings. Have some speech with my cousin Philip who is down from Larksleve with his brother Samuel. Philip more than halfway drunk at two of the afternoon. He offers to move into the shop and so protect us three defenceless females. Tell him that I sleep with the coal hammer next to my pillow, and Heaven help any man who dares to breach our door.

Brother William comes up to help with the garden. Visits also from Elizabeth and Ann. Good news from Patchwood. Mrs Dening is turning out to be a wise and kind stepmother to my sisters and brothers, especially to Ann. Not one stick of furniture moved by so much as an inch by Father's wife, her having a keen understanding of Ann's blindness, and leaving each room as it has always been. The three Dening girls said to be agreeable and qwiet.

The June days come in fine and warm. With Father in a good frame of mind, think it is time to mention that we have a sty standing empty, and it is a great pity that we have no weaner pig to fatten up for Christmas. A piglet brought post haste to us by Father.

There is a lilac bush outside our kitchen window. The scent makes me dwell on Mr Salter. I looked for his dark head among the butchers in the market, but no sign.

Now to my Book-Keeping, or I shall need to light the candle.

Business bad thru' the summer, but getting better with the onset of colder weather. Can now allow myself the expense of writing down a few private thoughts on Father's costly paper. Told Susanna no use worrying about lean times, we is bound to have our setbacks. She very sick and weakly in hot and thundery weather, also feels responsible for us, her being the oldest, and the grocery venture all her notion. Different stock, says she, is what we need. With the help of brother Will we make one part of the shop into a Sewing Corner. It looks very nice with bales of flowered material, cones of sewing thread, and packets of pins and needles. The pedlar, who comes to Buckland St Mary but once in a blue moon was most offensive when he found out that we was offering the self-same goods as him – but cheaper! Like I told him, the women of the Parish can choose who they buy from. All our Sewing Aids sold out within the week, and more on order. My Ledger will read well this month, and so please Father.

A big order brought up this day from Merriman's. Purchased many new lines, also two tubs of salt-fish what will be awkward to cost-out. Will they sell best by the pound or at so much per fish?

Thick fog down in Taunton. Persuade James and Mark to take me with them into the Cattle Market, lest I get lost in the great crowds. We meet Mr Salter. The frost is bitter in the streets and the men cannot go to the Inn because they have me with them. We go instead to the Coffee House beside the Praed. They three talk business and so I am free to gaze on Mr Salter.

He looks much younger without his hat. Would say he is no more than four and twenty! He is taller than my brothers. His dark hair waves back from a broad high forehead, and his features are very fine. His eyes are deepset and of a brilliant blue under thick brows. His speech is that of Dorset and funny to my ears.

He speaks to me, and I am tongue-tied. He asks about the shop and James answers for me. They fall to talking about America, but I do not listen. Our weaner pig is almost ready to be slaughtered and brother Mark, altho' a butcher, is not yet proficient in his job!

Will comes up from Patchwood this evening looking sheepish and much troubled. Susanna makes cocoa for him, what is a great treat. We all sit around the kitchen table. Father's wife, says Will, is with child. He thought we ought to know this. My brother sits silent and we know there is more to follow. His face gets very red. He says that he has asked Patience Bale if she will wed, and has been accepted. Will is unsure of Father's feelings in this matter, Patience being a servant in the employ of our Uncle John. We three maidens speak up for her. She has been at Newhouse Farm ever since she was orphaned, and is decent and hardworking. She is also the most comely girl in the Parish! Will takes hope from all we say.

I go with him as far as the front porch. I mention, as if it means little to me, that the pig is ready for slaughter. Perhaps, I say, he and Mark would like to see more of their friend from Dorset? Could not Mr Salter be asked to visit Patchwood, and put-paid to our pig at the same time? Will laughs. Romance, he says, pops up in the strangest of places. Even Father, at his advanced age, is behaving like a lovesick boy! Lay-in plenty of rock-salt, says my brother, and get ready the brine-tub. He is sure that Mr Salter will be willing to oblidge my odd fancy that he alone should kill our porker. Will is not so sure how the pig himself will feel about it!

I warn my sisters that a butcher friend of our brothers will be coming here soon for a certain purpose. Susanna busy with the

14

measuring-out and bagging-up of sugar pays me scant attention. The stricken face of Joan proves what I have long suspected. She has had sole charge of the pig for six months now, and has grown unwisely attached to the creature.

Mr Salter will be soon in Dommett. He is to attend Evening Service with Father and the family, and will spend the night at Patchwood. He will be here in the morning.

The shop, as always, is a joy to behold, and I shall take pleasure in showing it to him. Oh, but the state of our living quarters, and my hair needs to be washed, and my prettiest blouse lies unironed among a heap of laundry. Whatever will he make of us? Will he remember me?

Chapter Two

George Hodder Salter was a young man with a purpose, and the dream in his heart gave colour to his days. Even in sleep some part of his mind still worked on the problem of America and how he might best get there. He had heard, as a child, the legend of the early Salters, those Puritan ancestors who, in the year of 1623, had left their town of Dorchester, England, and taken ship from Plymouth Harbour to sail for America, where they were to form the settlement of New Dorchester, near Boston, Massachusetts. Money for this expedition had been raised by the Dorchester Patriarch, the Reverend John White. It was he who obtained a Charter for the colonists from King Charles I, and he who insisted that the building of a Christian church should be their first task on landing.

George had considered these long-dead Salters. He imagined them as dour and earnest Pilgrims, men who had gone out from Dorchester to break new land and spread their own brand of religion. As the oldest son in a farming family of nine children, George himself had no desire to own land. In view of the perishable nature of meat, wise yeomen always ensured that one son at least was apprenticed to the trade of slaughterer and butcher, and George had been so indentured at the age of twelve years. Now, at the age of twenty-four, he was skilled in his profession, well known about the markets of Somerset and Dorset for his ability to cut up a beast to the best advantage without any waste of bones or hide. Any farmer who employed him was always well in pocket on the transaction. But times were bad in Somerset and Dorset. Low prices in the markets meant a dwindling return for the slaughterer and butcher. And George was ambitious.

In November he walked by the river Frome; he stood on a low bridge and looked down into the silver waters. Yellow leaves drifted from the chestnut trees. Beyond him lay the misty water-meadows. He looked back to where the old town of Dorchester lay golden and hushed on that Sunday morning. George had not, until now, dared to face the degree of his dissatisfaction. He was not a Pilgrim, nor yet a Puritan. He had no desire to build churches and break wild land in the New World. But yet, America called to him across three thousand miles of ocean, and George knew his own worth, was sure in himself that given opportunity he could show a good head for business. He did not intend to sail as a single man, in an emmigrant ship, with a few pounds in his pocket. In the dream George saw himself embarking with a wife at his side, and letters of credit in his pocket of sufficient value to purchase a butcher's business in the State of New York.

He stood by the banks of the Frome and a chill little wind rippled down the waters. The last yellow leaves left the chestnut boughs to drift and fall around his ankles. George was gripped by a sense of urgency. The dream in his heart was no longer sufficient to give colour to his days. All at once he had a strange and bitter sense of time passing him too swiftly. It came to him then that his life would not be a long one; that at the age of twenty-four he had surely lived the half of it already? He shivered and then shrugged away the awful thought. He began to walk back towards High Street, to the church of All Saints where his family were at worship. He turned his thoughts, quite deliberately, towards the Greypaull family, and their recent invitation that he should visit Dommet.

The invitation had surprised him. Mark Greypaull, although not yet a proficient butcher, was more than capable of dealing with the family pig. Their friendship was of the casual kind between young men of equal status.

George had talked the matter over with his father. John Salter had grinned and dropped an eyelid. ''Tis a long ride into Somerset just to kill a pig. I've heard tell that William Greypaull have got a houseful of daughters, and four of 'em of

17

marriageable age! You had better go, boy. But tread careful when you'm up in Dommet. That place have got a funny reputation. Unwary men get bewitched there.'

He left home while it was still dark, taking his father's best black mare, and the case that contained the knives and tools of his profession. He came from Dorchester by way of bridlepaths and back lanes, riding hard when on level ground, moving slowly only when he reached the sharp tilt of the Blackdowns. The silver of hoar frost lay upon fields and hedges. He rode all day, and stayed overnight with a farmer uncle.

In the morning George followed the directions given by Mark Greypaull; he turned left at the Eagle Tavern, rode uphill to a cross-roads, and found the single signpost that pointed downwards into Dommett. He began the abrupt descent beneath whitened trees. Accustomed as he was to the lonely places of his native Dorset, there was a quality in this hidden hamlet that caused the skin on his face to grow taut, and his features anxious. He reined-in the mare, paused on the final descent, took stock of the house and farm known as Patchwood, then looked back towards the village of Buckland St Mary. The silence was unnatural; George was gripped by the fanciful notion that time had no rule here. He sat straight in the saddle, receptive to the significance of the place, convinced for no reason that here in these Blackdown Hills he would find the route that would lead him directly to New York.

★

The Grocery. Buckland St Mary.
January 1851

He comes to us riding horseback. He sits tall in the saddle and mounted on as fine a black mare as I have ever seen. He wears a cap and cloak of heavy green tweed, and carries the long case what holds the knives and tools of his proffeshun.

He bows from the saddle and doffs his cap at me. I stand by the door of the shop and hide my chapped hands beneath my apron. I am speechless as ever in his presence. He does not smile but has the look of a man who is keen to be about his business. I see that his hair has the blue-black sheen of sloes on the elder bushes. The frost has brought fresh colour to his face and his eyes are the bright blue of the winter sky. I close my own eyes against the glory of him, and think that I will forever hold his image. I have a wish to be noticed and remembered but shyness holds me rooted. It is Susanna who comes running to greet him, and offer refreshment.

I bide in the dairy while he is about his gory business. He stands in the doorway to say farewell, and the skimmer trembles in my hand as his long shadow falls across me.

The deed is done, the pig despatched, and we have fresh meat, and hams curing. Joan is puffy-eyed and mopey. Truth to tell, we all of us have small appetite for sausage and pigs-fry, and so send much of it to Father's wife at Patchwood.

A large order brought from Merriman's, which means many Ledger entries. Feel disinclined for this or any other effort. Mr Salter was here but a short time and the only word to pass between us was 'Farewell'. Lingered long this day beside the railings in the Cattle Market, but no sign of him. Think I may have caught a cold.

Spring comes early. It is almost a year since we went into business. There are primroses in the lanes. We are to make a small celebration of our solvent position, and Susanna's twenty-sixth birthday. It will be our first social occashun in our own home. Many relatives are invited. Also Mr Salter. Jacob Priddy, who pays court to Joan with out Father's permisshun, will also sit at our table.

We menshun to Father's wife that we have but three plates and cups, and knives and forks ditto. She sends up all the fine china and bone-handled cutlery that was our Mother's, including a lace-edged tablecloth that is her own gift.

Susanna says that we must *take stock* as do all shopkeepers at this time of year. We count every cotton reel, and weigh up the dry goods to the last ounce. I enter each item on a speshul page in this Ledger for the approval of Father.

Now we *take stock* of our ownselves and our living qwarters. There leaves much to be desired in all departments! With so much work in shop and garden, we have become careless of our appearance. We are in no fit state for company, says Susanna. She orders paint and limewash from the oil-and-colour man. I take three lengths of flowered cotton from the Sewing Corner and make new dresses for us all. Blue for Susanna because of her fair hair. Pink for Joan since it is Jacob's favourite colour. For myself I choose a soft olive green that is the colour of my eyes.

With the help of brother Will we paint and limewash all the rooms. I find a speshul soap down in Taunton that is garunteed to make our hair soft and shiny. When all work is done we rub grease on to our chapped hands and hope that they will heal in time.

It is Sunday evening and our visitors all gone. Father proud of us I think, altho' he does not say much. We set a good table: our own ham and eggs, jams and jellies from our fruit bushes. The house fresh-painted, the garden dug-over, and we three maidens looking spruce and dainty, and not a smear of paint left on any of us!

Father seems happy with his new wife. Their child is due any day now. Elizabeth is paid court to by Robert Vickery from Otterford. Jacob Priddy has asked for Joan's hand in marriage, and Father agreeable.

Mr Salter comes over from Dorchester at Mark's invitation. He has a different look about him when not employed on the business of slaughter. He is so tall and handsome that all other men look ugly beside him. First Banns are already called for Will's and Patience's wedding. With money left him by our mother, and help from Father, Will is to take on Burnt Oak Farm.

He says: 'I suppose you would like it if George Salter got an invitation?'

'Mr Salter,' I tell him, 'is your friend, not mine. You must do as you see fit.'

Will laughs. 'I see you peeping through the Cattle Market railings. It's not the fat cattle that you've got your eye on!'

Brother Will is too clever for his own good.

Susanna goes with us down to Taunton. We place an order with Merriman's, and then seek material for dresses. Will says that we are to wear silk at his wedding. Have orders from Joan to bring her pink for the sake of Jacob. Susanna chooses cream with a tiny pattern of blue flowers. The lilac bush is in bloom outside our kitchen window. The scent as always, brings his face back to my mind. I pick up a length of palest lilac silk and hold it against me. Susanna says it is not my colour. But I buy it anyway!

Will's wedding is but two weeks away and I must sew three dresses. Ply my needle every evening underneath the lilacs and face up at last to my joyus condition.

My heart is qwite lost to Mr George Hodder Salter!

Father's wife delivered of a daughter on the eve of Will's wedding. Infant's name is to be Zillah. Joan looks pretty in her pink. Menshun made by my brother that Mr Salter will be coming up from Dorchester, and stay overnight at Patchwood. Susanna's gown the prettiest I have ever acheeved. The cream and blue setting off her slenderness and ash-fair curls. The past months have seen a change in my cousin. She is full of zest. Does not lean so heavily on me when deciding small matters. The move away from Patchwood has been good for us all. It is like as if Susanna holds a preshus secret. Would think her frame of mind to be much like my own save for the fact that no handsome young man has come into Susanna's life, lest it be Mr Robbins the new Curate, who has taken to calling at the shop at all hours for what must be unnecessary items?

Will and Patience are married. A gathering of Greypaulls such as I have never seen. My aunt and uncle send Patience off with as much expense as if she were their daughter. They are such good people, altho' their firstborn, Philip, indulged and spoiled beyond belief. Poor cousin Eliza oblidged to dance with him altho' she does not like him.

Susanna looks charming in the cream and blue. I dance with Father and my many cousins. I do not dance with Mr Salter.

Mr Salter has eyes only for Susanna!

Time was when Susanna and I could tell each other all our secrets. She still as confiding as ever, but I have only this Ledger and the little gold key which locks it, worn on a thin chain about my neck.

I have been very foolish. Why should he favour me when she is so much prettier? I could have better borne it if my rival were Elizabeth or Joan, but my place must always be to bide behind Susanna, urjing her on, shoring her up against a hard world.

Mr Salter asks Father if he may pay Susanna court, and Father glad to give consent. Letters now pass weekly between Dorchester and Buckland St Mary. His visits here not many, due to distance and his work.

It turns out that *I* am the reason for so much of Mr Robbins' shopping, what is a pity. He has a red nose. I do not like him.

We begin this year of 1852.

Susanna is betrothed to Mr Salter on this her twenty-seventh birthday.

Father gives a big party down in Patchwood. The Salter family come out from Dorset. There is much talk about America and the fortunes to be made there.

Elizabeth dances wth Robert Vickery. Joan dances with Jacob. Brother Will and his new wife make a handsome couple. Susanna clings on to the arm of Mr Salter. The Curate is asked to the party for my sake. I dance with him but the once. He has damp hands.

I leave the dancing and go outside to cool my hot face. I stand in the Great Barn and recall the days of our growing-up together. Susanna and me always close. She being ever the one to make the first move into risks and danger, and me standing right behind her. I do not know how I shall bear this separation from her.

My brother Will comes to find me. He lays an arm about my shoulder.

'You are upset,' he says.

'No,' I tell him, 'it is the Curate. He *will* dance wtih me, and I do not like it.'

Will says: ''Tis not poor Robbins that you run from. Ah Rhoda, my heart aches for you. I saw how you felt about George from the very outset.'

'Did he see it too?' I ask qwickly.

Will is silent. 'No,' he says at last. 'No. I think not.'

'Susanna knows nothing,' I cry, 'nor must she ever. She could not talk to me so freely about him, if she suspected –'

'It will not be for long,' says Will. 'The talk is all of New York. George Salter will sail for America and take Susanna with him, just as soon as they are married.'

Spring has come early. There are many green buds on the lilac bush. I set myself to work from early morning to evening. It is the only way. I limewash the pig-sty and help Joan to plant the garden. I stitch new curtains for the parlour windows.

Susanna teases me about Mr Robbins. 'He will,' she says, 'soon be asking Father if he might pay you court.'

'It is too soon to think of that,' say I. 'Why I hardly know him.'

She smiles. 'I hardly knew George, but I was sure that I loved him at our very first meeting.'

I remember that meeting, when he came here to kill the pig.

'What was it,' I ask her, 'that drew you to him?'

'His looks at first, and then the plans he has to go to New York. His whole face lights up when he talks about it. He is daring and fearless. He is a strong man. We shall be all-in-all to one another.'

I walk at sundown towards Patchwood, but halt when I reach the crossroads. My brother Will no longer lives there, and Father's wife is again with child. I come up to the gate that leads into Dommett Wood. My cousin Eliza stands beneath the blackthorn thicket. She is looking for the gypsies but they are not yet come. We are of an age, we went to school together. She is musical and clever. She dares hardly to speak in her mother's presence. We fall to talking of many things.

'I hear,' says Eliza, 'that Susanna is bound for America when she marries Mr Salter.'

'Yes,' say I, 'they are to wed next January, on her birthday.'

'Would you like to be married, Rhoda?'

'Only if it be to the right man.'

Eliza touches the unlucky red hair that curls from underneath her cap. 'I fear that they will put me together with our cousin Philip.'

'You cannot,' I tell her, 'be forced to take a man if you don't want him.'

She gives me her strange look. ''Tis different for you. You have spirit, and you know your mind. You have all that brown and shining hair, and such sweet features.'

'It is not enough,' I cry, 'to have courage and dark hair!'

I am sore tempted to confide in her, but dare not. I walk away lest my hot face and unwise tongue betray me.

On Buckland Hill I meet the gypsies. They are making for their usual pitching-place in Dommett Wood. If I believed in such things, I would beg to have my future told me. But since I do not believe, it would be a waste of money.

Our cousin Walter is the village tailor, but Susanna will have her wedding gown made by me and no one else. She is so set upon it that I cannot refuse her. The dress is of lace-over-silk and the stitching of it very awkward. It is good that I must do this. As I sew, I become resigned to all what has come to pass. I see at last the childishness of my position Mr Salter has given me no sign of interest, right from the beginning. All the dreams of love have been in my own head. I turn my thoughts away from him and towards my cousin. Only now, with the packed trunks standing in the living room, and the tickets bought for the passage to New York, do I realise finally that she is about to leave me. It comes to my mind that my loss of Susanna is greater than my loss of Mr Salter, who was, after all, never mine to begin with. All my love for her is stitched into this gown, and I believe she knows this.

We try on the dress, and she is lovely in it.

She says, in a low voice, 'Come with me, Rhoda, to New York. I fear to go without you.'

'But you will have Mr Salter. You will have your husband.'

Her face is angwished. 'I will be homesick in a foreign country. You and I have never been separated. Oh please say that you will come with me!'

I have never refused her anything in life, but this I cannot do.

'No,' I say gently, 'this is something you must do by your ownself. Mr Salter would not wish my presence on his honeymoon, or later.'

'But he likes you, Rhoda! He often says so. He's fond of you. You must have noticed!'

I feel the heart twist inside me.

'No,' I say, 'I have never noticed.'

I pin the dress here and there, kneeling behind her to hide my face.

'There is the shop,' I remind her. 'How can I leave it? It is our home now. I am needed by Joan and Elizabeth. They rely upon me for the buying and pricing.'

Susanna weeps a little, but she is perswaded.

'Promise me but one thing, Rhoda. If I ever send for you, say that you will come!'

I hesitate.

I say at last: 'I promise.'

They are married on this eighth day of January, 1853.

Tomorrow they travel to Liverpool, where they will embark on the packet-ship *Endeavour*, bound for the City of New York.

Chapter Three

Another bitter winter. Snow lies deep in the coombes, and there is much sickness in the Parish. I grant Credit to many labourers' families. It will not read well in Father's Ledger, but they will die of hunger else.

I take Susanna's place as the Head of the Household. Father allows Elizabeth to leave Patchwood and join us. Of Father's daughters, Ann alone remains in Dommett. I believe it to be all for the best that Ann and Elizabeth are separated. I say as much and earn a sharp look from my sisters.

'Ann had become too dependent on you,' I tell Elizabeth. 'You could not be expected to be her eyes and her companion forever.'

Elizabeth says: 'It is my fawlt that she is blinded. I can never forget that morning in the orchard! We children were throwing the green apples at one another. Whoever would have thought that a blow upon the forehead would take her sight away for good? She was but six years old, and I but eight.'

'You have blamed yourself for too long,' say I. 'Ann bears you no ill-will. She is happy now with Father's wife. She is good with the new baby and with little Zillah.'

Elizabeth ponders my words. 'You are right,' she says at last. 'It is time for me to make my own life. With father's permission, I shall marry Robert Vickery at Christmas.'

We wait for the first letter from New York and it is long in coming. Nothing is the same. I wake each morning with a heavy heart. The loss of Susanna is like a small death. I follow her in spirit thru' every minit of that awful voyage across the Atlantic, and into the dangers of a foreign city.

At last, a letter! They are safe arrived in New York and lodged with a cousin of Mr Salter. They search for a house in a place called Charlotte, and find one straightaway. A butcher's business has been purchased. They are happy with their new home. The house is made all of wood and painted white, with green shutters. Susanna buys furniture while Mr Salter learns the ways of business in the New Country. She sees little of her husband, but is kept occupied with the painting of rooms and the hanging of curtains. We are all in better heart since the letter came.

It is Maytime and the lilac bush is bowed with blossom. I walk in the evening towards Dommett Wood, and glimpse the gypsies. I meet Mr Robbins on the road. He asks permishun to walk with me. We argue over many subjects. He hints that such forwardness in a young woman is not seemly, and comes of my being in business on my own.

A second letter from Susanna. The climate of New York State already hot and sultry, the air full of flying insects, the worst of these being the musqueto, a creature like our gnat, but bigger. The houses, she writes, are built in a funny fashion, the front hall serving also as the parlour. She has matting on her floor and two pretty red-plush sofas, a good mahogany table with matching chairs, and three handsome oil-lamps made of china, with shades of pink glass.

The Minister's wife has called upon her, and Susanna attends church with Mr Salter every Sunday. It is the Episcopalian, which she says is much the same as our own Church of England.

A meeting is held here in Buckland on the fifth day of May in the Lamb and Flag Inn. It is decided that our old church is to be taken down and a new one built in its place. A Notice is pinned-up by Mr Robbins, which promises money for the rebuilding. Of the eighteen promisory signatures of yeomen and farmers, I see that six of them are Greypaulls. Father much pleased at his own foresite in buying oak some years ago, and putting it to soak and season in the ponds behind the school house. Said beams and rafters are now well-seasoned, and Father granted the contract for the carpentering and woodcarving. Father is a good man of business.

It is over a year since they went away. Stocktaking is finished, and my Ledger figures show that our grocery still prospers.

It is as if I am two separate people. There is one Rhoda who wears the grocer's white apron, who measures out tea and sugar, and works out the profit to be had on a full cheese or a side of bacon. But Susanna's latest letter is always in my apron pocket. When the shop is shut I write letters to Charlotte, Monroe County. I let my thoughts go out across the seas to that little white house with the green shutters, where my cousin waits for her first child to be born. I know that house so well. She has noted for me every vase and curtain, how the kitchen door is hard to close; and the many plum and cherry trees that blossom in her garden. The climate does not suit her. She cannot take food in the sultry steamy weather of New York State. She is bad-bitten by the flying insects and dare not venture out in summer. Relief comes only with the winter, and this much colder she says than in Old England. Her child is due to be born in July of this year 1854.

My brother Will and his wife Patience have a little daughter name of Alice. My sister Elizabeth is soon to be wed to Robert Vickery, and go to live in Otterford with him.

An anckshus time, with no letters coming from Charlotte, New York. My distractshun noticed by Mr Robbins. He way-lays me on the road when I walk in the evenings, at a time when I would sooner be by my ownself. The nights are drawing in. The gypsies are making ready to leave Dommett Wood and move closer in to Taunton. I talk with my cousin Eliza underneath the blackthorns. She is sad to see the gypsies go.

A letter at last! Susanna delivered of a son on July twelfth of this year, 1854. His name to be John William for both his grand-fathers. My cousin says little of her own health or that of the baby, save that she is homesick and could wish to have her own kin around her at this time.

Elizabeth, now married to Robert Vickery, has gone to Otterford with him. There is much work for Joan and I to do, alone.

No private thoughts put down for many a long day! Joan and I kept on the run from daybreak till bedtime. The shop does good business. Think we must employ a girl to help us.

Father has a saw-pit dug and puts up a workshed in the Glebe Field. Our brother William works with him. The first part of our old church is taken down, what is said to be a dangerus thing, and likely to arouse the Devil and bring bad luck on them what do it!

I dream in the night about Charlotte, New York, and awake with such a crying and moaning that Joan is roused from sleep and displeased with me. In the dream I find the little white-painted house made all of wood, and standing among plum and cherry blossom. The green shutters are all closed. I go in at the back of the house and the kitchen door sticks fast, just as Susanna mentions. The rooms are all dark. I move thru' them looking for my cousin but she is not there. I find an empty cradle draped with muslin. I open a shutter in the parlour and see the pretty red sofas, and the china lamps with the pink glass funnels. There is thick dust everywhere, what is not like Susanna! I am so afraid that it causes me to wake and cry out.

Even as I pen this entry, a letter comes from New York. It is dated June twenty-sixth, 1855 and has been many weeks under-way. Susanna is again with child. Little John sits up unaided and has six teeth. He is fair-haired and grey-eyed and the living image of his mother. My cousin sounds happy. Her days are filled with caring for her family, and working for her church. It is the most cheerful letter she has ever written. Her second child will be born in November, in the cooler weather.

My dream was all a foolishness that came from tiredness and worrying about her. Will write back to her at once, and send kisses and hugs for little John's first birthday.

Dreadful news from Charlotte, New York. Cholera is raging in Monroe County. The baby John is dead. He died but two days before his first birthday. Susanna beside herself with grief. Parts of her letter hard to comprehend, the handwriting scrawled and ink run with her tears.

As soon as the shop is closed I go down to Dommett and aqwaint my Father with the sad news; he and I weep together. Poor Susanna, and her so far away from them what love her!

Father says in a fearful voice: 'I am engaged on the taking down of our old church stones.'

I say strongly, because his sorrow is so great: 'That cannot touch Susanna and her family in New York. The Devil has not so much power!'

But in my heart I am sore afraid.

It is November and the leaves are down. Go to Merriman's and place an order. I am poor company for my brother Will. On our return we pass the gypsies on their way into Norton Fitzwarren. They have so many brown and rosy children.

I say to him: 'Susanna must be near her time in Charlotte.'

He shakes up the reins altho' there is no need. He speaks sharply to me.

'You must not fret so, Rhoda. There is no call for it.'

'There is every call! Susanna begged me to go with them, and I would not. She is mad with grief at the death of baby John. I should be at her side at this time. Father is taking down the roof-beams of the old church. He has let loose the Devil upon us.'

Will pulls the horses into a qwiet place. We are in the covered cart because it is raining. The rain drips like tears from the canvas overhang. I would chew at the fingernails of my left hand, but they are already bitten to the qwick.

'You must bide here at home,' says Will. 'There is no other way. You cannot leave the shop now. Joan longs to marry Jacob Priddy, and in any case there is your own feelings to consider.'

I turn my face towards the hedgerow. 'I was mistook,' say I, 'about my feelings for Mr Salter. It meant nothing. He is a good man, but not for me.'

'So there is yet hope for poor Robbins?'

'I did not say that!'

'You will be all alone when Joan weds with Jacob.'

'I will bring Ann up from Patchwood to live with me.'

'And when you have run out of sisters, what then?'

I grow angry. 'Then I will live by my ownself. I will be an old maid, and keep my shop neat and tidy.'

Will turns towards me. 'You were never meant for that.' His gentle voice is my undoing. 'Oh Will!' I cry. 'Whatever will I do? How will this all end?'

We drive on thru' the rain. Will says that news must come qwite soon from New York, and that we must put our trust in our Saviour that all is well with Susanna.

This New Year of 1856 comes in mild and sunny. So smiles the tiger, says Mr Robbins, before he begins to devour his victim. Am surprised at the Curate's turn of phrase and unsettled looks. For myself, I keep busy. Take advantage of the unseasonable weather to work in the garden with Joan. We have a mind to try new lines in the shop. We make a space to hold writing materials. When down in Taunton I buy 1 dozen qwill pens, bottles of ink, and a few pounds of fine sand. I buy one of the new-fangled steel pens, but since I must price it at one shilling to make a profit, I do not expect to sell it.

Word comes at last from Monroe County. Susanna safe delivered of a son, his name to be William Edwin. So the empty cradle of my dream is filled. There is again a baby in the little white house with the green shutters. They are a family once more.

I ponder on the words I had with Will. I do not wish to be an old maid and keep my shop neat and tidy. Joan is to marry Jacob after Harvest Home. Mr Robbins comes into the shop. I smile at him, which puts him in such a confushun that he buys the expensive steel pen. I agree to take tea with his sister and him on this coming Sunday.

A letter from Susanna, what is so sad and homesick that it makes hurtful reading. A second letter from her within days, what is even more distressed. She goes back over all her life with us in Dommett. She writes of things I had forgotten. She makes menshun at the end that the infant Eddie is well and thriving.

I take tea with the Curate and his sister.

I am in grave danger from Mr Robbins. I truly do not know how this has come to pass, but he seems to think that we are about to be betrowthed. 'You have gained,' says he, 'the deep respect and approval of my sister, and she is hard to please.'

This last remark I can well believe!

I am twenty-six years old. It is time I was married. But not to Mr Robbins.

It is Maytime. The gypsies are back in Dommett Wood. One half of our old church is almost taken down and the new building soon to start. Late frost has caught the buds of lilac. There will be little blossom this year.

I am in a state what is betwixt dreaming and waiting, and I know not why. My mind will not latch on to business matters. I make mistakes. I purchase baskets down in Taunton, for sale in our shop. I find out within days that the gypsies' baskets are stronger and cheaper, and so I make no sale. That old understanding, what has been between Susanna and me since we was little girls, grows ever stronger since she went away. I do not need letters to tell me that something is amiss in Charlotte, New York.

The weather turns warm. Joan and I work long hours in the garden. We are as brown as the gypsies. Mr Robbins sees us.

'You would not,' says he, 'have to work like a labouring woman if you would but consent to be my wife.'

'I find no shame in the work of my own hands,' I tell him. I look up from the place where I am kneeling. I smile at him so as not to be offensive but I intend that he shall understand the manner of woman that I am.

I crumble the red earth between my fingers, and let it trickle thru' them. His face has a pained look.

'I am not parlour-bred, sir, like your genteel sister. My name is a great one, and of ancient lineage. But I am also come of farming generations. For you, this soil is but a nuisance what sticks to your clean boots. For me, it is a satisfaction. Without it, I would be but only half a woman.'

He does not understand. He stands over me, tall and thin in his cleric's black, and my heart is full of pity for him. I plant my beans in the narrow trench. When I look up, he is gone.

The autumn days pass slowly. I have a sense of waiting, but for what I do not know. Joan and Jacob plan a Christmas wedding. Soon, I shall be all alone here. No news yet of Susanna.

I close the shop and walk down towards Patchwood, in case a letter shall have come from New York to Father. On my way past Dommett Wood I meet the gypsy girl they call Meridiana. She bars my path, forcing me to halt.

'Your fortune told for a silver sixpence, my lady,' she says in her wheedling voice.

I speak sharply to her. 'I have to work hard and long to make a sixpence. As to my fortune, that rests alone in the hands of our dear Saviour.'

She darts at me, and grabs my wrist.

'You will pay me soon enough when I tells you your good news.' She peers into my palm and her expression changes. She speaks slowly. 'Word will come to your ears from a far place. Tidings what will split your heart clean in two!' She backs away from me.

'Go about your business,' I tell her. 'I am not my cousin Eliza to be tricked by your nonsense!'

She makes me no answer, and her gaze is still upon me as I walk into Dommett.

There is a strange horse tethered in the yard. I find Ann in the kitchen, the baby Arthur in her arms.

'Who visits Father?' I ask her.

'He is from America. He came straight from the ship, bringing letters to Father from Mr Salter.' Ann reaches a hand towards me. 'Ah Rhoda, it is bad news, I know it. I heard Father weeping.'

33

I go in to where the men are seated.

I find Will and James, Mark and Father, and a stranger dressed all in leather with a week's growth of stubbled beard upon his face. He stands up to greet me. He says he is a distant cousin of Mr Salter. That he is on his way to Dorchester having just returned from the goldfields of California. He has called on Mr Salter in New York State and promised to bring letters with all haste, when back in England. He points to the papers on the parlour table. I look into the faces of my Father and brothers, and a great dread fills my heart.

I try to speak cheerfully, as if this is a celebration. 'What news of Susanna and her husband?' I ask.

My Father and brothers say not one word.

I turn to the stranger. 'When were you last with them, sir?'

'I took ship for England on August twenty-first.' He looks towards Father. 'Tell her! Tell her for God's sake!'

I had thought that my Father would upbraid him for the blasphemy, he says instead: 'I cannot tell her.'

'Tell me *what?*'

I snatch at the leaves of paper. I move to the window where the light is better. I see for the first time the flowing script penned by Mr George Salter. I begin to read. I take in a paragraph or two, then I read no further. The four men of my family are weeping. I move back to stand before the stranger. I am like stone, even my voice is cold and hard to my ears.

'What happened?'

He leads me to the settle. We sit down together. His eyes are kind. 'Your cousin died,' he says, 'of grief at the loss of her firstborn son, and of homesickness for England. Doctors were called in by her husband, but there is no cure for sickness of the spirit. She lacked the will to survive. It was all too much for her.'

'You were there at the end, sir?'

He nods. 'She passed peacefully, in sleep.'

'What of her husband?'

'Poor George – he is brokenhearted.'

The man reaches into his jacket pocket, he pulls out a letter.

'This is for you. Read it and ponder upon it. It was not written lightly.'

I push the letter into the pocket of my skirt. I face my Father and brothers.

'*I* will tell my sisters what has come to pass. *I* will break the bad news.'

To the stranger I say thank you for his kindness. I walk into the kitchen. I tell Father's wife and Ann that Susanna is dead. I leave them to comfort one another. I go back to Buckland St Mary and pass the news to Joan. She at once sets out for Otterford, where lives Elizabeth and our oldest sister, Mary. Within hours the news is all around the Parish. My brothers and sisters weep together, and so ease their grief. I remain dry-eyed. For me there is no comfort. I had always feared that Susanna would not keep her grip on life unless I was close beside her. And so it came to pass.

A Memorial Service is held in the part of our church that is still left standing. I close the shop for a whole day and join my family in remembrance. It was less than three years ago that Susanna stood at this same altar in her wedding gown.

My heart is full of doubts. Why should a young woman such as she have been taken from life so unfairly? She had done no wrong. Had never harmed a soul. How could a loving Saviour be so cruel? He took first her child, and then herself! I feel the iron enter into my own heart. As we leave the church I stand for a time beside the heaps of torn-down stone. I feel Father's worried eyes fixed upon me. I am thinking now that it is surely the Devil who has brought this mischief on us.

Mr Robbins comes to see me. I send him away with bitter words. We have the sympathy of all the Parish. People speak kindly of Susanna what is a help to my sisters and brothers, and an easement for Father's sorrow. For me, there is no easement. The agony bides with me. Altho' I was the younger, I had always kept her safe, stood at her shoulder, ready to shore her up against disaster. When she needed me the most I was selling tea and sugar, digging in my garden, and taking tea with the Curate and his sour-faced sister.

There is a hatred grown up in me, and a great anger. People say that I am changed.

I was most happy in my life when I did not know that I was happy. There is no mistaking misery.

Father comes to see me in the evening when the shop is closed.

'This cannot go on,' says he. 'You are like to die of grief as did Susanna, and I cannot face to lose another dear one.'

'You have your new wife and your second family,' I tell him. 'My brothers and sisters have their wives and husbands. Joan is soon to marry Jacob. Ann is happy caring for your younger children.'

He makes me no answer. We look at one another. He says at last in a soft voice: 'What think you to the letter sent to you by Mr Salter?'

'What letter?' But even as I speak I remember the stranger, and the letter pushed into the pocket of my skirt. I look down at the black dress, worn always since that awful day.

'It must be still in the pocket of my blue skirt,' I tell Father.

'Then you must fetch it when I am gone from here. Read it in private and with great care. It is an important letter. It concerns your future.'

He lays a hand upon my shoulder. 'You are stunned with grief. It is natural. She was your favourite, always. But life must go on. There are those in the world who have a need of you, Rhoda.'

The letter is bound by an outer cover. My name is written on it in a strong script. I break the seal and unfold the single page. He begins 'Dear Miss Greypaull.' I lay the page down and can read no further. I remember his face, the sweep of dark hair, his bright blue eyes, and proud mouth. His voice was deep, his speech that of Dorset, and funny to my ears. I hear it now as I start to read his letter. His words are few and very clear, and still I cannot seem to find a meaning in them.

There is a motherless babe here in Charlotte, New York. Little Eddie is all that is left to me of my dear Susanna. He is cared for by a wet-nurse, and is at present in the house of the Episcopalian Minister and his wife. I see little of him. I must work many hours in every day, in order to gain a toehold in this new country. I am alone, Miss Greypaull, and heartsore. My hearth and home are cheerless, and my son without a mother. What I am about to ask may not be to your liking, and I shall understand that, but I beg you to come to New York and take over my household, and the care of my child. I have no wish to compromise you, or set you in an embarrassing situation. I should therefore arrange that we would be married straightway on your arrival here. Such marriage to be but a civil contract between us.

It is a lot to ask, and your heart and mind may be already settled elsewhere. Eddie will be weaned soon, and then other arrangements must be made for his safety and well-being.

I have written to your father on this matter, and I beg you to talk it over with him. Meanwhile, I remain

Your faithful servant,
George Hodder Salter.

The date is November. Susanna's child must be already a year old. Since the sad news came from New York I have given not one single thought to that little one and his condition. I lay aside Mr Salter's letter. I fall to thinking about my Father's second family at Patchwood. The baby Arthur has just seen his own first birthday. I have paid scant notice to Ann's chatter of him. Now I try to call to mind her mention of his progress. He has taken his first steps, speaks a word or two. He has eight teeth. He is a little person, and much like Father.

The hard place in my chest grows painful. I have wept not one tear yet for my sister's passing. I lay my head across the table. I am took by such a storm of weeping. How could I, because of my own grief, have qwite forgotten the sad plight of Susanna's baby!

To leave Buckland St Mary, to go among strangers, to live in a far land, is a hard prospect. I have never travelled further than

Taunton town. I know naught of the wide world save what I have read in books.

I have a need to be busy. I spring clean the shop altho' it is November. I find myself arranging the shelves as I would wish them to be seen by a prospectif buyer of my business. My hands move ahead of my mind and heart, to do those things that must be done before my departure for New York.

The Parish is afire with gossip. Even the gypsies know what has come to pass. The rain has held them fast this year in Dommett Wood, the wheels of their waggons sunk in mud above the axles. I walk down to Patchwood on the first fine Sunday afternoon. As I pass the woods there is a great cursing and noise as the gypsies drag their homes free from the wet ground. I stand for a moment and watch. Their life is hard, yet they do not shrink from it.

I am spied by the young one they call Meridiana.

'You owe me silver!' says she.

'I owe you nothing.'

She grows angry. 'I foretold that word would come to you from a far place. Tidings what 'ud split your heart clean in two.'

'It is none of your business.'

She looks at me with her great black eyes, and I am afeared tho' I will not show it. She holds her head to one side, and her earrings jangle. She says in her knowing voice: 'They be saying roundabouts that Miss Rhoda Greypaull is a saint to leave her family and business and go to a wild shore to bring up her dead cousin's baby!'

'I am no saint. It is my duty. Anyone would do it.'

'Methinks,' she says softly, 'that your heart *is* split clean in two. You grieve for the lost one — but 'tis more than duty what draws you towards the great ship. Your heart have already been in that far land this many-a-year.'

I turn upon her. 'Get away from me!' I cry.

She is not at all put out by my temper. She wags her head from side to side and the black hair moves across her shoulders. I see that she is beautiful in her wild way, and I wish that I had only half her good looks.

'Ah, dordi!' says she, ''tis a bad thing when a woman is too proud to call a spade by his proper name.'

She smiles and bobs a curtsy to me, but in a mocking manner.

'I wish 'ee luck, my lady, never mind your mean ways to a poor gypsy maiden!' Her face is full of craft. She nods, and the golden earrings sound like music.

'You's'll need my luck,' she whispers, 'for 'tis a risky thing when a woman holds back from the truth of her own heart.'

I meet Father on my way down to Dommett. He is bound for the saw-pit in the Glebe field. Even on a Sunday he is drawn back to gaze upon our pulled-down church. We walk together, it is easier to talk so.

He says, 'Your mind is made up, then?'

'What choice have I, Father? Susanna's child has need of a mother. I am the last unmarried daughter in the family, save Ann who is blinded.'

'George will be good to you.' Father hesitates. 'He will respect your feelings, he has said so in his letters to me. He knows that if you come it will only be from duty, and for Susanna's memory.'

We stand together by the saw-pit. I see the great hammer beams that are to hold up our new church roof. We go into the shed, and Father has started already on his carving of the pew ends. They are very fine, and I am sad that I will never see the finished church. I breathe in the smells of wood shavings and horse glue. I gaze at Father and see him as if for the last time. He is clever in many ways, a skilled carver of wood, and sharp in his brain as a Conveyencer of Land. He runs a hand across the carved pew. He smooths the grain as if it were a live thing. He says, 'I would not wish you to make this great sacrifice, Rhoda, if it should be done only to please me. I know that you and Mr Robbins have been sweet with one another . . .'

'I have not been sweet with Mr Robbins! Truth to tell, I do not much like him!'

Father is surprised. 'But I had understood that there was talk of a betrowthal?'

39

'Not by me! All the planning was on his side. We are not suited to one another.'

Father looks directly at me.

'Then it will not break your heart to leave Buckland St Mary and marry George Hodder Salter?'

Sawdust lies thick on the floor. I make patterns in it with the pointed toe of my black boot, just as I used to do in childhood when caught between lies and truth.

I say, 'No, Father. It will not break my heart to marry Mr Salter.'

Altho' we are a family still in mourning, Joan has married Jacob. Their plans had long been settled, and a farm made ready for them to move into. My shop is as good as sold. I am to leave it on the eleventh day of January. My dowry has been agreed by Father. A letter has been sent by him to New York accepting Mr Salter's offer of marriage to me.

The days are cold and dry, with blue skies and hard frost. Now that the die is cast I am full of impatience to be gone. I look at everything and know it to be for the last time. I shall never return to Buckland St Mary.

Brother Will stays with me, since I am alone now that Joan is married. He speaks of a longing to go to America. He says that our sister Elizabeth and her husband Robert have the self same longing. Give us five years, says Will, and the whole first family will have emigrated, and Father left alone in Dommett save for his second family. It seems that our brother Mark is also planning to take ship for New York. I would sooner that *he* stayed in Dommett.

They all come to see me in these last days, and it is hard to say goodbye to some of them. I part with extra regret from my cousin Eliza, she now betrothed to our cousin Philip. But as she says, no other farmer's son have offered for her, and the match with Philip already settled by their two fathers. We promise to write to one another.

Eliza asks, 'How do you feel about being a second wife?'

'I have not thought about it,' say I. 'Susanna's child is in sore need of a mother, and I am best fitted to do the job.'

Eliza is to be married on the first day of May, in the New Year of 1857.

A passage has been booked for me on the same packet-ship, *Endeavour*. I am, says Father, to have a Stateroom all to myself, what sounds very grand. It is arranged that I shall go by stage-coach to Liverpool. My brother James will travel with me. I kneel down with Father among my trunks and boxes, and we pray together for a blessing on my journey and the reason for it.

I hand over to him the keys of the shop, and the leaves of this Ledger what refer to Accounts. I beg for the green leather covers, and the little gold key what will keep my thoughts private. I confess to Father that I have oftimes used his Ledger for a Journal.

'Take it,' says he, 'take it and keep it for a rekord of your life in the New World with Mr Salter.'

Tomorrow, James will take me with my luggage to the stage-coach station in High Street Taunton. I shall go, for the last time, down the little winding lanes and steep hills of my birthplace. These are the final words I shall write before leaving England. It seems but yesterday that Mr Salter first came to Buckland St Mary, riding from Dorchester on his father's black mare. It was a coming what changed many lives, and there are things that I must know about him before my mind rests easy. But questions such as mine are best asked face-to-face. I shall be in New York within the month. I shall not give thought to Mr Salter until such time as I am in his household.

My sister Elizabeth and her husband Robert are also to take ship for America with their small son. They are bound for a place called Wisconsin. Father will have me travel with them, but no cabin to be had. So I must go by my ownself.

Much travelling and sad goodbyes what are better put from my mind. I now find myself abord the packet-ship *Endeavour*. It is the third day of our voyage and we begin to feel the full swell of the Atlantic ocean. Am seated in the Saloon on a wooden settle, and kept safe in this position by a bench table what stands direct before it, and bolted to the floor. The motion of the ship disagreeable, the weather fine but very cold. My living qwarters more cramped than the sty of our pig in Buckland St Mary, and much more evil-smelling.

There are five steerage and six cabin passengers on bord, so says our Captain Trentham. This is an American vessel, the speech of crew and Captain being slow and drawn-out, but all men are gallant in their manner towards me. Have seen nothing yet of the other ten who borded ship with me in Liverpool, they being laid low already with the sea-sickness. We seem not to make much headway. Enqwired of a sailor what is the name of the land to be seen on our left-hand side. Am told it is the coast of Ireland.

Have vowed once more not to think of Mr Salter before I step on to American soil – and I will not. Have a cabin all to myself what is a blessing. This Stateroom, so-called is not much bigger than a fair-sized coffin. There is a low cupboard with a wash bowl set in it, and a tall cupboard for my clothes. The bed is a piece of hempen sacking stretched and nailed on to battens and braced in the middle. What with the smell of bilge-water, and the noises from overhead, sound sleep is a thing of the past. Have unpacked all my thick crocheted shawls and wrap myself in them from head to toe; only in this manner is it possible to doze.

Am advised by a steward to go back to my cabin since a bad storm is coming.

Twelve days out from England. My hand so weak as to hardly hold the pen. Storms and gales for eight days, the ship rolled about like a cork. What with sea sickness, bitter cold, and being qwite alone for the first time ever, I almost lost my composure. Could only pray that the dear Lord would spare me for whatever awaits in the New World. Am much bruised about my person due to pitching from side to side in that dreadful cabin. Today we are becalmed and make no progress. I ask the steward what is our situation. He says we are blown off-course.

I take my first walk on the deck this forenoon. Am still weak

42

but clearheaded. 'Ah ma'am,' says the Captain, 'I see that you have found your sea legs. Has your stomach settled?' Scarcely know where to look or how to answer, the state of a lady's legs and stomach no fit subject for a strange man. But he is a sailor and American. Have already noted much familiarity by the crew what is all good natured, but of a sort never seen in England.

Fifteen days out from England. I sight land this forenoon. Am surprised at the strength of my agitashun. Knowing nothing of sailing matters, I am afeared that this is already New York – and it is *too soon*! Betwixt England and America, and alone upon the high seas, I feel myself to be still safe. In this ship of creaking timbers and flapping sail, naught can touch or distress me. I enqwire of a sailor what is our position. We are, says he, sailing off the coast of Newfoundland, and amongst the shoals and banks of those waters. It seems there is danger in our situashun. We are in such shallow seas that many soundings must be taken. Once clear of the banks we still find ourselves threatened by icebergs, the size and like of which I had never dreamed on. I spend much time on the foredeck gazing at these wonders. Am told by Captain Trentham that it is safer in my cabin. Do not heed him!

The weather closes in. It begins to snow. I find a sheltered place on deck and sit there, well-shawled and cloaked against the cold. The Captain begs me to 'go below'.

'No, sir,' I tell him, 'I am country born and bred. I cannot bear to be so hard-confined.'

It is not altogether true. The snow has brought me to mind of a winter's morning in Buckland St Mary, and we four maidens walking downhill into Dommett. I remember Susanna, her ash-fair hair looking almost white against the hood of her blue cloak. I see her halt and stand apart in the whirling whiteness.

'I intend to leave Father's rooftree,' says she. 'I mean to set up my own household. If any one of you is of a mind to come with me – then you is more than welcome. Otherwise, I shall go from Dommett by my ownself.'

'But,' say I, 'wherever will you go, maid, and what will you do?' I pause. 'You'll never manage by your ownself. You'll need to have me with you. If we go from Father's house, then we must to together.'

And here I am, on the foredeck of the same packet-ship *Endeavour*, sailing the same waters, gazing upon the same sights as did my dear Susanna but three short years ago, and she then in the company of Mr George Hodder Salter. I am indeed one step behind her. But only when it is too late.

The snow falls thicker. My black cloak turns white. I lose all feeling in my toes and fingers. There is a desolashun on my spirit. I go to my cabin caring little if I live or die.

Twenty days out from England, and we are sailing in bright sunshine. Two more days of such weather says Captain Trentham and we shall be in New York harbour.

Find all my skirt bands very loose about the waist. I must have lost weight, altho' the food on bord is good, a cow and pigs and several sorts of fowl being kept in steerage, and bread and biscuits of finest American flour baked fresh every day.

Twenty-two days out from England. Becalmed in thick fog. Am told we are in the Nantucket shoals, but am still none the wiser. Many sailors are aloft on the look-out for land. A wind springs up, our sails fill, the mist clears and there comes a great shout from above of 'Land ho!' My fellow passengers crowd the foredeck also looking pale and thin. 'Thanks be to God!' they tell each other. 'We are safe arrived!' they cry.

I stand alone and gaze upon the shore that is called Long Island. We are, I am told, still some fourteen miles from the harbour of New York City and shall be there tomorrow.

It is America. I am come to the place where my dear Susanna trod before me. I am keeping my promise.

PART TWO

Chapter Four

Whenever George Hodder Salter remembered England it was always to recall one certain hour in one particular season. In the time before sleep came, while drowsy thoughts wandered through his mind, he would stand once more on the low bridge that spanned the Frome, see ancient Dorchester lying hushed and golden on a Sunday morning. He would watch the yellow leaves drifts from the chestnut trees; smell the autumn sweetness of the water-meadows. George saw himself, still youthful and solemn in his Sunday black; twenty-four years old and never travelled further than Lyme Regis and Taunton. He hardly recognised the young man he had once been; could only marvel at the ease with which resolves are formed. The decision, made that morning by the silver Frome, to emigrate to the New World, had altered his own life and claimed the lives of others. Four years on, wise with hindsight, heavy with guilt, and lonelier than he had ever been, he would fall at last into heavy, dreamless sleep.

The moment of waking was the time he most dreaded: those first seconds of consciousness while his cloudy mind still believed that Susanna lay beside him, that he need only reach out a hand to touch her ash-fair hair spread out across the pillow. More than five months had passed since that day in August when they had laid her to rest in the little cemetery beside the Genessee river. George believed his demeanor had been, and was still, dignified in the face of this disaster. He rose punctually each morning, washed and shaved in the icy kitchen, put on a clean shirt and collar because these were the things a man did to show that he truly had the courage and strength of mind attributed to him by other people. It was said of George in this place called

Charlotte that he had come well through his sore afflictions. There had been the loss of little John his first-born son, only days before the child's first birthday. The ensuing months had brought him another son, but the birth of the new child had seemed only to deepen Susanna's melancholy. It had not occurred to him that she might die of sorrow. His own hold on life was strong and certain. He had not understood, still could not understand how she had slipped so easily away. He never spoke of these feelings, and his silence was respected by those around him and seen as yet another proof of his stoicism.

George alone knew the terror that possessed him in those hours when he was forced to be by himself. To his associates in business he was, as ever, the shrewd man of affairs. His ability to judge a situation, to take advantage of all it offered, remained unimpaired. Men recognised the capacity for hardness in him, the propensity for ruthlessness so necessary in this new, exciting land, where independence of spirit carried as much respect as the ownership of great wealth.

On the eve of his journey to New York, George assembled the trunks that still bore English labels. He stood before the closet that had been Susanna's, opened the doors with a violent gesture, grabbed an armful of dresses and tried, with head averted, to thrust them unfolded into the open trunk. The scent of lavender filled the room. He gazed down on a blur of sprigged cottons and dark velvets, on the blues and greys and creams that she had favoured. He lifted the garments and began to fold each one and lay it carefully into the trunk. He worked steadily and for a long time, until every smallest item that had been Susanna's was out of sight. He closed the trunks and locked them, and carried them up to the attic.

He came back to the bedroom, to the empty cupboards, the bare-topped dressing table; the scent of lavender alone remained to remind him of her. He opened a window, looked out on to a white night, in which a sickle moon lit from above the black branches of the cherry and plum trees. He thought briefly about Rhoda who must at this moment be approaching the shores of Long Island. He leaned his head against the icy casement and knew a moment of pure terror. He closed the window with great care as if the slightest sound on his part might shatter something precious. He turned back to gaze at the stripped room. The scent of lavender was not quite gone.

★

I had thought the village of Charlotte to stand but a mile or so from the City of New York, but such is the size of this land, so great the space between one place and another, that I am doomed to another three days and nights of overland travel; and in the charge of a man who shows no wish for my company or conversation.

I pen these lines in the comfort and privacy of my cabin, aboard the paddle-wheel steamer *Tecumseh*, and so begins the rekord of my life in the New World.

I come ashore on to a cobbled waterfront they call The Battery. I stand for a moment, looking seawards to the ship that has carried me from England. My fellow passengers are claimed by relatives and friends. I wait alone beside my trunks and boxes. The wind cuts like a knife and sets my bonnet-ribbons flying. I am afeared that I may have been abandoned; I look about me, and there he is in a sheltered corner of the jetty. I know him by his great height, and the green tweed of the cloak that he has worn in Buckland St Mary.

He makes no move towards me, so I seek him out. I hold out my hand and ask:

'Mr Salter?'

He growls in his deep voice: 'Miss Greypaull – you are so thin – I would scarce of known you.'

It is not his reason for hanging back and we both know it.

'You and I are much changed,' I tell him, 'since that day we first met in the Taunton Cattle Market.'

When he speaks again his tone is offhand. He points to a low stone building just beyond the quay. 'Here is Castle Clinton. 'Tis the Emmigration Depot. All foreigners must pass through it on arrival. You will need to have ready your credentials . . .'

'I have them, Mr Salter.'

I take papers from my bag and push them at him.

'Here is the letter from you what offers me marriage. Here is a letter of Credit from my father, for to pay you my Dowry money. There is another Note of Credit made out in my own name. I have private means. I shall not be any burden to you.'

I look to the porter who is loading my bags on to a handcart. I follow him to the Emmigrant shed. I say across my shoulder, 'I have been responsible for my ownself these many-a-years, Mr Salter. I see no call to change things now.'

The paddle-wheel steamer *Tecumseh* is a fine sight: she is painted overall in white, with her tall chimney stacks picked out in red. Her decks and holds are crammed with chicken coops and milk churns, with waggon wheels and ploughs. The last bales of merchandise are man-handled from what is called The Levee. Bells clang and whistles blow as we pull away from the slips. Mr Salter is at my side. He explains that the *Tecumseh* is capable of carrying six hundred passengers. That it is a boat both fast and up-to-date, as are *all things* in this land of opportunity. The river Hudson, he says, is navigable for a stretch of one hundred and fifty-five miles. On reaching Albany we are to transfer to the steamboat *Vermilion*, and so continue our journey by way of the Erie Canal.

'I only hope,' say I, 'that those baggage-handlers will be careful of my large crate. It holds a child's rocking-chair, carved in England by my Father's hand.' I think he will surely make mention of the baby, Eddie, but he says nothing.

As we come into the main stream of the Hudson river, the city of New York grows small against the morning sky.

He says, 'A fine sight, eh, Miss Greypaull?'

I look back to the clustered buildings. 'Fine enough I daresay for them as likes a fast life. I take poor heed of cities, Mr Salter. I have seen finer church spires in Taunton Town – and so have you!'

He guides me towards a stairway and down to a large saloon, carpeted in blue and lit by chandeliers. We are served with plates of sweet-cured ham and fried eggs, with a dish of hot buckwheat pancakes soaked in butter. The food is as good as I have ever tasted, but I have little appetite for it. His head is bent towards his plate, and I am able to study him unawares from beneath my bonnet brim.

Four years in America have changed George Hodder Salter. There are lines of pain about his mouth and eyes, hollows beneath the high bones of cheek and temple. He looks much older than his twenty-nine years. The mourning-suit of black serge hangs loosely from a frame that carries little flesh. His thinness serves only to show up his great height. A single white lock streaks the blackness of his hair. It is the most telling sign of all to mark his recent bereavements.

Pity for him wells up in me. I lay down my knife and fork, and my hand makes a move towards his hand. In that moment I might have found some words that would bind us together in our common sorrow, but his gaze does not meet mine, and so the impulse passes.

He has not spoken one word to me from which I might take comfort. He has not thanked me for the voyage of three thousand miles across dangerous ocean. He has not said that he is glad to see me. The name of Susanna has not been uttered by either of us.

We move from the saloon to a glass-covered observation platform, and sit down on facing leather-covered benches. The shared meal has not eased the awkwardness between us. I see how he turns with relief to a great range of rocks that appear around a bend in the river. They are known, he tells me, as the Palisadoes, and extend for a full twenty miles. All around us the American voices are raised in awe and admiration at this freak of Nature. I stand up and move away to the opposite side of the craft. He follows to stand one pace behind me. On this bank of the Hudson lies a pleasant land, with little hills and fields under cultivation. There are farmsteads with houses built of timber, wide barns and meadows where sheep will surely graze in springtime. Hope lifts my voice.

'This land is in good heart. See how well the trees stand. See how prosperous the farms look!'

51

He speaks without interest.

'They say the soil hereabouts needs only to be turned over once to bring forth bumper crops.'

'So how many acres do *you* have under plough in the village of Charlotte?'

'I own no land! I am not a farmer. I was raised on a farm and that was drudgery enough. I am a man of business, a butcher and slaughterer . . .'

'But you were bred to the soil! Why, I was certain that after four years in this country you would have marked out a square of it to call your own.'

'My "square" as you call it is a butcher's shop. I have a good yard and outbuildings, and plan to extend my premises when the cold weather eases. There is no other butcher on the Charlotte waterfront, so the franchise is all mine. Already I have brought one brother out from England to work with me. I shall soon have a need of extra hands.'

I gaze up into his face, and read anger in his features.

He says: 'But you are a shopkeeper too! You've been a grocer these many-a-years. I heard tell that you are an excellent Ledger-keeper. As to myself, well I have no head for figures. You will have no time, Miss Greypaull, to spare for farming notions. The state of my books will keep you occupied.'

I turn away from the patchwork fields and clapboard farm-steads. I return to the leather bench and face towards the Pali-sadoes. Crated in my luggage is the elmwood milking-stool, carved so long ago by Father. I remember Mr Robbins, the Buckland curate; the words I spoke to him that day when I knelt by the bean-trench. 'For you,' I have said, 'this soil is but a nuisance what sticks to your clean boots. For me, it is a satisfaction. Without it, I would be but half a woman.' The curate had not understood me and I felt pity for him. On George Salter I turn a face that is hot with anger.

'Keeping shop,' I cry, 'was never my own plan! I followed where my cousin led me, and I was glad to do so – but in my blood and bones I am a farmer. Susanna was a shopkeeper born, as are Elizabeth and Joan.'

52

I strike the bench with my clenched fist. 'I shall buy for myself a few fertile acres. I shall bear the full weight; it need be no charge on you or your brothers!'

His face grows so white that I am fearful for him. I have spoken Susanna's name and he is not yet ready for it.

When he speaks it is in such a quiet voice that puts terror in me. 'I think you have forgotten your purpose in coming here. There is a baby in Charlotte who will die without a mother. There is a house that has long lacked a woman's hand.' He swallows painfully as if the words stick in his throat. 'I was told,' he says, 'I was told that you once made a promise. That you would gladly come here if you were needed.'

He turns his face away towards the river bank, but I have seen the tears stand in his eyes.

Some women have a sweet way with men that makes the handling of them easy. I have no such sweetness. I cannot flirt or cajole, I cannot smile to get my own way. It is this lack what has kept me single while my sisters married, but I *will* be valued for what I am. If he cannot recognise my worth then the loss shall be on his side!

In the privacy of this superior cabin I have been able to bathe and change my clothing. I have taken down my hair and brushed it. The looking-glass on the wall has no good news for me. I am grown thin and sickly-looking from the bad voyage out from England and my grief for Susanna. He is in the same sad state, yet there is no common ground between us. He must surely know how much I loved her; what agony I feel in the making of this journey. Once again I am treading in my cousin's footsteps; walking in her ways, answering her call. He has made sure that I comprehend my posishun in *his* life. I am to be but a mother to Susanna's child, and the keeper of her household. For my self, I may have no little ambishuns. *I will not weep*. I need my ill-temper to carry me to Charlotte. It is my only defence against him.

The transfer from Hudson river to Erie canal has been made in darkness. I find myself in yet another *well-appointed cabin*. The superior worth of all things *American* is not allowed to escape my notice. Mr Salter is bound that I shall admit the grandness of all things in his adopted country.

From the upper decks comes the noise of men's voices raised first in anger, and then laughter. These river-boats are filled with rogues, card-sharps and gamblers, dressed in checked-suits and brown boots. As to the whereabouts of Mr Salter I have no knowledge. The sound of the paddle-wheels turning helps to ease my mind. I see now that my resolve to give no thought to George Hodder Salter, until he and I came face-to-face, was, to say the least of it, unwise.

We are come to Rochester! I sit on an upper deck while Mr Salter attends to the transfer of my luggage from steamboat to stagecoach. They say that this has been a mild winter, that it is not usual to find the waterways open so early in the year. For myself, I have never met cold of such a low degree; my fingers will hardly hold the pen.

Rochester looks to be a pleasant and prosperous town. I see many churches and large shops, what stand on broad streets lined with trees. There is a bustle of industry about these people. The stagecoaches gather at the river basin. They are said to leave frequently for all parts. Our stage, says Mr Salter, is the *Western Mail*. I see it clearly from this window. It is broader and more cumbersome than our English stages; carries nine inside, and one hardy soul upon top beside the driver. Have remarked to Mr Salter that the American vehicle has a dangerus and unwieldy aspect.

He explains that the road from Rochester to Charlotte is for the most part little more than an Indian trail. That on such a rugged and dangerous path, weight and strength of the stage-coach is necessary, if the way is to be made in safety.

Six weeks gone from England.

I scarce know how and where I should begin. Will set my confusion down on paper so that I may know what I am thinking.

54

The way between Rochester and Charlotte lies over rutted trails and through forests of tall pine. By three of the afternoon the daylight has almost worn away. The air grows even colder, and I shiver in spite of the footwarmers and fur rugs supplied to us in Rochester. Now is the time for the leather window curtains of the coach to be drawn and buckled down, but even as Mr Salter rises to perform this task he is well nigh overbalanced by the sudden violent motion of the stage. He sits down and holds hard with both hands to the seat edge. He commands that I shall do likewise.

'What is it?' I cry.

'We are come,' says he, 'to a corduroy road. I should have given you fair warning.'

I am bound to agree with this. Slow though our progress is, we are now bounced up and down, and thrown from one side to the other. Speech is impossible. When our torment ceases, and we are again on level ground, I say: 'And what may I ask is a corduroy road?'

We are come to a bend in the trail. 'Look back,' he says, 'and you will see it!'

I peer from the window. I see in the fading light that behind us is a road of logs, placed in close contact one with another, a genuine corduroy-rib, to be sure.

I feel a certain satisfaction at the sight.

'Well,' I say, 'I had begun to believe this country superior in all things. But this much I will declare. The state of the roads leaves much to be desired!'

His face takes on that patient look that means he will correct my thinking. 'The soil of these woods has no consistency save that of rotted leaves and vegetable matter. It cannot bear the weight of carriages at any time, least of all in winter. Because of the early thaw it is now no more than bogland.'

He warms to his subject.

'Don't you see the ingenuity of such a road? Here be trees – and here be bogland. The one is felled and laid edge-to-edge, in order to traverse the other!'

He could not look more triumphant had the corduroy road been his sole invention.

'I stand corrected,' say I.

Our fellow-passengers alight at intervals, and disappear into the night. There comes a time when Mr Salter and I are the only passengers within the stage. I take heart from the recent exchange of words between us. Perhaps he will be willing to part with some information of a more particular and personal nature, now that we are alone. The matter is a delicate one. I scarce know how to broach it.

I say, 'What plans have you for my future?'

When he answers, he stares at a point just above my bonnet.

'We are to be married at once, on our arrival in Charlotte. The Minister's house stands some fair way from the village, but fortunately it is on the stage-route.'

'But that is not a good arrangement! I could wish for time to change my dress...' His gaze comes down a notch to meet my own.

'It is all decided. I cannot take you to my house this night without a ring upon your finger. We shall be wed in the Minister's house. There is no more to be said.'

'But what of my luggage?'

'Your boxes will be delivered by the driver of the stage to my place of business. Do not fret so. There is no need.'

I see by the set of his mouth that there is indeed no more to be said upon the subject. I have such a longing to provoke him.

'Very well, Mr Salter. No doubt you know what you are doing. But I will take leave to fret about your child. After all, it is solely on his account that I am come here.'

'He is with the Minister's wife. She has been kind to him, but it could not go on for much longer. It is a mother that he needs.'

When he speaks of the baby his proud look softens. There is a tenderness in his voice. I am reminded of that day in Taunton when I first laid eyes upon him.

Rhoda Greypaull and George Hodder Salter were married on February tenth 1857.

I have written these words on the fly-leaf of my Bible. His ring is on my finger. I have wed with Susanna's husband.

★

I had thought to feel pain at this coming to Susanna's house, but there is a weariness that steals even memory away. Last night we rode to Charlotte over rutted roads and in darkness, and I so bone-tired as to notice nothing of the place, nor yet have a care for the meaning of it. A neighbour had lit the stove, a lamp burned in the window. My boxes awaited on the front porch.

I came into a room that held a narrow bed, a pine-chest and a child's cot. I sat down on the bed for but a moment to unlace my boots. I woke to find daylight; myself fully-clothed, the boots still on my feet.

When there is much to be done, my Father said, turn your hand to the first task that lies beneath it.

The house is cold, a thick layer of ice covers every window. Mr Salter has gone about his butcher's business. His sole fore-thought has been to leave a great stack of cut wood beside the box stove. I make fire and set a pan of water on to boil. A basket stands on the kitchen table. Under a white cloth lies fresh bread, a pat of butter, a jar of preserves and a small cheese. A note reads: *Here is brekfus. Welcom to Charlotte. Yrs. respectful. P. McCaffrey.*

The kindness of P. McCaffery brings me nigh to tears. I see her as a motherly soul in her middle years, and take comfort from it.

A tight rein must be put on all feelings. Tears will not scrub the grease from Mr Salter's kitchen, nor wipe the dust of months from every surface. There is tea in a wooden caddy, sugar in a jar. The water boils and I make a strong brew. The bread is good, the butter sweet. The room grows warm and I linger in it. Small creaks and sharp twangs sound all through this timber dwelling. It is the frozen fabric thawing.

I unpack the box that holds my working dresses, sackcloth aprons and stout boots. I wind my hair into a topknot and tie a kerchief round it. I slip the gold band from my finger and put it in a safe place. In a cupboard there are brooms and buckets, lye soap and beeswax polish. The last hands to touch these things must have been Susanna's.

Since I am to dwell in this place then every cupboard and room must be made familiar. I will not live with shadows. It is not a big house. There is a good dry cellar, a living room and kitchen. Stairs lead up into three small bedrooms. A stepladder brings me up to an attic.

Many pans of scalding water, much soda and soap are needed to clean up the kitchen.

Beneath layers of dust and scattered garments I find the pretty red-plush sofas, the pink-shaded lamps and the drugget matting. The dimity curtains are stripped from the windows, washed and hung to dry on clothes-lines in the attic. Last of all I come to the room that is used by Mr Salter. I drag grey sheets and pillowcases from the unmade bed. I am in a fury at his self-neglect. How could he have borne to live so! In a blanket chest is clean linen and fresh blankets, with sachets of lavender laid between them. I look into the wardrobes but find only men's garb. In the dust on wash-hand stand and dressing-table are marks where small trinkets have once stood. I make up the bed, sweep and polish, and allow myself *no thought* but of the work in hand.

Now the rooms are warm; there is sunshine at the window, the ice is melted. I gaze down on the bare branches of cherry and plum trees. The house stands on rising ground. Deep snow lies all around it. Beyond, lies a long row of bright-painted buildings in odd shapes and sizes; they have the look of a child's toys. Behind them lies a broad fast-flowing river. In the gaps between the buildings are just visible the masts of schooners, the red stacks of steamboats. To the left is a tall narrow structure made of grey stone. It has observation platforms and windows wherein shines a light. I saw many such buildings on my recent travels, but Charlotte lies miles from any ocean. There is a far blueness stretching out beyond the light house. Can this be the Lake Ontario that I heard mentioned?

So must my dear Susanna have once stood and wondered at this window.

Even as I write the daylight starts to fade, and still there are lamps to be cleaned and filled, a meal of some sort to be made from the scant provisions in kitchen and cellar. I will change my dress and braid my hair, and set to air before the fire clean sheets and blankets for the child's cot.

Chapter Five

It was said by those who travelled that no land in all this great continent was as beautiful as the terrain of mountains and lakes that lay to the north of New York City. On his brief excursions into Monroe County, George had found countryside that had a mystic quality; a place where the Gods dwelt. There were fertile plains and eligible farms, vast areas of timber. He had come to America with heart and mind wide open. The dream that had carried him from Dorchester to Charlotte, still sustained him. It coloured his days and gave purpose to his life.

The decision to settle in Charlotte had been made for the wisest of reasons. Letters from his cousin Jacob had described for George the thriving harbour village on the banks of the Genessee river, and told of the blue waters of Lake Ontario that lapped the northern shore. Waterways bring shipping, and ships carry hungry sailors; and provisioning of meat was George Salter's business.

He had come here with Susanna. They had walked through meadows of luxuriant clover, watched the harvesting of Indian corn, and marvelled at the abundance of grain and fruits. In the markets of Rochester he had studied prices; found that beef sold at eight cents the pound, a turkey cost a dollar, and a brace of fat ducks could be had for seventy-five cents.

From the very first day, George had loved the lusty atmosphere of the Charlotte waterfront. He worked to the sound of steamboat whistles, the cries of teamsters as they drove from The Levee, the bleat and low of sheep and cattle as the herds were unloaded from the jammed decks. From the Riverside Saloons came the tinkling music of a honky-tonk piano and the laughter of the bar girls. The stagecoaches halted at the American

Hotel. He had learned to recognise the gamblers who worked the riverboats. He did business with Indians and missionaries, with farmers and ship's captains. Blue-aproned and straw-hatted, the tall and handsome young emmigrant butcher had become a respected man of trade among the shanties and along the boardwalks of Charlotte's steamboat landings.

George had risen early on that Monday morning.

He walked down through fresh snow and in half-light to the shop on River Street. He went in by the front door, lit a lamp and made a swift tour of inspection. He found scrubbed and spotless counters, the knives and cleavers shining and hung on hooks in long rows. There was fresh sawdust on the floor, and in the rear rooms he found clean carcasses drawn and hung in readiness for that day's trading. His assistants were but boys, aspiring butchers just out from Home. One was his younger brother John, the other a Scots youth from Dundee. They had repaid his good treatment of them.

George lit the woodstove in the back room and set a pot of coffee on to boil. When the next-door bakery was open he would send brother John to fetch fresh rolls and butter. He tied on his apron and rolled up his shirt-sleeves; for a moment he stood in the open shop doorway. A keen wind came off Lake Ontario, taking snow clouds with it, and leaving a sky of bitter blue. He thought about the two graves: of Susanna and baby John, lying side by side in the little cemetery at the end of River Street. In a society that was accustomed to early death, his situation was not unusual. Bereavement was an everyday kind of sorrow and a man was expected to be strong. George clenched his fists and bit on his lower lip until the blood came. He considered briefly the girl who lay sleeping in his house on Latta Road: the strange and sharp-tongued Rhoda who, on the long journey north from New York City, had found not one single word of comfort for him. It was only now, when he had already stood beside her and taken vows of marriage, that George asked himself what manner of woman was this who had come out from England to be a mother for his child?

61

He went back that evening to find lamps and stove lit in both living room and kitchen. The warmth of the house wrapped around him so that he paused to enjoy the rare comfort of it; the clean smells of polish and soap.

She turned unsmiling at his entry. She wore a black dress trimmed with grey lace, and over it a white, starched apron. Her hair was neatly braided in the nape of her neck, her face was very pale, the green eyes bruised and puffy as if she had just wept. He stood like a visitor, the tweed cap twisting between his fingers.

He said: 'You've done wonders! You must have worked the day long.'

She did not look directly at him. She stirred the soup and laid a clean cloth on the kitchen table, poured water into a bowl from the steaming kettle and handed him a towel.

'Wash,' she commanded, 'before you sit at table! It's not much of a meal, but the best I can do until tomorrow.'

'I've brought bread and milk . . .'

'I was dependent on Mrs McCaffery for my breakfast.'

He frowned. 'There is no Mrs McCaffery.'

Rhoda pointed at the basket. 'I found that filled with groceries. There was a note pinned to it.'

George said: 'Oh – that'll be old Pete McCaffery. He runs the Riverside Saloon. He's a thoughtful sort of fellow.'

She said: 'Do you tell me that a publican came in here while I slept? That I have eaten food from a house of ill-repute?'

'The Saloon is no worse than the pubs of Taunton. You'll find that the people here are rough and ready, but there's not a man who will do you harm.'

She ladled soup into warmed bowls and sliced the loaf that he had brought. She sat down to face him across the table. He lifted his spoon, and dipped it towards the broth.

'Mr Salter,' she said, 'you will please to say Grace when we sit at table!'

He relinquished the spoon and put his hands together. He said a few awkward words that asked a blessing on the food. They ate in an uneasy silence. He looked towards the cot sheets and blankets that aired before the fire.

'Are you ready for the child? You must tell me when I should collect him.'

'Tonight.' She spoke in a tight voice. 'Bring him here tonight. The sooner the better. There is no sense in waiting.'

'You are well accustomed, I imagine, to the care of babies.'

'No,' she said. 'I had already left home when Father had his second family. I was myself a younger sister. I do not recollect having ever held a small child in my arms.'

The nursery was lit by candle and firelight. It held three cots and five small beds in which slept children of ascending ages.

'It should be possible,' Margaret Murray whispered, 'to lift him without waking. He always has his best sleep early in the evening.'

She laid a hand on Rhoda's forearm.

'You may have a mite of trouble to begin with; he is undersized for a child of fourteen months. He cannot say a single word. He often wakes screaming in the night and is hard to settle. What he needs is the sole attention of one person.'

She waved a hand towards the cots and beds.

'I have seven of my own and an eighth expected – even with two nursery maids . . .'

'You have done well with him,' said Rhoda. 'He has at least survived. And rest assured, from this day on he will have my sole attention.'

They drove back to the house through falling snow, the sleeping child enveloped in a fur rug. George carried him across the threshold and set him down gently on a red–plush sofa. At the click of the front door closing, Eddie came awake. He made no sound but observed them with round and thoughtful eyes. Rhoda knelt beside him and waited for his tears. It would, she thought, be only natural for him to cry out at the sight of a stranger. She became uneasy in the face of that unblinking gaze, and then she recalled that this child had suffered too many changes in his short life; and that those grey translucent eyes were those of Susanna, his mother.

Still kneeling, she laid aside the fur rug and the woollen

shawls. She touched his hair and the clustered black curls sprang back against her fingers. He had his father's fine bones and regular features. She slipped an arm beneath him and lifted him to lie against her shoulder. The little body, inert and yet almost weightless, offered no resistance; he stayed passive in her arms, but the pounding of his heart was like that of a wild bird.

To George, she said: 'Take the warmed sheets and blankets and put them on his cot.'

'You've come home,' she told the child. 'You don't know it, but this is the house where you were born; and never again will you be put among strangers.'

She took him upstairs, and they stood together, she and George, one on either side of the carved-pine cot which stood near Rhoda's narrow bed.

Rhoda lowered Eddie gently and covered him with shawls and blankets; and almost at once the dark-lashed lids came down. As she straightened up, she saw a look in George Salter's eyes that questioned her capacity to love, her knowledge of what mattered in the real world where he lived.

Downstairs, she unpacked the carpet-bag that held Eddie's few possessions. She found a small tin potty, to the use of which she had been assured the little boy was most thoroughly trained. His clothing was a shabby assortment of shrunken wool and yellowed cambric. At the bottom of the bag, neatly folded, she recognised a strip of well-washed silk. The cream stuff had worn thin, the pattern of blue flowers faded. She could not bring herself to touch it; she leaned forward and wrapped both arms about her body, and, in spite of the warmth of the room, she shivered.

The screaming began soon after midnight. Rhoda struggled up from sleep, lit the candle, and peered down into the cot. He lay curled, small fists clenched, his knees drawn up beneath his chin. She pulled back the covers and laid both her hands upon the taut little body. Gradually the screams diminished into a rhythmic sobbing. She found that he was warm and dry; she lifted him and rocked him against her shoulder; he had probably screamed, she thought, as do all very young creatures, without really knowing why. Slowly, the passion of his sobs grew less, but still his cheek was wet against her own.

Abruptly, the bedroom door came open, and the figure of George, tall and thin in a flannel nightshirt that reached down to his ankles, was making long shadows across wall and ceiling.

Rhoda forced her voice to be tranquil. 'He won't stop crying. I don't know what ails him.'

George said: 'Where are the things we brought back from Mrs Murray's?'

'Downstairs. In the carpet-bag.'

He went away, and returned with the strip of flowered silk. He bent over the child and showed it to him. Eddie clutched at the rag, his recognition of it instant. The sobbing ceased and even as they watched the swollen lids came down and he relaxed into sleep.

Rhoda lowered him into the cot. George covered him with blankets.

'That scrap of silk,' she said, 'just see how fast he holds it! What is the meaning of it?'

He turned away, towards the door. 'I need my sleep. I must rise at five and be about my business.'

The care of Eddie was now to become her main preoccupation.

To begin with, inexperience made her nervous and uncertain with him. He gave her no trouble; he was docile, used the potty without tantrums, submitted to her washing and dressing, her brushing of his tangled curls.

As her confidence grew, it was his indifference that disturbed her most. She noticed that he never smiled, made no sound nor any effort to move from the cot or chair where he was placed. His sole sign of recognition was in the way he followed her every movement with that grey, translucent gaze. The vulnerability of his eyes was so achingly reminiscent of Susanna.

Fresh falls of snow had made it impossible for her to leave the house and in fact she had no inclinaton so to do. In these first days in Charlotte, the house was world enough for Rhoda. She hung clean curtains at the windows; scoured cupboards and closets; made lists of her requirements and presented them to George. The child's need of proper clothing was becoming urgent. She ordered flannel and fine serge, woollen yarn that she might knit and crochet. She tried to recall her Father's second family: the tiny Zillah, Charles, and Arthur; and remembered them in smocked tunics worn over long flannel drawers, and in woollen caps and warm cloth jackets.

As she sewed for Susanna's child, she thought of herself sewing for Susanna.

It was late in the evening after they had eaten, when Eddie slept and George sat dozing before the fire, that she said: 'He won't be parted from that piece of rag. It grows dirty and I need to wash it. I've given him other scraps but he throws them down.' She paused. 'I don't want to upset him – I think he is beginning to trust me a little – but if I am to indulge him in this habit, then I must know the reason for it.'

George said, ''Tis nothing much. Just a strip torn from an old gown.' His voice was rough, his face averted.

'No, Mr Salter. There's more to it than that. You see – I recognise that material. I sewed that dress for Susanna. She wore it on the night when you first danced together.'

George leaned forward as if in sudden pain; his hands clenched into fists, his face drained of colour.

'The child is your concern,' he told her. 'This is why I brought you here. No purpose can be served now by talking of what is past and done with.'

'But there will be times when we need to speak of Susanna. She was your wife and Eddie's mother, and the person I loved best in all the world.'

Rhoda moved from her chair and went to stand directly before him.

'Look at me, Mr Salter,' she commanded, 'and recognise what manner of woman I am. I do not have my cousin's sweet ways, nor her patience. I have a need to know and understand things. Only then can I rest easy in my mind.'

His answer came slowly and in a harsh tone. 'The boy was

but eight months old when she died. Weak as she was, she still begged to the very end to hold and cuddle him. The gown had ever been her favourite. Each day she made me dress her in it. The child would lie in her arms and laugh, and touch the pattern of blue flowers. Afterwards – when it was all over – well, he was so little, it hardly seemed likely to me that he could miss her. But he cried. Oh, my dear Lord, how he cried! Nothing pacified him. The wet-nurse came in every day; she had no patience. Often, I found bruises on him. Then, one night, I recalled the gown. I found it and tore a long strip from the hem. I put it in his hands– and I swear to you, he recognised it. He went quiet after that, as if he knew that she had gone forever.' George paused. 'I've asked myself since then how much a young baby can recall of faces and voices. How can I tell even now, how often he still remembers his mother?' He sighed. 'Well after all that, I asked the Minister's wife if she would take him, just until you came from England. There's not much left of that gown. You'll find the remnants in a trunk up in the attic.'

Rhoda saw how the lines in his face had grown deeper. He was a man to whom such speech did not come readily. She also sensed the anger in him, at her probing; his resentment at this intrusion into his private grief.

He stared at her. 'Well – does that satisfy your curiosity? Is it what you must know to ease your mind?'

She felt an anger equal to his own, but something in his face, the whole defeated aspect of him, gave her deeper insight now into how much he had truly suffered; and here she was, in his house, capable and strong, young and healthy. The replacement for Susanna, a mother for Eddie, but never in any way a substitute for her gentle cousin. She moved closer to him. She placed her hand upon his shoulder.

'I'm so sorry, George.'

She had such a yearning to cradle him in her arms, to comfort him with the soft words that she used to Eddie. Alarmed at such a strength of feeling she drew back, suddenly self-conscious, and clasped her hands tight together. She moved towards the door.

He sat, shoulders bowed, his hands loose-clasped between his knees.

Without looking up he said softly.

'Don't go. Bide and talk to me a while. You said that a letter had come from your sister Elizabeth and her husband, Robert. How fares their farm in Wisconsin?'

'They have no farm. They are not yet settled. Robert works for a cousin in a place called Waupaca. My sister is again with child. When she is confined and her strength recovered, then they plan to buy land.'

'Pioneering will be a hard life for Elizabeth. She is an educated woman.'

Rhoda spoke sharply.

'All the women of my family are well-educated, Mr Salter. But that does not mean that we sit on silk cushions and sew fine seams! There is little use in book-learning without a capacity for hard work. We learned to milk cows and tend cattle when we were small girls. Elizabeth can swing a flail, make a cheese, and stack a hayrick! Her husband Robert is from a long line of Buckland farmers. Young though they are, they are both of one mind about this venture. Mark my words, they will prosper in Wisconsin!'

'Land costs money.'

'They have money. Old Mr Vickery made a handsome gift to Robert on his wedding-day. There is also Elizabeth's Dowry money paid by Father. They will have gold enough to make a start.'

Rhoda moved again towards the door. She said quietly: 'Would that my Dowry money was being put to such good use, Mr Salter. I have but little interest in the butchering business. In my heart I am still a farmer.'

Chapter Six

When Elizabeth Vickery smiled people tended to smile with her.

Of all William Greypaull's children it was she in whom the energy and fire had burned early. While Mary and Susanna, Joan and Rhoda, sat at home and waited for the young men of the district to come calling, Elizabeth had made her choice. At eighteen, she kissed Robert Vickery in Dommett Wood; at nineteen she was married to him. One year later she became the mother of a fine son.

Her resemblance to Rhoda was marked. She had the same slim and shapely figure, dark hair, pale skin and green eyes. Like Rhoda, the signs of good breeding showed in her bones; no amount of farm work would ever thicken her long, thin fingers, or bow the upright posture of her head and shoulders. Elizabeth had been a merry girl; she had grown to be a laughing woman, and the perfect partner for the earnest Robert.

The single shadow that had touched her life was one about which she could do nothing. A moment of boisterous play in her father's orchard, the throwing of an apple, and her little sister Ann had been blinded for all time. She would never forget the days and weeks that followed. The delight had gone from her; her plight, in a way was worse than that of Ann, who was at least blameless. It had come only slowly to Elizabeth, that the way to live with guilt is to admit it. She became her sister's eyes, her constant companion, and Ann, in turn, had mastered most of the skills of a sighted person. Guilt had come back with Elizabeth's love for Robert Vickery. But it was Rhoda who had seen and understood, who said: 'You have blamed yourself for too long. You cannot be Ann's eyes and her companion forever.'

69

When Robert talked of America, and the cheap and fertile land that lay fallow in Wisconsin, it was Father who had said: 'Go you with your husband. He is a good and sober man. I have made provison with my own hand for your little sister. Ann will always be secure.'

The first farmers to roll westward to Wisconsin were the native Yankees of New York State and Pennsylvania. They found a territory of open prairie, clovered meadow, broad rivers, and forests of basswood, oak and pine. With land selling at one dollar and twenty-five cents the acre, a man could purchase his full quarter section in the early springtime, work the breaking-plough over virgin prairie, sow his wheat, and in the fall gather in on that first harvest sufficient grain to repay the cost of his farm and its cultivation, and still show a profit.

Later there came the immigrants from Germany, Poland and Norway; strong young men, many of whom brought with them wives and children. By the middle of the century, the good flat prairie lands had been mostly taken up. What remained available for purchase was the thin and sandy soil of hard-to-work hill farms and the timbered territory of the Northwoods, that lay in the region of Green Bay, country that had until recent times been in the full possession of the Memominnee Indians.

The pioneers who first came to the forests of North Wisconsin were by definition a special kind of people: young men and women of determination and purpose. Robert and Elizabeth Vickery and their young son, John, left England in December 1856. Their first winter in Wisconsin had been long and hard. Like Rhoda, they had never seen snow of such a depth, or experienced cold of such low degrees. Their journey from England had been made in the company of a newly-wed couple from Buckland St Mary, Joseph and Louisa Maynard. It was on the farm of Joseph's cousin in Waupaca that they had lodged and worked in the bitter months since their arrival; and here, in this place of deep forests and many lakes they saw for the first time the Indian lodges, the squaws and their papooses, the redskin men on their coloured, fast-trotting ponies. Their second son, Charles, was born in the early spring of 1857. While Elizabeth regained her strength, Robert journeyed north to the Land Offices at Green Bay. Here he was told about the fertile soil and the wonderful timber to be found beside the banks of the Suamico river. He put down his twenty-five dollars and was given the Deed to twenty acres of prime forest. He returned to his wife and two young children in Waupaca and began to make preparations for the long waggon-drive up to Suamico, Brown County.

They started for Green Bay on a morning in early April, their main equipment for the new life contained in the covered waggon, the paired oxen that pulled it, and the hoarded dollars, contributed by both their fathers, that would purchase a sharp axe, a breaking-plough, and the first essential seed-corn.

As they travelled north the transformation of the land became apparent. Warm rains had washed away the last stubborn patches of lying snow. The sun had returned and grass came green. The great stands of basswood, of oak and elm, were coming into first leaf; between the timber openings woodland flowers blossomed, and strange birds sang unfamiliar songs.

They followed the Indian trails, narrow pathways trodden over many years by the red man to a depth of many inches, and hard to negotiate with oxen and waggon. They crossed crude log-bridges that spanned creek and river. The Indians of these parts were friendly. At night they slept undisturbed in the waggon; by day they rode through country of exceptional beauty. To the east they had glimpses of the blue-green waters of Lake Michigan. To the west the great forests of pine rolled clear away to the horizon.

They halted at the trading-post in Green Bay just long enough to ask directions to the settlement of Suamico, buy the breaking-plough, a set of harrows, the seed-corn, and a supply of food that would see them through the next uncertain days. Between Green Bay and Duck Creek they travelled easily upon a good plank road; but from the Creek to Suamico the way again wound over Indian trails and through deep woods.

They came at last to a place of scattered habitations, busy woodmills, and small holdings of land which showed fields already under cultivation. At a place where a bridge crossed over the Suamico river they found a tavern. The landlord, a friendly man, who introduced himself as Albert Sensiba, at once offered to ride with them to identify the markers that confirmed their piece of woodland.

In the year of 1857 on a morning in late April, Robert and Elizabeth Vickery stood together on the first twenty acres of American soil that was all their own. The journey from Buckland St Mary in Somerset, Old England, had been long and hard; but now they had a waggon and two oxen, and the tools that were necessary to tame this beautiful and wild land. Their two small sons already thrived and grew strong in the clear air of Wisconsin. As for themselves – well, they were very young and deep in love.

Robert Vickery had heard while in Waupaca about the kind of immigrant farmer who was bound to fail. He would be a proud man, determined to hoe his own row; one who held on to his native traditions and ways of doing things, even when those ways were not practicable in the country of his adoption. But all the same, his thanks to Albert Sensiba, for the kindness of his directions, were also a dismissal. The tavern-keeper made no move to leave.

He said, 'Your wife is very young. She looks kinda delicate too.'

Robert rarely smiled. The humour was in his voice and words. 'You don't know her, sir. You'll find out on better acquaintance that Elizabeth's looks are very deceptive.'

'That's as maybe! Even so, if you'll pardon the indelicacy – the babe in her arms is only weeks old. Your young lady was but recently confined. Now I don't know what you was planning on doing –?'

'We've been living over in Waupaca,' Robert said stiffly, 'and so I've seen how it goes in this country. First of all you buy

72

your land. Then you fell your timber, and use it to build your house.' His tone became defensive. 'I waited on purpose for the warmer weather, and for her to be strong enough to travel. We shall live in the waggon in the summer months. By winter I shall have a house built.'

Albert Sensiba smiled. 'You're English I guess?'

Robert nodded.

'Well ain't that something! Not too many English folks around here yet. Mostly Polish and Norwegian. Now I've heard about you people, 'specially your farmers. Sober and hard-working, but a mite too stuck-up and independent for their own good.' He grinned. 'Your plans do you credit, son. But we got diff'rent ways of doing things in these wildwoods. Suamico folk help one another. That way, we all get along together. When new settlers come in – why, we all pitch in and do our share.'

Robert said, 'My father is an English yeoman. I was born and bred to the farming way of life. I – we wouldn't want to put our neighbours to any trouble. If we need help, then we are able to pay for it.' He paused, 'I can turn my hand to doing most things.'

'You ever built a log-house, young man?'

'Well – no. But I've seen how it's done.'

'Seeing and doing is two mighty diff'rent things.' He looked towards Elizabeth who walked at the forest-edge, little John beside her. 'Your wife and children need a roof above their heads, and quick too. Living in a waggon ain't no joke, you'll have found that out on your way up here. Now this is how we do things in Brown County. The men hereabouts leave what-ever they happen to be doing, and we all set to work taking out the timber, and trimming it. That's known as a loggin'-bee. Then we have a house-raising. When the roof goes on we have a little celebration. Meanwhile, our womefolk take care of the new lady and her children. There's a room set aside in my tavern for that very purpose.'

He paused at the look of mutiny on Robert's features. 'And don't think it's charity we're offering you! Your turn will come

73

round quick enough, boy, to pay back every single kindness. When the next lot of settlers come riding in, you'll be expected to leave your ploughing and sowing, and do likewise unto others!' He clapped Robert on the shoulder. 'Now you just bring your lady and the little ones down to my tavern, and well before sundown, mind you! You'll stay here with the waggon and oxen. There's no fences to hold them creatures in, so you'll need to watch 'em. I'll put out the word, and by Wednesday we'll have started felling.'

People talked a lot about good times and bad times. To those immigrants who came to America in 1857 it seemed from the moment of their landing that the hard times had set in. In that year a labourer earned only fifty cents for a day's work, where in earlier years he had made one dollar twenty-five. For Robert and Elizabeth Vickery, the first months in the wilderness of these northwoods were to bring equal shares of sorrow and satisfaction.

The price of lumber they were told, had gone so low that it barely covered the costs of felling. The wheat crop no longer held its value. Rumours of war with the South had raised the prices of cotton and tobacco. The same Depression that caused them to leave England, had, it seemed, followed them across the Atlantic ocean. But this was the talk of the few old men who gathered round the fire in Albert Sensiba's tavern. The immigrant farmers, almost to a man, were well below the age of thirty. For Robert, who was only twenty-three, there was no tree he could not fell; no acreage of wilderness he would not tame. More important was the attitude of one immigrant family towards another. In this testing time the natural inhibitions between nationals of different countries were set aside. They were no longer English or German, Polish or Norwegian, but Americans, obliged for survival's sake to get along together.

The population of the northwoods, although growing, was still too low. If the citizens of the settlements were to prosper they would need a greater variety of skills among their people; and safety in isolated places must surely rest in numbers. The arrival of each new pioneering family was greeted with the brand of enthusiasm normally reserved for long-lost brothers and dear friends.

Many men had answered the call of Albert Sensiba. They came to Robert Vickery's land on Wednesday morning, bearing sharpened axes. Introductions were brief. There were the Dagget brothers, Charles and Samuel, John Lucia, Robert Tripp, Chauncey Wilmot and Joseph Ledger; all of whom, with Albert Sensiba, had moved west from Northern New York. There was John Donovan who was Irish, and a red-haired Scotsman named Munro. These men had accomplished much in the four years since their arrival. Robert was told about the blacksmith's shop, the grist-mill, and the cooper's shop owned by Christian Erdman.

They were glad to know that in England the newcomer had been both farmer and woodsman. The clearing of timber from his land, they warned him, would be a wicked business, and slow. Pine-stumps because of their resinous nature, never rotted clean away, but had to be burned and grubbed out, like old decaying teeth. But the land was good!

They worked throughout the daylight hours. A space was cleared on rising ground, and by Thursday noon the first of the logs were ready to be notched, so that they fitted together at the corners. By sundown the walls of a house, twenty feet by ten were in position. A load of roofing shingles had been hauled up from the woodmill. Friday morning saw the raising of that roof, and the final chinking-out with mud of the unavoidable gaps where log did not quite fit snug to log. A few small apertures had been made to let in daylight. A door was set into one corner, and a chimney built of smaller stones. The last refinements to be fitted were a lightning conductor on the roof, and greased-paper across the window openings. By Saturday noon ten weary men stood beside the finished house and shook their new neighbour by the hand.

There is a special brand of kindness found only in people who are lonely. The hospitality of the solitary person will be intense, an expression of deep feeling. The welcome extended to the little Vickery family came also from gratitude: the greatest fear of these first-footers, who had come to live among the tall pines, was that their outstretched hand might be rejected, and the new people turn away to seek some easier location.

Elizabeth came back to Robert on Sunday morning. She gazed at the little house, disbelief fighting admiration.

'All finished,' she said, 'and in only four days?'

'There were eleven of us,' he reminded her. 'They are all such good men.'

He led her through the door, proud as a child, eager to explain the cleverness of the construction. The most important feature was the fire-place; here she would cook, heat-up water, dry sodden clothing in the winter. In the exact middle of the floor stood a wide and solid table. Robert told how, when clearing the ground, a tree stump of extraordinary girth had been found and left in position, and the house built up around it. Sawn level, and topped by three smoothed planks it was he said, better than any shop-bought table.

Elizabeth remembered Dommett Farm, its fine furnishings, the polished mahogany of her father's pedestal dining-table.

She laughed. 'Now that's ingenuity of a very high standard. Something we shall talk about when we're very old people.'

'It's not what you're used to –'

She moved towards him and laid her hand upon his sleeve.

'It's the same for you. Don't look so worried. I can't bear it when you frown.' She pulled him to the doorway. 'Look out there! It's Paradise, a Garden of Eden – all we ever wanted, and every tree and acre of it all our own. There was nothing left for us in England. Never forget that, Robert. There's no turning back for us. Wisconsin is our home.'

He said: 'I'll help you to unload the waggon and get the children settled. Then I must start in felling, even though 'tis the Sabbath day. They tell me that, to get a good crop in the autumn, I must get my Indian corn sowed by the twentieth day of May!'

Chapter Seven

The sun also shone in Charlotte, New York State.

The snow and ice had melted, and Rhoda looked out for the first time on the sharp greens and misty blues of distant hills and mountains. She stood by the Genessee River and watched the brown torrent of its water; she lingered by the clapboard houses that were painted in soft shades of grey and pink and pumpkin-yellow, and she remembered the golden stone of Dommett Farm.

*

Walk out this day, Eddie in my arms, he being weary of the house and ankshus, I think, for to see the great three-masted schooners that lie at present off the river-mouth. (At least he looks at them when I point.)

It is three months to the very minit since I came to Charlotte. Great changes in some directions. None at all in others. The house now spic and span; all arranged to my taste and a pleshur to look upon. Have shaved a fraction from the kitchen door so that it *no longer sticks*. Have taken the small scythe and cut the grass beneath the fruit-trees; dug over a vegetable patch and planted it. Wait every day for some sign of interest from Eddie. He has taken his first steps, eats with a spoon, and does not wake so often in the night. He neither speaks nor smiles. There is no woman here who might advise me. To mention my fears to the Minister's wife would look like a criticism of her care of Eddie. I cannot speak of the child to Mr Salter.

I unpack the tiny rocking-chair made by Father. Sit Eddie in it, and set the chair to rocking. He shows no sign of pleashur, only watches me closely as he always does as if he is afeared that I might go away and leave him. His new garments suit him very well. Today he wears cherry-red. He is a handsome child with his dark curls and grey eyes, and is my sole companion in the days since I came here. I talk to him, hoping that my words might stir him to some speech. I point to Mr Salter and say 'Dadda', but so far nothing.

Have told Mr Salter that our attendance at church must be more regular, now that the weather has improved!

Letters come from my Father. I think often of Buckland St Mary. My cousin Eliza will have wed with our cousin Philip and gone to live with him on Larksleve Farm. My sister Elizabeth and her husband Robert will be, by this time, settled somewhere in Wisconsin. Oh, how we are all scattered!

Find work for myself every evening on the setting to rights of Mr Salter's Account Books, what are in *parlous state*. This work calls for much speech between us, his figuring not easy to read, and many explanashuns needed. We sit together at the table, after supper when the babe is sleeping. George's hand lies close to my hand. His face has that keen and earnest look when he speaks of his business. He is looking better, has gained a little weight, and seems less careworn. As for myself, I have got back all my strength and vigour. There is a shine on my hair and colour in my cheeks. I am not displeased these days with what my mirror shows me.

I ponder often on the words of the gypsy they call Meridiana. ''Tis a bad thing,' she said, 'when a woman is too proud to call a spade by his proper name – 'tis a risky thing when a woman holds back from the truth of her own heart.'

I lie in my bed, wakeful and uneasy. I take stock of what is in my heart and find scant comfort in it. For, truth to tell, altho' I have denied the love I bear towards him, that same heart of mine has been quite lost to George Hodder Salter for all of these many-a-long years.

★

George conceded only slowly that the coming of Rhoda had been a good thing. To begin with he had given her little thought, even less of his attention; she was merely a presence in his house, found most often in his kitchen, her dark hair tied up in a duster, a burlap apron around her narrow waist. Weeks passed, and the rooms had regained their former charm and comfort. He would find her in the evenings, seated close to lamplight, her coiffed head bent to the sewing of some garment for his son; the apron put aside to reveal her slim and comely figure.

They had not settled easily to the sharing of the same roof. It was only her love for the child, the anxiety of her devotion to him, that made it possible for George to tolerate that imperious little lift of the head when she spoke; her knack of making the simplest request sound more like an order; her condemnation of the bachelor habits into which he had slipped.

The winter days warmed into springtime, and with the sunshine there came subtle changes, things he would hardly have noticed in the stress of winter. The scent of lavender that had been so evocative of Susanna had quite gone from the house, and in a perverse way he felt resentful of it. Fresh sachets now hung in the closets, and between the clean linen. Rhoda had brought with her the pot-pourri gathered in her garden at Buckland St Mary; its distinctive perfume being the distillation of oil-of-lilac, made from the bush that grew beside that English kitchen.

Her practicality surprised him. She, like Susanna, had attended a Private School for Young Ladies, had learned music, and embroidery, and the finer points of etiquette. Yet he had seen her take a scythe and wield it skilfully on the long grass beneath the fruit trees; she had dug out a garden, and painted white the picket-fence around the house.

From the doorway of his shop on River Street he would see her walk, the child in her arms, towards the high ground where stood the Lighthouse. He would catch the speculative glances of his brother John, and withdraw again behind the counter. George knew that people watched him; it was the kindly curiosity of a small community towards a stranger that made them speculate on the sort of relationship that might exist between himself and this cousin of his dead wife.

There was an evening in late April when he had walked to the little cemetery beside the Genessee River, and looked down on the twin graves of Susanna and John. George stood for a long time beneath the cedar trees, his mind curiously empty, his heart quiet.

It was as he turned to walk away that the thought of a different face and figure came to taunt him. She would be waiting supper for him, her only sign of anger at his lateness the small force with which his filled plate would be set down before him. Because of her annoyance she would not smile. He had lately found himself envious of Eddie, who was the frequent recipient of her slow sweet smile.

He returned to the house on Latta Road by way of River Street's boarded sidewalks. A stagecoach arrived at the American Hotel, bringing gamblers from Rochester and Buffalo; professional cardsharps who would find easy pickings among the shore-going sailors who came from the schooners at anchor in the Bay. From the Saloon came the sound of the bar girls' laughter; the refrain of an old song picked out on the untuned keys of an ancient piano. George paused and gazed across the halfdoor; through a haze of cigar-smoke he could just make out the familiar faces of most of the property-owning citizens of Charlotte. His sense of isolation deepened. For a moment he was tempted, but he knew that the smell of whisky on his breath would bring on her most severe of frowns; and in any case, it was a remedy he had tried before, and which always failed him.

Her wedding-band still lay in the safe place where she had put it on that first day after her arrival. If George had noticed its absence from her finger he had made no remark upon it. He was not, she thought, an observant man in any respect save that of business.

When any two people live together beneath one roof, there are bound to be tensions. When the couple are male and female,

80

married only in law, then those irritations have a tendency to be explosive.

For the sake of Eddie, who was already of a nervous disposition, Rhoda limited her more obvious signs of displeasure with George to sharp gestures and hard looks. He, on his part, had developed a style of studied indifference towards her that was more insulting than any outright quarrel.

Their only visitor in three months had been his apprentice brother, John, who had lodgings in the village. Rhoda liked the smiling, friendly ways of young John Salter. Her disappointment on discovering that P. McCaffery was the keeper of the Riverside Saloon had been bitter. She had, on her brief walks through Charlotte, received smiles and nods from ladies of quiet and respectable appearance. But the innate reserve that marked Rhoda down as English had held her back from any move that might lead to an acquaintance with them.

Her prolonged isolation had been bearable in the short winter days when snow and freezing temperatures had made a haven of the little house. Her discontent had come with the flowering of the cherry and plum trees. It was on those mornings, when the breezes came balmy and sweet off Lake Ontario, that she thought most about Susanna: imagined her in the cream-and-blue silk gown, sitting under the trees, a baby in her arms. It was, in the evenings that she remembered Dommett Farm: when the breeze from the Lake turned chill, she would sit by the stove's glow and recall the inglenook in her father's kitchen, her sisters and brothers crowded in the high-backed settles, toasting muffins on a long fork.

If her absorbtion in Susanna's child was total, it was not surprising. But to a young woman of Rhoda's passionate and lively nature it was not enough.

The cones that held her sewing-thread came in varying sizes. They were made of polished wood, and hollow. A collection of empty cones had grown with each completed garment. Their use as toys for Eddie had seemed a good idea; Rhoda laid them before him, hoping to draw some sign of animation from him, but the shapes, like all her other offerings, remained untouched and barely noticed. There were times when she was almost persuaded that some sign of intelligence moved far back in those vulnerable grey eyes. She took comfort from his new skills of walking and feeding himself; but he never once smiled or laughed, or showed any hint of animation. If his father George observed this worrying lack, he said nothing on the subject. A dozen times in every day she would take the thin little body in her arms, only to feel him strain away, before he relaxed into his usual passive indifference against her shoulder. She would stroke his cheek and talk to him. All she could offer was her love. She could not bring back his mother.

It was on a wet May evening, when rain lashed the house, that they gathered close to the stove's warmth, looking, thought Rhoda, almost like a family. George read a newspaper, she worked on a strip of crochet; Eddie sat between them on the rag-rug, the wooden cones set down before him.

The first brief laughter was so unexpected as to be almost shocking.

Rhoda's fingers stilled among the bright yarn. The skin on George's fingers contracted to white against the newsprint. The sound came again, and this time there was a secretive note in the delighted chortle, as if it might at some time have been practised, but in private.

They gazed, first at one another, and then downwards. Even as they watched the small hands lifted one cone and fitted it inside another. Eddie smiled, unaware of their observation; he stroked the polished wood, and the gesture, so reminiscent of her father, caught at Rhoda's heart.

He looked up, the enchanting smile beamed first at Rhoda, and then his father. Eddie crashed the cones together, scattering them across the floor in his excitement. He spoke the one word that she had repeated to him more than any other. He held both arms up to George. 'Dadda,' he shouted.

The removal of one anxiety will often leave space into which other fears come crowding. The new normality of Eddie seemed only to deepen the atmosphere of brooding that hung about the white frame house on Latta Road. While the child played his game of fitting cones together, and rocked himself in the tiny elmwood chair, Rhoda, thought about George and the unnatural situation into which she had allowed herself to be persuaded; and wondered if her strength of mind was equal to the bearing of it. Her lifelong habit of directness, her lack of guile, her scorn of sweet ways with men, were now seen as a drawback about which she could do nothing.

She had done the things that she knew best: cleaned his house, cooked his meals, dug and planted his garden and darned his socks. She had brought his sickly child back to full health and spirits, but the satisfaction gained was no longer important to her. She still slept only lightly, even though the screaming bouts of Eddie had altogether ceased.

It was towards the morning, when the first notes of the blue-jay whistled from the plum trees, that she heard muffled sobs. The awful sound of a grown man's weeping, shocked her into stillness. She listened, breath suspended, to the agony of George, but made no move. Inadequacy was not her usual reaction to challenge, but still she hesitated.

Eddie stirred and moaned in sleep. She reached down into the cot, found the silk rag and tucked it underneath his fingers. The thin partition of the bedroom was but a sounding board; and no child, she thought, should ever hear his father's weeping.

She pulled on a wrap, shook the long and heavy hair across her shoulders, and trod softly to the door of the room George had once shared with Susanna. He sat on the edge of the bed, face pressed into a pillow, unaware of her presence beside him. Very gently, she took the pillow from him. He looked up into her face; he spoke her name but once, and it was all that she had wanted. There was, she now discovered, no need for guile and sweet ways. She said nothing, but cradled his head against her breast, stroked his hair, comforted him as she had so often comforted the little boy who was his son.

George put one arm about her, he reached up to touch her face, and then drew her down beside him. He kissed her, tentatively at first, and then with an increasing passion. He released her; he said, 'I believe that I might come to grow fond of you, Rhoda!'

'I lost my heart to you, George, in the minute I first saw you.'

She reached into the pocket of her robe, withdrew the golden wedding-band, and handed it to him. He smiled at its reappearance and for the second time in three months he placed the ring on the third finger of her left hand.

★

July 20, 1857

No writing done for many weeks. I scarce know where to begin. So much to tell. I thought at first that George had turned to me only from loneliness and heartbreak, but each evening on his return he bends to kiss me, even when his brother John is with him. I am so joyus that I think it must be sinful. Am afeared to meet the eye of others lest they see from my face that George and I at last are lovers.

Sometimes I fall to wondering if these days and nights for him are like the old sweet times with Susanna.

For me there are no old times. He is my first and only one.

August 1

I am with child. There is no doubt about it. The weather close and humid, what makes my head ache. Must stay within the house, screens at door and windows, or else get bad-bitten by the flying-insects. I am nauseated in the mornings, am brought quick to tears, what is *not* my habit. George enqwires if I am homesick. He is remembering Susanna, how it was with her at these times. I tell him lies. I say I hardly think of Buckland.

This is a time when I have need of my sisters. Even Father's wife (who has borne seven children) would be a welcome ear for my many fears. I talk to Eddie. He is my shadow. He walks well for his age, but knows only one word, 'Dadda'. We go out in the cool of evening. I take him for the first time to the little cemetery beside the Genessee. On our way back up River

Street we meet George, who is also homeward bound. He picks up the child and hoists him to his shoulder. He smiles to see us.

'And where have you two been roaming?'

I say, 'We have been to Susanna's grave to lay flowers . . .'

George halts in the middle of the boardwalk. In full sight and hearing of the populace he cries:

'I will not have him to the cemetery. He is but a baby. I will not have him weighed with sorrows.'

The blood flies hot to my face. 'Hush,' I says. 'Will you have the whole of Charlotte listen to our private business? It is his mother and brother who lie there. It will be better if he knows this from the very outset . . .'

'*You* are his mother! The only one he will ever know! Now you hear me, Rhoda! It is time to put away the past. He is *my* son, and I say that you will tell him nothing of these matters. I will not have him saddened.'

George looks up at the child seated on his shoulder. There is a fear in his face that I do not comprehend.

He says, in a low voice: 'Life will be short enough for him, and for me.'

He turns from me, and walks ever faster in his anger. His long legs cover the ground with such speed that I am obliged to run, so as not to pass from Eddie's sight. No more is said upon the subject, but in the night Eddie screams and will not be pacified; what he has not done for a long time.

Our difference of the past few days now all forgotten.

George no long calls me Rhoda. Altho' I do not wish it, he says instead 'Mama', when speaking to me.

Eddie learns the new name straightaway. There is nothing I can do about it. The word comes strange in the child's voice. He looks at me with his grey eyes and I see Susanna in him.

John Salter is to leave his lodgings; the landlady, being old, can no longer care for him.

I tell George: 'Better that your brother come to us. He is family. He should not be with foreigners.'

85

'They are not foreigners, but Americans. So shall we all be, when I take up my Citizenship Papers.'

I have a weariness about me at that moment. I am ravelled to my very nerve-ends. It is my condition. I say crossly: 'I am English. So are you. So will be our children. This will always be for me a foreign land. Why! I do not recognise so many of their birds and creatures, their trees and flowers! It is like another language – hickory and locust – loons and whippor-wills!'

George smiles. 'You will learn, Mama.'

'And if I do not choose to?'

His features change. 'I have seen that mistake made once before . . .'

'I go to him and put my arms about him. When we stand together my head scarce reaches to his shoulder. I know his mean-ing.

'I will learn,' say I. 'I will try to love this land if it be what you want. I will be an American if it please you!'

We sit down together on the red-plush sofa. He is so beautiful I can refuse him nothing. We go back to the subject of his brother.

'We shall be hard-pushed for room,' says George. 'This is not a big house.'

I have noticed how easy it is to add rooms on to these wooden houses.

'So fetch the carpenter,' say I. 'I will have the kitchen larger, and we will have a mud-room added for the leaving-in of dirty boots. Above, can be made two extra bedrooms. A hen-coop can be added, and a dozen beehives . . .'

'Hold on!' he cries. 'You will have me bankrupt.'

'Never make your wife the keeper of your Ledgers, if you would hold back on the state of your business! The shop pays well, George. You can afford to spend a little money for our comfort.'

He looks gloomy. 'There is a Depression coming. The farmers are worried. There is some talk of unrest in the South. I have heard mention of Civil War.

'Your brother John needs a home,' I remind him. 'There is word in Father's letters that my brother Mark will come here and bring Ann with him. It would seem that, in your letters to them, you have named an eye-surgeon in Rochester who might cure her blindness.'

He sighs. 'Very well, Mama. I will see the carpenter tomorrow.'

In spite of my aches and pains I have never been so happy.

No letter yet from Elizabeth. I grow concerned.

It is already late September, what is called The Fall by people hereabouts. Do not yet feel easy when using American expreshuns. George says I still use too many home-words. He fears this means that I am homesick, his speech qwite American after only five years spent here.

I had meant to keep a faithful rekord of these months, but weariness lies heavy on me. It is the hot and humid weather. It is all I can do to write to Father, who gets ankshus if no letter from me. He *will* know all about our church. I say it is a tiny wooden place, painted all in white, and having but the one bell. I tell him I have many friends there, what is not altogether true. These are good women. They seek my company, but I am not yet ready for their cups of tea and gossip. I have overheard their conversashuns. The talk is all of money, of births and deaths and weddings, and who is in the family-way. It is just like Buckland St Mary. They have spied my condishun and would call upon me. They are admiring of Eddie, saying how it is a miracle that he has 'come on so fine', after all his sad beginnings. Their talk creeps ever closer to Susanna and I cannot *bear it*.

Mr Joshua Allen the carpenter has done his work. It took but days to nail-on our new rooms. (Would that Father could have seen this!) Now, all our outside timbers must be painted before winter sets in. George is content to have it white again. I say no! I have such a fancy for the pumpkin-yellow shade. He can refuse me nothing these days.

Because of the added rooms, the whole house feels like a new one. It *makes a difference*. Eddie's little tongue is never still. It is like as if the words were in his head already, only waiting for the right time. He walks well, but grows heavy. George says I must not lift him anymore. I go alone to Susanna's grave. It is a mistake. You may have Eddie call me 'Mama', I tell George, but the day must come when he hears the truth. Even now it grieves me to take his baby-kisses, what should have been all for her.

John Salter moves in with us. I have the men shift furniture and beds. John now has the room that first was George's. My child will be born in the brand-new bedroom.

Oh, how much I like this John! He is a merry presence in the house. He sings and whistles the day long. He has a look of George about him, but not so tall and proud. George feels his posishun as the eldest brother. Just you wait, he tells John, until you are in business on your own. Then you will walk and not run. Then you will sigh and not sing. It is hard to find a toe-hold in this new country. George is coming thirty, but already weighted-down with worries. Not everybody pays their bills up. But still, says he, it is better than Taunton Market on a wet day!

October is a sweet month in Charlotte. Feel more like my old self in the cooler weather. We four ride out in the 'buggy' (my newest Yankee word), after church on Sunday. George ankshus to find level roads, what is not easy in this county. He is so careful of me.

Nice to get away from all that lake and river water, and into deep country. The farms roundabouts are a perfect picture, all so neat and tidy. John plays with his nephew. Eddie learns the names of strange birds and trees, and they romp and run about. George and I sit qwiet together. The wind is in the west, and George says: 'Listen, that roaring sound is the Falls of Niagra, a full thirty miles from here, and the wonder of the Western World.'

The farmers are still about their Harvest. The crop is called Indian Corn, what is the very last one to be gathered in. The grain is in many lovely colours, such as I never saw before. They call this time of year the Indian Summer. It will ever be my favourite Season in this country. We come across another farm where fields are newly ploughed. The smell of the fresh-turned earth is like a tonic. I ask George to halt and, as we sit and gaze upon the furrows, I feel the movement of my child for the first time. It is like the stroking of tiny fingers. I say to George: 'Our child lives.'

Worked yesterday in sunshine in my garden. Had mentioned my love of lilac, so George begged a few roots of the blue and white sorts from a customer of his. Planted these by the kitchen door – and now, from one day to the next it is winter. Woke to find snow. Fear the worst for my lilac roots, tho' John says snow is a protecshun.

Find much to do inside the house. Have talked with the midwife (who is a very stout old body name of Sanchez). Was told by her to at once get ready all things needed for my confinement in January. 'Best to be prepared early,' says she. 'You little skinny women usually give birth well before-times.' I set aside the tall chest-of-drawers for to hold the oldest sheets and towels; make a plait of cambric as instructed by Mrs Sanchez, for to pull upon when my time comes. Make four dozen tallow candles.

Look out with Eddie from an upper window; show him the snow falling thick above the Lake. As we watch, I see John Salter come running up from River Street. He waves a paper packet to me. I open the window. He shouts: 'You have a letter, Rhoda. It is from Elizabeth.'

Elizabeth says that her second child is a boy and already aged seven months. They are all healthy and content. She menshuns that Suamico is a good place in which to settle. Robert has built a small house and harvested his first crop. They work side-by-side. She begs a letter of me. I straight way pen many pages, so that she may know what is my life here.

November 18, 1857

It is Eddie's second birthday. Oh, how he is changed in the months since I came here. George says the credit must be mine.

I bake a speshul cake. John brings for Eddie a little wooden horse, and the child will not be parted from it. It must stand by his plate while he eats his supper. He lately learned to call John 'Uncle', what pleases that young man very much.

George late home from business on this of all days. Eddie falls to sleep, and John carries him to bed. I am much afeared. The fur-traders are in town. George has said that they often lie drunk on the boardwalk beside his shop. I light the storm lantern. Fresh snow has fallen, but no wind to speak of. I beg John to go out and seek his brother. John says there is no need. 'Then I will go!' say I. 'My husband may well lie murdered in this wild place!' John will not meet my eye. When I press him further he lets slip that George is to the cemetery, and will be straight home. George comes in, and he is in his dark mood, as he was so often when I first came here. John goes to his bed; he pats my shoulder and kisses my cheek before he goes.

'I say to George: 'Eddie fell to sleep waiting for you.'

He makes me no answer.

'You should not go to the cemetery in darkness,' say I. 'It is dangerous.'

He does not look at me. He says: 'I should never have brought her here. She would still live, and so would her first child, had I only stayed in England.'

'She was happy to come with you. She was never strong in health, but how were you to know that?'

He turns upon me such a face of angwish. 'And what of you? Will you also leave me?'

I go to him, and put my arms about him. I feel the movement of our child. He feels it too. 'No,' I say, 'I will never leave you, George. I am strong enough for both of us.'

He holds me close and kisses me, and I am content. To myself I think: Brave words, Rhoda. Please God that they may be true ones!

December 24, 1857

It is my birthday. I am twenty-seven years old. Letters come from Father and my sisters, what bring me nigh to heartbreak. Oh, how I long for English voices, for the peal of our old church bells on a Sunday in Buckland; to look from a window and see the dark coombes and green hills of the Blackdowns.

My eyes are sore from weeping, and from the whiteness of the snow that will bide with us until April. George brings a fir-tree and we tie it up with red ribbons. Eddie dances for joy. John gives me six handkerchiefs, lace-trimmed. George gives me a pretty gold ring set with rubies and emeralds, what explains last week's journey to the town of Greece, and his secretive looks ever since. It will be the first Christmas that we four have celebrated all together. Shall attend church tomorrow morning no matter if a blizzard!

January 15, 1858

Woke this morning with a backache. Not knowing what to expect, I paid it little heed. George and John went to their business. George returned mid-morning, he knowing more about these matters, and being over-anxshus. He is gone now to fetch the midwife, tho' I told him it is but a backache!

January 30, 1858

My backache the first sign of a long, hard labour, but a beautiful son the result of my travail. George stayed by my side throughout. The midwife very good. Did not need the doctor. George and John take turns at keeping house, there being little business done at present due to river and harbour being fast-frozen.

Eddie comes often to my bedside. He strokes and pats his baby brother and calls him 'Uncle' what is his favourite word, and so sets us all a-laughing. The ladies of the church come calling. Laid-up as I am, there is nothing I can do about it. George is no match for such strong-minded females. He says they all but push him off the stoop, so keen are they to come upstairs and see me. They are all so kind. They bring gifts of

91

crochet, and fine smocking for the baby, and do not miss a single item of our furnishings and fittings. They notice that I have been confined in the *new-built* bedroom. The house is not unfamiliar to any single one of them. Each was here qwite often in Susanna's time, altho' no word is said about it. It makes for an awkwardness on my part. I wish they would stay away.

My son is so beautiful, and the image of his father. He has the fine Salter features, the bright blue eyes, and dark curling hair. Have come downstairs today for the first time, the three weeks of my lying-in being over.

Must take the reins of the household back into my own hands. Must write to my dear sister, Elizabeth, and aqwaint her with my good news.

Chapter Eight

The skills of Robert Vickery were not exceptional in a community of farmers. But among men who were used to assessing character on short acquaintance, he was easily nodded in as a young man of industrious nature; an Englishman who was willing to learn new ways.

To the farm wives who first spoke to Elizabeth, it was apparent that here was a rare gem come among them; an Englishwoman of refinement and superior education. Her smile and ready laughter charmed all who met her, and it was not only the quality of her dress, or the gold-and-ivory cameo brooch pinned at her throat, that had impressed them. They saw the pretty, high-cheekboned face, heard the preciseness of her English speech, the clipped consonants and pure vowels; they spied the leather-bound volumes among her crated luggage, and felt respect.

In a community where money was of little value, and continued existence dependent on a system of barter, Elizabeth Vickery could offer a service that was unique. There were those to whom the writing of letters did not come easily, native Americans who, through poverty, had received little or no education. Then there were the Germans and Norwegians, the families from Denmark and Poland, for whom the language of English was to be spoken only when necessary, and was still impossible to set down on paper. Because of Elizabeth's confinement, the Vickery family had come late in the season to the northwoods. If a first crop was to be planted by the end of May, a logging-bee must be held on this wild twenty-acres. A service for which Mrs Vickery could pay, if she so wished, by the penning of letters for certain of her neighbours.

The undergrowth had needed to be taken out before the big trees could be felled. Robert chopped down bushes and small trees, working by day and moonlight in that month of May, so as to clear the greatest possible acreage before his neighbours came to his assistance. When felling began there was no time to saw trees into logs and save them for winter. The great pines were brought low in windrow-fashion, chopped in straight lines, so that one tree toppled on to the next. At night the trees were burned where they lay, lighting up the landscape, crackling and sparking, and giving off a scent of resin. A careful watch was kept on the new loghouse, in which slept Elizabeth and her two children.

When the land was cleared the stumps remained; the breaking-plough, so Robert was told, would be impossible to use at this stage of cultivation. His instinct was to plough, as had his father and grandfather in Buckland St Mary. He talked the matter over with Elizabeth.

'They say I should use only harrows in this first season. That the plough is hard to wield amongst the tree-stumps.'

'Then you be guided by these men, Robert! You can plough next season. First of all we must get some crops sown. Our English ways don't do in this land!'

Five times he put the harrows to the ground and drove the oxen between the pine stumps. Then he sowed the seed, harrowed it in, and still he was doubtful that such casual treatment would bring forth corn. But the warm moist earth was all that had been claimed in the Land Office in Green Bay. Within days, there were strong shoots of green; within weeks, the crop was knee-high. He bartered his best leather shoes for a sack of seed-potatoes, and pumpkin and squash seeds. By mid-June fifteen acres were put down to corn, and five to potatoes. Between the potato drills he planted his squash and pumpkins, Indian-fashion. Only then did he find time to build a larger privvy, and a shed big enough to house the oxen and the milch-cow he had purchased. He stood with Elizabeth beneath a wild crab-apple tree that had somehow been missed by his axe; the last pink and white blossoms drifted down upon their heads and shoulders. Deep in the woods, in the fragrant twilight, a whippor-will called, and was answered by a screech-owl. He pointed at the stumpy clearing.

'Not much like a farm, eh?'

'Be patient, Robert.'

He said: 'The hardest time is yet to come. Remember winter in Waupaca?'

She linked her arm through his, and shook him, gently. 'We have a roof above our heads, flour in the bin, fish in the river, meat on the hoof. Our children thrive – and God is with us.'

He said: 'The time has come to mark-out what is ours.' He pointed to an opening where a few straight oak trees had been granted to him. 'Tomorrow I'll take them out, cut them into lengths, and split them into quarters. Then I shall build a fence around us.'

For Elizabeth, this first summer in the new land was sweet with discovery in a way that no other season would ever be. Indelible upon her memory was the bank where the wild strawberries grew; the finding of a whippor-will's nest, the chatter of katydids and crickets. There was also the emergence of strengths within herself, both physical and mental. She carried wood and water, wielded saw and axe; learned how to use the shotgun and hit a moving target.

She began also to learn how to be alone with the children, in the long daylight hours when Robert was absent. New settlers had come in to claim their steadings. In that summer came the families of John Cook, David Danes, Peter Baker and his brothers Nelson and David, Isaac Burdeau, and Charles and Pulaski Fraker. Eight log houses needed to be built, eight tracts of forest cleared. Now was the time when Robert would take his place in this community of farmers; when he would show unto others the same kindnesses that had been shown unto him.

It was always in the evenings that certain neighbours walked the rough tracks that lay between one steading and another. People came to Elizabeth with requests for offical letters to be written; to the Land Office in Green Bay, to an Attorney, to the Board of Supervisors of Brown County. Payment was made in proportion to the length and urgency of the letter. A brief note merited a jar of preserves; an involved one could bring a piece of pork, or a pitcher of maple syrup. Then there were the sad little missives: the young wife separated for the first time from parents and sisters; a son writing to his father, for whom she must find the words that would allow him to boast of his ownership of land, while begging the loan of a dollar to buy medicine for his sick wife. It was in this way, that Elizabeth formed friendships that were to last lifelong. With notepaper costing three cents for two sheets, letter-writing was listed as a luxury among a settler's priorities. Three cents would buy a man a good cigar; for a woman it meant a bunch of ribbons or a quarter-pound of coffee.

For the sake of economy, Elizabeth learned to write exeeding small.

Wisconsin in the fall was a time of warm days and cold nights. The sun hung low in the western skies, it dappled the ground beneath the sugar-maples; seemed to set alight the crimson sumac that edged the pathways. There were scents of ripened apples and wild plums; the heavy musk of cut crops and turned earth. At night a red moon lit up the corn-shocks that were Robert Vickery's first harvest. The yield was heavy beyond belief, the quality of grain first-rate. The potato crop had been exceptional, the pumpkins still lay huge and golden on the vine, waiting to be gathered in.

There was a purity in the light of these October days that they had not seen in any other place. It roused in Elizabeth and Robert a sense of reverence. The saying of family prayers, learned in Buckland St Mary, was now to become a daily habit. If God was not with them in Suamico Brown County – then He was nowhere!

They had experienced a winter in Waupaca, and so believed themselves to be prepared. On summer evenings Elizabeth had sewed warmer garments and mended old ones. Robert patched worn boots, and stacked firewood up against the house. Meat had been salted down, potatoes stored; the cow provided milk and butter. The system of barter between neighbours had made good the deficiencies of this one difficult year. When the first snow came, they were not dismayed.

But the winter in Waupaca had been passed with a well-to-do farming family, long established in the region. The cold had not seemed too severe in a frame farmhouse with lined walls, glass fitted at all windows, and a stove in each downstairs room. They had landed in America in mid-January: within ten weeks the snow and ice had melted. Now they were to sample the full length of a winter in the Northwest.

The gales of November came roaring through the trees, seeking every unplugged chink in the loghouse, every gap which had been overlooked in the summer warmth. Elizabeth gathered moss from the forest floor, and, as each crevice made its presence known, she filled it. There were other hardships not so easily overcome. The small predators of the forest would find a way in, and make a meal from any unguarded food supply. Greased paper across the windows was no defence against a blizzard. Robert carried logs down to the mill, had them sawn into planks and made strong window-shutters. Each new crisis demanded its own remedy; but all their ingenuity and skill could not replace the money already spent. The crops had been heavy, there was grain enough to last until harvest time came round again. But self-sufficiency did not extend to a doctor's call, or medicine for a sick child. There were always some items that must be bought-in, and Robert Vickery had neither beast nor corn that he could sell. Their last few cents had been spent in the blacksmith's shop to purchase nails for the fixing of the window-shutters.

The Vickerys had not come to America as poor people came, sailing in an overcrowded, immigrant ship, all their wordly goods tied up in one small bundle. Like Rhoda, they had booked a stateroom on a packet-ship. They had brought money with them, sufficient for a good start; and still they believed that money had been wisely spent.

The harrows had been a necessity. The breaking-plough a

good investment. Without the purchase of a waggon and a pair of oxen, the recently-confined Elizabeth would have travelled up to Green Bay in a convoy of strangers and in great discomfort. The milch-cow was essential if John and baby Charles were to keep in good health. Most settlers, they had found, slept on mattresses filled with corn-husks or straw. Elizabeth's purchase of a fine feather-bed while in Waupaca, might be seen as their single extravagance; but it was done now, and they at least slept easy, without constant scratching.

It was the outlay of a few cents here and there, the small purchases of cutlery, cooking-pots, and earthenware dishes, that had in sinister fashion added up to several dollars. Then there were nails, and shoes for the oxen.

For the first time in their lives, Robert and Elizabeth Vickery knew the lack of the smallest of copper coins to jingle in their pockets.

In England, pride was seen as a virtue. The proud man set his standards high and then maintained them. Robert had only lately come to accept with grace his neighbours' aid. The concept of working for pay in another man's employ was hard to swallow.

'They call it hiring yourself out for labour,' Elizabeth explained. 'It pays fifty cents a day. According to the wives, all their husbands take paid work in the winter.'

Robert's look was mutinous. 'I never came here to be a labourer.'

'You worked for your father.'

'That was different. That was on family land.' He knew that she was right, but still the charade must be played out that would salve his pride. He said reluctantly, 'What kind of paid work?'

'They're taking men on at the woodmills further down the river. Or there's logging at the big camps – but that would take you away from us for weeks at a time – I heard howling in the night – they say that at this time of year wolves come close to the houses; I wouldn't care to be alone here after dark.'

'Nor shall you be! I'll go to the woodmill in the morning and ask about paid work. Meanwhile, we've a deal of sorting still to do. The seeds from the pumpkins must be laid away to dry, and the best of the potatoes saved for next year's seeding, the corn grains likewise.'

The fire of logs gave sufficient light for them to work by; they knelt, one on either side of the great stone fireplace, and sorted seed. The children slept, curled together like puppies in the one wide cot. Close by the fire two pails of ice melted into water; a piece of thawing deer-meat hung from a hook and dripped blood into a pan.

Robert paused and looked to where Elizabeth picked corn for turture sowing, her long and slender fingers moving swiftly among the grain.

He said: 'Are you content?'

She said, surprised: 'Do you have reason to think otherwise? What I said about wolves, about not wanting to be left alone here . . .'

'No,' he interrupted, 'not that. It's just – well, the way we live now. The hardship of it all.' He gestured towards the log walls.

'It's not much like Patchwood, is it?'

At his mention of Patchwood, her shoulders straightened. She rocked back upon her heels and gazed directly at him.

'Why,' she asked, 'do you think I was so anxious to get away from Buckland? Oh, don't look so discomfited! We've never talked about Ann's blindness, have we? I found it hard to watch her, Robert! Many's the time I've wept to see her stumble, knowing it was my fault. I would have given her my own eyes. Every happiness I ever knew was touched with guilt – can you understand that?'

He said: 'You were but a child when it happened. You did not intend it.'

'But I grew up with the result; her blindness was *my* blindness. It was Rhoda who talked to me in the end. But for her I would still live under Greypaull rule.'

'Greypaull rule?' Robert's lips twitched at their corners, he almost grinned. 'Your father is no worse than mine, when it comes to laying down the law. All these old chaps shout and bluster, they usually come round in the finish.'

Elizabeth, to whom laughter came easy, did not smile.

'You're a Vickery,' she said. 'There's no taint on your family; no burden laid upon you.'

'What taint? What burden?' His tone was full of disbelief. 'Why the Greypaulls are one of the first four families in the Parish!'

'Did you ever,' she asked, 'hear the story of our royal blood? Father tells how his ancestors are buried in Westminster Abbey. Some are said to have been imprisoned in the Tower of London; one or two knights among them were beheaded.' She paused. 'In the beginning there were Greys and Paulls. Two separate lines loosely related. Then they began to intermarry, cousin wed to cousin, uncle to niece, aunt to nephew; and always to keep land and money in the family. After a time even the two names were joined together.'

Elizabeth fell silent; she began to lay pumpkin seeds out in long rows on a strip of sacking, placing them precisely, at an equal distance one from another.

Robert watched and waited.

She said, her tone deliberately even: 'My father suffers seizures. Did you know that?'

'What kind of seizures?'

'He falls to the ground. He lies unawares for many hours. When he wakes he remembers nothing save that he has seen bright lights and suffered tricks of eyesight just before his fall.' She looked down at the pumpkin seeds, their deep colour and neat rows. When she spoke again her tone was bitter.

'They call it epilepsy. It passes down in families. Sometimes it goes together with idiocy in children. So much for the blood of kings, eh Robert?'

Robert said: 'But not you, Elizabeth. Not you, and not our children!'

'No. I am well enough. Our boys are bright and healthy.'

'Then what other burden do you carry?'

'It is only when the letters come from home that this mood comes on me; it is like a strong hand reaching out to pull me back to England. James says that Ann is to come to Rhoda in

100

the spring. There is an eye surgeon in Rochester who might cure her blindness. But what if he fails, Robert? How much worse will Ann feel then?'

Chapter Nine

William Greypaull walked slowly down the slope of path that led to Dommett. The first stars showed in a washed sky, and darkness crept among the deep coombes; he felt that tightening of the scalp that always came on this particular stretch of incline. An experience invited deliberately by his refusal to ride home in the dog-cart.

There were times when William saw shafts of brilliance streak across the night sky; his head would feel curiously light, his limbs weightless. Sometimes these manifestations were so severe that he would fall to the ground, and lie there, until found by his frightened family. The doctor had said that it was all to do with his affliction, the malady from which he had suffered since childhood; but William knew better.

By nature he was a man both humble and exalted. He preferred to go on foot where others of his rank and station rode horseback, or travelled in a conveyance. William saw his habit of walking as being comparable to that of the old-time Prophets and Disciples. He read often the Biblical account of Saul's journey to Damascus; this saint, who was later to be called Paul, had also been vouchsafed direct communication with his Creator, by means of a bright light.

The sickness had showed itself more in the past year than at any time in his life. It came, he noticed, only in those hours when he was deeply troubled in his spirit. William knew that by this means the Lord both chastised and communicated with him; although there were occasions when His precise intention was hard to comprehend.

He paused on the incline and gazed down upon Patchwood. The stone of the fabric took on the colour of old honey in the fading light. He saw the lamps shine out in the many mullioned windows; admired, as he had done a thousand times, the exquisite proportions of the house, the way it lay snug and side-on into the hillside, as if it had not been built by the hand of man, but had grown there by Divine Will.

The names of his children trickled through his mind as they so often did at the day's end. He was able to pass with confidence over that of James, who was clever and dependable and showed no inclination to leave his father's rooftree. The name of Mary was abandoned with equal compliance; only fleeting thought was given to the decent industrious woman who was married to farmer Daniel Crabbe, and already the mother of several children. To think of Mark was to invite fear in. Words came too readily to mind and described the solitary rogue male thrown up by the Greypaulls in every generation. Charming and lazy; deceitful and glib. A young man who, in appearing to please others, served in fact his own selfish ends. Then there was Will, his namesake; the son who was closest to his heart, the boy who had inherited his father's passion for wood and the carving of it.

Darkness came down upon the Blackdown Hills, stealing over fields and hollows, deepening like the disappointment that crept across his heart whenever he considered the five girls who had been the flowers of his family. Unbearable was the memory of Susanna, his niece. Hers had been the light heart in his house. Why had he not seen her dependent nature, her inability to stand alone? Her brief life in the New World was a disaster upon which he could not dwell.

Elizabeth and Ann came bracketed together. In his mind William always saw them, arms linked and made inseparable by the guilt of one and the neediness of the other. It was he who, after the accident, had told the child Elizabeth Ann that was to be her special charge. But now, even these two had been separated. Of the girls, it was Joan, with her love of colours, her flair for the making of pretty dresses, her happy marriage to Jacob, who gave William the least cause for concern.

Rhoda was the deep one. In her, William had sensed the

banked fires, the passionate nature that lay far behind the calmness of her green eyes. She was, he thought, in every sense a womanly woman, strong, capable of deep love and limitless endurance; the kind of partner sought out by men of vulnerable spirit.

He came at last to the pain that had all day lain dormant. That morning he had watched the carriage out of sight, had waved goodbye to Ann and Mark, to William and his wife and child. He had instructed James to see the four of them safe aboard the packet-ship in Liverpool, and then to return home with all haste.

Save for James they had left him, every one!

They seemed not to know how much he suffered at each parting. The ministrations of Grace, the fondness of the babies of his second marriage, could not compensate for the loss of these, his older children. He had always foreseen them as settled close around him, working the farm lands he had purchased for them, seeking his guidance. He paid-over the several Dowries, gave up the lump sums that would ensure a foothold for his sons in the land of America; and all with a good heart. But he would never understand what beckoned them across three thousand miles of ocean. Why, even Ann, her blindness long since declared incurable by two specialists in London, had seized at once on the hope held out in George Salter's letters, and gone willingly to Rochester, New York State. Wherein, William felt sure, lay only further disappointment.

He began to walk slowly down towards the sanctuary of Patchwood. When James returned from Liverpool they would talk about the drawing of a Will. How convenient it was to have a son who was a student of the Middle Temple, Lincoln's Inn.

William knew that his malady could kill him. He had witnessed it in others of his family. The day would come when he would not return from the dark and secret place of his convulsions, when his tired heart would bear no more seizures, or his spirit further disappointments.

James Greypaull had designed his life to fit his nature. Caught between his father's Biblical devotion to the begetting of children, and his own childish mistrust of each successive sibling, James had chosen early not to be a rival, but to stand apart from this growing brood of farmers and carpenters; to be the acknowledged scholar amongst them.

He was by instinct a schemer, a weaver of webs, a spy in the camp of his unsuspecting family. He had, in his youth, developed a look of sagacious interest, an inclination of the head, a judicious pursing of the lips that impressed the elderly and moneyed members of his family. His hands were white and soft, his fingernails clean; his tall and slender figure well suited to the frock-coat and striped trousers that were his daily garb. He was thirty-seven years old and knew his own mind well enough to state with truth that he would never marry. On weekdays, he occupied a suite of elegant rooms in Taunton; at weekends and holidays, he came home to Patchwood. In Buckland St Mary and in his family, James was shown respect, his opinions deferred to; and in matters of business and law, his father was totally dependent on him. But it was not enough. As his brothers and sisters moved out towards new lives in the Western World, James Greypaull had decided that his profession of Solicitor and Conveyancer of Land no longer satisfied him.

His unease had begun with the marriage of his oldest sister Mary. James's instinct warned him to beware of women, and his loathing for Mary was so strong that he could not conceal it. He had witnessed the Letter of Credit that paid over her Dowry and told himself that money was well spent if it rid him of her presence at Patchwood.

Then had come the wedding of Susanna, and the stirring of a more powerful resentment. He had pointed out to Father that she was but a cousin and therefore no strict obligation devolved upon the family; but William had been set upon the matter, and so a second Dowry had been handed over.

Father's marriage to the widow Dening had shocked and depressed James. He suspected that William's lustiness had not waned with the years; that a new line of Greypaulls was soon to be produced. But, while weathering the births of Zillah and Arthur, further drains were made upon the family purse. Two

105

more Dowries were paid over, first to Elizabeth and then to Joan. Three fields and an area of woodland had needed to be sold off; and almost at once had come the marriage of Rhoda to George Hodder Salter.

James had argued with Father that no further financial debt was owed to George Salter. The man had already been paid a substantial sum on his marriage to Susanna. But a Dowry, William had said, was Rhoda's birthright. It was this final, uncalled-for expense that had decided James. He made his own wishes known; four hundred pounds, he told William, would be the entrance fee for a student of The Middle Temple. He wished to become a Barrister, and to live in London.

London suited James; he liked the dignified aura of the Inns of Court; the prospect of wearing a wig and gown appealed to his suppressed love of drama. But Buckland St Mary drew him back. He had returned for that Christmas of 1857 to find further Letters of Credit awaiting his witness. Will and his wife, and Mark and Ann, were, he discovered, about to depart for New York. Ann to seek a cure for her blindness, the other three to squander what remained of Father's fortune.

The journey to Liverpool had been made merry by a bottle of Father's finest whisky. James had joined in the laughter, encouraged the grandiose notions of his younger brothers, expressed hopes for their success in the New World. He had watched the packet-ship out of sight on that grey February morning, waved regretfully to the four who waved to him, and privately wished them gone forever from his life and England.

He returned to London, to the quiet dusty rooms of Lincoln's Inn, to the books that held the mysteries of Inheritance, and how a father's Last Will and Testament might best be worded so that the faithful son was given his just reward.

In late March James went down to Somerset.

He chose a Sunday afternoon to saddle-up the bay mare that was now to be kept for his sole use. He rode slowly through the lanes of early springtime, pausing briefly to study the half-completed church, the contract for which had provided so many passages to New York City; so many Dowries. He spoke to neighbours, to his father's tenants, and all the time he made inspection of every last cowshed and privvy, every unsafe rented roof, each stone and stave of the boundaries that marked the Greypaull land. On his return to Patchwood, James knew to the final penny the precise value set on William Greypaull's estate, should it ever come to public auction. Knowing also how his father loved to walk, James suggested that they might stroll together after supper. They came up to the blacksmith's shop which was in the tenancy of Matthew Matthews.

'He complains of his roof,' said William, 'but a thatcher comes expensive!'

'Does he pay up his rent?'

'Every Ladyday without fail.'

'Then perhaps you should oblige him, Father. It is not wise policy to let your property fall into disrepair.'

William sighed. 'My affliction has troubled me greatly these past months.'

James said: 'Your wife – Mrs Greypaull – is concerned about you.'

'I grow old and clumsy, James. I have too many sorrows. Why, even Ann has left me, now.'

'The subject of Ann weighs heavily on my mind, also. As I watched her sail away she looked so frail – so helpless. It occurred to me as I stood upon the quayside that no proper provision has ever been made for Ann. I was wondering, Father – do you not think . . .?'

William smiled. 'Ah, James, you and I think alike. Whatever would I do without you! Your concern for your poor blind sister does you credit.' He turned from his study of the blacksmith's shop. 'How long are you staying with us this time?'

'As long as you have a need of me, Father. If there is any service I can render . . .?'

William's tone was careful. 'As a matter of fact – before you

107

go back to London — there is a matter that should be settled. I think it is time for me to make my last Will and Testament — what say you, James?'

James nodded slowly; his forefinger laid across his pursed lips, he surveyed his father's anxious features.

'You will, of course, live for several years yet. Of that, there is no doubt in my mind. But a wise man employs forethought in these matters. Your estate and its disposal is not exactly a simple matter, is it Father? You have two quite separate families to consider, and of your older children — why three daughters and two sons are in America, and, as we have already said, Ann is blind and can never fend for herself. There is also,' said James, 'the question of your own peace of mind. The doctor has said that you should have no worry, that tranquillity is essential in the case of your affliction. The making of a Will would ease your heart. I know how you worry about your absent children — and them so young and inexperienced in the ways of this wicked world. It would never do to allow your estate and monies to fall into careless hands.'

A note of diffidence crept into his voice.

'As your son, and a possible beneficiary, it would hardly be proper of course for me to have the actual wording of the Document placed in *my* hands. There is a reliable solicitor in Chard . . .'

'No, no!' cried William. 'I have no need of other legal men. The drawing of my Will shall be a private matter. It shall be our first task in the morning. You are a Barrister, James. Who else can I trust in this world, if not you!'

Chapter Ten

March 16, 1858

Ann is come, and there is much tears and laughter. She is quite worn-out from the awful journey. I lead her to the room I once shared with Eddie. After she has bathed and eaten she sleeps for many hours. John Salter agreeable to share his room with Mark. My brother also very tired.

They are rested and much recovered. We are a merry household! I had not known how much I lacked for company until their coming.

George says: 'Why, Rhoda, I have never heard you talk so much or laugh so hearty!'

'They are my kin,' say I, 'we shared all our lives together until I came here.'

'You are not settled with me, are you?'

I look at Eddie and the baby in my arms, at the ankshus face of my dear husband.

'My home is where you are,' I tell him, 'and will always be so. You and I have been together for but a short time. We grow closer every day. Soon, I shall not dwell so much on England and my family.'

I speak in a strong voice, and he is content. But talk of Father and Buckland St Mary brings tears often to my eyes. Ann has much news of Mary and Joan; we admit to fears about Elizabeth, who still writes only short notes from Suamico, Wisconsin. I ask about our brother James. Ann says he was affable upon their departure from Liverpool, most espeshully to Mark. Our cousin Eliza now married to Phillip Greypaull and living on Larksleve. The building of our church still a long way from compleeshun!

Ann makes much of the Children. She settles in qwickly, and is soon at home.

'We must,' I tell Eddie, 'not leave anything about the floor that your aunty might trip across. Her eyes are poorly, she cannot see, so we must be watchful of her.'

He looks at me, and I see Susanna. 'Eyes all open!' he says.

'Yes,' say I. 'But she cannot see even though her eyes are open.'

He thinks about this. He says, 'All better soon, Mama?'

He asks the single qwestion that none of us have dared to face.

April 2, 1858

A letter from my brother William and his wife. They are staying in New York City. They are seeking advice as to prospekts before they travel further.

The snow has gone, the air mild. I dare to take baby Georgie outdoors for the first time in his life. Ann goes into my garden. I see how she bends to touch each bush and leaf, how she listens to birdsong and the sounds that come from the waterfront and lakeside. She will have me describe Charlotte to her, so I speak of the blueness of Ontario's waters, how the Genessee foams and rushes in a brown froth, and brings business to my husband. I picture for her the American Hotel and its fancy stoop that seems always to be missing a few vital boards. Ann can hear for herself what goes on in the Riverside Saloon. I explain the dry-goods store that stands on the corner of River Street and our own meat-market that makes up what George is pleased to call the Business Section of our little town. I describe the coloured clapboard houses, and how our own house stands high on Latta Road; how the tall stone Lighthouse can be seen from out windows. How the roar of the Falls of Niagra can be heard when the wind is in a certain quarter.

Ann listens. She makes pictures in her mind.

She says: 'You speak of this place as if you love it, Rhoda.'

'Oh no!' I tell her. 'It is so American, so foreign! It is in no single instance what I have been used to!'

I begin to describe the other side of Charlotte, the aspekt of which a lady is aware but does not talk. I explain about the fur-trappers and the loggers who lie drunk across the boardwalks; about the brawlings and stabbings that occur from time to time. I whisper to her of the painted girls who dance and sing in the Riverside Saloon. Such goings-on, say I! They have upstairs rooms where men may visit them! The ladies of the church have had many words with Mr P. McCaffery, but all to no avail. Because I do not wish to paint too black a picture, I speak also of Charlotte's fine, stone-built houses wherein live our Justice of the Peace, our Doctor Jones, the shipbuilder and other wealthy citizens.

Ann smiles. 'For all that you say against it, I do believe you have *some* affeckshun for this place. It is in your voice. The lilac beside your kitchen door has taken root. You always loved the lilac, Rhoda!'

Our brother Mark is out and about a great deal. On his return he smells of whisky. He talks each night with George and John. It is clear to me that he is listening too much to the words of the riverboat gamblers and the drifters who pass through Charlotte. He speaks of mining for gold in California, of pioneering in the far West; of keeping a fancy saloon in downtown Chicago.

'You had better,' I warn him, 'have a thought for poor Father's hard-earned gold what is burning a hole right through your britches pocket! It will soon be all spent in this land of temptations. Hard work is the watchword in America! That is something you have never buckled-down to!'

'Very well,' says he. 'If that is how you think about me, sister dear, then I had best be on my merry way!'

'There is always a place for you here, Mark, whenever you should want it.'

I make this offer because he is my brother, and for the sake of Father. But in my heart I know him to be a vagabond and rogue.

Mark has packed his bags and sailed westwards on a lake steamer. He kisses Ann and my little boys before he goes.

111

He says: 'Don't fret about me, Rhoda dear. I shall probably grab myself a rich wife.' He laughs, and I see how handsome he has grown. Fair hair and blue eyes, and a charming tongue may even yet prove to be his fortune.

Ann listens. I see that she is fit to weep as his footfalls grow less upon the pathway.

'He is gone,' I say, 'and it is better so. He is a man. He will do exactly as he pleases. As do all men.'

April 20, 1858

Ann is to go to Rochester with George. They will take the stage early in the morning. Tonight, I wash her hair and pin it in a coronet of braids about her head. We choose a travelling costume from the many outfits made by Joan. I advise the wearing of the dark blue, with a white blouse ruffled at the throat.

Ann questions me as to her looks, what she has never done before. I know what is in her heart. She is hopeful of tomorrow's verdict. It would be better if she forget all hopes of marriage, but I cannot lie to her. She is pretty as a picture.

'You are charming,' I tell her. 'Your hair has kept its gold colour, your eyes their deep blue. You are as slender as I am – but a little taller.'

We have never spoken of her blindness.

'Do not raise your hopes too high, my dear.'

She smiles and says, 'I have borne other disappointments.'

But this is different, think I! This is New York State, and you have journeyed long and hard to come here. There is in England such a faith in all things American as if here be miracles just waiting for to happen!

I see the way Ann holds my baby; how her fingers trace the features of little Eddie, how her head turns to catch his every word and chuckle. She has such love of children. Oh, I am so fearful for her!

They are returned. It is late, but still I must set down what has come to pass. George comes in, he holds Ann by the arm; he shakes his head towards me, but says nothing.

Ann says only, 'We will speak tomorrow, Rhoda.'

She goes up to her room; I hear how awkwardly she stumbles, but I dare not go to her, when she does not wish it.

George comes into the kitchen. He sits close to the stove altho' the night is warm. I make tea, a strong brew. I sit down beside him. He is so pale and drawn in his face. I put the cup into his hand. I loose his cravat, and the laces of his boots.

'You had better tell me all,' I say. 'You will not sleep else.'

George finds speech hard. He is much moved by the happenings of the day. He lays a hand to his chest, and I hear the breath rasp in his throat. I take his hand, and it is like ice.

He says at last, 'I should not have meddled, Rhoda. I should not have written to your father.'

'You did it for the best.' I hesitate. 'How bad is it?'

His breathing becomes tighter. He says with difficulty: 'It could not be worse. The surgeon has told me that it is the optic nerve that is destroyed by that single blow to her forehead. There is no operation, no treatment that can ever restore it. It pained him to give a hopeless prognosis to one who is so young.'

George paused.

'There is but one suggestion – but it will involve some considerable expense . . .'

'My father,' I remind him, 'was willing to pay for her operation.'

'So he was. But this is something different. In New York City there is an Institution for the Blind, a sort of hospital-and-school combined where such as Ann can be taught new skills. The surgeon explained about something called Braille. It is a system of raised dots on thick paper, whereby the sightless may be taught to read. They also teach a writing method. Paper is pinned across a ridged board, and the letters formed within the ridges. He mentioned several things . . .'

George leans forward in his chair, which movement seems to ease his breathing.

I say: 'What is it? Have you taken cold?'

'It's nothing. Just a tightness in my chest.'

I see the way his hands are clenched together, the hard line of his jaw.

'Well,' say I. 'This is indeed good news! It will be a new life for Ann if she can read and write.'

His breathing eases. He says: 'It was not the outcome I had hoped for.'

'You have done your best, George.' I go to him, and put my arms about his shoulders. I push the hair back from his forehead, and see how the white streak has grown thicker among the black curls. 'Go up. I'll be with you soon. You are worn out with so much worry.'

I watch him go. He feels the hurts of life so much more than do most men. He is also ambishus. The two do not sit well together.

The lamp burns low.

I think of Ann who has lost her final hope.

I think of Father who waits ankshuslly in Buckland.

I think of Elizabeth in Suamico, Wisconsin. I scarce know how I shall word that particular letter.

May 10, 1858

We sit on the front porch in the cool of morning. I peel potatoes and shell peas. Ann sits in the rocker, Georgie in her arms. Eddie plays in a corner of the garden. Since her return from Rochester, Ann has spoken little of that day. I cannot tell what she is thinking. Even as we sit, John Salter comes running with a letter. It is addressed to Ann in Father's hand. I begin to read aloud his words, and it is as if he has come to sit among us. I have a picture clear of his gentle face and kind eyes.

My dear Ann,
On the other half sheet of paper is a Letter of Credit in your favour for five Pounds, which I trust you will get all right and trusting at the same time you are well and comfortable in your new situation. But since you has left me I have been sore afflicted, but am thankful to say am now recovered. But since that, I had the misfortune to put out my ankle which laid me up considerably, and just as that was well I met

114

up with another misfortune-to-wit, a piece of wood fell on my little finger, which were ten times worse than my ankle. Such a bruise as I never met with before. The pains were so acute that I scarcely knew what or how to manage, which lasted for six weeks, and during that time was obliged to wrap it twice a day. And I have pleasure now to tell you I have just left off the finger-cap.

Mr Salter stated he was about to take you to an Eye Infirmary in Rochester very soon. Have you been there?

Mary was up here a few weeks ago and kindly enquired after you. Joan wrote me a letter and feels much hurt that you haven't written her so much as a line since you left. She is much pleased that you were so compatible with your dear sister and your little Nephew.

I have no particular news to tell you more than I have stated. Wishing you will be a good girl and make yourself generally useful, believe me I have your interest at heart. In my house oftentimes you have always been uppermost in my mind, and during that time I have with my own hand made provision for you amply to carry you through this life in a respectable manner after I am no more.

Therefore, keep up your spirits and put your trust in your Saviour whose glorious rising from the dead we commemorated yesterday.

And now my dear child I bid you farewell for the present, trusting you will bear in mind what I have written to you, and that you will lift up morning and evening prayers in the name of your Eternal Redeemer, for yourself, and for your very dear absent father − and not forget to write me on receipt of this, and all the news you know. And may the blessing of peace rest upon you, and believe me to be your ever dear and affectionate father.

Wm. Greypaull.

I look to Ann and see that the floodgates are at last open. She weeps, and it is good that she can do this. I take the sleeping baby from her, and lay him in his crib. I kneel beside her and hold her hands in mine.

She says, 'Joan is angry that I have not written.'

'The fawlt is mine, Ann. I have not made time for your dictation. I should have been more thoughtful.'

Her weeping ends. She says in qwiet voice, 'This cannot go

on, Rhoda! I am as a child in Father's house and in his mind. He will protect my every step, and it is hard to bear.' She reaches out her hands, her fingers touch my features, she finds the wetness of my own tears. 'I have caused enough sadness in this family. I am dependent in so many ways. Father calls me his child – he bids me to be a good girl, but I am a woman grown, twenty-three years old! Oh yes, I had hopes of Rochester, but it is better to know the truth. Now I must build on what is left to me of skill – I have two feet, two hands, I have a brain. Maybe it is time to use them.'

'What have you in mind?'

Ann speaks in a new voice. 'There is an Institute for the Blind in New York City. I am resolved to go there. I will learn to read Braille, to write my own letters.'

'Father will miss you. He tells much about his accidents; about his affliction. You were ever the one who fussed around him when he was indisposed. He will have you home.'

Ann says: 'I am happy here with you and George. You make a welcome, Rhoda, for all who come here. I have given it much thought. In America I have found the courage to walk by myself in the New World. I shall go to New York, with all speed.

'This evening you shall pen one final message for me. Father must be told that I shall not return to Buckland until the day he receives a letter from me – written by my own hand!'

September 30, 1858

No entry made for such a long time. Many letters written and received. We wait in the summer months to hear from Buckland. The news comes at last that Father is agreeable to Ann's plan, tho' he is much saddened that she should wish to stay away so long from him and England. He sends Letters of Credit to cover her expenses, and more is promised.

Ann has been here but a short time, and she is much changed. Her courage shames me. She has put disappointment behind her, does not bide inside the house as she did at Patchwood, but walks out, hand-in-hand with Eddie who is not qwite three years old. These two are seen often on Latta Road and River

Street. Eddie guides his aunt across the boardwalks, saying, 'Step up – step down.' The very roughest of men are considerate of her. I think I may say that in her time among us my little sister has become much loved.

Arrangements are made for Ann's journey to New York. She is to go in the company of two other young ladies who are also afflicted, and whose parents are to travel with them. She is happy and excited. We spend many days getting ready her gowns. In all her life she has never met another blind person. We walk to the cemetery on the eve of her departshur. Ann lays the purple daisies of Michelmas upon the two graves. The Genessee River runs close beside this place. Under the cedar trees there is a rough bench. We sit down in the cool of evening. Ann is very qwiet.

She says at last: 'That must have been hard for you, Rhoda, when you first came here?'

'It could not be otherwise,' say I. 'My situation was painful. You know how much I loved Susanna.'

'And now you love George?'

'With all my heart.'

'He depends upon you in all things.'

'I make my voice light. She cannot see my face.

'Ah well! He is but a man; they are not so sturdy as we women. I keep his business books and records, as I did in our shop in Buckland St Mary. But I know nothing of the butchery trade, that side is altogether his, and he is skilled at it.'

It is the last time we shall speak privately together, or even meet in this life. I take her hand in mine. I say:

'Can you keep a secret?'

She smiles, and says in the American fashion:

'Well now, I will surely try, ma'am.'

'I believe I am again with child. Georgie is but eight months old – but if it be a daughter then I shall be well pleased.' I pause. 'I shall not tell my husband until I am absolutely certain.'

'Oh Rhoda! How lovely if it be a little girl! If she has the dark Salter curls and blue eyes, and the rosy complexion. You have described George, and his sons and brothers, in such a way that I can see them in my mind. You must write and tell me all that comes to pass!'

Now it is Ann's turn to grip my hand. A pink colour rises in her face. She says:

'Can you also keep a secret?'

I say:

'Well, I will surely try, ma'am.'

'Do you remember the Curate who came courting you in Buckland?'

'Mr Robbins?'

'The very one. After you left he was much cast-down. He came often to Patchwood. His sister died suddenly. He is a very lonely young man. We talk together often. He has led me home from church a few times.'

'Do you mean to tell me . . .?'

She nods. 'He will marry me, Rhoda.'

'But that is the best news you could give me! Does Father know about it?'

'No, no! And neither must he. Father does not see me as a woman, but only as a blind child.'

All at once I understand.

'This is why you were so set on coming here. Why you will take the great step of going to the Institute in New York.'

She smiles. 'A Minister's wife must at least be literate. We are promised secretly to one another.' She sighs. 'I am not worthy of him.'

I bite hard on my lip. It is on my tongue to say that she is worthy of a great deal better than the red-nosed Robbins. But Ann sees people with an inner eye. Her judgement may well be surer than my own. I have an admiration for handsome men, tho' I would never of course, look further than my beautiful husband.

I say; 'You are more than worthy of the Curate. But, oh my dear, I am so happy for you!'

We walk home arm-in-arm.

I ask; 'May I tell your news to Elizabeth when I write?'

'Just so long as she does not pass it back to Father.'

We come into the cosy room where sit George and John, a sleeping child in each man's arms.

George says: 'You two look very happy?'

Ann puts a finger to her lips. 'We have been exchanging women's secrets.'

I had feared tomorrow's parting from her. But now it will not be so bad.

November 29, 1858
It is near on midnight and the men not yet to home.

We have many orders from the ships that lie at anchor; their Captains seek provishuns before the harbour freezes over. For a week now. George and John must slaughter beeves and sheep, skin carcasses and dress them, and all with but a few hours' sleep and never time for proper meals.

I have only the children for company since Ann left us. Georgie walks and talks already, what is very early for a boy but much due to Eddie who will have his baby brother for a playmate. They grow so fast. I must sew for both boys, and the expected one. George says he will go to Rochester next month and buy a sewing machine for my birthday. John has fixed runners to a wooden box, and a rope to pull it thru' the snow; wrapped up well against the cold, Georgie loves to ride inside this. Eddie and I have coats and hats made all of black fur, what is very smart. I write of this to my Father and sisters. I say nothing of the lonely hours. I knew George for an ambishus man before I came here, and a business cannot prosper when the master sits to home with his wife and children.

A letter from Elizabeth, who is both sad and happy to have Ann's news. Robert's harvest was so good that they have flour to take them through the winter, and several bushels left to sell. This year he has grown wheat, and such grain as was never seen in England. They work side by side on their twenty acres.

My child has qwickened early this time, I have already felt movement in this fourth month, which means that it must be a girl. I long so for a daughter. George plans to employ another butcher who will live with us and share John's room. Then there will be five male persons in my household.

March 29, 1859

My daughter came punctually into this world on the twenty-second and a more exqwisite child was never seen. Our Dr Jones says she is like an English rose, with the fair Salter complecshun, bright blue eyes and a cap of tight dark curls. When it came to the choosing of her name – why what else would suit her father but to call her Rosalind Rhoda? George stays at home to care for me and mind the children. He says it is harder work than butchering, and how do I manage? He is all set on hiring a maidservant to help me.

Do not much care for the thought, altho' he means well.

June 10, 1859

One week has passed since our crisis and I set these words down in a spirit of humility, so that I may not forget the lesson I have learned. I was Churched the fourth Sunday after my confinement, this custom of purificashun of a new mother being held to in America as it is in England. All arrangements for Rosa's baptism one month hence being made at this same time. Was also told while at church that a measles epidemic is rife in Rochester and in Town of Greece. Had small fear for my little family, my sons mixing little with the children of the village.

The disease must have been passed on while we were in church. Some days later both boys showing a dark-red rash, swollen eyelids, and a high fever. My fears for Rosa very great. Kept her from them, but the damage already done, says our Dr Jones, and measles often fatal in a babe of only six weeks. Had seen more than one tiny coffin being carried out by grieving fathers from houses roundabout us, and on discovering her fever and rash I am as a woman demented. The boys by this time much recovered, what was a blessing.

The crisis comes on a Sunday evening. George fetches Dr Jones away from his family supper, and our worst fears soon confirmed. On being informed that our treasure was not yet baptised, we are told to bring a Minister to her with all haste. George, much affected by this news becomes very pale and is scarce able to draw breath or move from his chair. I am at first impatient with him until I recall that he had lived before thru' a similar agony in the loss of his first-born son, John.

It is my dear brother-in-law who rides out to Rochester, to Christ Church Cathedral, and brings the Rev Henry Neely to us; our own Pastor being absent on a visit to his mother. I pray that I might never have to live thru' such a night again, this baptism seeming more like the administering of the Last Rites.

I sit all night in my rocking-chair, the babe so still and white in my arms. I feel the presence of Susanna in the house. The beam from the Lighthouse swings regularly across me, and I know for certain that she also sat in this, selfsame chair, thru' a dreadful night, and waited for her child to die; and now I am made to understand so many things. I stand chastised before my God for my lack of percepshun. This is how it feels when a mother loses the child of her body. It is like the bitterest of birthpangs, but with no happy outcome. I had wondered often at Susanna's weakness of spirit, her lack of will to go on living. Now I understand.

George sits in his chair, qwite helpless, and fights for every breath. His brother kneels beside him. They are like shadows to me. The feeling of Susanna's presence grows ever stronger, and now it is *her* strength that sustains *me*.

The sun comes up. I hear the bluejays fighting in the garden. I no longer feel my cousin's spirit. I look down at my daughter's tiny face, and see that there is colour in it; she opens her eyes and waves her fists.

I turn to George. I say:

'She has survived the night. She will live now.'

Chapter Ten

Late spring was followed by a short, hot summer. October came around and in Suamico, Wisconsin, the first frosts already rimed the grasslands. In the woods a pair of redwings bickered, a killdeer called; Elizabeth gathered the blue wild grapes, and the apples of the sweetcrab that were improved, so people said, by having frost upon them. She felt the loosening of home-ties, thought less about England, with the passing of each season. It was good to be able to speak of last spring's sowing, last year's harvest; to note the earlier flight of the wild geese, and how late the peepers had lingered this fall in her patch of woodland. To belong was to survive.

As for Robert, he was, she thought, even more securely rooted in the rich earth of Brown County. A winter spent working in the lumbermills had taken away the more obvious signs of Englishness in him. Small things but significant; a difference in the way he thought, his attitude to other men. The rhythm of his speech was changing; she noted with a smile his use of American expressions. In a few years Robert Vickery's country of origin would be forgotten by all but her; and even she would not strive overhard to remember England.

The days grew short, the evenings long; it was her favourite time of all the year, because it brought him home from field and shed to be at her side and with the children. She never tired of watching him: his body had grown lean and hard; his face, which seldom revealed the nature of his thoughts and feelings, was as inscrutable as ever. But there was about him lately an air of satisfaction, a pride that he had never shown when working in Buckland for his father. And he had cause for that satisfaction. In the two years of their occupation a miracle had been wrought in these wild twenty acres. The pine-stumps had all been grubbed or burned out; now the plough could cut sweetly through the good earth. A neat fence encompassed what was theirs; the cow and the pair of oxen were safely housed against the winter. A ceiling of pine planks had been fitted in the log house, creating a second room beneath the rafters. Robert had built cupboards and small chairs for the children. Elizabeth had learned from the older women of the community how best to store food against the winter. She remembered the grocery shop in Buckland St Mary, the Monday trips to Taunton made by Rhoda and Susanna; their return from Merriman's Wholesalers with sacks of sugar and flour, boxed soaps and candles. In Suamico she gathered the wild-rice that grew in the autumn marshes, made her own tallow candles and boiled up lye soap in a kettle. The writing of letters for her neighbours had ensured a supply of small luxuries. They would survive the winter.

Survival, for Robert Vickery, was not enough. He noted that a loghouse was a settler's first option; he saw how in a few years the successful farmer built a larger, more elaborate dwelling of pine planks, which was warmer in winter and had separate rooms.

He could never forget that Elizabeth was a Greypaull; her love for him was a wonder in which he could never quite believe. For her sake he wanted a frame house, blue-painted, with glass-panes in every window and a stylish porch. Their third child was due at the end of December.

Last winter he had worked in the lumbermill. He had hired out his labour and team of oxen to haul loads of cordwood and shaved shingles to Green Bay and De Pere. He had been absent from home only one night in any week, and earned but a couple of dollars for his trouble. Robert had no wish to leave his wife and children in the hard times of winter, but a spread of twenty acres would not support a growing family, and a man could do no more than the power of his muscles and physical strength allowed. He had learned to appreciate the subtleties of certain American phrases. 'Getting along' meant a roof above one's head, and food, however meagre, upon the table. 'Getting along pretty well' signalled new shoes for the winter, a set of matching china dishes, a piano in the parlour. 'Prosperity' was what you aimed for. On American lips the word had a new sound, a full rich taste upon the tongue. The status of 'well-to-do' put a man up in a carriage, his wife in silks, his children in expensive boarding-schools. All Robert really wanted was to 'get along pretty well'; to be able to hold up his head among this company of strong men; to be a part of the growing settlement of the northwoods. He would, in time, like to hear himself described by some knowledgeable person as 'Robert Vickery, townsman of Suamico, Brown County'.

These were his thoughts as he harvested his wheat crop, as he fashioned a rocking-cradle for the expected child, and counted out the few silver dollars that remained, when bills were paid, to see them through the winter.

The strangers had come into Suamico at the summer's end, two tall and rangy men wearing buckskin trousers and distinctive woven shirts of a red-and-yellow Scot's plaid. They passed close by the Vickery's cornfield. Robert, intent upon the cutting of a clean swathe, did not see them. It was Elizabeth, tying up sheaves, who noticed the bright shirts and heavy backpacks approaching on the trailpath.

It was the shorter, red-haired man who called out: 'Hi there! A word, if you please!'

There was thick dust on the boots that came across the stubble, a stoop of weariness, a drag of the heels that meant exhaustion. Robert laid down his scythe and shook the extended hands.

'James Black, sir. Glad to make your aquaintance!'

'Matthew Black, sir – and likewise!'

Elizabeth moved to stand beside her husband; John and Charles, who had played among the corn-shocks, now clung shyly to their mother's skirts.

'Robert Vickery – and this is Elizabeth, my wife. Can we help you, gentlemen?'

The men eased the backpacks from their shoulders. Robert looked towards the setting sun. He pointed towards the log-house.

'We were just about to eat our supper – won't you join us?'

James Black said: 'We'd be very glad to, Mr Vickery. It's been a long walk from Green Bay!'

In this land, little interest was shown in where a man had come from; in fact, it was considered impolite to ask. The first question, Robert had noticed, was always what was the stranger capable of doing, and where was he heading?

The men had washed the dust from their hands and faces, eaten their fill of Elizabeth's cornbread, pork and gravy, and blueberry pancakes. From his backpack, Matthew Black produced a small locked box of polished wood that held tea. He gave it to Elizabeth.

'Make a good strong brew, ma'am. According to our mother, 'tis only the Scots and the English who can make proper tea.'

She looked at the plaid shirts.

'Are you Scots, then?'

It was James Black who answered. 'Canadian by birth, ma'am. Pure Scots by blood. Our grandparents and parents came from Dundee.' He grinned. 'From your speech I'd guess you folks are English?'

'We came from Somerset,' Elizabeth said. 'We've been here but a short time.'

Robert listened to the conversation. He drank the good tea, and studied the two men. In offering them hospitality, he was keeping to the traditions of the northwoods where doors were never locked, and a place by the fire was made for any stranger; where no Indian or his squaw was ever turned away without a gift of bread or corn.

He said in a tight voice: 'So what brings you to these parts, Mr Black?'

'Call me Jim why don't you! and this here redhead is known as Matt! Well – there's not much to tell about us. I'm thirty-three years old, and he's twenty-seven. We're bachelors still. Guess we never stayed long enough in any one place to settle down and marry. We lived on the home-farm in Kingston, Ontario, until we were big and strong enough to go lumbering on the Ottowa River. We work winters in the pineries, in spring we ride the log-rafts down-river to the mills. In summer we do whatever comes along – we've both got itchy feet I reckon!'

Matt said: 'We're not usually this far south. While we had family we stayed in our own Province. Father died when we were kids. Our mother passed away in June. It felt like the end of things for us in Kingston. We sold up the farm and decided to take a look at America. We put into Escanaba on the lake-steamer *Oconto*. Since then we've been looking at the country-side along the Bay. You chose well to come here, Robert. This is good land, well-watered. No Indian troubles. Good hunting in the woods, plenty of venison and wildfowl.'

Robert said: 'There's still land to be had at a dollar twenty-five the acre.'

It was three days later when mutual trust had been established that Jim Black said: 'If we decided to buy – say a lot of forty acres – would you be willing to clear and work it for us, for a couple of years? All the crops would be yours, of course, and we'd pay you for the work of clearing.'

'Well – yes, I'd be willing to do that. But why won't you stay here, build a house and settle?'

Jim said: 'Guess you folks don't hear much news out here in the backwoods. There's a big war coming – if Abe Lincoln gets elected it'll come for sure!'

Elizabeth said: 'But what has that to do with you?'

Matt grinned. 'Why, we're Scotsmen, ma'am. 'Tis in our blood to fight for the underdog. Nothing we like better than a good scrap!'

Jim said: 'Aye, there's that. But we'll also be fighting for a just cause. Abe Lincoln is an Abolitionist, he's our kind of people. His parents were pioneers, could hardly write their own names. There'll be an end to Southern slavery if Abe gets into Office.'

126

Elizabeth said: 'What slavery? I never saw slaves anywhere in this country.'

'It goes on in the Southern States, ma'am. Down in Virginia and Alabama, in Georgia and Kentucky. Why in some States the black slaves outnumber their white masters by as many as four to one!'

Robert said: 'I don't think I ever saw a black man.'

'Yes, we did, Rob. There were negroes on the quay when we landed in New York.' She turned to the brothers. 'But this is the land of the free. That is why we came here.'

'You just happen to have the right colour of skin, ma'am. If you were a negro, you'd have a chain around your ankle.'

Matt said: 'We reckon there'll be Civil War before much longer. We mean to be where the action is when Lincoln gets elected. Meanwhile . . .'

Jim said: 'We'd like to have someplace to come back to when the fighting is all over. A piece of Suamico would suit us very well. Tomorrow, we'll go back to the Land Offices in Green Bay. Make the whole thing legal.'

They picked up their blankets and walked to the door.

Robert said: 'You're welcome to sleep tonight beside the fire. There's little comfort in my lean-to shed.'

Matt smiled. 'Reckon we're not used to so many home comforts. But thank you for the offer. The nights are not too cold yet. We'll be just fine on that good heap of clean straw. We'll be gone before sun-up.'

James and Matthew Black returned one week later with a Deed of Purchase for the forty acres of wild land that lay to the right of the trailpath, and within view of Robert Vickery's own spread. They also brought with them a length of green silk for Elizabeth, tobacco for Robert, a claspknife for each small boy to be given to him when he was old enough to use it; and news-sheets. When the evening meal was finished, and the children sleeping, Robert wanted to talk about the newly-purchased land.

'How long do you think to be away?' he asked Jim Black. 'What crops do you want me to raise in your absence?'

'Do whatever you think best, man! You're the farmer. We're lumberjacks. We also made a deposition while we were in Green Bay. If we don't come back within seven years – then the land is yours.'

'But of course you'll be back,' said Elizabeth. 'I can't believe that a Civil War can come to this peaceful place.'

'Oh it won't happen here, ma'am. It'll all be fought out in the Southern States.'

Robert said: 'You're a very political sort of fellow, Jim. You seem to know a lot about it all.'

'I keep myself informed. I read every news report I can lay my hands on.'

He pushed away his empty plate. He said politely: 'I must thank you, ma'am, for a real good supper – and now, if I may, I'd like to tell you what is in the news-sheets we brought back from Green Bay. Maybe then you'll understand what it is that beckons Matt and me to go South.'

Matt said: 'We're Republicans. We're making our way down to Chicago. The Republican Convention will be held there next May. Lincoln's bound to be selected as candidate for the Presidency, and once he's in power – then the fireworks will begin!'

Jim rustled the news-sheet.

'It's started already,' he said, 'down in West Virginia. According to this report there's been big trouble in a place called Harpers Ferry. A man named John Brown went down there with a company of seventeen white men and five negroes. They seized the United States Government Arsenal, rounded up the biggest of the plantation owners, and told their slaves to rally to John Brown.' He paused. 'Says here, that the very next day a Colonel Robert E. Lee took a force of eighty Marines into Harpers Ferry and wiped out all but Brown himself and six of his men. There's to be a trial in Charlestown. It's expected for sure that all seven men will hang.'

Matt said: 'Why can't they see that slavery is ruining the Southern States? Why, we're way ahead of them in farming, in every kind of business. They depend entirely on cotton – but without slave-labour they'd be sunk without trace.' He tapped the news-sheet. 'If they string John Brown up, then we'll have a martyr to our cause, and that man's name will live forever!'

The time was November; it was too cold now, said Robert, for them to sleep on straw in the lean-to shed. Wrapped in their blankets, the Canadians lay down on the pegged rug that covered the hearthstone.

They started for Green Bay early the next morning; they would take the first river-steamer that was Chicago-bound. The house seemed very quiet after their departure. It had all happened in a short space of time, thought Elizabeth, this miracle that would keep Robert from the logging-camps and enable him to stay with her for another winter. At the moment of leaving, James Black had laid ten silver dollars on the table; for expenses, he had said, for any unforeseeable problem concerning the wild forty acres. There had been tears in Elizabeth's eyes, a huskiness in Robert's thanks.

'I won't let you fellows down. When you come back there'll be a thriving farmstead waiting for you. Good luck with your war, wherever it may be. We shall be thinking of you every day, and praying for you.'

It was a long speech for Robert Vickery to make; the closeness that had grown up between himself and the two brothers had a warmth that was akin to love. It could not have happened in Buckland St Mary. It made bearable all the deprivations, all the heartaches.

William Greypaull Vickery was born four days before Christmas, a solemn baby, his tiny face a replica of Robert's sober features. Arrangements had been made that a neighbour should attend Elizabeth at her confinement, but a blizzard and a short, swift labour had obliged the father to act as midwife this time as so often happened in the northwoods. In the days of Elizabeth's lying-in Robert build great fires against the aching cold; cooked pans of venison stew; whittled wooden cows and horses for the amusement of John and Charles. It was a time when they were all together, dependent only on each other. The stories told by James and Matthew Black, of slavery and injustice in the far South, had little meaning for them.

Elizabeth said: 'Civil war must be a dreadful thing. It means brother fighting against brother. Rhoda said in her last letter that Mark and Will are settled in North Carolina.'

In May 1860, Abraham Lincoln was voted in as President of the Union of American States, the first Republican ever to hold this high Office. In December, the State of South Carolina declared an Act of Secession from that Union and made clear its intention to elect its own President and Legislature. Eleven months later the first shots were fired in the Civil War that was to divide a nation. The wooden barracks of Fort Sumter fell to the Confederate Armies of the Southern States. At once, the call went out from President Lincoln for 75,000 three-month volunteers to rally to the Union Flag.

The spring of 1861 brought rain and flood to northern Wisconsin; many roads and trailpaths around the area of Green Bay were barely passable, rivers overflowed, Duck Creek became a torrent of white water.

The forty-acre lot, now spoken of by Robert as 'the Black farm', had been cleared by him of brush and pine trees and stood ready for cultivation. It was on a day in late April, while he wrestled to put ox-drawn harrows to the sodden earth, that word was first brought to him of the Civil War. The recruiting officers had come by in a horsedrawn buggy. They asked for directions to the nearest tavern. He had pointed the way to the Rough and Ready House. A meeting, they said, would be held at the Inn that evening. All able-bodied men would be expected to attend.

The oath of Service and Allegiance to the United States was sworn that night by lumbermen and loggers, and by many farmboys. As Robert told Elizabeth, 'They were interested only in signing-up the single fellows. It'll be an adventure, they said, and since the South will be whipped in less than three months, it seems hardly worth taking a married farmer from his land and family.'

The letter arrived on the day that the last of the Indian corn was harrowed-in on the newly-cleared land. It was headed May 24, and was written in the sprawling hand of Jim Black.

Dear Friends Robert and Elizabeth Vickery.
A few lines from me so that you know what has happened to me so far. I enlisted in a Pennsylvania Regiment of Volunteers, but, that State having filled its Quota, I was then assigned to company A, Second West Virginia Volunteers. I am a sargent which suits me mighty fine! I am hoping to see action pretty soon. They say it will all be over in a matter of weeks, so could be seeing you all again real quick. Matt hurt his foot a while back, so I left him with a pal to recover. Had word from him yesterday that he has joined the Twelfth Regiment, Wisconsin Volunteer Infantry.
  Matthew sends his regards and so do I.
                      Your friends,
              Jim and Matthew Black.

June came in hot and dry. With sixty acres of good land under cultivation the Vickerys laboured long and hard underneath the sun. The little boys grew brown and strong. William, at eighteen months, was already an independent child who walked and talked, and was his father's shadow. News of battles and blood-shed in the Southern States came only slowly to Suamico, Brown County.

  But for that single, cheerful letter, nothing more was heard of James and Matthew Black.

Chapter Eleven

News of the war came to Charlotte with every river-boat Captain, every drover of cattle, every travelling missionary who stood before George Hodder Salter's scoured-wood counter. In Rochester and Town of Greece the fever of approaching battle was running high. Boys of sixteen years lied about their ages, dragged rusty weapons from their father's sheds, stole meat cleavers from their mother's kitchens, took the Oath of Allegiance before a doubtful Sergeant, and then put on the oddly assorted military garments with which the Union clothed its soldiers.

The madness had spread to men of more mature years. After the first battle of Bull Run was fought, and won by the Confederate Armies, George said to Rhoda, 'At this rate they'll be in Washington before the month is out. They're still saying it can't last more than ninety days. I think I should volunteer. After all, this is our country of adoption. We owe it our support against the enemy in times of peril!'

'You've been listening to the talk of those recruiting-sergeants.' Rhoda's voice was bitter. 'It's one thing to provide meat and sausage to the Army – quite another to throw up a thriving business, leave your wife and children, and run to join the mob! You're thirty-four years old, George, and this is *not* our country. I say let the Yankees fight their own wars. Remember that Census gatherer who came here last year? He refused to describe us as English on the form. He put us down as Aliens – we who pay up our dues and taxes regularly – if we be Aliens on paper, then we will be so in practice!'

He did not understand her woman's logic. 'It's a matter of pride,' he said, 'to volunteer, to at least show willing. When this is all over, would you have me remembered as the only man in Charlotte who turned his back upon the Union Flag?'

'I would have you remembered as a man of sense who did not desert his wife and three young children.'

'And suppose Abe Lincoln's armies are defeated? Would you want to live as a subject of Confederate rule?'

It was not often that she defied him openly, but now her right hand came down with a sharp slap upon the table. She said, 'Union rule or Confederate, I see little difference in them. They're all customers, aren't they? They all eat meat, don't they?'

George had long since recognised the futility of argument with Rhoda, but he remained uneasy in his conscience. It hardly seemed right to be prospering at such a rate when other, younger men were dying in battle. He admitted that soldiers in training needed to be fed, and that he was known to be a purveyor of the best meat and sausage in the district. As recruitment continued, his business with the Army increased in proportion. His standing at the Bank had never been higher.

Time passed; the year dipped into autumn, winter came and each traveller who passed through Charlotte had his own story of the horror and deprivation that was being endured by Union soldiers. George had heard talk of a practice whereby a man of sufficient means could pay a poor man to enlist and do his fighting for him without any loss of face or damage to his reputation. He also heard that abusive letters had been received through the postal system by certain prominent business men in Charlotte and Town of Greece who had not yet made a move to do their Duty.

On a day in May 1862, he read accounts of the Peninsula Campaign that was being fought out beside the Chickahominy River down in Virginia.

In mid-afternoon he told John, 'Hitch my horse up to the buggy. I have some business to attend to in Town of Greece.'

The enlistment office was a disused warehouse that still smelled of the half-cured pelts and furs that had once been stored there.

George stood in line among boys who were almost young enough to be his sons. Their excited chatter increased the nervousness that had been mounting in him since the moment he left Charlotte. The tightness in his chest grew worse as he approached the officer's table. When asked his age, the reply, 'I am thirty-five, sir,' came out on a wheezing breath. The Captain looked keenly at him, and gestured towards an adjoining table. 'See the Doctor! You don't sound like a fit man to me.'

George saw how the young men stripped off their shirts, were tapped on the chest, asked a few questions, and passed on to be fitted out in uniforms of blue. As George stood before the old man in the white coat, the sound of his breathing must, he thought, be audible to every youth in the long room. He struggled with a growing panic; the desire to rush outside, to seek fresh air, was overwhelming.

The doctor did not touch him.

He said, 'How old are you?'

'I'm – thirty-five, sir.'

'What made you come here?'

'Seemed – the – right – thing – to – do.'

'The right thing for you is to turn straight around and go home. We can do without middle-aged asthmatics in this man's Army.'

George gasped 'I'm – not – asthmatic. Whatever that is!'

'The hell you are! How long have you been having these attacks?'

'It – only – comes – on – when – I – get – nervous.'

'Sure it does! That's asthma, and you'd better get yourself to a doctor pretty damn quick, mister! Unless you've got a wish to choke to death one of these fine days! A quiet life is what you need.'

George drove back to Charlotte, going slowly through the sweet May morning, allowing the horse to find its own way. Seated in the buggy, shoulders bowed to ease his breathing, the awful rasping sounds gave way; the fear of sudden choking death receded. Asthma. He had neither heard of, nor witnessed it in others. On either side the tidy farms stretched out to the

134

horizon. To own such a quarter-section was what Rhoda wanted. A quiet life the doctor had said. George remembered his father's farm in Dorchester, England. The drudgery of milking, early and late; the disasters of failed crops and sick beasts. There were easier and more interesting ways of making money. Recent prosperity had turned his attention towards the business of wholesale dealing. Rhoda was a business woman born. If he explained it carefully enough, she would surely see the wisdom of expansion.

George straightened his shoulders, took up the reins, and drove at a brisk trot into Charlotte.

Life with George was never settled. Rhoda seemed always to be perched uneasily upon one foot while the other sought for some equally uncertain toehold. She still yearned for the certainty of land, for stands of hardwood timber at her back, orchards, at her left hand, a solid barn upon her right. On the subject of such a purchase George would not even speak. He provided her with advantages she had not even known were lacking.

She almost regretted the ease with which rooms could be added to a frame house. In the years since Rosa's birth the wooden structure had encroached upon her vegetable garden. The engagement by George of a servant had called for another extra bedroom, and then there was the little place he called his 'office', but where in fact he sought refuge from three lively children.

Once trained to Rhoda's exacting standards, Bridget Reilly had proved a cheerful and reliable addition to the household. The illiterate Irish girl, at Rhoda's instruction, had learned to write her own name. Further than that she would not go. But her presence meant a few precious hours when walks might be taken with the children, letters answered, and sewing done. The writing of the Journal had become a compulsion, and now she possessed both time and paper.

★

Geeorge does not confide in me as he should do. He is sick tho' he will not own it. His tender conscience leads to such foolishness! John tells me, confidenshully, that my husband has tried to join the Union Army, but was declared unfit. Can only hope that now he will be content to attend to our ever-growing business.

It has not, thank goodness, even crossed the minds of John and Rignold to volunteer for this senseless war. Every day more wives and mothers are oblidged to put on mourning-black. Our two butchers feel as I do, that as citizens of England there is no call upon them to go to a fight that is none of their making. I spend a few hours of each week rolling bandages and packing parcels for those poor boys who follow the drum. Photographs of Mr Lincoln show him ever more careworn and shabby in his appearance, as well he might be! That man has much to answer for! Even Eddie and Georgie play at nothing but soldiers these days. The worst insult they can shout at one another is 'Johnny Reb', what I have now forbidden them to do.

'Don't you know,' I tell them, 'that your uncles Mark and Will are somewhere in the Southern States? They both have the sort of wild natures that make men volunteer to kill one another. Civil War is an evil, and an abomination in the sight of God.'

My boys do not really understand, and, tho' they look chastened, a few hours later, and the wooden swords are again heard crashing in the backyard.

September 15

Already we are into autumn. Many shortages due to the War. Oh, how our menfolk do grumble without their tobacco. Made a quantity of lye soap today with Bridget. Tomorrow we begin to put down preserves and pickles to last the winter.

A letter comes from Father. He says he is sick and will have Ann to home, since no one tends him better than she. He asks for news of Mark and Will. They have written him not one word since leaving England. He makes no menshun of our

War, but asks for a Portrait of the children. George says there is a Photografer in Rochester who makes very tasteful pictures.

I sort thru' the children's clothing and nothing is good or fine enough for a picture that will be seen by all in Buckland St Mary. I spend an evening measuring them and making patterns. Georgie very naughty, will not be measured and hides from me. Eddie brings him back. I hear him say, 'It is for a likeness – for Grandpapa in England, because he won't ever meet any of us.'

I go to Rochester with George. While he is at the Cattle Sales I visit the city's finest Drapers. My list is long. I enqwire as to what the children of fashunable people are wearing these days.

For Rosa I buy pale pink velvet with many feet of burgundy velvet ribbon for to trim it. For Eddie I buy a length of green-and-white worsted in a small check-pattern, for to make his trousers, and a piece of plain green cloth for his jacket. I take also a ready-made bow-tie in green watered-silk; this out-fit must serve a double purpose. He will be seven in November – and go to school. Georgie is five. I am told by the shopkeeper that such little boys are dressed often in knee-britches made of blue velvet, with long white socks, and jackets made of silk. Fashunable shirts have frilled-lace jabots down the front. Buy material enough for all this, and a bow-tie for Georgie in matching dark-blue.

Many hours spent at my sewing-machine. Rosa qwite cheerful to be fitted-up in pale pink velvet. I make a dress for her doll from the left-over scraps, what, she says, will also have its picture sent to England.

Eddie likes his dark-green, espeshully the checkered trousers what are a true copy of some worn by his Papa. He stands qwiet to be fitted. Not so Georgie! My little boy will not have the knee-britches at any price. He wants proper trousers like his brother. He says the long white stockings are for girls and make his legs itch. He will wear the frilled-lace shirt-front only because Eddie has the same. Have ordered a pair of soft black leather boots to be made for both boys, and a pair of pumps with silken pom-poms to fit Rosa. Tell Georgie since the knee-britches are already stitched together he will *have* to wear them.

Such a day as I have *never lived thru'*. Was never so shamed in a public place by all three children. George says if my Father wants to see them in the future he can come to Charlotte for that *dowtful pleashur*!

They are not ushully so naughty, but it seems that taking a photograf is something like baking a cake, and it must 'cook' for som many minutes until it is ready. Meanwhile, the sitter *must not move a fractshun*! Oh my poor darlings! Eddie did his best as oldest in the family, but he must laugh at Georgie's antics and so make all *much worse*. At first Georgie scratched to ease the itching of his stockings – what spoiled the first photografic plate. Then the lace-jabot made his chin itch, or so he said. He wriggled and so fell off his chair, the blue velvet knee-britches covered now with dust, and Eddie laughing fit to burst. Rosa must copy both boys – like always! She now suffers from both itching and laughing – drags at the neck of the pink velvet frock, and tries to kick her naughty brothers.

The photografer comes out from under his blackcloth and says if I cannot control my children I had better not bring them out in future. I say it is a pity that such an expensive salon cannot keep cleaner floors, and if he wishes to be paid he had better practise patience! If it turn out to be pleasing to my poor Father I shall be surprised! All three *looking mutinous as Lincoln's soldiers*, and Rosa still dragging at the neck of the pink velvet!

The photograf has come. Three copies made and all of them hand-coloured. Cannot say that I am pleased, all three look tearful, but their outfits showing very *fine* and *splendid*. George says we can be proud of our little family!

George reads aloud to me from the newspaper after supper is finished. Many slaves have been set free by the Union soldiers.

'Free to do what?' I enqwire.

He is not sure, but thinks on the whole that it must be a good thing.

November 18
Eddie is seven today!

All three children have the tall and slender Salter build, the charming looks and ways of their father, his blue eyes. The likeness between the two boys espeshully strong. It is only on these birthdays that I remember that Eddie is not my child.

December 1
Eddie to school! The two who must stay at home are fretful without him. Georgie and Rosa do not *get on* together without peacemaker Eddie. Much time wasted by Bridget and me on settling their sqwabbles. Heavy snow. Lake and river already frozen. Bridget knits woollen caps, and mufflers and gloves, in bright reds and yellows for each child. We go every day to meet Eddie from the Schoolhouse. The young ones like to take the small sleigh, and we pull Eddie home after all his hard work. All goes well for a few days and then I see the marks of tears upon his face. He is very qwiet. I touch his face and forehead but he has no fever. I ask if he is nauseus, since he does not eat. Eddie says he is not sick at all.

When bedtime comes I cannot find him. We scour the house, but no sign. As I come from the children's bedroom I look upwards, and there is a chink of candlelight showing underneath the attic door. There is nothing up there save the boxes I brought here from England – and the trunk that holds Susanna's dresses.

All at once I am so fearful that I scarce find strength enough to climb the stairs. I go softly, push open the attic door, and there he is, knelt by candlelight among her gowns.

He turns his white little face towards me, and the grey eyes are changed to a lavender colour. He speaks in a voice high with anger, what he has never used to me before.

He says: 'So this is where you hide things.'

He is holding what is left of the blue-and-white flowered silk.

'I used to have a piece such as this when I was a baby. I bet you thought I wouldn't remember!'

I say: 'Oh Eddie, what is it? What has happened to upset you?'

He turns his face away, but I have seen his top lip tremble. I go closer. I make to hold him. I say: 'Can you not tell your Mama what is the trouble?'

He pushes my arms away. He turns upon me. 'How can I tell my Mama,' he shouts, 'when she lies dead in the graveyard!'

'Who told you this?'

'Luther Denman.'

'He is at the school?'

'He's one of the big boys. He knows all there is to know. He said so.'

It is in my mind to bring George to him. He has made this tangle of deceit, let him unravel it. But I dare not leave the child in such a state.

I say: 'I am the only mother you have ever known. Is that not good enough?'

He seems not to hear me. He says: 'I want to know about her. I want to see the place where she lies.'

I take his cold hand. 'Let us go down to the kitchen. You shall have hot milk and cookies, and then I will tell you all about your mother.'

George makes to speak when we are in the kitchen, but I put a finger to my lips. Eddie will not face his father, but sits on a stool, and looks to me. I sit down. I say: 'Your mother's name was Susanna. She was my cousin and next to your Papa I loved her best in all the world.' I tell him how she came from England, that she was his father's first wife, and how pretty she was, how merry; how she loved to dance. I tell Eddie that he had a brother called John who died of the cholera. I say that God had need of them both to be angels in Heaven because they were so good. I say that God sent me to America to care for the baby Eddie and his father because they were so all alone. Even as I speak I pray that it might be the right words. I tell him that he is as preshus to me as Georgie and Rosa. I hear the rasp of George's breathing; he is upset, what always brings on the asthma attack.

Well, it cannot be helped. *It does not do to lie to children.* I recall how hard-won was the baby Eddie's trust. I say: 'I am your Mama in every way that matters.'

He says: 'Will you take me to her grave?'

'Tomorrow,' I promise. 'We will go tomorrow.'

George leaves the kitchen. The front door opens and closes. In a bad attack he is best left to himself. He seeks fresh air upon the stoop.

Eddie says: 'Is he really my Papa?'

Oh George, you meant only to protect him from life's hurts – but see now the damage you have done!

'Come stand before the mirror, Eddie!' I put my hands upon his shoulders, we gaze at our two reflecshuns. 'Look at me,' I tell him. 'My hair is brown and straight, my face is pale, my eyes are green. Now look at you! You have the same face as your father and your Uncle John, as your brother and sister. You are truly a Salter.'

I take him to his bed. I cossett him, what I have not done for a long time. I hope it is enough.

George comes back into the house. His breathing is eased but not qwite normal. He sits in his chair and reads the newspaper. He says not one word upon the subject of Eddie, and I see by his face that I would be wise to hold my tongue!

I have often noticed that it is in the nature of most men not to let pain in, and so, when awful things happen – they seem to mind less.

Chapter Twelve

The Indians still used the traditional trailpaths which led to Menominee hunting and fishing grounds, even where those paths passed over and close to the white man's habitation. To begin with, Elizabeth had feared the red men. In summer they would encircle the house, stand on tiptoe and peer in at her open windows, inspect and laugh at the undergarments hung out to dry across the adjacent bushes. At their approach she would run with the children to the ox-shed and hide until they went away. In winter, when times were hard, they would hammer on her door and demand food. She always gave them a loaf even when she could not spare it. It was the custom thereabouts, and made for peaceable living.

Other fears were more persistent and not to be cured with a loaf of bread. She had grown accustomed to the cry of the loon, the honking of the wild geese, the sinister rustle of racoon and bear as they prowled around the house in winter. But the howling of wolves in the night raised in her such a terror that she would cover her head with the pillow and pray to God for them to go away. In this year of 1862 the howl of the wolfpack had been heard in late September. People said that it meant a bitter winter and a late spring. In October the days were crisp, each breath streamed white across the cold air. Birds came to feed on the orange bittersweet berries. Robert finished his ploughing of their arable acres, repaired fences, hauled his stack of swamp-hay closer to the house and sheeted down his straw-stack. A few hours of every day were spent on adding to the log-pile. The cow had calved, and Elizabeth made butter and curd-cheese. This year their stocks of food were high. The war had caused a rise in the prices of farm products, and a system of barter was still practised in the northwoods. Items purchased in the dry goods store in Green Bay could now be profitably paid for with a few pounds of butter, a crock of cream, the surplus honey from an industrious housewife's beehive, the preserves and pickles from her kitchen.

The loghouse had gradually taken on a more comfortable aspect. By means of barter and exchange Elizabeth had acquired a number of fur rugs. Curtains of blue gingham now hung at the windows, coloured cushions made comfortable the chairs and benches. She had made her 'wall of honour' on which hung the portraits of her family and Robert's; racked close to the door was their most valuable possession, the shotgun which provided venison and wild duck, and the sweet meat of the black squirrel.

The wind was in the northwest quarter and had been so for many days. A brilliant sky arched above the pinewoods but in the west thick clouds of white built ever higher; clouds that held a core of ominous blackness at their centre. Robert, coming from the gristmill with several sacks of flour and meal, urged the oxen hard along the trailpath. He had learned to read the snow signs, and the clouds to his back and the rising wind made him fearful. He reached home as the sky overhead began to darken. He housed the oxen and waggon, stowed the flour and meal, and then fastened the shutters across every window. He filled water buckets at the stream which had not yet frozen over. The boys helped Elizabeth to bring logs into the house and stack them beside the fireplace.

It was the noon hour, on the day before Christmas, when the snow began. It came gently at first, such tiny flakes like a powdering of fine flour; and then, quite suddenly, the temperature dropped. A wind came from out of the north, more fierce and bitter than any they had ever known, and now the snowflakes were thick, and sharp-edged enough to flay the skin. It snowed for two days and one night. At intervals Elizabeth and Robert were obliged to go outside to milk the cow and feed the stock. In the unpredictable manner of drifting snow, they found the loghouse buried to its topmost timbers, while a convenient pathway had been left open between house and sheds. It was not the Christmas they had planned. As more land was taken up and the community grew, strong bonds had grown between disparate neighbours. The many nationalities lived comfortably together, tolerating the idiosyncrasies brought from each one's native country, and appreciating the new and good things that each separate grouping had to offer. Parties had been planned to celebrate this Christmastide. Coffee and cake would have been served by the settlers from Germany; panny-cakes and pea-soup by the French. The Dutch among them were already famous for their excellent doughnuts. From England Elizabeth had brought her skills of cheese and cider-making. But this year's end was to see very little of visiting and the parties that made tolerable their awful isolation. Each family must struggle now with its separate privations, and not all of them were equal to the task.

On January the first the temperature dropped to the lowest degree ever known in that section of the northwoods. People woke to find a rim of ice across their blankets where breath had frozen overnight. Even as fingers were dipped into the wash-bowl a crust of ice formed around its edges. The raging winds found new chinks in the loghouse; Elizabeth built great fires upon the hearthstone and prayed that their stock of fuel might last until the thaw came. On that first day of 1863 milk froze in the pail even as she carried it from shed to house. Grey shadows moved at the edges of the clearing. The timber-wolves were very close now to human habitation.

The weather eased. A rise in temperature made living bearable again. Trailpaths opened up between each farm and its neigh-bour. Men gathered at the Inn and around the blacksmith's forge. Robert learned how some homesteads had been ill-prepared for such extremes of weather. For others, tragedy had come through isolation. In this place, more than any other he had ever known, people needed one another.

There would, he told Elizabeth, be many funerals, and it was

144

the very old and the very young who had not survived. In the case of the old, a sheaf of corn saved from last summer's harvest for an eventuality such as this, would be laid upon the plain oak coffin; a symbol of fulfilled years and a soul safely gathered in. For their nearest neighbours there would be no such panacea. Twin girls, born prematurely to the young Wagners, had not survived those days of blizzard and extreme cold.

On hearing this news Elizabeth at once set out for the Wagner house, taking her three children with her; for she did not believe in shielding them from life's hard truths. God, she explained, would always see fit to call Home the weakest and oldest in times of great hardship. He had taken them to be angels. They were happy now in Heaven.

It was harder to believe as she stood beside the little coffin. Perfectly preserved in the icy air of an upper room, the babies lay side-by-side looking like two waxen dolls, and dressed in the fine baptismal robes that Inge Wagner had brought with her from the Old Country. Even in death they would not be separated. Elizabeth went down to sit by Inge's bed. She held the hand of the young mother but there was no comfort she could offer.

Inge said: 'We should not have come here. At home I would have had my mother by me, my sisters. They said we would not manage on our own, and they were right.'

Elizabeth said: 'You will have other children. They were your first, and so very tiny.'

The ground stayed frozen to a depth of feet. The dead could not yet be buried, nor mourning properly begin. Coffins were closed, and loved ones whatever their beliefs were taken to the Roman Catholic Chapel. The path leading to that Chapel passed close beside the Vickery spread. Elizabeth came to dread the sight of a laden sleigh, its cheerful bells removed, or a slow-walking father who bore a tiny coffin in his arms.

Spring came tentatively that year. Johnny, who was eight years old and knew every bird by sight and name, came running to her in April to report a bluebird, a killdeer, a flock of redwings, a pair of jacksnipe. Chas, who was six, carried little green frogs in his britches pockets, and wept when forced to set them free. Willum, who found it hard to pronounce his name, was a sturdy three-year-old with a tendency to roam, and now Elizabeth could hardly bear to let them from her sight, so dear and precious were they. Each child had his daily chores; even Willum, whose task it was to feed chickens and collect eggs. He would bring the eggs to her one by one, each in a nest of straw and carried in his woollen cap. She would take the egg and place it in a bowl, then hug the child so fiercely to her that he would struggle to be free.

Robert said that sons must not be mollycoddled; and already these three boys showed promise of the men they were to be. But at secret moments, at bedtime or in the early morning, she held them close and kissed them. They were, she thought, the good harvest of her body, more valuable than any crop that could ever grow in Suamico, Brown County.

The post came to Suamico twice weekly. It arrived in Green Bay by way of Escanaba, and was carried from the Bay by Toussant Tellor, a sturdy young man of French descent, who journeyed to bring it through the very worst of weather. It was many months since the mail-pouch had held post for the Vickery family. Now came four letters, all together, three of them bearing English postmarks.

Elizabeth approached news from England with hesitation and pleasure. It was gratifying to be remembered, but experience had made her nervous of the bad news and grumbles that seemed invariably to come out of Buckland St Mary. Had the Greypaulls, she wondered, always been so gloomy, so full of complaints, so concerned and inclined to dwell on the trivia of their own small troubles? Letters from her oldest brother were especially irritating. Since becoming a Barrister he tended to be pompous and inclined to lecture. It amused her sometimes to imagine the impeccable James, set down in his frock-coat and brocaded waistcoat, without warning or assistance, in the middle of the deepest pineries, and obliged to fend for himself. Nobody at Patchwood, save perhaps her father, had any notion of what was true hardship or hard work!

She studied the handwriting on each envelope. First came the tall and elegant script of James; every i dotted, every t crossed. There was a black-edged envelope addressed in her sister Joan's quick and sprawling hand, and a third written carefully in childish unformed letters. The fourth envelope, much stained around its edges, was in a strange hand and bore the postmark of Memphis, Tennessee.

It was not until much later, when the children slept, and Robert sat with her on the stoop of the loghouse, that Elizabeth found courage enough to open the mail. It was her habit to read aloud to him the Greypaull letters. The June evening was filled with the sounds of katydids and crickets. A little breeze rustled through the knee-high corn, and brought with it the sweet smells of clover and new hay. Robert had laboured since sun-up, dividing his time between their own land and the Black farm; for many of those hours she had worked at his side. Weariness had overcome him; now he sat in his chair, eyelids drooping.

She said: 'The news can wait until tomorrow if you'd rather . . .'

He sat upright. 'No. – let's hear it all. Read out the home news to me.'

The black-edged envelope came first to hand.

Dear Sister Elizabeth and your husband Robert,
Have not written to you for a long time, and now must tell you my bad news. My dear Husband Jacob died suddenly at Christmas. He was ill but a few days with inflammation to the lungs. He was but thirty-four years old. I have no child for comfort. I miss him sorely. But I must earn my living, and since I have no liking for farming I have sold-up house and land and bought a draper's business down in Taunton. I keep very busy. I make dresses for a few select ladies. I often think on our happy days in the little shop in Buckland St Mary. Do you recall the Sewing Corner made by poor Susanna? How good it was when we were all together.

147

Ann is back in England. I wanted her with me in Taunton, but Father will not let her from his sight. She is much improved in many ways, but has no will to stand against him.

I hope you are both well, also your dear Children.

Your loving sister,

Joan

Elizabeth laid down the single black-edged sheet of paper. She said: 'Poor Joan! I must write to her at once.'

Robert said: 'Jacob and I went to school together. He was a good fellow, one of the very best!'

Unspoken dread coloured both voices. Their secret fear was always that the other one would die early.

The letter from James had the feel of a speech delivered from a high place. It told of parties to which he had been invited, young ladies to whom he had been introduced. He spoke only briefly of family. *Father,* he wrote *has aged much in the past few years. The absence of Ann was a great sorrow to him, and seems to have accomplished little. It would have been better had George Salter and our sister Rhoda not meddled in Ann's affairs. The jaunt to America has cost a great deal of money – and all is as before.*

'They still blame me,' Elizabeth whispered. 'He does not say it outright . . .' Her fingers fumbled with the third envelope. She held up the single sheet of paper, bemused by the level spacing between each line of rounded writing, the unfamiliar aspect of it.

My dear Elizabeth and Robert,
You will be surprised at a letter in my own hand. I learned much of value in New York City, can both read and write now. The Braille was hard to master, but it has given me a new life. I am now betrothed to Mr Robbins the Curate, but Father is not well, and so we shall not marry until he is improved. Please write me a few lines. I think often on our happy times together. You were ever dear to me, Elizabeth.

Robert took the letter from her. He said: 'Don't cry now! This is a miracle, the like of which we never hoped to see! Ann reads and writes – she is to marry the Curate.'

148

'So it is true. Rhoda wrote me something of the sort, but I thought it but the fancy of a blind girl.'

Elizabeth spoke softly.

'I had prayed that God might give her sight back, but He had done the next best thing.'

'– and your brother James dares to say in his letter that little was accomplished in New York – that all is as before?'

Elizabeth sighed. 'James thinks only in terms of hard cash. He is a strange man.'

She looked thoughtful.

'Now that Joan has gone to live in Taunton only James and Mary see very much of Father. There is Ann, of course, but Father will always treat her like a child.'

The letter from Memphis, Tennessee, had taken two months to reach Suamico. The single sheet bore a few lines of shaky script.

Elizabeth read,

Dear friends Robert and Elizabeth Vickery,
I was wounded in battle, got shot through the stomach. The surgeon patched me up, but I am no more good for fighting. Was this day discharged the Army and paid-off all money owing to me. Have had no news of Jim in a long time.
Shall be making my way back to you in easy stages.
Your good friend,
Matthew Black

It was August when Matt returned. He came up through fields that were tall with crops and white with moonlight. He leaned heavily upon a hickory stick, and rested many times along the trailpath. They watched him come, and there was that about him which held them rooted with a new kind of shyness that was almost fear. It was not only his emaciated frame, the strange angle at which he held his body; in those long minutes as he walked towards them, it seemed to Elizabeth and Robert as if the smell of battlefields, of death itself, was strong upon him. It was not until he spoke their names, held out a hand towards them, that they were released sufficiently to embrace him and draw him into the house.

All his wounds were to the stomach. It was, so the surgeon had told him, a miracle that he had lived. Now he could eat only light foods. For a month he rested-up, eating the milk-puddings and coddled-eggs Elizabeth made him, but gaining not one ounce of weight, nor sign of strength. In the fierce heat of the day he stayed within the house, at night he slept on a straw-filled mattress out on the front porch. Neighbours visited, bringing small gifts for the returned hero, but on the subject of the war he would not be drawn.

Robert showed Matt the tidy fields that were known in the village as the Black Farm. He explained his system of rotated crops, attempted to hand over one half of the profits made from those crops in the brothers' absence, only to have the money pushed back at him across the table. Matt said, as he did to every proposal, every question about the future: 'It must wait until Jim gets back. Without him I don't even want to think about it.'

His disability pension was paid monthly. He gave the ten dollars to Elizabeth; with it she purchased boots for him, new clothing and tobacco. As winter came on he was able to do small chores about the house and yard. Together he and Robert made a proper staircase which led to the upper storey of the house. The space beneath the roof was partitioned now into two rooms; one for the occupation of the three boys, and the other for Matthew. Twice weekly he walked to the Postmaster's house to collect the mail. It was at Christmas that the letter came from Lieutenant James Black. The address at its heading was that of the Libby Prison for Officers, Richmond, West Virginia. It was dated September 25, 1862. The envelope bore a spattering of brown stains, but no stamp. He paid the excess postage and hurried to Elizabeth. He placed the letter in her hands as if it were a great gift.

Matthew said: 'I'd given up hope.'

'This news has taken fifteen months to find us,' Elizabeth warned him.

She saw his anxious face.

'We won't wait for Robert to come back. I'll read it to you straight away.'

They sat down, at midday, one on either side of the banked fire; an unusual happening, which added drama to the reading.

Dear friends Robert and Elizabeth your wife,
More than a year has passed since you last had word from me, but little time to spare for letter-writing in this War, and whenever time allowed, I fear I lacked the inclination. As you will see from the above, I am now in 'Durance Vile'. Was captured while acting Officer of the Picket Guard near the Rapidon River on August 15 of this year 1862. We were brought to the Libby Prison at Richmond, Virginia, and expect to remain here, unless we are fortunate enough to be exchanged.

I was enrolled with a rank of Sargent, and was promoted to 2nd Lieutenant on March first of this year. I was injured a while back, just before my promotion to Lieutenant. I was in command of a Scouting party near the Green Briar Road, in Green Briar County, West Viriginia. There had been heavy fighting thereabouts and we were missing several men. I feared that some lay injured, and found that such was indeed the case. While searching along the edge of a precipice I heard a man cry out for help. I managed to drag him to safety, but in so doing, overbalanced and fell myself from the precipice in the darkness, sustaining thereby a severe hernia to my right side, and a partial loss of the sight of my right eye. On another occasion my horse took fright and threw me. Unfortunately, my foot stuck fast in the stirrup and I was dragged for a quarter-mile before being released. This time I took flesh wounds and bad damage to my shoulder, but managed to stay on duty throughout. Seem to feel all these aches and pains more severely since being here in Libby Prison.

Well this my news up to date. Wish I could say that I hope to see you all real soon, but fear that we are some way off still from the winning of this war. I have had no news of my dear brother Matthew since I heard of his enrolment in the 12th Wisconsin Volunteers. At least he is fighting for what we now think of as our Home State.

When things get bad here I call to mind Suamico, Brown County, and all your sweet kindness to us. What wouldn't I give now to be out of this sticky Virginia summer, and swinging an axe in your pineries on a cold and frosty morning.

151

I trust this letter reaches you in safety. I am giving it to a comrade who is to be exchanged tomorrow, and he has promised to post it for me. May the good Lord keep us and preserve us until we meet again.
Your true friend
Jim Black

Matt picked up the brown-stained envelope.

'I wonder,' he said, 'what happened to Jim's comrade?'

'Don't think about that,' Elizabeth said quickly. 'It seems that men sometimes get exchanged from the Libby Prison. If Jim had died or been killed in action we would surely by this time have had word from the Army.' She paused. 'He'll be back. I have this strong feeling that some things are meant to be. God sent you both here for a certain purpose. I don't know what it is, but Jim will return. This is where his home is.'

The farm boys of Wisconsin were said to be the finest soldiers in Abraham Lincoln's armies. In that final year of war the people of Brown County began to count their losses. There were many who would never return; others who came back, discharged as no longer fit for service, with empty sleeves pinned across their tunics, others with shattered legs that would never again walk behind a team and plough.

On April 9, 1865 General Lee, with his army of 27,000 men surrendered to General Grant at Appomattox, Virginia. Lee's soldiers were permitted to go at once to their homes, taking with them their horses, which, as General Grant so generously said, they would need for the spring ploughing.

Three million men had been engaged in Civil War. Of that number 620,000 had died of wounds, or diseases contracted while on military service. But the Union of American States had been saved; the slaves had been freed. In the days that led up to Good Friday the people of Washington began to celebrate the victory: the churches and bars had never been so crowded. The President and Mrs Lincoln attended the performance of an English play at Ford's Theatre on Tenth Street. While the drama was in progress an actor named John Wilkes Booth placed a derringer to the back of Mr Lincoln's head and fired it, inflicting a wound from which he died twelve hours later.

The passing of Abe Lincoln had a profound effect upon the minds of people. In his lifetime he had been both loved and hated, many threats had been made against his life. But now, for the rest of their days, the people of America would remember precisely where they were, and what exactly they were doing, when reached by news of the assassination.

Word came to Suamico brought by Toussant Tellor, who had heard the tolling of the church bells while collecting the mail in Green Bay.

Down in Nashville, Tennessee, Jim Black heard the news in the Paymaster's Office, as he drew his severance pay from the Union Army.

Chapter Thirteen

In a time of great change, among a shifting population of many nationalities and colours, the Englishness of Rhoda remained unaltered. In church affairs, in stores and markets, in all her dealings with the local people, that clipped yet quiet speech was listened to with an unusual respect. When she walked through Charlotte, the roughest of teamsters and traders still tipped their hats and moved aside for her to pass along the boardwalks. In her presence men tended not to chew and spit, and were later surprised at their own forbearance. There was about her a confidence, a conviction of her own rightness in a violent and disturbing world.

George took pride in Rhoda. She was his only certainty in a world of fluctuating standards. With her, a man would always know exactly where he stood, how far he dared to venture, what risk he might attempt. He could not imagine life without her. His dependence upon her, he secretly admitted, was greater than that of any of their children, who were already showing strong signs of separateness and self-will. His present prosperity had much to do with her wise counsel, and yet ambition burned in him more strongly than ever. He had, Rhoda said, caught the American fever. They had made for themselves a good life in Charlotte, she was as content as she was likely to be, why could he not be satisfied?

But George now dreamed of living in Chicago as he had once yearned to come to Charlotte. There was a restlessness in his nature that would always keep him striving; he had a mind that schemed and planned in a reckless way that paid no heed to the severity of his attacks of asthma, or the dangers of living in a city. In the hours when his breathing was most laboured he would banish fear with an image of a signboard, painted in letters that were a foot high. On it was the title for which he longed, and meant to have.

GEORGE HODDER SALTER and SONS. MEAT PACKERS
OF CHICAGO

They walked to church on that Easter Sunday morning. Rhoda, her left hand touching George's elbow, carried prayer-book and parasol in her right hand; the three children walked silently before them. She noted absently how a small, black-booted foot strayed towards a stone that lay waiting to be kicked on the sidewalk. She saw the warning nudge from Eddie that saved Georgie from her anger. This walk to church, along tree-lined Latta Road, was always the testing time of her success or failure. The appearance of the children, spotless and creaseless, with shining boots and faces, every curling hair subdued beneath straw hats, was as faultless as it could possibly be. Eddie, who at nine years old was conscious of his position of older brother, would keep Georgie in order for the span of the service. Rosa, a born lady, and loving every flounce and ribbon of her new pink dress, was never any trouble to her mother.

Rhoda glanced sideways and upwards, and a small line appeared between her eyebrows. George was wearing his new suit of fine black broadcloth, with the velvet waistcoat and the cravat of blue figured silk, that was kept in place by a diamond-tipped pin. She herself, dressed in a simple gown and cape of dark green, thought the tie-pin ostentatious. She did not altogether approve of the black velvet waistcoat; even the black broadcloth, when worn by George, had a dashing, slight rakish air about it. Oh, but he was handsome! Even when standing behind the counter and wearing his boater and butcher's apron, the charm of George remained undimmed. Young housewives fluttered their eyelashes at him across the sausage-links and pork chops; substantial matrons ordered bigger joints of beef than they had originally intended while enjoying the brightness of George's blue eyes.

Her hand tightened on his elbow. He felt the pressure and

155

smiled down at her, and she at once forgave him his stylishness, his unselfconscious good looks. The ambiguities of her own nature sometimes troubled Rhoda; by instinct she still tended towards the puritanical and plain. But as they walked from sunshine into dimness, and filed into the pew that bore their name, she began to compare the looks of her four beautiful Salters, the Englishness of them, with the solidity and plainness of these worshippers of Charlotte. Quality, she thought was unmistakable and God-given. If pride in her family should be reckoned sinful, then she would pray to be forgiven for it. It was said by Baptists and Methodists, and the Irish Roman Catholics, that those who belonged to the Episcopalian Church believed that they alone had been granted a first-class ticket into Heaven. It was true that the Episcopalians were the acknowledged superiors among such social orders as existed in this land of opportunity for all. Church members came mostly from business and professional people, and the best of the emmigrant English; which, as Rhoda said to George, was exactly as it should be. There was, in her opinion, far too much familiarity about in these days. Since the onset of the war, quite ordinary people had grown smarter and gave themselves airs that were undeserved. Even Charlotte itself was no longer the simple village to which she had first come. Rhoda talked to missionaries who knocked upon her door; she read the newspapers bought by George. She learned that it was in the homesteads, in the backwoods, in the wide and lonely places of the American States, that the Hand of God lay hardest and heaviest on the people. On Sundays their little clapboard churches were filled with believers. Their faith was simple. They knew that God alone could bring order to their risky lives, that without him they were helpless. Farming men and women who laboured long throughout the week found in church a certain drama and excitement. If times were good they came to thank Him. If times were bad they accepted that this was God's way of punishing them for past sins.

In Charlotte faith was not so simple. This fertile plain that lay on the shores of Lake Ontario had always been good growing soil for psychic experience and mysticism. At intervals a kind of passion seized its people, and from among them there would come forth a prophet. People still spoke about William Miller who had prophecied that the world would end on October 24, 1844. There were those of Rhoda's neighbours who re-membered how many farmers' crops had been left unharvested that summer; how long lines of believers had climbed to the highest place in the Pinnacle Hills, and waited for the world to end. They also recalled the cold and bedraggled Millerites who came down from the Hills the next morning.

As the Pastor climbed into the pulpit, she saw that instead of the white and gold vestments of Easter Sunday, he was wearing a set of black robes. Even as he began to speak the single bell that denoted mourning began to toll above them.

★

April 14, 1865

No rejoicing in our Church this morning. Was told by our Pastor of the awful murder of President Lincoln, what comes as no great shock to me, this being such a wild and lawless country. Told George and the children that such a thing could never have come to pass at home in England. Our dear Queen Victoria being held in *reverence* and *awe* by *all* her people. Cannot help but see the Hand of God in all of this. Still feel that George's diamond tie-pin much too showy to be worn to Church, but cannot bring myself to say so, and spoil his pleashure in it. My boys qwite the opposite of their dear Father, cannot wait to rip off what they call their 'Sunday-duds', put on their old things and sneak off to the fields where are kept the horses. They beg for a pony. In this alone do I see the Greypaull blood in them, every man in our great family is born with a strong passhun for horses, and a wish to ride them. All too often do Eddie and Georgie come late from school, their britches torn, their faces muddied. Better buy them a pony I tell George! They are like to be killed or maimed while trying to ride that wild creature that grazes in Liebermann's field. George complains that both boys hang about in the harness repair shop,

157

and around the blacksmith's forge. How, he asks me, shall I ever make business men of either of them, while they so neglect their studies? Forbear to say that so far neither child shows any sign of interest in butchery or money-making, what is not too surprising since Eddie only nine years old, and Georgie seven. Would like to point out that both are country-boys, with a love of birds and flowers, and all animals, *espeshully horses*. Could it be that they are farmers born, and not butchers? Shall say nothing further on the subject since Eddie whispers after supper that he has prayed in Church, and now thinks that Papa 'is coming round' to the notion of a pony.

May 12
George grows restless and nervous, what is not good for his asthma. All he thinks of is Chicago and the fortunes to be made there. He is keen to go into the wholesale business of meat-packing – but not here in Charlotte. Since the Union Stockyards opened on Christmas Day he talks of nothing else but the transport of carcasses by railroad, the possibilities of buying cheap ice, the best ways of pickling pork and salting beef. Cannot see a more dreadful prospekt than to live in that wicked and godless Chicago! Bridget says if we go from here she will not come with us, she now walking out with Liam O'Connell who works in the boatyard.

Was very nauseous again this morning. The fourth time in a week. Shall say nothing to George until I am certain. Six years have passed since the birth of Rosa. Had begun to believe there would be no more babies.

July 5
My condishun confirmed this day by Dr Jones. Am still nauseated every morning. Lie very qwiet in my bed and Will it *not* to happen, but the minute my two feet touch the floor I am sick enough to *die*. Have grown weak and thin as a result. Tell George qwite strongly that any move to Chicago is *out of the qwestion*. Unless of course he is prepared to be a widower for the *second* time in his life. I am nearly thirty-five years old.

158

Many women have babies at a much more advanced age than this, or so says Bridget, and no trouble at all.

September 14
George says no more on the subject of our going to Chicago, but he reads pamphlets about the wholesale business. In the evenings he and John talk much about the putting-up of hog-meat. As I try to eat my supper, for which I have no appetite at all, I must listen and learn much about the statistics of the meat trade. It would seem that the State of Illinois is the Qween of Butchers. In the year of 1862 a half-million hogs were slaughtered and packed, what was a rekord, and outdid that of the State of Ohio. George looks at me with *meaning* and says offhand, that there are now fifty-eight packers in business in Chicago. I try to take some interest in the matter since it is so important to him. I learn that to 'pack' meat is to cure it or smoke it, and place it in barrels. I push the food around my plate, and Bridget clucks and grumbles at me. The men go on to talk of lard what is extracted from the carcasses by means of steam-tanks. George then tells John about the risks of packing, and how in warm weather one small mistake can cause fermentashun in the pickling brine and so turn rotten whole batches of hog meat. It is at this point that I excuse myself from their company, and make haste to the stoop and my chair in the cool of evening. A strong stomach is needed when married to a butcher, and I am no longer in *good health*.

December 20
Have not left the house for many weeks. Deep snow has lain since early November, and my limbs very swollen. Mrs Sanchez shakes her head above me, but Dr Jones says all is well, and my confinement expected in mid-January. Today I send Bridget up into the attic. She brings down the crib, and the little rocking-chair I brought from England. We have made all new baby clothing, and George has promised me one of the new-fangled baby carriages on sale in Rochester.

The children are making all ready for Christmas. The house

looks so pretty but I am low in spirit. George wants so much to live in Chicago, altho' he does not say so.

January 12, 1866
Our new son is five days old. He does not have the Salter looks but favours more towards the Greypaulls. A long and agonising labour with much haemorraging. George much frightened. He wept for joy when Dr Jones said we should both 'pull through'. The baby's name is to be Jonathon.

I must write letters to Elizabeth and Father, but weakness too much for me at present. Whatever should we do without the help of Bridget?

September 7
Jon is eight months old today. A good, contented baby, hardly know that he is in the house, so qwiet is he, save for the convulshons. Dr Jones says it is nothing, some infants always suffer fits when they are cutting teeth. He does not yet sit upright, but all children do not develop at the same rate. He has my exact looks, pale complecshun, green eyes, and much brown and shining hair. He has such a sweet smile, and is much loved by us all, most espeshully by Rosa.

April 4, 1867
Many months have passed since my last entry. My fears so great that I can scarcely write them down. There was a time in my life when to write things down was to know what I was thinking. Now, I no longer wish to know my own thoughts.

It is April. In Buckland St Mary the gypsies will be back to Dommett Wood. Their waggons will stand, green- and yellow-painted, underneath the blackthorns. There will be primroses and violets showing in the churchyard and the lanes. There will be a smell of damp moss in the woodlands, and soft sweet air such as only blows in Somerset in springtime. Oh, how much I long to be in England, to feel the loving arms of Elizabeth and Joan about me. If I could but run to the shelter and wisdom of my father – but how could I do that, even if it were possible to

160

take the voyage home? How could I say to him: 'My beloved child has inherited your sickness. My darling baby Jon is epileptic. Three doctors in Rochester have said so. That old curse of the family, which missed my own generation, has come out in my last child.' Such words cannot be written in a letter. My father is an old man, now, and must never know what has come to pass, here in Charlotte.

Jon now fifteen months old, and so contented and good. He sits up lately, but does not stand or speak. But then, neither did his brother Eddie, when I first came here. Some children are slower to develop than others.

April 20

Weather still very cold. Frost night and morning. A long, sad winter. Try to bide cheerful for the sake of the children, but so much of my time taken up by Jon.

Spent most of last evening on our Account Books. George comes in and sees my occupashun. He stands beside me and fidgets from one foot to the other, as do my boys when they have transgressed.

'What is it?' I ask.

He hands me a Money Draft. It is addressed to the business of G. H. Salter, Slaughterer and Butcher, and is in the sum of two hundred dollars.

'Enter that up in the Ledger, Rhoda!'

His eyes are merry, his breathing deep and easy, what is always a good sign in George.

'So what is this?' I scold him. 'If it be the payment of some riverman's bad debt – then you know you should never have allowed so much credit to those rascally steamboat Captains!'

He pretends contrishun.

'It is not the payment of an old debt, but rather the birth of a new business.' He is set to tease me, but I am wary.

'Then you have sold the carriage? You have left us without transportashun?'

He places his hands upon my shoulders.

'Look at me, Rhoda!'

161

I look at him. I take time to study his features, and now I see what I should have noticed these many weeks gone. Inside himself, George is fired with a fever of excitement. He is like to burn up if he does not soon tell me all about it.

'What have you done?' I ask him.

He pulls up a chair, and sits beside me.

'It was last Fall,' he says, 'and you were so concerned with Jon. I thought it better not to tell you until my venture had succeeded. I bought-in a stock of hog-meat and some hundreds of barrels. I also had an ice-house built at the back of the store.'

'You have gone into the wholesale business! You are a packer!'

He snatches up the Money Draft and waves it like a banner.

'And ain't that just fine and dandy?' he cries. 'The easiest two hundred greenbacks that I ever made.'

I do not like it when he speaks American and he knows this.

'You never told me,' I accuse him. 'You did all that and not a word about it. What lie would you have given me if you had lost that money?'

'But I didn't lose it, Rhoda!' He grows qwiet. He says: 'I had no wish to deceive you, but you have so much to do these days with Jon and his – his illness. I would not put another burden on you. But we have four children now, and one is very sickly. There are doctor's bills, medicines. We are not living in Buckland with our families around us. In this country there is but one way to go – and that is upwards!'

'And that last remark,' say I, 'is the nub of the matter. You are not content to get along pretty well, as are most of our neighbours.'

'No,' says he, 'you are qwite correct. Prosperity is what I aim for, I will build up a business for my sons. I will have the name of Salter mean something, whether it be here in Charlotte, or in Chicago.'

'It is enough,' I say, 'if the name of Salter be respected.'

He looks downcast. I take the Money Draft from him and enter it up in the Profits column.

'This time,' I tell him, 'all went well. You are to be congratulated. But I am hurt, George, that you saw fit not to tell me of this risky venture. Only very rich men can afford to take such chances.' I smile. 'I would have found out anyway, I expect, that you had been up to something, just as soon as my Ledger figures did not balance out.'

It is the wrong thing to say. I know it the very instant the words are spoken. He measures me with a long look. His tone gives me warning that now he is set upon a certain course, and I had better resign myself to it. 'I have,' says he, 'been studying the packing methods used in Chicago, and I find that it is possible to process hog-meat in the summer months.'

July 1

Little time for writing in the past weeks, each evening being swallowed up by the costing-out of the prices of saltpetre, sea-salt, barrels, and whatever else is needed for this business of 'packing' hog-meat. I am *not happy at this venture. Winter*, I tell George, is the only time safe enough to pickle pork.

'Are you,' he says, 'now trying to tell me how to run my business? Your place is to keep the books, and run the house. I will not have your interference!'

I am vexed. I say: 'Your business is founded mainly on the Dowry monies paid to you by my father. Surely this fact must give me some say in the managing of it!'

His breathing becomes short. His face is stony. I disregard the danger signals. I say: 'In England people have more sense than to attempt to preserve meat in the summer. In fact, George, in England all things are better done, and with a deal more style and decorum, than in this brash and reckless country!'

He speaks with difficulty. 'I am sorry, Rhoda, that you consider your father's Dowry payment to have been mis-managed by me. It is true that he was generous, but don't you forget how I work for some sixteen hours in every day? Butchering and slaughtering is not exactly light labour, and I am no longer one of the youngest – I was forty years old last April.'

He is gasping and in some distress. 'I will have a better life for my sons. The owner of a packing-house is able to employ men for the heavy labour. He has no need to swing the cleaver with his own hand.'

I regret my hasty words about the Dowry money, but on all else I must stand firm. There is now a coolness between us. George speaks only to his brother John about his plans, these conversashuns held always at the supper table, what he *knows* is *distasteful* to me.

George addresses his brother, but the words are aimed at my head. 'How lucky we are,' says my husband, 'to be living in Charlotte, on a busy shipping line which gives us easy transport. Most packers,' says he, 'buy-in meat that is already slaughtered and dressed, which makes it so much more expensive. We shall have the advantage of them when it comes to profit-making. The whole operation from living hog to pickling vat – and so to sealed-down barrel – will be done in our own packing-house, and no middle-man involved!'

It makes sense. I apply myself to my plate, but find little taste for roast meat, what is hardly any wonder. What George says is all true. As a slaughterman and butcher he *is* in a *prime* position. Find myself qwite unable to stay silent. There is still a flaw in his reasoning, and I must speak it.

'That's all very fine,' I burst out, 'but why must you try to "pack" meat in July?'

'Because,' says George, 'that is when it will fetch the highest prices. Men who wait for the first long spell of cold are forced to sell in a glutted market.'

I clear the dishes, but qwietly. I make no clatter as I wash and dry them. They talk of the almost-built sheds where they will do their work; about the shipment of ice they are expecting to arrive at any moment. George has spoken to me in that old way of his which is meant to give instructshun to an ignorant woman.

Make a vow that I will say *not one word* more to him upon the subject.

July 3

Jon now eighteen months old. He is the sweetest-natured of all my children. The convulshuns much worse in this hot and

164

humid weather. Dr Jones gives him mixtures and cooling draughts. Mrs Sanchez brings herbs. Nothing helps.

I read back in this Journal the rekord of my early days in Charlotte. Eddie, at eighteen months, did not even smile. Jon smiles and laughs. I begin to collect the wooden sewing cones that worked such magic with Eddie's slowness. I tell myself it is not a matter for being downcast or despairing. My father, in spite of lifelong epilepsy, is a clever man of business and has had a good and long life.

The boys come straight from school to home, without even looking-in at the blacksmiths or the harness-repair shop. They are bursting with news. They find me in the kitchen.

'Pa bought fifty fat hogs,' cries Georgie.

'More than that,' says Eddie. 'Could be eighty or a hundred! They're in the new stockpens, back of the store. According to Uncle John he and Pa'll be slaughtering tomorrow. The shipment of ice just came, all packed in straw and sawdust. There's big sacks full of salt, and at least a thousand new barrels!'

Georgie says: 'Aw shucks, Ma, do we have to go to school tomorrow? Why can't we go and help Pa?'

I tell them to wash their hands and faces, and sit down at the table. I give them lemonade and cookies. Think a thousand barrels must be an exaggeration. I say: 'You are not to use words like "aw shucks". We speak English in this house, Georgie, as you very well know! As for helping your Papa, you are not yet old enough, and if I find out that either of you has been anywhere near to the slaughterhouse, then you will be in great trouble!'

Rosa, who started to school but a few months ago, plays at being teacher. She sits on the stoop and instructs Jon and her many dolls. The boys go to the backyard. They play at being slaughtermen, using logs from the woodpile as fat hogs.

August 14
Something is wrong. George and John both very downcast, but nothing said in my hearing. George suffers many severe attacks of asthma. Because of the heat and the state of his breathing, he

can no longer sleep within the house. I make him a bed on the front porch. His suffering is much eased by the night air. My worry about him so great that I also lie wakeful. I go down to the stoop. I say: 'Something is amiss besides your asthma. Better that you tell what it is. We have always faced our troubles together.'

He says nothing for a long time. When he speaks I have to bend to catch his words.

'We have never,' says he, 'had such troubles to face as we have now. I don't know how to tell you of it.'

I say: 'It is the meat-packing project. It has bankrupted us just as I knew it must do.'

'No,' he cries, 'we are not totally ruined!'

He is much distressed. I bring him brandy and water. I sit down beside him and take his hand in mine.

'What went wrong, George?'

'We did everything right,' says he. 'We were so very careful. It was an order for the Army. I supplied them all through the war with fresh meat. They were keen to do business with me. John and I have gone over every detail of our processing – from the slaughter of the hogs right down to the final closing of the barrels.'

'So what was the trouble?'

'The meat was rotten on arrival at the Barracks in Ohio. Every single barrelful. They made a bonfire of it. The agent said the flesh had a speckled appearance.'

'What causes that to happen?'

He sighs: his grip tightens on my hand.

'It is a disease in the meat known as "measles". It happens when joints are put into the brine before they are thoroughly cooled-down. This causes a fermentashun in the pickling-brine and makes the meat unwholesome.' He turns to look at me, his face so white that I am fearful for him. 'I had ice especially shipped in,' he cries. 'I was so careful with the cooling process!'

I say, as gently as I am able: 'But it *was* July, George.'

'But it can be done, Rhoda! Packers work all summer through, over in Chicago!'

'In the morning,' I tell him, 'we shall work out on paper exactly what and how great are our losses. Whatever economies are needed, then we shall have to make them. Meanwhile, my dear, you must try to sleep. It will be the final blow for us all should your health break down.' I counsel sleep, but for me there is no rest this night, nor I think for many nights to come.

August 16
It is very bad.

As to expenses. There was the building of the stockpens and extra packing-sheds. Then came materials, saltpetre, ice, and so forth. There was the cost of barrels. The fee to the commishun agent. The price of shipping the consignment to the Army Barracks in Ohio. Worst of all, the check still owing to the farmer for some hundred fat hogs. Some of these costs already known to me, but not all. Have completed my reckoning. All our savings swallowed up. Shall need to sell the carriage and horses, my gemstone ring and George's diamond tiepin. We shall *not* be what people roundabouts here refer to as *dirt-poor*, but it is as well that Bridget is about to wed with her Liam. I would not have wanted to dismiss her, but truth to tell, we shall be hard put to it this month to find her final wages.

August 20
Weather very hot and humid. Electric storms what last for many hours. My fear of fire very great at such times among so many wooden buildings. My boys show no fear of lightning, but Rosa and I hide in the linen closet.

Bridget has wed with Liam O'Connell in the Roman Catholic Chapel. I stitched her bridal dress with my own hands, and made a small celebration for them. They are to live with Liam's mother, who is in poor health. Bridget promises to visit us often. The children weep to see her go, tho' she is but on the other side of Charlotte. I miss her too. The presence of another woman being such a comfort in this household of men.

News of our finanshul loss spreads like wildfire around

Charlotte. Would that we could keep it private, but the President of the Bank is also our Churchwarden, and his wife not famous for a qwiet tongue! Our lowering of standards, in any case, not possible to conceal. The sale of a man's carriage and horses being the most certain sign of his failure in business. Overhear Eddie say to Georgie that 'now we are poor folks' they stand no chance of getting a pony. Georgie says to Eddie that 'Pa is still hell-bent on moving to Chicago, and won't it be just dandy to live in a big City?' Should reprove my Georgie on the subject of his speech and ideas, but Jon now suffering a long bad spell and I must attend to him every minute, lest he choke to death in the convulshuns. Do not dare to call on Dr Jones, tho' he would come to us without hope of payment. But his bill already more than we can settle, and I have *some* pride left. Can only be watchful of Jon and pray for an easement of his condishun.

August 22
My father is dead.

I set down the words so that I may believe them. The news from my brother James comes as a great shock. It is like walking upon safe ground and coming, unawares, upon a black abyss. I had thought my father would always be there for me, a firm rock set in England, a sure hope in an unsafe world.

The manner of Father's passing is disturbing, espeshully to me, and in view of Jon's condishun. Death came to him by means of epileptic seizures, what followed one upon the other until his tired heart could stand no more. I cannot weep. My grief for Father is all mixed up with fears for Jon. Do not understand my feelings. Have a longing to behave like Georgie, who oftimes smashes things in temper. It was the same with me when Susanna died. I was angry for such a long time.

It is wrong to doubt the wisdom of the Lord, but why should this old Greypaull curse have been laid upon my blameless baby? What purpose can it serve in Heaven that Jon should suffer so? Our Pastor comes to me. He speaks of resignashun and acceptance. To be resigned is not my nature. Once, there was comfort to be found in just remembering Patchwood, and Buckland St Mary. Well, that has been taken from me also. Poor Father, he was so good to us, always.

I *will* be thankful, I tell George, when this awful year of 1867 is *ended*.

Chapter Fourteen

In Suamico, Wisconsin, Elizabeth read several times the stilted phrases written by her brother James, before the meaning of his words took on reality for her. She studied James's description of the manner of her father's dying, then turned to the healthy, sunburned faces of her sons, and had a sense of disaster narrowly avoided. She lay wakeful through the night, and slept briefly and too deeply towards morning.

Elizabeth's grief was uncomplicated. All that day she wept at unexpected moments. She had not striven to remember England, which made doubly poignant the memories that crowded on her now. Father's love of Patchwood; the way he had stroked beams and lintels when a storm was coming; the way he cared about them all. The help that never was refused; the little, unsolicited kindnesses.

Only last Christmas he had sent shoes, a pair for each of them, handstitched in fine brown leather 'so that you may all go well-shod through the winter'. There had been a dress for her birthday, a gown so fine that she rarely had worn it. Made of stiff silk, and of a deep crimson colour, it was, he had said, stitched by Joan in her drapery business, and in the very latest London fashion. The gown, with its leg-of-mutton sleeves, tiny waist, and full, ribbon-trimmed skirts, had been the wonder of every wedding and christening she attended in Suamico. An exact copy of the dress had been sent also to Charlotte. Sometimes, when Elizabeth put on her plain cotton gingham, when she washed dishes, scrubbed floors, tied-up corn-shocks in the harvest, she would think of the crimson silk and feel a warmth, a little secret pleasure that both she and Rhoda, on occasion, would be wearing identical and elegant outfits. She had known in her heart that she and Father would never meet again in this life; and yet while he still lived there was always the sense of a door not quite shut.

She read again James's account of the funeral procession. and how the whole Parish had turned out to mourn. Of her father's first family, only three of the eight had remained in England to walk behind his coffin. The final page of the letter was all to do with the reading of the Will. It was couched in the complicated and repetitive legal language which James so loved to use. She had not understood one word on her first reading of it. She laid it aside; her father had always been a fair man and to pursue such a subject on this of all days seemed to her to be indecent.

But the images of Buckland were not so easily put away. Elizabeth counted years, and found that more than ten had passed since she and Robert first came to Wisconsin. They had known good times and bad times. There had been bitter winters, spoiled harvests. But they were still strong and healthy; their boys were good and decent children. She took down the portrait from her Wall of Honour, the family group requested especially by Father 'so that he might study their likeness and take comfort from it'. It showed herself and Robert seated, the three boys standing up behind them. She noticed for the first time how the hand of each rested on the other. Her own fingers touched Robert's sleeve with a possessive gesture. The hands of the boys touched their parents' shoulders. She smiled through tears. The portrait had the comforting look of a family, loving and united.

Captain James Black had taken his severence pay, had the order of release stamped into his Paybook, and, still wearing the dark-blue uniform, high boots, and peaked cap of the Union Army, had begun the long journey north. His progress was deliberately slow. Sometimes he travelled on the railroad; in certain States he would spend the night in a country tavern, and in the morning take a northbound stage, or hitch a free ride on a farmer's waggon. Some instinct warned him against hurry. He willed the tightness in his mind to slacken; he talked to

171

disillusioned Confederate soldiers, to frightened negroes who, in their unexpected freedom, found no place to go. He wondered what it had all been about, the bloodshed and the dying, the horror of the Libby Prison for Officers, which would stay with him forever; the new weaknesses of his own body, which had appeared like cracks in a hitherto reliable structure. In Chicago he boarded a lake-steamer that was bound for Milwaukee. In Milwaukee he took a stage, the final stop of which was to be Fond du Lac. In a bar in Fond du Lac he found a wheelwright who was delivering a new waggon to a farmer in De Pere, and that town was but a few miles from Suamico. In Chicago, and in every town and farmstead on that journey north from Tennessee, people talked of little else but the murder of Abe Lincoln.

Jim had come with relief from the enervating South to the crisp nights and mornings of a springtime in the northwoods. He recognised Wisconsin by the great, red-painted barns, the blue valleys of hepatica flowers; that special quality in the light that he had never found in any other place. It was early May; a few days later and he would have missed this most beautiful of seasons. He watched the last blossoms blow from the wild sweet-crabapple trees, saw a farmer tilling soil on a far hillside, caught the smell of growing things, and felt an easement in his mind.

His final ride was hitched with a teamster who was on his way to Green Bay. It was early evening when they approached Suamico. Jim left the waggon and struck out along a trailpath that passed through deep woodland. He walked very slowly, all the weariness of four years' soldiering seemed to gather now and fall across him. The damaged left side of his body ached from the long journey over rough terrain. He had deliberately held back from all thoughts of those people who awaited him at this journey's end. In a world where so many things had changed, where so much had been lost, and even a President had been murdered, he no longer dared to hope for the continued survival of good people; sweet places.

Jim emerged from the trees on to rising ground. He stood on

the hillside and looked out across the sudden cluster of lighted windows. From this point it appeared that the houses stood close together, but he knew that a mile or more would separate one steading from another. Through the dusk he picked out red barns and windmills, shingled roofs and tall stone chimneys from which smoke was rising. He located the silver thread of river, the long low bulk of the Rough and Ready tavern. There had, he remembered, been a cooper's shop, a blacksmith's, a little schoolhouse; the impaired vision of his left eye made it hard to focus on the exact spot where stood the Vickery loghouse. Suamico. More thickly-peopled than he remembered, more lights ashine in settlers' windows. Even at this distance he could sense the safety of it; could imagine the sweetness and scents of apple and plum blossom in newly planted orchards, the hum of bees about hives that were almost hidden in deep grass, the good-cooking smells that had not meant home to him since he was a very young man.

He felt the wetness of tears, but did not wipe them away; and that was also a weakness not experienced since boyhood. He thought, for the first time in years about his mother and father, and the good life they had made together. This brought him, unavoidably, to think of Matthew, who might – or might not – have survived the Civil War.

It was Willum, coming back from his last call of the day on the just-hatched chickens, who saw the tall thin man limping down the trailpath. He ran to the house.

'Mama! Stranger coming! Looks like a soldier!'

She knew at once that the man was Jim Black. In the three weeks since the War's end, Elizabeth had, almost without thinking, cooked a little extra supper every evening against his return.

She said: 'Is your father close by?'

'No, Ma. He's still over at the Black Farm.'

'Where's Matt?'

'Just across the yard. He's trying to finish off the corn–crib before dark falls. Can't you hear him hammering?'

173

Even as Willum spoke the sound of hammering ceased. Elizabeth moved to the rear window. She saw Matt set down the hammer, saw him peer through the dim light, sense from the lift of his head his recognition of the approaching man.

They faced one another beside the corn-crib. Each man took stock of the other's altered appearance, and struggled to make the impossible adjustment.

Jim said: 'Guess you've changed a mite, boy!'

His voice was as offhand as he could make it. He grinned. 'But hell – you don't look all that different. Now me – well, I feared you'd never recognise me.'

'Knew you straight away, Jim. Four years don't make a man look all that much older.'

They fell silent. Jim Black moved one step forward, he clapped both arms about his brother's emaciated body; for a moment they stood in a fierce embrace.

Matt said: 'What took you so long? Where've you been? What have you been doing? It's good to have you back, Jim.'

Jim laughed.

'Slow down, man. Why, I wasn't even sure that you would be here.'

'I wrote you.'

Jim said: 'I never got your letters.'

Matt peered through the dusk. He touched the silver crowns on his brother's shoulder, and grinned.

'Well, that's all right now, Cap'n Black, sir! Guess you've found yourself mighty busy lately, a-giving out orders and suchlike, eh?'

'Don't get sassy with me, little brother. I could always whip you in a fight!'

They began to shadow-box, but awkwardly and without enthusiasm. After only a few minutes they gasped and leaned against the corn-crib, then turned and walked towards the house, their arms about each other's shoulders.

Early morning was Robert Vickery's good time of day. He came alert at the moment of waking, and left his bed as the first light crept at the rim of the world. He dressed, pulled on his boots, splashed cold water on his face and head, and dragged a comb through his straight brown hair. He left the house at once, no matter what the weather, to walk through his yard and fields. Sometimes, as he walked, he would have a thought so significant and powerful as to pull all other random thoughts tight together.

In the grey dawn of this late October he could feel already the keen edge of winter; the increasing cold sharpened up his mind, he had a clear sight of all that must be done. There was stubble yet to be ploughed-under. A few late pumpkins to be gathered, fences to be mended. He planned to raise a barn, to build a bigger hog-house, maybe sink a second well; and then there was the house, the walls of which must be chinked-out again with clay against the winter storms. He came up to a slope of ground from the summit of which he could look down on the Black Farm.

Three summers had passed since the return of Jim Black. In that time a loghouse had been raised on the tilled forty-acres, the brothers had settled down to a batchelor existence. In winter Jim worked as foreman-logger for Martin Tremble, the sawmill owner, while Matt kept house and fed the stock. They were, thought Robert, the kind of men who by their very presence brought a warmth, an extra dimension of pleasure to quite ordinary matters; he remembered the summer night when they had first walked into Suamico, his feeling of instant kinship with them. He hoped that they would stay, but as Elizabeth said, with single men one could never know – he began to walk downhill, towards breakfast and his day's work. Robert thought about the set of harrows that must be repaired; the finding of suitable wives for Jim and Matthew Black. He failed to notice the horse, and the rider who observed him from a distant stand of sugar-maples.

The little school opened up when the harvesting of grain and fruits was over; even then there would always be those pupils who could not attend because of family crisis. Elizabeth believed in education. On one occasion only, when Robert had suffered a broken ankle, had she kept Johnny and Chas at home to help out with the chores.

On this October morning she packed lunch-pails, checked ears and necks for cleanliness, and warned her sons to 'come straight home when school is out!'

The black-edged letter from Buckland St Mary still crackled in her apron pocket. A second letter from her brother James stood on the shelf above the chimney-breast.

The house was quiet; she set a bowl upon the table, filled it with hot water from the kettle and began to wash the breakfast dishes. At a sound from the door she called: 'Come on in,' thinking it was Matt who had lately become ambitious in his cooking, and would call to borrow her receipt-book. But the voice that spoke from the doorway was English.

'Tidy little place you've got here, Elizabeth. How Father would have approved! But then – he always had a high opinion of Robert.'

She did not need to turn around to know that it was her brother Mark who stood there. She took in the shabby appearance of him, the tightness of his face and body.

She said: 'Are you hungry?'

'Haven't eaten in two days.'

She looked beyond him to the yard.

'That's a valuable horse you have there.'

He grinned. 'Borrowed – not stolen. I left a note on the stable door that I'd have him back to Oshkosh come next Sunday.'

'You don't change, do you?'

He shrugged. 'I don't have the same talent for hard graft as the worthy Robert.'

She said: 'Where have you been? We heard that you were in Carolina? You look sick. What's been happening to you?'

He sat down, suddenly.

'Food first, Elizabeth. Talk after.'

She reached for the largest skillett and set it on the stove. Into it she sliced salt-pork; when the fat was hot she broke three eggs

176

and watched them flutter and sizzle beside the meat. She took the last piece of bread from the crock and buttered it for him.

As she started to pour coffee, he said: 'You must have something stronger than that tucked away in a cupboard?'

'I've put down a few firkins of cider. We mostly take it mulled in winter, for bad head colds, like we did at home in England. It's not ready yet for drinking. Robert rarely touches anything alcoholic.'

'Where is our farmer Plod?'

Elizabeth slid meat and eggs on to a plate and set the dish before her brother.

'Don't mock my husband, Mark,' she warned.

'All right – all right! No offence intended! He's worth a dozen of my sort, but there's not much joy in his life, is there? I saw him earlier this morning, walking his estate, surveying his acres. He looked a bit like Moses on the mountain.'

Mark began to eat.

At the far end of the table Elizabeth completed her washing of dishes; she cleared a space, assembled flour and water, and the tins she used for baking bread. The bread-sponge had been set on the previous day; all night the mixture had sat in a wooden trough close to the fire, swathed in a scrap of clean blanket. Now, as she unwrapped it, a wonderful yeasty smell filled the house. The risen dough was placed upon a floured board. Elizabeth began to knead with firm and regular pressures of her slender hands. She looked to her brother.

'I want to know,' she said, 'all that has befallen since we last saw you.'

He took a briar pipe from his jacket pocket and waved it at her. He said: 'A fill of tobacco first – if you please, dear sister. I talk better when I'm smoking.'

She said: 'Help yourself. The tobacco-jar is on the shelf. You won't find much in it. We can't afford such luxuries for Robert very often.'

When the pipe was filled and drawing to his satisfaction, Mark pulled his chair close up to table; he leaned both elbows on it. He smiled. 'So what exactly do you wish to know? I've done a lot of things you won't think very nice . . .'

177

She said: 'What have you done with the money Father gave you?'

'Ah,' he said, 'now there speaks a true Greypaull! It's money first and last and always! I do declare, Elizabeth – you've become every bit as bad as Rhoda and dear brother James. Joan too is probably as avaricious by this time. It was all that shop-keeping when you were younger. All that counting up in farthings and ha'pennies!'

Elizabeth said: 'I count now in cents and dollars, and every single one of them is earned in sweat and tears.'

She waved towards the sheds and land beyond the window.

'It's taken us ten years to get this far. I'm not avaricious, Mark, but Father was always so good to us. It seems to me that we owe it to him to do well.' She hesitated. 'I've had bad news from Buckland.'

She said with difficulty: 'Father is dead. The epilepsy killed him.'

Mark said: 'Oh I know all about that. James wrote to me while I was still in Carolina.'

Elizabeth kneaded dough with unnecessary vigour, formed it into a long roll and began to break off pieces of equal size and put them into tins. Her actions lacked their usual rhythm.

'So what,' she asked, 'brought you so far north and with such speed?'

'Would you believe that I had an urgent need to see my kith and kin?'

'No, I would not.'

'Well, it just so happens to be true. What has happened to you, Elizabeth? I recall you as always laughing – a merry girl – but not one smile have you given me since I walked in your door.'

She began to clear the table. She tested the oven for tempera-ture, and placed the tins of bread inside it. The face she turned to him was flushed and angry.

'I am sad because of Father. Seeing you, after all this time was quite a shock. You have still not told me what brings you to Suamico, and in such a state!'

Mark pulled a letter from his pocket.

'This screed,' he said, 'came from our learned brother James, the Barrister. It makes fascinating reading.' He nodded towards the chimney shelf. 'I see that you also have been favoured by him.'

'We've had two letters within six weeks.'

Mark laughed. 'Our James becomes a most devoted correspondent when money is in question.'

Elizabeth frowned. 'But nothing is in question. James sets out the terms of Father's Will quite clearly. One part has been set aside for Father's second family. The remainder is to be divided between the surviving children of the first family with Susanna's portion coming down to her son Eddie.'

Mark said: 'Has your husband read that letter?'

'I read the home letters to him.'

'And he asked no questions?'

'Well – I didn't trouble him too much with all that legal detail. I don't understand it myself – and in any case it hardly seemed fitting to mention the subject so soon after Father's passing. Patchwood and its land must go of course to Father's widow and her four children. It is their home. What is left cannot amount to much. If all is sold-up and divided between eight of us – why we shall receive but a few pounds. Father,' she insisted, 'was more than generous to all of us in his lifetime. There cannot, says James, be much for us now!'

Mark said: 'Let me see your letter.'

She handed it to him. He laid the two pages side by side upon the table. 'They are almost identical; word for word they are the same. Oh, but our James is a wily bird!'

He began to read aloud.

Dear Sister Elizabeth and Robert Vickery,

I have posted three letters at one time. One for Rhoda, another to Mark, and the other to you. I directed Mark's and posted it without a stamp or paying the one shilling and a penny for a stamp. Mark seldom pays the post on his letters to me. I paid one shilling to send your letter to you.

Father, by his Will, which he made in 1860, devised or gave the

*Houses and Lands at Dommett, and Allottments at Buckland Hill, to
me and my Heirs, upon trust, until any time when I may think proper
to sell the same by Public Auction, or by Contract, or to Let the same,
and divide the Rents.*

I intend to LET *Father's properties for some time to come. There
must be thatching and plastering done on all the premises, roofing and
patching. After paying the Mortgage Debt of £290 and the interest,
our shares of the Rents will not be a great deal. I will send you your
share of the rents at the proper date, one year from Father's decease.*

Your affectionate brother. J. P. Greypaull.

Elizabeth said: 'It seems to me that James had our interests at
heart. He is doing his best for us all. He is a clever man, Father
trusted him and was guided by him. He will send us whatever is
due on the proper date. He says so in his letter.'

'How can you be so gullible, Elizabeth? Don't you see what
that man has done? He is a lawyer. He had the wording of this
Will entirely in his hands. In effect, James has control of
everything that should be ours – on Trust, he says – until any
time he may think proper –'

'But we shall have our share of the Rents, Mark.'

'And how much will that be when he has paid out Mortgage
and Interest, plastering and thatching?' Mark stood up. He
waved both letters close to Elizabeth's face.

He said in a low voice: 'Have you any notion of how much
land and property our father owned in Buckland St Mary?'

She shook her head.

'Well, you can be sure, my dear, that, before that Will was
drawn, our brother James had worked out to the very last
penny just how much the Estate was worth. Can't you see the
cleverness of him? *He* will be the big man in Buckland now. *He*
will be the owner of farms and cottages, the blacksmith's shop,
and all the rest. Our father was a wealthy man, Elizabeth. If the
properties are sold we should all be rich!'

Elizabeth said slowly: 'But that selling all devolves on James –
and in his letter he has no intention of putting anything to Sale
or auction.'

'Exactly!' Mark went to his sister. He laid an arm about her shoulders. He said: This could mean the loss of thousands of dollars for us all.' He paused. 'Something will have to be done about brother James, and quickly!'

She said: 'You had best talk to Robert about it. He's working in the lower field.'

'I can't stay,' Mark interrupted. 'I have to return to Oshkosh. Pack me a slice of pork and one of your warm loaves. I'll be back before too long. I suppose,' he said carefully, 'you keep in close touch with Rhoda and George Salter?'

'But of course! We write regularly.'

His face grew thoughtful.

'I wonder,' he said, 'how those two are taking the news of brother James's deception.'

'Leave them alone, Mark! George has business troubles, and Rhoda's youngest child is sore afflicted.'

Mark rode away. She watched him go, then turned slowly back towards her baking. He had stayed no longer than it took to make a batch of bread, but in that time he had, by his very presence, evoked the old days and ways of life in Buckland St Mary; had forced her to acknowledge loss, and the jealousy, well-concealed during Father's lifetime, which had always been felt by the two older brothers of her family towards their sisters.

Chapter Fifteen

Eddie had grown in a space of months. Soon after his twelfth birthday he was measured by Papa and found to be as tall as Rhoda, and almost as big as his Uncle John. He was a handsome boy, sturdy and well-muscled, but shy and just sufficiently hesitant in manner to win the approval of his parents and teachers. The shyness was instinctive. Since that day when he had learned that his true mother lay in the Charlotte cemetery, he had felt an apartness from the other children. Sometimes, when sent on an errand to his father's place of business, he would take the long route home. He would run the length of River Street, leaping from one shaky boardwalk to another, past the American Hotel and Mr Wood's millwright shop, until he came to the little gate which led into the graveyard. He always paused then to tidy his appearance. He would pull up his long woollen stockings so that they covered the cuffs of his moleskin britches and revealed no unseemly stretch of bare skin. He wiped a handkerchief, first across his face, and then once over the toecaps of his boots. A hand thrust through the curls that hung upon his forehead, and Eddie was prepared to make the visit. He knew by heart the words engraved in gold on the white stone.

SUSANNA SALTER. DEARLY BELOVED WIFE OF
GEORGE HODDER SALTER, BORN IN SOMERSET, OLD ENGLAND.
DIED IN CHARLOTTE. NEW YORK STATE.

He had been told about the baby who had died of cholera soon before his own birth. He never allowed himself to think about that; it was nicer to see himself as her one and only precious child. He knew that she had loved him. Mama had told him so.

His visits to the grave of his mother, Susanna, had been longer and more frequent lately. With Eddie's increased height had come a new and bewildering sensitivity of feeling, a strain of melancholy, a reluctant awareness of the troubles that complicate the lives of grown-up people.

There were hours when the company of Georgie was a childish torment from which he must escape; times when to roam the waterfront with the younger boy, to lurk with him in a corner of the harness-repair shop, and listen to the old men's stories, held no further fascination. At such times Eddie walked to the higher ground where stood the Lighthouse. He sat on a stone wall and listened for Niagara's roar; looked down on the familiar sprawl of Charlotte, the brown rush of the Genessee river. He measured the length of River Street, located the precise spot where at one end lay the cemetery, and at the other his father's meat-market, with its new sheds and cattle-pens. He came last of all to Latta Road, and the pumpkin-yellow house that stood among fruit trees. The triangle formed by these three locations had seemed, until lately, to protect him; now it held a vague threat.

He tried to talk to Georgie about it.

'Pa's lost all his money. We're poor folks now like the Denmans and O'Brians.'

Georgie looked up from the sling-shot he was trying to make from a forked stick and a stolen length of Rosa's hairband. He said hopefully: 'Guess we won't have to go to school then! Luke Denman gets to stop home most of winter. He's got no proper boots or britches.'

'Not that poor, silly!'

'How poor then?'

'Well – Pa's already sold the carriage. He took his tiepin and Mama's ring to a shop in Rochester, and got money for them. Mama's been making-over Pa's jackets and trousers so that they'll fit me – hey, Georgie – have you noticed – we don't get to eat so good these days?'

Georgie had lost interest. The sling-shot had no spring in it; he threw it to the ground and stamped upon it.

Bravado, and a need to gain attention made Eddie say:

'Uncle John is going home to England. Maybe I'll go with him? Maybe I'll leave school and get a job? I'm old enough for work. There's not much more that school can teach me. I'm twelve. 'Most everybody goes to work at twelve.'

Georgie said: 'What d'you bet we never get a pony, now?'

'Oh I'll be allright. I'll have more ponies than I can ride. I mean to go to work at Brandon's.'

It required, George now discovered, no more than a hint of business troubles for a man to find himself beset by other traders. Those who had formerly allowed him to owe small sums of money, without pressing for payment, now presented their bills, hand-delivered after dark fell, with a request for immediate settlement.

George himself was no longer able to offer credit. The few faithful housewives who paid-up promptly still brought him their business, but the river-boat Captains and provisioners of larger vessels took their trade to meat-markets further down the Genessee, where extended goodwill was easier to come by. The small slither in his fortunes, caused by the failure of the meat-packing project, now became an avalanche, and there was nothing he could do to halt it.

Rhoda was angry; and it was not altogether their new state of poverty that enraged her, but the fickleness of people. On the eve of that Christmas of 1867 she wrote in her Journal.

★

December 24

From one month to another we are poorer. Only in America can such things happen. George says our plight would have been just the same were we still in Buckland, but I have noticed that in this place a man may make friends of many people. These friends will praise and applaud him in the good times, but let bad times come and it is as though we suffer plague. Now they are knocking at our door, calling-in on the very smallest of debts, and threatening us with litigashion. There is the matter of repairs to a fence, new parts for my sewing-machine, little bills outstanding at the feed-merchant's and the dry-goods' store. Separately, these sums are trifling. Six months ago I could have paid them from my small-change; added together, and prompt payment of them now demanded in Law, these tiny amounts could see us altogether ruined.

Christmas this year will be as good as we can make it. The children fill the house with green and berried boughs. The boys set a little fir tree in a tub, and it fills the space in the sitting room where until lately stood my piano. Rosa trims the tree with ribbons. John is coming three years old. I do believe that he is on the very verge of speech. If he would but say one clear and distinct word it would ease my heart and mind in these trying times. Today is my thirty-seventh birthday.

January 1, 1868
George to Rochester this day to sell my gold and ivory cameo brooch. It was my father's gift to me on my twenty-first birthday. I do not part easily with it. George returns to say that he has but pawned the brooch and will redeem it for me when times are better. Have no hope of ever seeing it again, but do not say so.

It is only the *English* of Charlotte who are still *with* us. Great friendship and compasshun shown by the Gillingham family, themselves not long out from Somerset, and struggling to get along in their proffeshun of Carriage and Waggon makers. The rest of our neighbours seem to have forgotten the leeway allowed them by George when they were not able to pay-up their bills. Rignold Powell, our assistant, has departed for Chicago – where it seems, is to be found a paradise on earth for ambishous butchers! My dear brother-in-law John Salter is to take ship for England. It is for the best. George does so little business lately that he is well able to manage the shop alone, and, in any case, we can no longer afford to pay out wages. All our bills now paid up with money from my brooch, thus saving us from bankruptcy.

February 10

Eddie is to leave the school and go to work at Brandon's. It is all his own wish and suggestion. Joel Brandon is an Englishman. I would not think to put my Eddie in his care were the man and his wife anything other than our *own sort*. In my heart I am against this move, but George says it will be for the best. It will, says he, be one mouth less to feed, and Eddie doing little good in school these days, he being, as always, qwite taken up with horses and all to do with them. Boys in the Charlotte school *seldom* stay there after their twelfth birthday. Eddie profishunt now in reading and writing, and fair in numbering, is *keen* to work in Brandon's stables.

Our friend Mr Gillingham will drive Eddie out the five miles to Brandon's. I pack a box with all his warmest clothing. I forget to put in his flannel nightshirts. When I go to include them I find, tucked down into a corner, the last scrap of the blue and white silk that was Susanna's gown.

When they drive away I think my heart will break. I remember the promise I made him when I first came to Charlotte. 'This,' I have said, 'is the house where you were born, and never again will you be put among strangers.'

George sees my distress. He says that Brandon is a friend to us, that Eddie goes to a good situashon; he will live-in as family and be paid thirteen dollars the month; that for one week-end in every three months he will be allowed home to see us.

That, say I, is all very fine. To me Eddie is a child. He is but twelve years old!

March 14

Have word from Eddie. He says the food is good and plentiful, he loves the horses, but gets very tired. He asks, do Georgie and Rosa miss him? What must mean I think that he is missing all of us.

A letter from Wisconsin. Elizabeth much troubled, what is not ushally her way. She writes of a visit from our brother Mark. What thinks George, she asks, to the letters that have come from Buckland St Mary? Mark, she says, is of the mind that James intends to cheat us of our inheritance from Father.

186

Truth to tell, I have paid scant heed to my brother's letters, each one being written in a style of legal language what is meant to hide his true thoughts. James is a stranger to me, he being always studious and straightfaced, and never a part of our merry crew of younger children. I return to his letters, of which there are three since the death of Father. I study the wording of them. It is as I first thought. The yearly Rents of all the farms and properties are to be divided equally between eight of us; what cannot amount to any great sum. I consult George. Together we see what I had overlooked.

Father's properties, says James, have been left to *him* in *trust*, to Sell or Rent as he sees fit. He does *not* intend to Sell and pay us our share of the money. Had I been less concerned about our business failure and the plight of our children, I should have seen this for myself. George says to his brother John: 'You sail for England on April fifth. Perhaps you will go to Buckland for us, and see what James Greypaull is about? This money could be the saving of us. If it be properly explained to the man what has happened here, then surely he will reconsider?'
George much cheered-up by the prospekt of my inheritance, but it is clear that my husband has had little dealings with the Greypaull family. They do not give up easily what they consider to be theirs.

March 21
Bridget comes to see me. She enters thru' the kitchen door. I am busy at my baking. She, being qwite at home, is happy to brew tea for both of us.

I say: 'You will not mind if we drink it here, at the kitchen table? I have a batch of bread rising in the trough, and pork roasting in the oven. It is a tough joint and must be basted often.'

She looks surprised. She says: 'Well, 'tis glad I am that you're eating so well, ma'am.'

She sits down; as she pours the tea she looks towards the closed doors that lead off from the kitchen. Tears stand in her eyes. She says, in the maudlin and sentimental manner of the

187

Irish: 'Oh, ma'am, I just had to come over and visit with you. Like I said to Liam' 'tis such a shame, that poor little Eddie being put out to farm work, and, if what I hear is true, all your fine furniture sold off to keep food in the cupboard, and your jewels sold in Rochester to keep the bailiffs from this house!'

It is hard to keep dignity when basting pork. I turn from the oven and the redness of my face is due only to the fire. It is my habit to grow pale in temper.

I also sit down. I drink the tea she has poured out. I keep my voice qwiet.

'Tell me,' I murmur, 'is this what people say about us?'

She is uneasy. 'Well – not the Episcopalians.'

'But all the others?' I ask. 'The Baptists and the Methodists, the Wesleyans – and the Irish Roman Catholics?'

She begins to weep.

'Not me, ma'am. I never said one word against you and Mr Salter. A fine family, I tell people, what don't deserve the misfortune what has come upon them.' She turns a streaming face towards me. 'I only come here because I felt so sorry. We was together, you and me, for so many years, and never a hard word betwixt us!'

I see that I have wronged her.

'Forgive me, Bridget. I am a little touchy lately.' I rise; I throw open the doors that lead off from the kitchen.

'Come,' I say, 'look around you. We still have our sofas to sit down on. The carpeting is yet nailed to the floorboards; the pictures hang on the walls, the china is in the cabinets gathering dust!'

I attempt to smile at her.

'Only my piano is absent from the roll-call. I never have time to play it anyway since you left me to get married. I must say that I miss you sorely, Bridget.'

She is comforted.

'As for Eddie,' I continue, 'he has obtained an apprenticeship at Brandon's Stables. It is well-paid, and what he himself chose to do. You must recall how much time he always spent among horses. Why, he was more often in the blacksmith's and the harness-shop than he was here at home!'

She looks doubtful.

'Going out to work at twelve years old is all right for the sons of labourers,' says she. 'It don't seem right somehow when it's the gentry what does it. Poor boy – he was never brought up to expect such a thing.'

I go to the bread trough. I remove the cloths and find the sponge well-risen. I flour the board and begin to knead dough with all my might.

I say: 'We are not gentry, Bridget. We are business people.'

She speaks with a dignity that she must have learned in her married state.

'Beg pardon, ma'am. I am well-turned forty years of age. I worked for the nobility of Ireland when I was a young thing. Give me leave to recognise blue-blood when I see it. Even without your brooch and rings and your piano, you are a lady-born, Missus Salter. So was Missus Susanna who was here before you, and your sister, the one who was blind. 'Tis in all your children too!'

Bridget leans confidenshully across the table.

'People recognise that you are "Class", Missus Salter. That's why they crow when you has a setback.'

I say, surprised: 'But in America all men are equal, Bridget.'

She shakes her head. 'Oh no,' says she, 'don't you never believe that, ma'am. Blood always tells – in the end.'

May 29

Eddie comes home for the weekend. George and Rosa qwite overjoyed at his arrival. Jon smiles at him and hugs him. Eddie looks well. He says that he is content, that he is glad to be with horses. He is footsore, having walked the full five miles from Brandon's. He hands to George a packet what holds thirty-five dollars. It is his wages of the past three months. Eddie explains how four dollars are kept back from each apprentice to cover the cost of boot-repairs and so forth. He now speaks to his father as does one grown man to another. George hands back one dollar, this sum says he to be used for postage or any small thing needed. They are earnest together, father and son. In their looks they are much alike, but the eyes that look up at George are those of Susanna.

That night my husband suffers the most severe attack of his malady that I have yet witnessed. At one time I fear he is altogether lost, no breath seeming to come from him, and his colour awful.

We miss church on that Sunday morning. Eddie also weary. In the two days he is with us he all but sleeps the clock around.

On Sunday evening George borrows Mr Gillingham's bay mare. He and Eddie will ride back out to Brandon's. I pack a small satchel with cinammon cookies. The bag what holds clean linen and darned socks is hung from the pommel; Eddie sits before his father on the Spanish saddle.

In the moment of farewell our boy looks down upon me; only I am witness to the tears that are standing in his eyes.

June 12

A packet comes this day from my brother James. It holds yet another stern letter. He trusts that we are working diligently in the New World. He hopes that George attends closely to his business; that our children are respectful and good to their parents. It is plain to see that James imagines himself as having taken Father's place. He is all admonishments and strict warnings. There is again much legal language with which he will confuse me.

Contained in the packet are several sheets of parchment. In a separate note James explains that this is a copy of our Family Pedigree, obtained by him, at great personal expense, from Historical Archives. I learn that we have a Coat of Arms; that some Knights of our name were beheaded in the Tower of London. We are, it would appear, descended from a long line of important persons. Numbered in the pages are Earls and Bishops; Members of the Parliament! James cannot know what a *service* he has done me! The papers have come at a low ebb in my spirits. I had never qwite believed my father's stories of our descent from Kings and Princes, now I idle away a pleasant hour in the study of my noble ancestry. I reflect what a pity it is that poor Bridget can neither read nor write. But I will show the parchments to her. She is bound to be impressed by our Family Crest. She will, without a doubt, spread the word thru' the length and breadth of Charlotte!

July 2
George does hardly any business. I know not how we shall go on if this state of things continues. He is very low in spirits, and misses his brother John most grievusly, they having worked and talked so nicely together for so many years.

I miss John also. So many times was he my stay and bulwark against my husband's changeability of moods, the worry of the asthma attacks, my ankshusness about little Jon and his convulshuns. Our household has grown small. Without Eddie, John, and Bridget, the rooms seem full of empty corners. Without much company I am soon fearful and nervy.

Dr Jones calls in on his morning rounds. It is a friendly visit. He comes only, so he says, to drink a cup of my good tea, his American patients offering only much-boiled coffee, for which as a Welshman he has little fancy. We sit on the porch. The doctor looks to Jon, who is in the garden.

'How has he been of late'

'He is never well in the heat of summer.'

'And his speech?'

'He has his own way of talking to me.'

Dr Jones sets down his teacup. He says in a gentle voice: 'Mrs Salter – do not expect too much of Jon. I have seen other children, similarly afflicted. He will never be altogether . . .'

'He is not afflicted,' I interrupt. 'He is worn-out with the convulshuns. This makes him slow. Eddie was also late in talking.'

'Eddie,' says Dr Jones, 'had suffered at the hands of wet-nurses. He lacked a mother's love and close care. Your coming cured him.'

'My father,' I say, 'was also epileptic. But he was sound in his mind and a clever man of business.' I pause. The doctor is a kind man and I do not wish to offend him, but it must be said. I

191

continue in a firm voice. 'Jon will recover from this setback. In a year or two he will be as bright and active as his brothers and sister.'

August 1

A letter comes today from John Salter, the first news we have had since he left Charlotte. John says he arrived safe back in England, and looks around at present to buy a butcher's business for himself. In July he was to Buckland St Mary to see my brother James about the matter of Father's Will. He aqwainted my brother with our situashun here in Charlotte, and told him that we are in want of money to make another start in business, that George wishes to go in for wholesale meat-packing but lacks the necessary capital.

It seems that my brother said very little on the matter of monies due to Father's children in America, save that *he* is the Trustee of all farms, lands and properties, and will administer them as he sees fit, and for as *long* a time as he *chooses so to do*.

John says he was offered refreshments by my brother, and then instructed by him on the state of farming in Australia, where it seems, land costs one pound an acre, and mutton is steamed into tallow and shipped to England. All of this having *nothing whatever* to do with the plight of us here in Charlotte!

When George comes to his supper I tell him the bad news from England.

I say: 'John Salter did his best for us, but my brother will not share the money with us.'

George says: 'Then there is nothing we can do. We are at the whim and mercy of James Greypaull, and that is a demeaning situashon. Have you thought,' he asks me, 'of what the future holds for us if we continue to stay here in Charlotte? We limp along from week to week, we grow ever poorer. Money breeds money in this country. Because my capital is gone I am refused credit. We need to move west – to Chicago!'

I say: 'It is a city of bad reputashun. I will not take my children into such evil and corrupshun.'

George says: 'Chicago is known these days at the "Queen of the West".'

192

'Not by me!' say I.

'Then have you considered the alternative, Rhoda? I may hold on to my meat-market for another year. Then I shall be reduced to a jobbing slaughterer and butcher. Eddie is already put away from us – soon it will be Georgie's turn to earn his own bread. In a few more years we shall be seeking a domestic situashon for Rosa. Your children will be scattered, and if my health should fail what will become of you and Jon?' He speaks qwietly but with great purpose.

'It is not what I meant when I came to this country. I wanted a good life for my children, and for you, my dear. You must see that we shall never again get on our feet here in Charlotte?'

His words affect me deeply. He is not a man of long speech, what can cause sometimes misunderstandings between us. Now that I know what is his reasoning, I must confess that he is right. I am near to tears at his descripshun of our children's future path in life.

He sees by my face that I am softening. He says: 'I need to have you with me in this new venture. There is a house and packing business to be had in West Chicago. The sale of our present house and business will furnish a deposit. The rest of the money can be had on mortgage. It is a risk, I know. But better to risk all on one bold move than to sit here in Charlotte and do nothing to save ourselves from bankruptcy.'

He pauses. He says 'If you will but say yes, I will sell-up straight away. Eddie can be brought home tomorrow. The boy is homesick, Rhoda.'

I am perswaded. Nay – I am convinced! I go to him and put my arms around him.

'Go,' I say, 'sell-up your shop and this house, and buy steamer tickets for Chicago. But first of all, go borrow Mr Gillingham's bay mare and bring Eddie home!'

September 1
Four weeks of high excitement. Eddie is home; the children talk of nothing but the coming move. George now stands straight and tall. He makes plans, he is once again the man of affairs. He

193

is Chicago-bound, this very day, on business. For myself, I am not so sure of the wisdom of it all, but I have given my word and cannot go back upon it. I am alarmed at the very thought of dwelling in a city. Taunton town, on a market-day was more bustle than I cared for. I viewed New York from the window of a river steamer, and thought little of it. The very word *Chicago* has a raffish aspekt. I speak to our Pastor, who has travelled West, and he says there are many churches and misshun-houses in that city. He also reminds me that 'a man may touch pitch and not be defiled'. I hold-on to this thought. I have four children who must at all costs be protected from this world's evil.

Our house and business sold to a stranger. The business, because of a lack of goodwill, brings us very little. The house, extended as it is, with land and orchard, and standing upon high ground, is a valuable asset, and brings a much larger price than George and I could have ever hoped for. We sell the house with the furniture in it. But for personal posseshuns and our clothing, we take nothing with us to Chicago save our hopes and prayers.

The trunks, made by my Father's hand and brought from England, are dragged from the attic and now stand open to receive our treasures. I pack the little rocking-chair, what *must* be an *heirloom*, and passed down to them that come after us, for the use of their children. Have allowed one small trunk for dolls and toys, the contents of which seem to alter daily, one shabby favourite being discarded in favour of another. My own choice of treasures limited by space, our clothes and household linen having first-call! But my little elmwood milking-stool, branded with the letter R, has been mine since childhood. It seems a strange item to take into a city, but I cannot bear to be parted from it.

September 28
George returns! He is a new man. As the Americans would say, he is 'full of vim and vigour''. A business has been purchased in Chicago with facilities for trade both wholesale and retail. He has found a large old house in a quiet street; the house to be

rented and not *bought*, since we shall need every cent of our capital sum to once again get on our feet, and trading.

I qwestion him on many subjects. I ask about his health. He says he has not suffered one breathless moment while in Chicago; that the air in that city blows from both prairie and lakeshore, and is always fresh. He is like a young man again. He seizes me by the waist and dances me around the kitchen.

He tells me, in a qwieter moment, what are his thoughts and feelings.

'I came to this land,' says he, 'with a dream in my heart of achieving great things, I pictured grandchildren and great-grand-children, who would carry with respect the name of Salter. I saw myself as a – a Founding Father, like those first Salters who built up New Dorchester in Massachusetts. I wanted to be remembered with pride for generations.'

'Perhaps it is pride,' say I, 'that has been the undoing of you, George.'

I speak gently, but *certain things must be said*, and this is a salutary time in our affairs.

'The Lord God,' I say, 'saw your small vanity and deemed it a risky thing. He has chastened you, and brought you low. It is far better you should be remembered for your kindliness and goodness.' I put my arms about him, so as to soften my words. '*Good money* comes only from long and steady labour,' I say. 'But you have been granted another chance. We know not what awaits us in Chicago, but if it be God's Will then we shall prosper.'

He smiles at me. He says: 'You are a rare woman, Rhoda. I don't really deserve you.' From his pocket he draws a case of dark-blue velvet. I open it and find my gold and ivory cameo brooch.

'I have,' says he, 'redeemed this pledge, at least!'

October 1
All has been done that can be done. Our trunks are packed, tickets for railroad and steamer have been purchased, farewells have been said. It is that qwiet time that comes just before a

final departshur, and I would that we were already begun and upon our journey. I occupy myself with small tasks what are trifling, and yet seem to be of great importance.

I dig out, with difficulty, a root of the lilac at my kitchen door. I wrap it in moist paper and a strip of burlap.

George says: 'There is no call to take the garden with us. There will be lilacs growing in Chicago.'

'But not this one,' say I.

I walk alone to the high ground where stands the Lighthouse, and remember the times I have come here with my children. I look down upon Charlotte, and the pumpkin-yellow house among the fruit trees has a safe and kindly aspekt for me. It has been home to so many of my dear ones since the time when George first came to this land. It is a house I will think of very often in the years to come.

The children are restless. Eddie comes late to his supper and I scold him. He is defended by his brother.

Georgie says: 'You can't be vexed with him, Mama! He was only saying goodbye to his real mother.'

So great is my shock that I have no words. I look to George but his gaze is fixed elsewhere. It is on my tongue to say: 'How did *you* know of these matters, Georgie?' I study the face of each child and find them unconcerned. I see that Georgie, too, is growing-up. How long has he known that I am not Eddie's mother? I feel a pang of guilt. I should have been the one to tell him all about it. I butter bread to calm my nerves. I say: 'Tomorrow will be our last day in Charlotte. Perhaps we could go all together to the cemetery?'

Eddie looks at me with his mother's eyes, and I know that for once in my life I have said the correct thing at the significant moment.

*

They left Charlotte in the mild and mellow days of Indian Summer. In the moment of going, and quite unexpectedly, the house became a place she could hardly bring herself to leave.

Their boxes and trunks were already standing at the stagecoach depot; the children waited impatiently beside the gate. George frowned, uncomprehendingly, Jon in his arms, while she still prowled the empty rooms. At last she closed the kitchen door quietly behind her. She looked thoughtfully at it.

She said:

'It used to stick when I first came here.'

George said, in a voice so low that in years to come she would not be sure that she had truly heard him:

'But that was in Susanna's time.'

He walked away from her towards the children. Rhoda turned for one backward look at the pumpkin-yellow house. She heard a rustling among the fallen leaves in the long grass of the orchard, and thought she saw her cousin's pale shade slip away between the trees.

PART THREE

Chapter Sixteen

Chicago
October 30, 1868

It is evening. The children are asleep and George not yet come to his supper. I sit in the kitchen, what is the only room to have chairs and table, and, with the curtains drawn and the stove aglow, I might almost think myself still back in Charlotte. Save that in this place I keep bolts slid fast across the doors.

Today I unpacked the green leather covers that hold the many pages of my Journal. It is time to set down my thoughts, and pull my scattered wits together.

The journey I have so feared turns out to be full of little pleshurs. The boys are much taken up by the novelty of steamboat and railroad, and qwite forget to argue. George is good with the children. He explains the passing scenery to them. Jon is happy just to be carried in his father's arms. It is a time of companionship I shall long remember.

We go first from Charlotte to Buffalo; this part of our trip made by stagecoach. We come to a corduroy road, and George describes its purpose to the children. When we are once again on level ground he says to me: 'Do you recall that night when you first came to Charlotte?'

'I remember that corduroy-rib of pines, and how hard it was to cross the swampy place and come on to firm ground.'

We are alone on the stage, but for the children who chatter beside the far window.

George asks: 'Are you contented with me, Rhoda?'

His words confuse me.

I say: 'I have never thought about contentment.'

He smiles.

'Perhaps there will yet be time for us to reach our firm ground in Chicago?'

In Buffalo we board the lake-steamer *Superior*, which takes us across Lake Erie and into Detroit. Both boys delirious with joy to find the last part of our trip will be made by railroad.

Had not thought to be ever grateful to see the name CHICAGO writ in foot-high letters, but almost weep for *releef* when we pull into the Depot. We are come in the afternoon of an overcast day. A keen wind blows off Lake Michigan, and it seems to me that all the summer sweetness will forever lie behind us in our old home. The city streets are choked with traffic and I am fearful for our safety. The driver of our buggy whips his horses to a lather and we come into Green Street at full gallop. George pays off the man, who then throws our baggage to the ground and is *fast away*. I stand on trembling legs and take in the extraordinary house that is to be our home.

George says that Number 96 Green Street had been built by a farmer to house his growing family, in the early days when the South Side of the city had been rural in aspekt, with cattle grazing under trees and tributary streams from the Chicago River running thru' green fields. In this year of 1868 the street is green in name only, save for a patch of grass that grows before each dwelling, and the hickory and maple trees that have been spared the axe.

As time is measured in Chicago, the house is an old one. It has a sturdy frame-clad structure laid over pine logs, and is painted a robin's-egg blue that has faded in places to a silvery grey. The house stands alone, separated from its smarter neighbours by an area of hardpacked ground where only weeds and brambles flourish. A succession of careless tenants have left the place with a ramshackle appearance. George says he has chosen to rent it because of its size and the quaintness of its location, tucked away as it is between the busy thoroughfare of West Madison and West Monroe Streets. I hear his words, but nothing has prepared me for additions made across the years, the fancy gables, the curving balconies, the intricate carvings;

202

least of all for the tiny turret room from whence a flock of birds fly in and out.

It is Eddie who will try to reconcile me.

'Well,' says he,' at least it's heaps bigger than our old place in Charlotte.'

Rosa speaks painful truth. 'Oh Mama!' she wails, 'it's so awful old and shabby!'

Georgie, who has been uncommon qwiet, comes to sudden life.

'Hey Mama!' he cries, 'did you spot all those raggedy little kids and people as we drove up from the Depot? Did you catch all the fancy shops and stores, and the great high buildings?'

He turns to me and holds out both his hands in the exact way that was my father's. His face is awestruck.

'I guess that Chicago is the boss-city of the whole world!'

Eddie says: 'It's this house that we're talking about – perhaps you've not yet noticed we've arrived?'

Georgie grins. He straddles wide his legs, and grips his lapels like a river-boat gambler.

'Why,' he drawls, 'if you folks want my opinion, this here is the cutest old shack in the State of Illinois.'

I look to George, I shake my head.

'Ten minutes in this place,' I say, 'and he is worse than ever.'

'Come boys!' George orders, 'You shall help me with the luggage. Rosa, you keep Jon safe by you while Mama unlocks the door.'

The iron key turns stiffly in the lock. The hinges creak as the door swings open. I step across the threshold, and altho' I am not a fanciful woman I find myself moving as one who is caught fast in a dream. It must, I think, be want of food and weariness that causes me to feel lightheaded, and yet, in that moment of entry, I know this house to be a certain haven. I stroke the knotted pine of doors and lintels and feel strength flow out into my body. I have a premonition that when all about it falls to ruin, this structure will still stand.

I come back, very slowly to my right mind, and although the light falls dim thru' dirty windows I can see festooning cobwebs,

203

and rusted box-stoves in the two large rooms that front the street. In the kitchen stands the table and chairs, the serviceable china George has purchased. There are cupboards a-plenty; a north-facing pantry with stone-slabs for coolness. In an inglenook stands an iron range, also rusted. I come last of all to the *most delightful* feature. I stand before it and can scarce credit what I see. A pump-handle curves above the brownstone sink! At a touch of the hand I shall draw water! No more carrying of pails on washdays. No more journeys to a back-yard pump on winter nights. I press on the handle and the water flows, slow and brackish to begin with and then fast and crystal clear. I feel mirth rise inside me, in fact I laugh out loud. Here I am, in the wicked city of Chicago, and all my concern is for stoves that need a good blackleading, and the idle pleasure of pumped water.

The staircase rises in the exact centre of the house. I climb the treads that are broad and shallow enough for the safe use of Jon. The unexpected mirth stays with me. Overhead, swift footfalls and shrill voices mark the passage of the children; Jon's unsteady footsteps can be heard among the others. I pause to listen. Bedrooms are being laid claim to, further staircases discovered, attic rooms explored and window sashes raised. Released from the pressures of long travel they fly like happy birds from one corner to another. It is so good to hear their laughter after so much constraint.

George comes in to stand beside the staircase. In his hand he holds the final piece of baggage.

'Those boys,' he grumbles, 'were supposed to help me.'

'Let them be,' I say. 'They also have a need to acqwaint themselves with their new home.'

'And what of you, Rhoda?' His face is ankshus. 'It's not much, I know, but the best to be had in the circumstances. There are houses fronting Lincoln Park that are more to your –'

I go to him. I reach up and place my fingers on his lips. 'No more dreams, George,' I say qwietly. 'Number 96 Green Street is exactly to my taste. It needs but soap and water and a deal of beeswax polish.' I hesitate, but some things *must* be said. 'The

204

door does not stick in this house, it only creaks. If there be ghosts then they are happy ones. I ask but one favour of you, George. Let this be *my* home.'

November 6
Eddie is to work with George and learn the business of butchering and slaughter. A church school, suitable for Rosa and Georgie, stands but two blocks from us. Meanwhile, in these first days of our occupashun, my husband allows the children to bide with me. Eddie oils the front door hinges; together he and Georgie blacklead all the stoves until they gleam. Rosa helps me with polishing and scrubbing. Beneath the grime we find floors of polished pine. The boys begin to saw the cord of firewood George has purchased; they build fires in every stove. The house comes alive beneath our fingers. So far we have but beds, a table and six hard chairs, but I am content. The boys run all neccessary errands. I do not care to step further than the back yard. The curtains brought from Charlotte fit these windows very well.

Eddie digs a hole in the packed earth beside the kitchen door; it is a hard task and he skins his fingers. Together we plant the lilac root that travelled with us from Charlotte. When we are finished I cannot meet his grey eyes. I know that he is thinking of Susanna. I put salve upon his damaged hands, but there are other hurts I cannot ease. I doubt my lilac will survive the winter. Eddie's thirteenth birthday in a few days. Must make a little celebration.

November 22
Much has happened in the past days. I have been curious to see our place of business but George forbids me near it until all refurbishment is done and he is trading. We go at last to West Adams Street, all of us together, on a Sunday morning. The shop is very fine, double-fronted, painted dark-blue, with a sign picked out in gold-leaf above the door. Georgie and Eddie stand together on the sidewalk and read aloud: 'GEORGE HODDER SALTER and SONS. MEAT-PACKERS OF CHICAGO.'

I say: 'But you are not yet . . .'

George interrupts me.

'In this city,' says he, 'a man must state his position, declare himself, make absolutely clear what it is he is about.' He stands between his sons, a hand on each boy's shoulder.

'Meat-Packers stands above our place of trading, and Meat-Packers we shall be!'

We go inside the shop. I admire the counters of white marble, the scales of shining brass, the new blue paint. In back, there is a cold-room, and beyond lie sheds and pens, and an open-sided structure which, says George, will be suitable for packing. I am much impressed by the wisdom of his choice in all things.

December 1

Worked late last night on our Ledger figures. Am dismayed at the cost of refurbishment. Surely, I tell George, those carpenters who fitted up your place of business must have used silver nails and a golden hammer to justify a bill of this length! He says that all things cost more in Chicago. Am releeved to find, when all bills paid-up, that we are still solvent. George does brisk trade in these first weeks of his opening. It must, I tell him, be due to the novelty of an *English* butcher behind the counter, and a *clean meat-market* in this grubby town, but he will hear naught save good said about Chicago. He is masterful and energetic, and so far no sign of his breathing troubles.

I tell him the good news about our finances, and he says at once that new furniture must be bought, that he can no longer see us live in such great discomfort. I fear to spend our capital. It will serve only to stiffen our spines, say I, if we sit awhile longer on hard-backed chairs; and we are unlikely to have any fashionable callers knocking on our door. But he is *insistent*. He tells me about a store on Madison Street where bargains may be had. There is a Bohemian cabinet-maker who is clever at his trade. In a rear room, and apart from the new goods, this man keeps restored items that have known one careful owner.

'Then go purchase some,' say I.

'I cannot make such choice alone,' says he. 'Whatever I buy you will have it different.' He looks at me in a keen way. 'It is a month or more since we arrived here, and you have left the house but once in all that time. You are become a hermit. There is no more danger on these streets than those in Charlotte! We shall shop for furniture this very evening.'

'It is December,' I cry. 'Jon cannot stand the night air.'

There is a point of argument with George beyond which I dare not venture. I see now that I have reached it. He has a way of smiling which means he will no longer keep his patience.

'Your fears,' he says, 'are beginning to infect the children. They are not yet started to the school. How much longer will you keep them by you? My Rosie is unwilling to go far beyond our own yard. Even Georgie, for all his manly swagger, will run fast to the nearest store and scuttle quickly back.'

He pauses, but I make no answer.

He says: 'You understand me, Rhoda. We go a-marketing. This very evening. All of us. Together.'

December 4
The Bohemian cabinet-maker speaks little English, but his furniture is of the finest I have ever seen. It is almost worth the long walk beneath those great high buildings, and the press of people on the streets, to witness such a master of his craft. The store is long and narrow. It reaches back thru' many rooms. We begin to move between stacked tables and what-nots; from the ceiling hang row on row of hardbacked chairs. Around the walls stand wardrobes, chiffoniers and bureaux, and bow-fronted tallboys (known as highboys in this country). There are sofas and armchairs, button-backed and upholstered in the finest velvets and brocades. I pause to touch the grain of unfamiliar woods, there are items made in hickory and locust; oh how my father would have loved this store, and its Bohemian craftsman – and oh, how sorely I am tempted to spend money!

I whisper to George: 'There are no prices marked on anything.'

He says: 'We have to make the man an offer. He will refuse it. Then we haggle for a spell until we reach the figure he first had in mind.'

'But that is outrageous! It is the way of a cattle-sale between English farmers.'

'This is Chicago, Rhoda. Everything is different here.'

At once I move sharply to the rooms which hold the once-used items. Even these are superior to any we have ever owned. I choose wardrobes and highboys for the children. For our own room George urges me towards a full set of mahogany bedroom cupboards, with a triple-mirrored ladies-table, and a matching bed with a headboard upholstered in rose-brocade. I am lost; all resolution vanished. 'Go haggle with the man!' I whisper.

With nods and gestures, and a final handshake, the bargain is struck. Meanwhile, I have strayed back among the brand-new chairs and sofas. There is a suite of five pieces in some dark unfamiliar wood, and brocaded in my favourite shade of yellow-gold. Jon is qwiet in my arms. I say to him: 'Don't you just love that pretty colour?'

George says: 'How fine that would look in the sitting room that fronts the street!'

'With matching curtains,' I agree. 'And a flowered carpet, and perhaps a . . .'

I halt my dreaming.

'It is too soon, George. Already we have spent too much. We are in need of so many more practical items. We were obliged to leave so much behind us in Charlotte.'

He looks keenly at me.

'But I thought,' said he, 'that was your wish – to put away all the things that were not your choice? To start over, and make *this* house all yours?' There are times when George reads my mind too well. But he is a man, and cannot be expected to understand a woman's private feelings.

We do not buy the yellow chairs and sofas.

December 6

A Bank Draft comes this day from my brother James in England! It has been long underway since he has addressed it first to our old place in Charlotte.

It is the first payment of the share of the Rents of Father's

208

properties in Buckland. When changed into American money the Draft yields *twenty dollars and five cents*. In his letter James explains that there is no money due to Eddie, since his share under Father's Will cannot be paid over until Eddie reaches the age of twenty-one. It will be a more joyus Christmas than I could ever have hoped for!

George is to go forthwith to the Bohemian cabinet-maker, and purchase the yellow sofas and armchairs.

Chapter Seventeen

The Draft on Messrs. Stuckey's Bank of Chard, Old England, had arrived in Suamico at the end of a disastrous harvest. Robert made the journey into Green Bay, and returned the next day with a sum of twenty dollars and five cents. He placed the money in Elizabeth's hand. She counted out the silver coins.

She said: 'It's much more that we could have made in profit, even from a truly bumper harvest. More than you could have earned from many weeks of hauling timber at the woodmill.'

Robert said: 'With that much cash in hand and the bit we've put away, we can really start to think about the building of a frame-house. If our neighbours be willing, why, we could even have a house-raising in this fall. With the walls and roof in place, I could be working on the floors and staircase over the worst of the winter.'

'For that sort of building Robert, we should need to employ a carpenter, or maybe two.'

'Well I know for a fact that Ephraim Lutz will be glad of the employment, and Matthew Black is a handy fellow with a framing-chisel.'

Elizabeth said: 'And what of this house?'

'Why, we just take out the dividing walls, and there we'll have a good stout barn that'll stand for generations.'

His lips twitched almost to a smile.

In a fortunate family the babies came along at the rate of one each year. Allowance needed always to be made for the loss of an infant or two at birth, or soon after. Epidemics of cholera, of croup and enteric fever; the accidents of frostbite or snakebite might carry off a further two or three in childhood. When a final count was taken at the end of her child-bearing years, a pioneer mother considered herself well-blessed if her surviving children numbered seven or eight.

Elizabeth had borne Robert three fine and sturdy sons. Her health was good and theirs was a close and happy marriage. But for nine years the rocking-cradle had stayed empty; she was the sole female in her household; their nearest neighbours were the bachelor brothers Jim and Matt; and it was women's talk for which she yearned. In the early years she had been cheerful. Busy from sun-up to dusk with her little boys, with learning the farming ways of the new country, there had been no time for vague regrets. But now, when she went with her family to the logging, the husking, the sugaring-bees, and all the other shared-work tasks which brought Suamico folk together, she saw mothers older than herself who still had a babe-in-arms. Elizabeth found it increasingly hard to look upon these infants, to hold the warmth of a tiny body against her shoulder, and feel the ache for possession that pierced her heart. She feigned interest in the ceaseless talk of croup, the teething problems, the speed or lack of it with which a baby crawled and spoke.

Just returned from the baptismal celebration of a neighbour's seventh daughter, she had said to Robert, 'The Lord has seen fit to make me barren. It is a punishment for past sins.'

Her tone was abrupt, the words forced from her by a bitter anger.

He had placed a hand, awkwardly, upon her shoulder. He said, intuitively: 'The last letter to come from Buckland St Mary said that Ann had married with the Reverend Robbins. That they are well-settled at Rook's Farm. That she had never been so happy.'

She looked into his face and saw only puzzlement and deep concern. Although he tried, Robert could not comprehend her true feelings. How could he? He was but a man, concerned only with a man's affairs. The men of Suamico rubbed shoulders frequently with one another. They met together at the black-smiths, the harness-repair shop, the grist and lumbermill, the

211

cooper's shop, the Rough and Ready Tavern. Even Robert, who was not an imbiber, would make the occasional call to Albert Seniba's bar, to acquaint himself with the current price of corn and hay in Green Bay, and to learn the weather prospects as forecast by the old men. It was the women, shut away on the homesteads, tied down with the endless tasks of yard-work, the twice-daily milking, the churning of butter, the making of cheese, the harvesting of fruits, the picking of meats that must see them through each severe winter, who suffered the torments of near-total isolation.

He said: 'There was a time when you were always smiling.'

His thin face reddened underneath its tan, but his tone was gentle.

'Guess it was your laughter that made me love you in the first place. Sometimes, when I see how low you are, I get to worry.'

She turned quickly to him then; she said: 'It's allright. There's no call for you to fret. What with corn rotting in the shocks, and the apple-harvest blighted, a wife with the vapours is something you can do without.'

Elizabeth pushed away her dreads and fancies; she resolved to fight the fears that came when she was by herself, and the silence of the great woods brought her near to screaming. It was not only the twenty silver dollars, paid from England, that had set her dreaming. It was the letter just received from Rhoda.

The lake-steamers of the Goodrich Line plied their trade between Green Bay and Chicago. A trip of sixteen days, and a small portion of that twenty dollars, could be the means of bringing her together with Rhoda. But Elizabeth believed that if she practised self-denial, that if she was sufficiently stoic and uncomplaining, the Lord, in His wisdom, would smile once more upon her, as He had on the barren Elizabeth of the Bible story, who had conceived, miraculously, in her old age.

She took Robert's hand. She said: 'Tell me more about the building of this frame-house.'

Relief smoothed the deep lines from his forehead; his shoulders straightened. He looked at her with the gratitude of recognition.

They walked together to the highest point of land on all the spread.

'*Here!*' he said. 'From this rise our windows will look clear out across Brown County. And remember this. We are building for our children, and their children.'

A cool wet summer was now followed by a dry fall. The carpenter came with his three sons; plans were made and measurements taken. The frame was first constructed in its several parts, the carpenters working on level ground, joining up the stout timbers by means of mortice and tenon, and pinning together the whole framework with hand-made, white-oak treenails.

By November all was ready for the house-raising. The whole community would be there, a feast must be provided. It was time for the Vickery house-pig to be slaughtered. Elizabeth baked great batches of corn-biscuits and pork roasts; her store-shelf was robbed of her best preserves and pickles. She made English muffins and fruit-scones. Two kegs of her best cider were rolled out and set beside the laden table.

The lifting was done in mid-morning of a cold but fine day. A hundred hands gripped the timbers, and as each side of the frame swung into position a great shout of triumph went up from every man, and a sigh of relief from each watching woman. With the most dangerous part of the raising now completed it was time for the younger men to show off their climbing skills. The afternoon saw the pinning together of the topmost timbers and the nailing of heavy rafters into position. By the time dusk fell, the bare bones of the new Vickery house stood proud and high. The already-cut floor planks were laid down, and dancing began to a fiddler's music. Bonfires had been lit all around the clearing.

Robert stood with Elizabeth; they watched the laughing, whirling couples. He said: 'There's still a whole lot to be done. The roof must be shingled, and each side-wall clad. We don't have much time before the snow comes. I hope our money

213

won't run out before the job is finished; it's a much bigger undertaking than I first figured on . . .'

For the first time in many months Elizabeth smiled.

She said, thoughtfully: 'Rhoda and George must by now have reached Chicago, and be settled in their new home. It's possible, I guess, for a woman to be just as lonely in a city. But Rhoda has her daughter, and people all around her.' She waved a hand towards the dancers. 'Tomorrow, all our friends will be gone back to their own steadings. It may be months before we have visitors again. I've given you a hard time lately, Robert. I'm resolved to do better in the future.'

He said: 'It's been a long hard road for both of us. But by spring we'll have the house completed. Just think of it! Sash windows that pull up and down, with panes of real glass we can see through! We'll have an elegant front parlour like our parents had in Old England.'

He reached out to touch a corner-post of the skeletal frame. His next words were those of a shy man, embarrassed by his own emotion, yet compelled to speak. He struck the post a light blow with his bunched fist.

'This will still be standing here when you and I are long gone. We came out from England with little more than our willing hands and a mind to work hard. We're farming folk, you and I. We don't look to make a great fortune. All I truly want is to make the Vickery name as well-respected in Suamico as it has always been in Buckland St Mary.'

Elizabeth took his clenched fist; she stroked his fingers until they lay pliant in her hand.

'Come,' she said softly, 'let us join the dancing.'

Chapter Eighteen

Eddie's thirteenth birthday had passed almost without notice. Georgie had yielded up a treasure once found on The Levee in Charlotte, a forbidden knife-blade the ownership of which had long been in dispute.

'Guess you'd better keep this in your pocket,' he had muttered. 'Mama reckons you're likely to get murdered, running errands like you do for Papa on all the big streets.'

Eddie had known that he would not be murdered, but he took the blade anyway, and thanked Georgie for it.

Rosa had knitted mittens, bright green in colour, and of thick scratchy woolyarn. 'To keep your fingers warm,' she said, 'while you carry those parcels of cold meat to rich folk's houses. You must be awful brave, Eddie, to go about the way you do. Me and Georgie reckon you to be a wonder.'

Respect from Rosa was unexpected. He exploited the moment.

'Oh well,' he said, offhand, 'I've been about the world you know. Just remember that I left home when we still lived in Charlotte. I worked almost a whole year out at Brandon's Stables. Chicago comes as no big surprise to me.'

Papa had measured Eddie's height against his own.

'Why, he's up to my top waistcoat button already. I do believe he'll be the tallest of all the Salters.'

Mama, who was herself a tiny, tireless woman, said: 'And he'll outgrow his strength, George, if we're not careful. It's a dangerous time for a boy's health when his legs are shooting upwards at a great rate.'

That image of himself, his legs shooting ever upwards, was a comfort to Eddie on the winter mornings when he walked with

Papa through the windy darkness. He would look up towards the stars and be thankful for his height, the broadening of his shoulders, the fact that he looked older than his years. His ambition was to be as tall and strong as his father; to live up to the gold lettering that declared the new business to be that of *George Hodder Salter and Sons, Meat-Packers of Chicago.*

Away from the house, his father talked to him as one man to another. Their retail customers, said Papa, had been inherited from the meat-market's previous owner, and still needed to be served. Many of them lived in the great mansions that fronted La Salle Street. They preferred to deal with an English butcher. Eddie's task was to deliver to them daily the finest cuts of fresh meat. But the true purpose of the move to Chicago was to set up a packing business. First Eddie, and then Georgie, were to learn their father's trade of slaughterer and butcher. By the time they were both proficient, said Papa, the packing enterprise would be well in hand; as each son reached his majority at the age of twenty-one, he would be made an equal partner with his father. They would no longer wear a butcher's apron, but be themselves employers of men; would own seats on the Board of Trade, wear business suits and sport a fresh flower daily in their lapels, as was the custom in the City.

It was a description of his future that seemed unlikely to Eddie, as Papa adjusted the canvas straps which held the heavy delivery basket in position on his shoulders. Papa had warned him, in his first days of employment, that he should speak to no one, should pass quickly by if ever accosted, and Eddie had seen, straightaway, that it was the puny and trusting man who came quickly to grief on Chicago's streets.

Papa asked if he was homesick for their old place. They never spoke together of Eddie's true mother. Eddie sensed the unasked question behind his father's concerned words. They exchanged a long look, each one knowing that the other was remembering the two grass-covered mounds underneath the cedar trees in Charlotte.

He said: 'It's allright here in Chicago because we're all together. I missed you awful bad, Pa, when I was living at Brandon's.'

'I know, boy. There was a time, once before, when I had to put you in the care of others. But never again.'

Eddie trudged through the bitter streets of the December morning, head bent into the wind that never ceased to blow. He trod the uneven boardwalks, alert for upstanding nails and loose slats. With each delivery he made, the load grew lighter. Gradually his shoulders straightened. By the time he reached Monroe Street he was able to walk upright. The hot coffee, given to him by the cook in the house of his final call, had warmed his chilled body. He came back to West Adams Street by a circuitous route, dawdling pleasurably on river bridges, and lingering beside the stables where lived the horses which pulled the city's street-cars.

The early-morning talk with Papa still occupied his mind; it confirmed the private thing between them, the bond that was never mentioned. It was since the move, and when he was out and about like this, quite alone among the city crowds, that the image of Susanna came most strongly to him. A scrap of her blue and white gown was always close to hand. He transferred it, surreptitiously, before a washday, from the pocket of one pair of britches to another. Sometimes he imagined her wearing that special gown, himself a baby in her arms.

There were spells when Mama was unapproachable upon the subject of Susanna. He had learned caution across the years. But lately, by gentle manoeuvres, he had come to know a younger vision of his mother: a white-aproned girl, with fair curls falling loose about her face, who kept what Mama called a "grocery shop", in Buckland St Mary, Old England. Since coming to Chicago, he had taken to peering in through the windows of dry-goods stores. But the young women who clerked in the stores around La Salle street were the dark-haired daughters of Italian and Greek immigrants. So he thought instead about the place called Old England, the country of his parents' origin, the land to which his beloved uncle John Salter had recently returned.

They had taught him in school about the many nationalities which made up the population of American States. He was coming, slowly, to recognise the varied names and habits which distinguished one culture from another. In the few weeks since their departure from Charlotte, Eddie saw how determindly American his father had become. The blue-striped butcher's apron and straw hat had been abandoned for a white smock coat. His speech was now indistinguishable from that of his children. Unlike Mama who had retained her precise, clipped accent; who still drank afternoon tea from thin china teacups, and baked English muffins, and something called steak-and-kidney pudding which was boiled-up in a cloth for several hours.

Eddie's admiration for Mama was wholehearted and secret. He practised, in private, her English way of speech, the inclination of her head, the little regal air which could put in his place the most obstreperous of men. He liked to see himself as being English, it made of him a certain kind of person, one who valued privacy, who was honourable, of whom was said: "He is an Englishman; his word is his Bond."

He had tried to talk to Georgie about it all, but his brother was still too young to make the fine distinction. His obsession nowadays was with Chicago. Every night, before they slept, he questioned Eddie about the day's events.

'So where did you get to today, huh?'

'Go to sleep! I'm tired, and so will you be when it's your turn to carry that heavy errand-basket.'

'Aw, come on then, Ed! I don't never get to go downtown. Ma won't let me budge further than Green Street. Why – we don't even get to go to church these days.'

Georgie thumped his pillow.

'Even church'd be better than cooped up in this house with pernickity Rosa.'

Eddie said: 'Today I was up on Clark and Monroe. I watched the horses pull the street-cars. Don't seem right somehow. Bet they've never ate a single blade of fresh grass, nor galloped in a field.'

Georgie said: 'Hey, that's awful sad about the horses. But tell about the street-cars. Say, Ed – how do they keep the iron tracks from falling off the plank roads?'

'With metal spikes, of course!' Eddie yawned. 'I should have thought even you could figure that much!'

Georgie chuckled in the darkness.

'Guess I'll be a street-car driver when I'm old enough.'

'You can't be. You've got to be a butcher and a meat-packer, like Pa and me. It already says so on the sign board, so you'll have to do it.'

'Not me. I don't have to do any job what I don't want to. Mama said so. I'm gonna climb up to that old board and scratch out that letter S on the end of SONS.'

'You'll break Papa's heart if you do that.'

Georgie looked up across the pillows. His face had a new, more convinced expression, as if he had just learned an adult truth. He said: 'He won't even *notice* if I'm not around to chop dead cattle up in little pieces. He'll aways have you, Ed.'

★

December 24

It is Christmas Eve and my thirty-eighth birthday. The children say how unfair it is that my birthdate should fall on a day when it is bound to go unmarked. This year they are set upon a celebrashun. Rosa bakes her specshul biscuits. The boys (aided by cents from George) bring me a box of coloured ribbons. From my dear husband I get a set of six white collars and matching cuffs in a heavy watered-silk. To buy such items, ready made, comes expensive, but he knows how much I love to trim my dark gowns with them.

The new furniture is arrived. Such excitements! I am more then middle-aged yet today I feel as a new bride in her first home! As to the bedroom pieces, my conshence rests easy. They have already known one careful owner, and altogether cost but four dollars and eighty-five cents. It is the two sofas and three armchairs that are my sinful indulgence.

George says: 'The money came from your father's Estate. He was himself a maker of handsome furniture. He would be glad to see us off those stiff-backed kitchen chairs and comfortably seated.' George has a way of reasoning that oft-times has me almost perswaded.

'But,' say I, near to tears, 'each sofa cost a whole three dollars – and I chose *two* of them. Together with the armchairs and bedroom things, why, the full bill comes to seventeen dollars and thirty cents.'

'And you have not yet bought the matching window-drapes,' he laughs, 'nor the flowered carpet-square, or a what-not for the corner, or a . . .'

'Halt!' I cry. 'Or you will truly vex me!'

George looks to the boys. The children are all smiles, even Jon, who is also privy to some secret. They go from the room, and return heavy laden, the boys with a carpet roll, Rosa with a bale of yellow brocade, and my baby Jon, very carefully, in both his hands, brings to me a lamp of brass with shade of engraved glass. It is all too much. I am overcome. I weep.

George throws up his hands.

'So what do we have to do to make your mother happy?' he asks the children.

'I *am* happy,' I sob. 'But it is such extravagance, and we cannot afford it.'

George no longer laughs. 'Sometimes,' says he, 'it is good for the *soul* to go beyond safe limits.'

I look swiftly to where the children are unrolling carpet and unfolding brocade. I take the lamp from Jon and kiss him. I offer up a devout prayer that none of them has overheard the rash words of their Papa.

December 27

Was to Service on Christmas Day, in the Congregashunal Church which stands but two blocks from us. Altho' George had told me it was so, had not thought Salvation to lie *qwite* so close at hand. Was pleasantly surprised at the Minister, a young Englishman who preached a *deep* Sermon against the perils of gambling and loose living. His name is Smith, his wife is a very plain but nice young woman, who is soon to be confined. Am bound to ask her what has brought them, of all places in this land, to a city like Chicago.

220

'Why, Mrs Salter,' says she, 'we go where the need is greatest. As you have surely noticed, wickedness and degradashun are to be found here on every street corner.'

Her words confirm all my worst fears, but do not care to admit lack of firsthand witness, since I have left the house but once since our arrival, and then only in the company of George.

After Service we are introduced to the small, but select congregashun and discover that another English couple, Mr and Mrs Bristol, are our very nearest neighbours. He is a shipping clerk who works for the Goodrich Line. George at once engages him in business talk. We all walk home together. Before we part, an invitation comes from Mrs Bristol, that we should take tea with them next Sunday.

George notes my improved spirits.

'There you are,' he smiles. 'You have walked but two blocks today and found two most superior English families.'

'I do not,' say I, 'expect to find that every two blocks in Chicago is so well endowed as to population. Green Street is especially favoured!'

But I cannot conceal my satisfaction. Find myself humming *Once in Royal David's City* what was my father's favourite Christmas hymn-tune; and *this* while I am basting the roast!

George says: 'It is as well that we bought the sofas and armchairs, the carpet and the what-not. Invitations will have to be returned, and it would not look well to have a Pastor and a shipping-clerk sit on the hard chairs in the kitchen.'

I suspect him of mockery, but he is straightfaced and earnest.

'Oh, how right you are, George!'

I have an awful thought.

'We have only this thick but serviceable ware. I cannot serve tea in anything but real bone-china.'

Another terror strikes me.

'You must unpack my sewing-machine this very instant. I have not yet made-up the yellow brocade. We have no curtains at the front-room windows!'

'It is Christmas Day, Rhoda,' he reminds me. 'It will be New Year before we are obliged to return hospitality.'

'Well, Rosa can help me sew the curtains,' I go on. 'And Eddie can look out for some inexpensive china while he does his deliveries . . .'

'I had thought,' says George, 'of having calling-cards engraved. We could put them on a silver salver. Perhaps Georgie could act as butler?'

There is laughter bubbling in his voice.

January 3 1869

George and Eddie are to business, and Rosa and Georgie are to the school.

I am alone with Jon, who is also lost without them. He goes from one room to another, hunting for them. At last he stands before me, tearful and much vexed, I see his lips part and expect a shout of anger – to my astonishment he says: "Where 'Osie?" His little face is puzzled, his cry comes from the heart.

I kneel down. I take him in my arms and lay my cheek against the smooth brown hair that is so like my own.

'She is to school. She will be home soon.'

I can scarce find the words so great is my emotion. He will be three years old on Thursday, and these are the first words he has ever uttered. Were I not so fearful to be abroad in this wild city I would run to West Adams Street and acqwaint George with the miracle.

As it is, his foot is hardly across the threshold before I am telling the good news. George goes straight to Jon and lifts him up. I see tears stand in my husband's eyes. He says: 'Perhaps, after all, there is some hope for him.'

I am nettled by his lack of joy.

'Do you not recall,' say I, 'how Eddie first uttered in the selfsame manner?'

Jon nestles in his father's arms. George strokes his cheek. He says: 'Why will you not admit it, Rhoda? It is *not* with Jon, as it was with Eddie. Jon's trouble goes much deeper. There is a doctor's office on West Adams. He is said to be good with backward children.'

'He does not need a doctor! Today he has shown that he *can*

222

speak when his need is urjent. He is devoted to Rosa. When he could not find her he was forced to utter. I will not have you dub him backward! I will not!'

George says: 'We have here a sweet and loving boy. He shows us more affectshun than the other three put all together. They are always keen about some matter of their own. They care for us, but have no time to show it, which is only natural for their ages. With Jon it is different. Why can you not be content to take what Jon offers? To accept him as he is?'

'Because your view of what he is does not match my own. I am the one who must be always with him, who must watch his every step and move. I see his small improvements. Your concern is only with your business!'

George turns away.

The moment, which should have been one for celebrashun, has ended in conflict.

January 15

Today my Georgie is eleven years old. He is the liveliest and cleverest of all my children. There are times when I could wish him less spirited and stubborn, but Eddie keeps him well within bounds. My husband marks the date by saying to him: 'One more year, young fellow, and you will also rise at five every morning.'

More snow comes this morning to cover earlier falls. Cannot venture forth even should I wish to do so. All goods delivered from nearby stores. Jon and I stay snug within the house. Today sees the finishing touches put to my front parlour. The yellow curtains are in position; the stiff brocade, looped-up at each side by means of silk cords, reaches to the floor, which is all but covered by the flowered carpet. The stove is flanked on either side by the pair of sofas. The armchairs take up most of the remaining space. The new lamp stands on the mantleshelf. The what-not holds bits of treasured china. It remains only for me to choose my Wall of Honour. This I do when school is out, since I have promised Rosa that she shall help me.

We decide upon the wall behind the box-stove, since it is the first to meet the eye on entering the room, and is most prettily lit by the red glow from the fire. We unpack the Portraits. The tinted likeness of our Dear Queen must, as ever, be given the central spot. Have long since instructed the children in the history of the English Royal Family.

Georgie, who is ushually inattentive to such subjects now asks: 'Who is she, then? Is she our Grandmother in England?'

Rosa, who is much given to laughter at her brother's nonsense, rolls about in mirth on the new carpet. Jon, who mimics all her actshuns, doing likewise.

'Don't be silly,' cries she.' 'If the Queen of England was our kin, why, Mama would be a princess, and you would be – well – a duke or something!'

I grow thoughtful. I go to my writing-box where are kept our business papers. I take out the parchment Pedigree sent to me by Brother James. I say: 'Since we are on the subject, you may be interested to know that there *is* a loose connection between my family and the Royal Line. It has been discovered lately by your Uncle in England, who is a Barrister and a most important personage.'

At last I have Georgie's full attentshun.

'You mean he's like the President, or Mr Armour the meat-packer that Pa is so keen to meet? Or is he like Black Hawk maybe?'

I try to see James in mocassins and feathered headdress.

I say, nonplussed: 'Well, no, not qwite like that.'

I delve into the trunk. I hold up the Portrait of my brother. The children gaze in silence on this recent likeness. I go to the kitchen to check on the roast of beef. As I return, Georgie says to Rosa, 'Why he's just a stout old party in a too-tight frock-coat. I don't like him. His eyes are too close together. He looks awful mean!'

I say, from long habit, 'Now, Georgie, don't be so disrespectful to your elders and betters.'

I hang James's picture below that of my Monarch, and beside that of my father. I reflect as I fix the frame upon the hook that I too perhaps have never cared much for the looks of my oldest brother, but have lacked until now the spirit to so much as *think* it.

January 16

As if my thought had beckoned him to me, a letter comes this very day from Buckland St Mary. James writes about his Stewardship of Father's Estate. He makes much of the roofing and plastering that must be done; the thatching and patching. I am surprised to learn that Father's property has been allowed to fall into such a sad state of repair. It was never so in my time.

I read aloud the letter to my husband in our qwiet hour when the children are a-bed. I come to the part where James hopes that 'George has got back into business in Chicago, and is showing more prudence and wisdom in his undertakings.' James also hopes that our children are industrious at school and good to their parents.

I see anger in my husband's face. He says: 'The man has no child of his own, yet he presumes to know all about the raising of them!'

'There is yet more,' say I.

'Read on!' cries George. 'I might as well know all at once.'

'My brother trusts that you are a good husband to me, that I am well provided for and contented with you.' I hold down the merriment that bubbles in me.

The wrath of George is mighty to behold. 'How dare he! He is himself too mean to marry, too set upon self-advancement.'

George hesitates. He says: 'I have never mentioned this before, but it has long been my belief that your brother begrudged me every penny of the Dowry money paid me by your father. On the night of my betrowthal to Susanna, he presumed to give me "wise advice". "Young man," said he, "I believe that you intend to sail shortly for the New World? Well, think on this. He travels fastest who travels alone."'

My laughter dies unuttered. George must truly be disturbed that he should raise Susanna's name.

I say: 'He is my oldest brother. He is an earnest man.'

'I too am the oldest of the Salter family! But I have never

225

presumed to patronise and preach – I tell you, Rhoda, it is as well for James Greypaull that the Atlantic ocean lies between us at this moment . . .'

I hear the breath rasp in his throat. I go to him. I put my arm about his shoulders.

I say: 'Do not distress yourself. I will tell you something most amusing. When Georgie saw James's likeness yesterday, he described him as being a stout old party in a too-tight frock-coat.'

George smiles, then he begins to laugh. Our mirth is so great that we must needs cling to one another.

★

Eddie's duties were of the menial kind. Papa had shown him how to deep-scrub benches and counters, how to scour chopping-blocks, and scald knives and cleavers. Every morning he must lay a depth of fresh sawdust on the front shop floor. He must never, said Papa, come to serve in the shop in anything but a clean white apron. Several items had been inherited from the meat-market's previous owner. An elderly horse and ramshackle dray lived in a shed behind the shop. A young Latvian called Joe, in the final year of his apprenticeship also came with the business. On a wharf of the Chicago River, a small slaughter--house and packing shed were also a part of the same bargain.

'We won't speak at home,' his father said, 'about matters to do with the packing. Since my venture failed in Charlotte, your mother worries overmuch about money. She is finding it hard to settle in the city. She frets about Jon. It will not do to place another weight upon her mind.'

Eddie's features took on the gravity required by this exchange of confidence between men.

'I reckon you're right, Pa. Mama surely has her hands full, what with the three little ones and all.'

Papa grinned at him then, in that way he had that always made Eddie feel that he was special to his father.

He said: 'We understand each other, Ed! All we need now is a batch of hogs and you and I will be really trading. We shall start in a small way to begin with . . .'

'But Mama keeps the books. She has every last cent accounted for. How can you buy-in extra stock without her knowing?'

'*Credit.*' There was wonder in the single word. 'Remember Charlotte, Ed? It was a mark of shame in that place if a man should owe money. In Chicago, a man of affairs is considered a failure if he is not in hock above his ears. We can borrow all we need, any time we want it, without a single entry showing red in Mama's Ledger.'

The pressure of his father's hand fell on Eddie's shoulder.

'Remember this, boy. Women are frail creatures. They have a need to be protected from the rough and tumble of real life.' He paused. 'Your Mama is a good and cautious woman. But you and I are moving towards big schemes. Can't you feel it in your bones, Ed?'

Slaughtering was carried out twice weekly in the months of winter. It needed but a light tap on the shoulder to bring Ed awake on those mornings. He would lie for a moment while his sense of vague unease deepened into shameful dread. In the kitchen his father prepared bowls of bread, soaked in hot milk and sprinkled with brown sugar. They ate quickly and in silence. The food lay uneasily on Eddie's stomach, but he dared not refuse it.

Out in the street, clad in thick coat and stout boots, he felt marginally better. Walking at this hour, in a freezing darkness lightened only by starshine, required more concentration than dodging pickpockets and streetcars in full daylight. They picked their way through the icy ruts of unpaved Green Street, and across the varying levels of the Halsted Street boardwalks. Most roads in the city stood dangerously higher than the buildings which edged them.

He could smell the river long before they reached it. The stink of the Chicago Basin was unique, even in winter, when prevailing north-westerly winds took the worst of the stench towards the lake. Together with the smoke and reek from slaughter-houses and stockyards, the pollution was a cause for complaint as far away as Crosby's Opera House and Jefferson Park.

The first streaks of dawn showed red beyond Lake Michigan as they came down to the wharfside. A scum of grease rippled into rainbow colours on the sluggish river waters. Eddie stood aside while Papa unlocked the heavy double doors that led into the slaughter house and stockpens. He thought about Charlotte, the sweet waters of the Genessee which flowed between clovered banks in summer. As the doors swung open the stench of twenty penned hogs was overpowering; they had arrived by railroad on the previous morning. Pa had explained the import-ance of resting an animal for twenty-four hours before slaughter. The creature must always be watered and fed and allowed to recover from its journey, or the meat would turn out to be 'fiery', and there was no sale for pork of an unpleasant shade of red.

The Latvian apprentice Joe had come to join them on this special morning. A notice, informing customers that the business would not open until ten am, had been pinned to the shop door. Six hours, said Pa, should be time enough to "stick" twenty hogs and hang them to cool in the inner room. They would return that evening to complete the pickling process. Mama had already been warned that due to press of business they would be late home for supper.

As children, Eddie and Georgie had been forbidden by Mama to go near to the yard and sheds when killing was in progress. Now, Ed must herd the hogs into a special enclosure; he must lift the trapgate that allowed a single creature to walk through and wait its turn before the hog hoist. He must stand before that hoist and attach a loop of chain to the animal's hind leg, and then fix the other end of the chain to a hook on the outer rim of the great wheel.

Papa would wind up the hoist until the squealing hog was hanging head downwards. He would then, with one sure stroke

228

of the cleaver, sever the larger blood vessels of the animal's neck. The hog was left to hang until it was utterly dead. Eddie's task, meanwhile, was to prepare the vat of scalding water into which the carcase was plunged.

The subsequent scraping-off of hair and bristle, the removal of the head, had become a routine matter and caused him no distress. It was that lifting of the trapgate, those final, trusting steps of the first unsuspecting victim; that hoisting of the living creature upon the hooked wheel; the sounds and smells of the act of slaughter, that he found difficult to bear.

Eddie knew that Papa had noticed his revulsion. A face of stone might be assumed at the moment of actual execution, and impassivity was in fact the only weapon he possessed. But there was nothing to be done about the sudden pallor of his skin, the threatened nausea, the fine cold sweat that broke across his forehead. This treachery of the body was so severe that after several killings he became clumsy and slow, with such a trembling in his hands that he could scarcely fix the hoisting chain about the poor beast's leg.

Oh yes, Papa had noticed, but said nothing. He had looked hard at Eddie in those first shaming days. Now the hip-flask was passed between the spokes of the wheel as a matter of routine. 'A nip of brandy to keep out the cold,' was how his father put it, 'and don't you ever let on to your Mama that I treat you to it!'

The number of things which Mama must not be told seemed to increase daily. The need for secrecy was indicated lately by no more than a gesture. A finger to the lips, the droop of an eyelid, and Eddie felt singled-out and proud. Not that conspiracy came easy; there was, he discovered, little satisfaction in this new role of sole repository of Papa's secrets, when no one but Eddie was conscious of the honour. The temptation to hint, if not actually tell, was most severe when he was with his brother. Georgie's inquisition still began with the removal of their bedside candle. Even as the door closed on Mama's 'Goodnight boys. God bless you,' Georgie was already sitting upright in his bed.

'So what did you see downtown today, huh? What did you and Pa do? How many hogs did you put paid-to? Say Ed, how does it feel – you know – to watch Pa use the cleaver?' It was only the faint tremor in his brother's childish voice that made it possible for Eddie to reply in tones of unconcern.

'Nothing much to it, boy. All in the day's work.'

When pressed harder for explicit details he would say at first: 'Kids don't have to know about such things. It's only for men like Pa and me.'

But Georgie pleaded in the covering darkness until Eddie answered. In the newly acquired accents of Chicago, he said with assumed glee: 'You really sure you want to hear this? Well – dem old hogs sure do set up a hollering and a squealing when they swing up on the wheel. The first one comes in quiet enough, but hogs ain't as dumb as people think. Once they smell blood they kinda know that their turn's coming next.' He added, his stomach churning, 'O'course, our Pa sure is a good, neat slaughterman. He finishes 'em off with but the one clean stroke. He don't never get more than a splash or two of blood across him. Now me – if I don't dodge quick enough – I get a real hard soaking of it.'

'Aw gee,' Georgie whispered, 'that must be just awf – just stoo-pendous!'

Successive slaughter-days brought other questions. Georgie pushed him ever further. Eddie found himself describing, in fine detail, the process of scalding and skinning, the method of evisceration and dissection.

Satisfaction was finally gained on the night when his interrogator stumbled retching and moaning from his bed to seek Mama. Eddie grinned in the darkness to hear her scolding voice, and Georgie's violent rejection of the dose of brimstone and treacle.

Later on he whispered: 'Hey, Georgie, what ailed you? Was it the thought of the nice pork chops you ate for supper?'

From across the room a weak voice said: 'Aw, shut up, why don't you? Bet you're dead scared, too, but you don't dare let on.'

February 21

Waited supper until half-past ten last evening. The food by this time qwite spoiled from overcooking. This has happened often in the past weeks. I stand in the darkness, by the front-room window and keep a watch. At last I see them, walking very slowly, George supporting Eddie. They come into the kitchen. The faces of both are paper-white. Eddie sways and would fall but for his father's arms. I think straightway of murderers and footpads.

'Who has set-upon you both?' I cry. 'Whatever can have happened?'

George says it is naught but weariness what ails them.

I make hot milk with a dash of brandy in it. I tend to Eddie. I take off his boots and jacket. As I loosen his shirt collar I find that garment dark with blood. I cry out: 'He is hurt after all, George.' George says: 'It is but hogs' blood. We have had a heavy day's slaughtering. You have been a butcher's wife these many years. The sight of a bloody shirt should not alarm you.'

His tone is sharp and I am nettled by it.

'*Your* son,' I tell him, 'has but thirteen years. Tall he may be, but he does not yet have a man's strength. You *shall not* make him work like this. I will not allow it.'

George says: 'I was but nine years old when I started working with my father, and that was farm-work which is harder than butchering, and gives longer hours!'

'We live in more enlightened times, George! But still I do not understand this need for frequent slaughter. Has pork become such a fashionable dish in this part of Chicago that you and Ed must needs work a day of eighteen hours to keep up a supply?'

George yawns. He says they are both worn-out and will I please be qwiet and let them go peaceful to their beds. I look at Eddie's grey eyes.

I say: 'He was left to me in trust.'

Eddie says: 'It's allright, Ma. Pa tried to send me home lots of

231

times but I wouldn't go. Don't be mad at him. It's not his fault. Anyway, the last of the pork was packed and shipped . . .'

He claps a hand across his mouth.

George groans.

Eddie cries: 'Sorry Pa! I never meant to tell. It just slipped out.'

I pour more hot milk into their glasses. This time my hand is extra-heavy on the brandy. I wait while they drink.

I say, but gently: 'I think you two have not been altogether truthful, lately.'

George pulls a sheaf of papers from his pocket; he pushes them across the table.

I spread the papers out. The first to meet my eye are the Notes of Credit, from various banks, and all of them for small sums.

'You have been borrowing,' I say, 'and without my notice!'

'I do not need your notice, Rhoda. In any case, you would have tried to stop me.'

He sighs.

'If you look more closely you'll see those Notes have been repaid in full.'

I come next to bills for railroad freight, for drayage; there is a cooper's receipt for a hundred barrels, there are chits for marine-salt and saltpetre. There is a record of extra hours worked by Joe, the apprentice-boy. I try to calculate within my head, but it is too much for me. I rush to pen and paper. I add the figures. I say: 'This venture has cost us a small fortune!'

George brings out a final slip of paper from his top waistcoat pocket.

'That pork,' he grins, 'sold for twenty-five dollars on the barrel.'

'And you had a hundred barrels filled?' I whisper.

'A straight profit, Ma, of two hundred dollars.' The smile on Eddie's face is broad. I know not whether I should laugh or weep.

March 2
With two hundred dollars now safe in the Bank of Chicago, I

232

sleep better nights and awake more hopeful. Not that I have forgiven George for the decepshun. I trust this lapse of faith will not become a habit with him. I will not be looked on as a weak and helpless female fit only for the darning and mending, the washing of clothes and dishes!

'Back in Buckland St Mary,' I remind him, 'I was a full business partner with my sisters.'

'But that was in a little dry-goods store, in an English village.' He smiles. 'Come, Rhoda – it was hardly a matter of high finance, was it? You four did not require to belong to the Chamber of Commerce, nor sit on the Board of Trade.'

His words confuse me. I know nothing of these Boards and Chambers what he speaks of. I do believe it is his intention to undermine me with such menshun.

'I balanced the Books,' I say sharply. 'I was never short in my accounting, no, not even to the final farthing!'

'And in Chicago you balance *my* Books to the last red cent!'

His tone is condescending. He will indulge the 'little woman'. Were he not so handsome, and his smiles so sweet, I could be very angry with him. As it is, I take silent note that since his recent *secret* packing venture, the Ledger Books have been referred to as being *his* and not *ours*.

March 20
Our Pastor's wife safe delivered of a daughter. On the evenings when I was obliged to wait-up for George and Eddie, I have fine-smocked an infant's lawn gown. I go now to the Vicarage in the company of young Mrs Bristol. As we walk, she remarks that in Chicago the word Vicarage hardly fits the yellow frame-house wherein lives our Pastor. Can only agree with her, the Buckland St Mary Vicarage being built of limestone and very fine! Enqwire what does she think might sound more fitting? She has not the faintest notion; nor have I.

The baby is a pretty little thing. She resembles her father, what is fortunate for her according to Rubina Bristol. Can only reflect that the *same* is surely said behind my back of my own children, they having inherited the beauty of the Salter family.

233

We sit cosy by the fire in our Pastor's bedroom, the period of lying-in being not yet over, and the weather still so bitter cold.

'Do not dream of coming downstairs,' I tell Mrs Smith, 'until the sun shines. There will be toil enough once you are on your feet.' The smocked gown is much admired. Admit that I have learned fine-stitching in my Boarding School for Young Ladies, in Chard, Old England.

Cannot help but let my eye wander round the room as we are talking. Am qwite gratified to note that my own mahogany bedroom set is finer than theirs. Compare my own rose-brocaded headboard to the plainness of our Pastor's bed. Chide myself for being worldly. Pay attenshun to the conversashun, and find that young Mrs Bristol is confiding to us that she herself is lately in 'an interesting condishun'. As the oldest mother in the room, I feel myself well qwalified to speak upon such matters. A fassinating talk, what qwite restores my self-esteem! Until our Pastor's wife makes menshun of my *four* confinements. Cannot answer all at once. Feel their gaze upon me and know that my strange looks have made them curious about me. The colour in my ushally pale face has betrayed me to them. There is no hope of passing-over what is, after all, a very private matter, but since I insist on truth in others, I would be a hypocrit if I did not toe my own line.

I say at last: 'Well, as a matter of fact, I have been confined but the three times. Eddie is not my child. My husband was first married with my cousin Susanna. She died when very young. The baby was left to me in trust.'

To my surprise, there are tears in the eyes of our Pastor's wife.

Altho' English-born she is qwite American in speech. She says: 'Oh, my dear Mrs Salter, that is surely the most touching and beautiful story I have heard in a long while. Why, I was saying to 'Lija just the other day, that Mrs Salter sure is the very soul of goodness. Well, I never knew the half of it, I do declare!'

Mrs Bristol is likewise overcome. She says: 'Oh he does you

234

credit, Mrs Salter! Ed is such a fine young man, so polite and handsome. The very image of his father – but his nice manners so clearly learned from you.'

It is all most gratifying. We talk at length upon the matter of a motherless child and how it is best dealt with. After all, who is better qwalified to speak than I?

'If I were to die this instant!' cries our Pastor's wife, 'I could only hope for a mother like you for my preshus babe!'

'Oh yes,' says young Mrs Bristol, 'we will keep your confidence of course, Mrs Salter, but it is such a beautiful and romantic tale.'

Am surprised at these words. Have never seen my marriage to George as being in the least romantic. Walk home in a *glow* of satisfacshun.

When Eddie comes in I reach up to him and kiss his cheek.

He blushes.

'Why Ma,' says he, 'whatever brought that on?'

'Because,' say I, 'you are my very own dear son. It is high time I said it to you, lest you doubt the way I feel about you.'

April 22

Rosalind Rhoda Salter is ten years old today! She does not have an easy time I think, placed as she is between two smart older brothers, and Jon who will not let her from his sight. It is her first birthday in Chicago. The choir master has informed us that her voice is very fine and should be encouraged. George finds for her a small pianoforte so that I may play and accompany her singing.

To mark the day we make a Portrait. Rosa and I together. I wear my crimson silk with the two deep frills and the white watered-silk cuffs and collars. At my throat I pin the ivory and gold cameo brooch given me by Father.

'When I am gone from this world,' I tell Rosa, 'this brooch is to be yours.'

'Oh Mama,' she cries, 'don't talk about such things, 'specially on my birthday!'

We sit for the Picture, Rosa standing by my side. She wears a

235

dress that I have made her in white broderie-anglais, with a wide sash of blue, and six starched petticoats beneath it. About her neck hangs the gift from Ed and Georgie. A necklace of coral, what they tell me is very fashionable right now in the city of Chicago.

At the crushal moment both she and I recall that other Portrait, with the three small Salters looking tearful and cross. We grin at one another.

'No smiling, *please*,' orders our photographer. 'Let us have you two ladies looking dignified if you *don't* mind!'

Rosa asks if I will make a small tea-party for her and three chosen school friends. At first I say no. I have seen the girls at her school. I fear for my new furnishings and china. She pleads and I give in. I have never known her so set upon a thing. She promises to warn them about spilt tea and cake-crumbs.

Jon and Georgie are banished, grumbling, to the kitchen while their sister entertains her guests. I have laid out, in *trepidashun*, my best china service; and just refrained from covering my brocade chairs with dust sheets. I admit three large and heavy-footed sisters who look clumsier than ever at close qwarters. Rosa begs that she alone might serve the tea. Her face is so ankshus that I can but agree.

I listen at the door, but hear only the murmer of voices and the chink of cups. They thank me nicely on their departshur, all three looking much *subdued*. Rosa comes into the kitchen.

'Oh Ma,' she says, 'they were so knocked-out by just every little thing! They couldn't stop looking at your Wall of Honour and our fine-looking kin. I showed them Queen Victoria's portrait. I said she was a relative of yours.' Rosa smiles in a satisfied way. 'I bet they don't have brocaded sofas in their house – I could tell by the way they hardly dared to sit on ours. Maimie said she'd never seen such a lovely flowered carpet, not in all her life! Bessie was wild with envy at my new piano.'

'Rosa,' say I, 'such an attitude towards your friends hardly does you credit.'

She looks downcast and is close to tears.

'Well – I guess they won't snub me so bad in school now that they know that we're not poor trash!'

'Poor trash?' I reach for the nearest chair. I sit, astonished.

'Their father, they say, is an up-and-coming business man. They look down their noses at me because I'm just a butcher's daughter. They'll soon be off to a fancy boarding school, so they tell me.' She grows thoughtful. 'But for all their fine words, they were mighty impressed with my home and my mother.'

'Sit down,' I say. 'It is time we talked together, you and I. There is a deal of boasting goes on in this city. In fact I would say it is a *habit* of Chicago people. Now I am not a wordly woman, I do not go about much, but I have eyes and ears. Pay no attenshun, Rosa, to your braggart school mates. They most likely live in a hovel and sit on herring-boxes. The values of this city are altogether false. Even I have lately caught in myself a tendency to worldliness and empty pride, and anyway, good taste cannot be bought with dollars.'

I wipe away her tears. I say: 'Never let yourself feel snubbed by *any* person. You have much to be *justly* proud about.'

'But it's so hard at school among city kids. Oh Ma – why did we ever leave Charlotte?'

'Listen,' I say. 'If a little boasting is reqwired then you have my leave so to do. You may inform your classmates that your father is not just a butcher but a Packer of Meat; that he is familiar with the Chamber of Commerce, and intends to sit on the Board of Trade.'

May 1

At last a fine warm evening, after many weeks of rain and storm. Take a turn about the yard, what is most depressing, it being no more than a wild patch, and overgrown with weeds. Decide it is all a hopeless prospekt and best left alone. Eddie comes to join me. He stoops to search among the nettles that grow thick beside the kitchen door. He calls me to him.

'Mama – have you seen our lilac root, the one we brought from Charlotte? Come quick and look – it has green shoots!'

I go to him. We kneel together on the damp ground. It is true. Our lilac, against all odds, has rooted itself in city soil. Ed

237

goes into the kitchen, he finds an old glove in my ragbag. He begins to clear away the weeds.

He says: 'That sure is one determined bush, eh Mama?'

I say: 'Would that I, too, could find such heart. I have lost my love of gardens among these busy streets.'

He looks strangely at me. 'You're tired. Jon has been pretty sick just lately. If you like – I could help you clear the yard. I saw flower-seeds for sale in a store on West Halstead.' He grins. 'Guess it's true what they say. There ain't nuthin' you can't buy in the city of Chicago!'

'Can you take me there, to this store?'

'Anytime that Pa can spare me.'

I stand upright. 'It's qwite a big piece of ground after all, Ed. Seems a shame to leave it lying fallow. We could make a vegetable plot.'

'We could,' says he, 'have a few plum and apple trees –'

'No!'

I speak so sharply he is startled. He walks a short space from me. He says: 'Your're dead-set on changing everything, aren't you? Don't ever think that I don't notice. We've got yellow chairs and sofas now instead of red ones. The drapes are hung all diff'rent.' He turns away and will not look at me. 'In the Charlotte house I still felt my mother's presence. Sometimes, when I felt awful low, I sorta used to see her in the orchard.'

'So did I, Ed.'

'You did?'

'Eddie,' I say, 'your mother was the dearest person in my whole life. When she died I all but lost my mind. Can't you see, how painful it has been all these years, for me to live in her shadow? Can you blame me if I used the move to Chicago to try to change things a little?'

'But I never knew her!' His mouth is trembling. 'You never want to talk about her, and, when you do, it's like you're telling me about a stranger. I don't even have her grave to go to any more.'

I sigh. I must be careful what I say; he is at an age when feelings are fragile. I say: 'You know that I keep a Journal of our doings?'

238

'I've seen you writing sometimes.'

'I have done this since the day I left my father's rooftree. When you are a little older I will let you read it.'

'You promise?'

'I promise.'

September 2

A letter comes this day from Buckland; it is in the hand of my oldest sister Mary. I know not what is the hardest to comprehend, be it her scrawled handwriting or the bitter anger of her words.

It appears that she is at odds with brother James in the matter of *the Will*. She is no longer content to receive her share of the Rents from Father's properties, but will have James sell-up the entire Estate, and so receive her part of the *large* sum what will result from such a Sale.

It would seem that James has given her short shrift on the subject. This I can well believe, those two oldest of my father's children having been at loggerheads since childhood!

She reqwests an immediate answer from me. What, she asks, do George and I mean to do about James, conserning Father's Will? If we stand firm, all eight of us together, we can *force* a *sale* and so outwit James. A letter, she says, has also been sent to Elizabeth in Wisconsin on this same subject, and one to our brother Mark in Oshkosh.

I do not show the letter to my husband. It is Greypaull family business; and after all, George has also, lately, kept his confidence from me.

September 10

Eddie and I do a little yard-work each fine evening. We clear the brambles and pile-up rubbish in a distant corner. It is too late for flower-seeds. He brings instead two seedling-plum and three young apple trees. Next spring, I tell him, we will have hollyhocks and wallflowers. My sister in England can send us seeds from her garden. We talk as we work.

By careful wording, and a show of lukewarm interest, I learn to my releef that George has no intenshun of trying *summer* packing of hogmeat for some years yet to come. It is, says Ed, a venture what is done by bigger packing-houses with good results. But great qwantities of ice are needed, and ice-blocks come expensive, as I well know, having bought one such to place beneath Jon's bed in this hot and sultry weather. Wrapped in thick burlap, such a block will help to cool him, and so lessen the convulshuns.

October 5
Much shaken by the events of yesterday.

Eddie and I had qwite cleared the yard of all rubbish. The resulting heap being so unsightly, I resolved to make a bonfire. Had not realised how tinder-dry was everything after this long, hot summer. Leaves also lying ankel-deep across the yard from surrounding trees. A spark from our fire – and the fence was alight! Fire spread from the fence to the hickory-tree, which went up like a torch! To my eternal shame the Fire Brigade was summoned. George *very* angry! He is aware, he says, that I do not care overmuch for Chicago – but there is no call for me to burn it down!

*

In a span of thirty-five years Chicago had grown from a Frontier village of three hundred souls to a city which numbered three hundred thousand people. Men came there to make money. It was the place where a thing was no sooner said than done.

It was the Chicagoans' proudest boast that this was a city of 'fast horses, faster men, falling buildings, and fallen women. Everyone comes here – anything goes here!' Yet there was a simplicity among the brashness; a kind of charm in the very absence of sophistication. On the main streets, wealth and squalor stood unselfconsciously together. In the shadows of many proud buildings stood wretched two-roomed shanties which housed the immigrant poor and their cow and chickens.

Chicago, in this year of 1870, was a mix of cattle-yards and opera houses, of gambling-dens and marble-fronted churches; and Georgie Salter, twelve years old, and newly apprenticed to his father's business, loved it with his very soul.

A second delivery basket had been purchased. The broad straps chafed his bony shoulders; he found this obvious badge of the errand-boy to be demeaning, but since brother Ed bore his load of meat without complaint, Georgie must do likewise. The twelve years of his life had been spent in catching-up with Eddie. It was on Saturday bath night, with Mama excluded from the kitchen, that he was forced to remove his flannel undershirt and reveal the rawness of the weals.

Eddie said: 'Whyn't you tell me, you little fool? I would have carried part of your load for you. It takes some getting used to, and you're so durned skinny!'

'No! I don't want you to help me, and if you breathe a word of this to Pa or Ma, then I'll have to kill you!'

Ed fetched a jar of Mama's home-made salve from a kitchen cupboard. His fingers were gentle. He said: 'There's a heap of clean rags in Mama's sewing-bag. We'll make pads, and I'll fix 'em underneath your shirt before we start for work on Monday. Nobody will know about it.'

'You never needed no old pads under your shirt.'

'I'm built diff'rent than you. We only look alike in our faces, that's all, 'ceptin I've got grey eyes and you've got blue ones.'

Eddie looked at him and grinned.

'Say, kid, you'd better eat more of Ma's suet-puddings. You're as thin as a rail, I can count all your ribs, you got legs like beanpoles!'

They began to scuffle, but without enthusiasm. The days were past when, out of sight of Mama, they would fight until one of them submitted. Deterred now by the soreness of his shoulders, and a dropping weariness induced by one week's labour for his father, Georgie turned, unexpectedly from combat. He pulled the stripped nightshirt over his head; a few months ago it had reached down to his ankles, now it barely met his knees. Ed dragged the tin bath to the kitchen sink; he began to bale out the water. It was a task that should have been shared between them.

He said: 'Get off to bed. You can take your turn next week.'

The affection between them was of the rough kind, found between one sibling who has learned, early on, to make allowances for, and sometimes take mean advantage of, the frailties of the other.

January was prime slaughtering time in the pork-packing business. In the weeks that followed, Georgie also left his bed at five in the morning. On killing days three bowls of bread and hot milk were now made by their Papa. Ed never reached the bottom of his dish. A fellah, thought Georgie, could learn a lot about another fellah, just from watching. Ed went unwilling, those mornings, to the packing-house on the wharf of the Chicago River. It showed in his rigid spine, in the braggadocio he adopted when obliged to speak about the job. On the other hand, he owed his own preparedness to Ed. The act of slaughter held no sense of shock for Georgie.

Spring in Chicago meant a shorter workday. Packing ceased in the smaller plants with the onset of warm weather. His shoulder healed; his skinny frame was toughening into muscle and sinew. He was less weary when he left his bed. By the end of May he had recovered sufficient energy to be obnoxious; that old childhood curiosity of his came back to shame his older brother. Their deliveries made, Georgie lingered on the crowded streets. He stood and gazed upwards at the Potter Palmer building where Marshall Field had his great store. He peeped into hotel vestibules, remarking loudly on their marbled grandeur, and was chased away by the negro porters. He loved the street-cars and the horses which pulled them. He said, aloud, that large people should pay higher fares than thin ones, since they increased the load for the poor nags, who might be better fed and housed in consequence. He embarrassed Ed whenever he could, and took delight in so doing.

When asked by Mama if he was contented to be working

242

with his father and brother, Georgie said: 'It was tough in winter. But now that summer's come why it's a barrel-load of fun!'

Mama said that work was a serious matter, and not to be viewed in a spirit of lightness; and what *exactly* did he mean?

The taking of the Census of 1870 had commenced in January, on the north side of the city. By mid-June the count of heads had reached the west side of the Chicago River. On June twenty-sixth it was the turn of the inhabitants of Green Street to declare the essential details of their lives.

Rhoda peeped from behind the yellow drapes at the black-garbed Enumerator and his Clerk. She was familiar with the procedure of Census-taking. In his time, her father William Greypaull, had acted as Enumerator for the Tithing of Dommett in Buckland St Mary.

★

June 26

Weather overcast and very hot. Jon is fretful. He whimpers and shakes his head, and seeks out a dark corner of the front parlour. He huddles there as is his habit just before a convulshun. The Census officers are with my neighbours. I resolve to move Jon from the corner and lay him on his bed. His is upset by strangers at such times, but they are already at my door, and it is too late.

The men come in. The Clerk who holds the Book is a young man. He spies Jon in the corner and, thinking it some game, he bids him come out and tell his name. Jon makes no sound or movement.

'Is the child deaf?' he asks me.

'No. He is not deaf. The sultry weather does not suit him. He must needs seek a cool place.'

I distract them from Jon with an offer of my homemade lemonade, which they accept. But the Enumerator, who is an older man, still studies Jon. He asks if I have had him to a doctor. I tell him, no, it is not necessary. The qwestions begin. I confirm that George Hodder Salter is the Head of the Household; that he is forty-three years old and was born in England. His business is that of butcher. He holds no real estate, but his personal fortune amounts to five hundred dollars. I give them my own details. Then comes the listing of each child. The two boys, I tell them, are employed by their father; Rosa is at school, and Jon, who is four years old, still at home with me.

I speak qwickly, so as to have the matter done with. Jon is now holding his head and rocking from side to side. He makes sharp little cries, then becomes very qwiet. Again, the Enumerator calls to him, but he makes no answer. I recall that in the English Census there is a category that pertains to health. The condishuns listed are those of Blindness, Deaf-mute, Idiotic or Insane. I sit very still. I await that final qwestion.

The Enumerator says: 'Are all in this household sound in mind and body?'

'Why, of course,' say I, 'we are very well, thank you!'

The Clerk looks keenly at me.

'Mrs Salter. I think you misunderstood the qwestion.'

He looks towards Jon. 'Surely we have here a very sick child? I am surprised that a woman of your intelligence has not sought a doctor.'

'He is not sick. He suffers, sometimes, from convulshuns.'

The men exchange long looks. The Enumerator says: 'Bring him here, please.' I go to Jon and lift him. I sit as far from the men as I am able. Jon rocks from side to side. He grips his head, and I know the seizure is not far off. They study my child's face. The older man says gently: 'How long has he been like this?'

'The seizures began,' I say, 'when he was but weeks old.'

'Does he speak?'

'He says his own name. He does not have clear speech, but *we* understand him.'

'Mrs Salter, I am sorry to press you on this matter, but my rekords must be accurate. There are but two categories for such as Jon, and he is clearly not Insane.'

'I know them well, sir. It is the same with the English Census.'

'Then you will understand my problem.'

'He is not of unsound mind,' I burst out, 'he is just a little slower than my other children, but that is due to epilepsy. I will not have you list him Idiotic.'

There is pity in the young Clerk's eyes. The Enumerator nods to him. The entry is made in the Book. They rise and take their leave.

I stand at the window, Jon in my arms, and watch them go. I have been robbed this day by thieves. My tears drip on Jon's face. His eyes are closed. The convulshun is upon him.

October 4

We are come at last into the cooler weather. Jon much improved. 'What,' I ask George, 'is the name of that doctor you once menshuned?' He says it is a Doctor Hahn. He has a suite of rooms on West Adams, and is said to be very good in children's ailments.

'I am thinking of taking Jon to see him. He has such bad chest colds every winter.'

Dr Hahn has grey hair and a kind face. He reminds me of Father. He takes Jon on his knee, and gives him his silver watch to play with. I say we have come from Charlotte, New York State; that Jon suffers from bronchial trouble every winter. The doctor says nothing, but studies Jon. My gaze follows his, and I see how the watch slips repeatedly through the child's fingers, and would fall to the floor but for the chain what holds it.

'I think,' says Dr Hahn, 'that you have not come to me about bronchial problems.'

I hesitate. I remember the Census-takers.

'My son is epileptic. He is slow for his age. I am conserned about him.'

'What had your Charlotte doctor to say about Jon?'

'He said that he would never be like my other children.'

'And what do you think, Mrs Salter?'

'My father was also epileptic. But he was a man of strong intellect and good brain.'

Dr Hahn lays his fingers on Jon's head. He says: 'This little one has more troubles then just epilepsy. But I think you know that. I cannot tell you what you wish to hear.'

I say: 'My husband is not a poor man. An inheritance is due to me from England. No matter what it costs, can you not . . .?'

He interrupts me. 'If it were only a matter of dollars, my job would be easy.' He looks keenly at me. 'The first step is up to you. Until you accept that Jon is hindered, then I cannot help you.' He raises his hand against my protest. 'I know how you feel. You believe that if you treat your child as if he were normal, then he will grow to be so. In the case of Jon that will never happen. Your only course is to face the truth. Take him as he is, Mrs Salter.'

December 24

It is Christmas Eve and my fortieth birthday. George spies me before the looking-glass.

He says: 'You are hardly changed since that day I came up to Buckland to kill the house-pig. There is scarcely a line in your face. You have not a single grey hair. Your figure is as trim as any young girl's.' He drops a kiss upon my head. 'I don't know how you do it, Rhoda!'

'It is not for want of worry!' say I. 'If my troubles showed up in my face then I should be a *crone*. Instead, it is my nerves what suffer.'

He laughs. 'You have no cause to be ankshus, these days. The business prospers. The children keep well. Even Jon is more content since you are less pushing with him. I rarely suffer asthma any more. It is Chicago that has worked a miracle in us!'

★

The Chamber of Commerce stood on a corner of Washington and La Salle streets. It was built, so Pa had told them, of Athen's marble. The two impressive storeys stood ninety feet high and had a total frontage of two hundred feet. With lofty windows

246

and a mansard roof it resembled a small cathedral. In this year of 1871, the Chicago Board of Trade carried on its business on the second storey of this building.

Monday, being left-overs day, was the one morning of the week when no deliveries of meat were made. Ed and Georgie went with Papa to the Chamber of Commerce, riding as a rare treat on the horse-drawn street-car. They stood in the sunshine and drank the hot coffee bought for them by Pa from a street-vendor. They watched as Papa climbed the marble steps, and entered the great oaken door.

'Hey, Ed! What's a-Seat-on-the-Board-of-Trade?'

'Well now – I guess it's a kinda bench thing – what business men sit on while they make their fortune. That's why Pa's come here this morning, to buy his own bench, so's he'll have somewhere to sit down while he's making money.'

Georgie said: 'Seems to me like a waste of dollars. Reckon I'll stay standing up when I'm full-grown, and buy a horse an' saddle instead.'

'Papa's getting old. His hair gets real grey these days.'

Georgie snickered. 'Guess he'll catch it hot and strong from Mama, when she finds out he's been buying hisself a bench to sit on. They've been arguing every night about it. You're getting too ambitious, George! That's what she said. Hey, Ed, what's ambitious?'

'It's when you want to get on in life. Di'nt you learn anything in school? It's why Pa brought us with him, this morning. He wants us to see how it goes on with a man-of-affairs – and before you ask – a man-of-affairs is one who deals on the floor of the Board of Trade. They make bids for whole elevators full of grain, and whole freight-cars full of hogs – sight unseen!'

'But that's stoopid! I would never buy anything I hadn't first looked at.'

'Oh sure. You already drive storekeepers crazy poking in among the candy and the apples to find the biggest for your money.'

'So? It's what Mama does when she goes marketing. I reckon Ma's smarter than Pa when it comes to trading.'

247

'No, she ain't then!'

'Don't let her hear you say "aint", Ed.' Georgie giggled. 'You know that ain't proper English.'

They scuffled briefly on the sidewalk, coming dangerously close to the brazier over which the coffee vendor boiled his kettles.

'Look out, you kids,' he shouted. 'You want to burn Chicago down?'

They sat down on the lowest of the marble steps.

'Guess it would burn real well,' Eddie said. 'I never really noticed it before, but 'most everything here is made of wood.'

'And tar, Ed. The cedarwood blocks what make the roadway is all set down in black pitch. You can see it squeezed between the cracks. Then there's the boardwalks, and most of the houses – bet I can find more wooden things than you can!'

It was a game they played, while Papa bought his seat on the Board of Trade.

★

January 10, 1871

Money comes in these days what never passes thru' *my* Ledger. I still keep accounts of the meat-market trade, but a new set of books is now kept by Eddie conserning the packing side of the business. I learn from my sons that casual labour is being employed in the packing-shed. That George has put in machines to make the work go faster. I see little of him, and when he is at home he talks only of the price of grain and hogs, and how instructive it is to stand shoulder to shoulder on the Chamber floor with giants like Cyrus McCormick and Phillip Armour, who bid in hundreds, oft-times thousands of dollars. It all sounds to me less like *business* dealings and more like *gambling*. I hope George knows what he is about!

The nights now bitter cold with severe frost. The little lake in Jefferson Park is fast frozen. The young folks make up a skating party. They light bonfires around the lake, and toast muffins and marshmallows. George buys skates for Rosa and the boys.

Jon and I wrap-up warm, and go to watch their antics. All three are black and blue from bruises until they master the knack of staying upright. Eddie skates hand-in-hand with a young girl who clerks in her father's drygoods store on Halstead Street. She has long fair curls and is very pretty. Must make sure that George has *spoken* to Ed about certain aspekts of *growing-up*.

March 3
George talks now of a brick-and-stone manshun fronting Lincoln Park, of entertaining, and being seen in the 'right' places, among influenshul people. He will make life easier for me, he menshuns a servant or maybe two! He receeves dinner invitashuns and will have me go with him; what I refuse to do.

It appears that in Chicago there are no *soshul* distinctshuns. Store-clerks and packers sit down to dine at the selfsame table as emminent poets and historians, this mix being made by the wealthy barons of the Chamber of Commerce. This being the case, I take leave to wonder what other company is present at these 'evenings'. Have read in the *Chicago Tribune* that singers from Crosby's Opera House are popular guests at certain 'festive boards'.

Matters come to a head as I have known they must. George shows me an engraved card which reqwests the company of Mr and Mrs Salter at a party to be held in a Michigan Avenue manshun. 'I cannot go,' say I, 'I am a plain and simple woman. I would not fit in among the bedizened females of such company. What is more, I have Jon to look to.'

'Mrs Bristol will come in and mind him for you. It is but for one evening, Rhoda. I will give you money for a new and stylish gown . . .'

'. . . and paint for my face I suppose, and feathers for my hair? I have seen the wives of your new friends, George. They ride in their carriages thru' Green Street. I would not wish to break bread with such worldly women.'

'You are qwite wrong,' says he. 'Why, the wives of my friends are most devout and qwiet ladies. You and they would find much in common.'

'I am sorry, George, but my mind is qwiet firm upon the matter. I will not go and that is that!'

March 20
He has gone to dine *without me*! Two hours were taken up with his bathing and dressing, the trimming of his whiskers, the pomading of his hair, the tying of his bow-tie. He looked so *very* handsome. Am inclined to weep, and probably shall when the children are abed. Meanwhile, I have much sewing to occupy me. The boys need new trousers, and store-bought clothes poor in qwality and very *dear*.

April 15
George goes to other dinner parties. Alone and without me. There is a coolness between us, not to say *coldness*. I qwestion the boys, but discreetly, about what goes on in the packing-house. Further sheds have been erected so they say, and an ice-house built. I fear he will embark once more on the summer packing of pork what was so disastrus in Charlotte, and brought us close to being bankrupt. But my lips are sealed on this subject, as on many others. Oh! how I wish that we had never come to this licenshus and wicked city!

Eddie says that Papa goes in mostly for Futures dealings. That he is known on the Board for being 'lucky'. That next winter will see a great expanshun in the affairs of George Hodder Salter and Sons.

June 14
A letter from Elizabeth in Wisconsin. The new frame farmhouse is complete, she says, and looks very fine. She writes about crops; they have bought a horse, but will still keep their team of oxen. Her oldest son, Johnny, is coming seventeen, and taller than Robert. All at once, I am homesick for Buckland St Mary and my sisters; I long for the old days, when control of events was not *altogether* out of my own hands. A letter from my sister Mary serves to remind me how powerless we women are against determined and *ambishus* men. She is also upset that I

have not yet answered last year's letter from her. But England is so far away, and what happens in Buckland seems hardly real to me, when set against the life here in Chicago.

Mary's letter is again all to do with our Brother James and his refusal to sell-up Father's properties and share the monies with his brothers and sisters. Mary writes that she and her husband are in dire need; that things are very bad in England. She and Daniel have been out of business for two years past, and no hope of ever getting in again. She has young children, still at home and dependent on her. It would appear that Mary and Joan are in league against James and qwite set on forcing him to sell and share the proceeds. She has written to Elizabeth and Robert, pleading that they will stand with her against James; she asks the same of George and me.

I have little heart for family feuding, but I am sorry for Mary. I lay the letter to one side. How I wish that Elizabeth and I could talk together!

August 15
No rain for many weeks. They say it is a drought what is come upon the States of the mid-west. Everywhere is tinder-dry. Hear the clang of the fire-bell a dozen times each day. My garden withers and dies in the prolonged heat. Only the lilac root manages to flourish. A 'Society for the Promotion of Social Purity, to help the Fallen Women of Chicago' has been formed by our church. We are sewing and knitting in order to raise funds for this worthiest of causes, what is much needed in this evil and godless city. Surely, the patience of the Lord will one day soon be at an end, and this place will be destroyed as were Sodom and Gomorrah!

September 2
George came in last night with news that fire had destroyed a great warehouse at the corner of Sixteenth and State streets. When told that this building housed barrels of spirits and strong liquor, I could not find sympathy for the owner's loss of three hundred and fifty thousand dollars. Our Pastor has many times

251

foretold that the judgement of God is about to come on men who make profit from the weakness of others.

October 5
A hot wind blows from the southwest. No rain, nor hope of any. Dr Hahn has found a soothing draught that seems to calm Jon, and so make less the number and strength of the convulshuns. As to the rest of us, the sultry heat makes tempers short. Even I lose my control. Have high words with George about the way my Georgie is allowed to roam alone in certain streets and witness unsavoury sights.

George says: 'The boy is about his normal delivery route. He must needs walk with both eyes open. Would you have me keep him in leading reins? He is coming fourteen years old!'

'Oh, he keeps *both* eyes open,' say I. 'Why, only yesterday he was in Randolph Street, a place which decent *men* avoid, never mind young boys. He described for me last evening the gambling houses and saloons on Hairtrigger Block, and how in the afternoons the gamblers and a "certain type" of woman, promenade arm-in-arm up and down the boardwalks. Even as he walked my poor child was witness to the shooting of one gambler by another!'

George has the grace to look troubled.

*

There had been a time when smoke was a fragrance, evocative of garden bonfires in autumn and log-fires on winter evenings. In this fall of 1871 the smell of smoke had become a potent signal for alarm. Awareness came slowly to the citizens of Chicago. Three months of drought had drawn moisture from every wooden structure. It had crisped the roofs of pine shingles, and melted the tar of felt-roofed houses. The trees which grew on every street had already shed their leaves. On city pavements and in every backyard lay a depth of drifting tinder. Rhoda remembered her own disaster of last October when she and Ed had burned the garden rubbish, and in so doing had destroyed the fence and the hickory tree. She swept up the leaves, but almost faster than she cleared them, the hot winds brought in a fresh deposit.

People grumbled about the heat, the dust and flies. Thoughtful men eyed the sawmills wherein was stacked huge piles of timber. The city's most prestigous buildings were built of wood and stucco with a thin veneer of marble on their flimsy frontage. They feared for the libraries of valuable books, the works of art. Of Chicago's sixty thousand buildings, more than forty thousand were constructed of combustible pinewood. There was but one water-pumping station in the whole of the city, and only fourteen fire-engines to spray Lake Michigan's waters over any conflagration.

Saturday evening was the time when serious men of business dined together. Even had Rhoda been willing to accompany him, George could not have taken her to Gunters. Important deals were settled there across gourmet delicacies imported from New York. Fortunes were made and lost while he pushed frogs' legs around his plate, and sipped the sour Chianti wine which was the current fashionable drink.

He had dressed with care on that particular evening. Clothes sat well on his tall, lean figure. He wore a suit of light-grey English worsted with a shirt of white pleated-silk; his waistcoat was a deep-blue satin, which exactly matched a broad and flowing bow-tie. Wings of silvering hair among the black curls, premature lines about mouth and eyes, gave a look of distinction to a face that was still arrestingly good-looking. The hint of English accent, his considered way of speaking, brought respect from men of varied origins, who believed that the British always honoured their commitments.

This particular gathering of men, this evening's exchange of confidential information, could put him in a privileged position when dealing opened on Monday morning. George listened to the talk of grain and railroad shares; the price that pork was fetching in Milwaukee. He studied the faces around the table, and placed them in more familiar surroundings; he thought of the Board of Trade apartment, its lofty position, the tall windows that looked out upon the finest buildings in Chicago, the fresco paintings on its walls. He had come to live for that moment when the gavel sounded, and into the silence a secretary's voice intoned the latest telegrammed prices from the markets of London and New York. His next deal could mean a modest mansion built of stone; a servant for Rhoda; the end of meat-delivering for Ed and Georgie.

Raised voices brought him back to his surroundings. The word '*Fire!*' passed swiftly from one man to another. Fire on the West Side of the river, out of control and moving towards West Adams Street.

It had started, so people said, around ten o'clock in a woodmill that stood on the west bank of the Chicago River. George pulled out his silver hunter; thirty minutes had elapsed since the onset. He rose and pushed back his chair. He said to the man on his right side: 'My packing-house is on the western wharfside! My meat-market stands at the corner of Halstead and West Adams. My wife and children are at home in Green Street!'

The smell of smoke had become so familiar in past weeks that Rhoda could no longer be certain of the need for alarm. A constant pall of yellow drifted over the city from distant conflagrations. But people said that the new waterworks could pump more gallons to the minute than would ever be needed to quench the most persistent blaze; and after all, the firemen had all of Lake Michigan from which to draw! She sat alone on that October evening. The children were abed, but not yet sleeping because of the continued heat and sultry air. Rhoda wept briefly, and in anger. An old argument with George had flared between them as he had dressed for yet another business dinner.

It had ended, as it always ended these days, with a cold farewell on either side, and no loving kiss.

The cabby offered to take George as far as Canal street.

The vehicle and horse, as the man pointed out, were his only means of scraping a living, and he was too poor to carry fire insurance. Even as they drove, the wind swung around to the south-west. The western heavens were brilliant with orange light. As they came closer to the river-basin, a sudden rain of glowing cinders burned holes in the new English worsted. The cabby held his nose against the smell of smouldering wool. 'Hey, bud,' he said, 'you stink worse than this here river! Guess I'll have to let you walk from hereon. This wind'll carry the flames right up Jackson and Adams. Shouldn't be surprised if it don't reach as far as Van Buren. Did you say you lived on Green Street?'

George nodded.

'Well, if I was you, pal, I'd get back there pretty damned quick. You can't never tell with fire!'

George paid the man. He watched as the driver whipped up his horse, and in a silhouette of scarlet, headed back across the bridge towards the North Side. As they passed from his sight George still hesitated. On the one hand lay his packing-house, the sum total of all his ambition; the substance of the dream he had brought with him from Dorchester, Old England. On the other hand were Rhoda and his four children. Ed was responsible and steady; in another month he would be sixteen. Georgie was intelligent and resourceful. But they were only boys, and fire was the business of grown men.

He turned away from the burning wharfside, and began to run towards Rhoda, and Green Street.

The ironing could have waited until morning. It was a task self-imposed in order to heighten the sense of her injustice. Rhoda thought of George, dining at Gunter's in the new shirt of pleated silk that would be tedious to press; she sprinkled water on too-dry linen, wielding the flat-iron with unnecessary vigour. The doors and windows stood open to the night air, which had hardly cooled since midday. Moths flew in and beat their wings against the glass chimney of the oil lamp. As she worked, the smell of smoke came sharp and acrid; she stood the iron across the trivett and walked out towards the yard fence. Her neighbour's upper storey windows stood several feet higher than those of surrounding buildings. Frederick Sangren had appointed himself in recent weeks as chief fire-spotter for Green Street. In moments of stress he reverted to his native German. His voice came clearly now from an attic window.

'Feuer! Feuer am West Adams Strasse!'

With an urgency that was never heard on a Sunday morning, the single bell on the Congregational Church Tower began to toll.

Rhoda leaned for a moment, both hands against the fence. The glow in the western sky grew brighter as she watched. She became aware of the pinewood fence-planks beneath her hands, and behind her the timber structure that was her home. Underneath her feet, a depth of dry leaves rustled. She turned and ran into the house. She went from room to room, closing doors and windows against thickening smoke. In the children's rooms only Ed was stirring.

'Come,' she whispered, 'but quietly, mind! The fire is yet some blocks away. Let them sleep if they can.'

She returned to the kitchen and began to assemble every bucket, every crock and jar that would hold water. Ed worked the pump. Within minutes they were as prepared as she thought it was possible to be.

He said: 'Is Pa at Gunter's?'

She nodded.

Ed said: 'The very second word gets to him he'll be back to guard the shop. The minute fire starts on any street the looters are out in full force!'

'I should hope that his family and home would be your father's first thought.'

Her voice was sharp, her features tight with fear and anger.

Ed said: 'But you've got me, Mama. Pa knows he can rest easy when you've got me around you!'

She looked up into his face, still pale from interrupted sleep, the black curls tumbled in his eyes; those eyes that were not Salter blue, but the calm grey of his mother.

'I know, Ed. But your father's place is to be here at home, with his family. It's something he's forgotten a deal too often in the past year! It would look well if we all burned to cinders while he was off closing a deal to buy hogs from Milwaukee!'

Ed said: 'We could soak blankets and sheets so as to be ready if the blaze gets to Green Street?'

'But I've only just washed and aired my blankets, and put them in lavender ready for next winter!'

'But, Mama,' he said gently, 'if the fire gets to us we won't be here to need any blankets for next winter.'

George ran awkwardly; his long legs covered the ground at a speed that surprised him. It was his straining lungs that forced him to slow, and finally to halt. He leaned against a shopfront, his shoulders bowed, the breath rasping in his throat.

A voice said: 'Stay right there, or I'll shoot you.'

George turned his head, but carefully. The shop was a jeweller's, the elderly owner stood foursquare in his doorway, a derringer held chest-high, his finger on the trigger.

George said, with difficulty, 'Don't be − a fool − man! I'm − asthmatic I − mean you − no harm!' Slowly he straightened, until, standing upright, the white silk shirtfront and expensive suiting showed up clearly in the fire's glow.

The derringer was lowered. The man, a Jew by his looks and accent, said in a shamed voice, 'I'm very sorry, sir. It was the way you came running. Don't suppose I would have shot you, anyway.'

George said: 'Couldn't really have blamed you if you had, friend! There's a mob down on Canal Street breaking into a liquor store as I came by.' His breath came more easily now. He said: 'I own a meat-market on the corner of Halstead and West Adams. Guess I shall find myself short of a side or two of beef, come morning.'

The old man laughed. 'Fire keeps on like this, sir, you could even find that beef ready roasted for you, come the dawn.'

George began to run on.

The clanging fire-engine bells, the tolling churchbell, had wakened all of them, save Jon. Rhoda had her forces ready

257

marshalled and instructed. The yard had been cleared of leaves. Every sheet and blanket in the house lay in the kitchen ready to be soaked in water should the need arise. Every household tool suitable for digging stood together with garden implements beside the kitchen door. Ed had heard that a ditch dug around the house could act as an effective break.

Rhoda said: 'If the fire moves one block closer we begin to shovel for dear life!'

She smiled as she spoke, making it a game, at least for Rosa.

Ed walked at intervals to the street corner, ostensibly to check the progress of the fire, but in fact to seek his father among the throngs of frightened people. At last he saw him, coming at a shambling run into Green Street, both hands pressed to his chest, his face paperwhite.

Ed stood directly in his father's path.

George gasped: 'It's reached Jackson and Van Buren – the Adams Street viaduct has gone – it's getting into Halstead –'

Ed said: 'I know Pa, I know it.'

He put his arm about his father's shoulders, and realised among the panic and the flying cinders, that they were finally of equal height.

George said: 'Your mother – Jon – I should not have left them.'

'They're all right, Pa. Ma is acting like a three-star general.' His voice shook a little: 'Hey, but Pa – I sure am glad you made it home. I was gettin' a bit – anxious – you know – with Georgie being such a goshdarned kid an' all.'

George said again: 'I should not have left you.'

'You couldn't know there'd be a fire.'

They came into the house.

George gazed at the ranks of water-filled utensils, the piled-up linen, the shovels and large spoons. Rosa knitted fiercely at some long and highly-coloured garment. Georgie played a game of checkers against himself at the kitchen table. In a corner Jon slept on an improvised bed. Rhoda, neatly dressed, hair smooth, features calm, said: 'Why, you've quite ruined that new suit, George. As for that expensive pleated shirt – oh well, at least I'll be saved the chore of trying to iron it.'

He caught the hint of tremor in her voice.

He said: 'I'm sorry.'

She said: 'What of your packing-house?'

'I don't know.'

'And the shop?'

'I don't know that either.'

'Then for pity's sakes, George, get yourself round to Halstead Street, and find out what's happening! Do you *want* our meat to be looted? We could be free-feeding all the Irish in Conley's Patch if you don't stand guard. Take Eddie with you!'

George hesitated.

'No. Ed stays here. You need a man beside you.'

He laid a hand on Georgie's shoulder.

'Come on, my lad! How good are you at scaring looters?'

'Me, Pa?'

His grin was pure delight, the look he sent to Ed, triumphant.

The West Side fire burned for fourteen hours. Four blocks of the city were destroyed, many people were made homeless. It did not reach Green Street although it came uncomfortably close; and but for a few cracked windows and some smoke damage, the Salter meat-market was unscathed.

The people of the district slept late on that October Sunday morning; church services were missed, the Sunday dinner eaten in mid-afternoon. The exhausted firemen dampened down the smouldering ruins, rolled up their hoses, harnessed the horses to the firewaggons, and departed homewards.

George had kept vigil with Georgie until daylight had brought policemen in to guard the business section of Halstead and West Adams Streets. They came back to the house, and Georgie returned to his bed. Rhoda said: 'You should also get some sleep, George. Everything is safe now.'

'I must get down to the wharfside. I doubt my packing-house still stands.'

'Then a few hours sleep will make no difference, will it?'

He slept uneasily, in an armchair. He awoke, pale and

breathless, still suffering the effects of the night's unaccustomed running, and the inhalation of so much smoke. It was five in the afternoon before he was able to rouse himself sufficiently to go to the river basin.

Rhoda said: 'You're not well. You're not fit to stand, George! Why won't you leave it until tomorrow? So at least take Eddie with you! We shall be quite safe now. Lightning never strikes twice in the same place; in this house we have the Lord's protection. Last night's fire was a warning to the gamblers and imbibers of this city.'

George still wore the scorched grey suiting, the spoiled silk shirt.

He said to Ed: 'I'd be glad of your company, boy. There may be something we can salvage.'

To Georgie he said: 'You be good, now! Mind your mother. Watch out for your sister and Jon.'

He turned to Rhoda. 'I have this feeling,' he said. 'I've had it since the instant I awoke. I believe that the Lord God is not yet done with punishing Chicago!'

It took time for them to work their way across the burned streets which lay between Green Street and the Chicago River. A drift of yellow smoke hung upon the humid evening. Heavy cloud had massed above Lake Michigan; there was that tension in the air of a storm that could not quite bring itself to break. George halted frequently to catch his breath. Ed stood beside him at such times, uneasy and anxious.

'Better we go back home, eh Pa? You already know what we'll find. You can see how the destruction gets worse as we come closer to the river.'

But George would not be turned. 'I have to see it for myself,' he gasped. 'For twenty years that packing-house is all I've dreamed and worked for. If it's gone, I have to witness it, Ed.'

'But you'll get the insurance money.'

'Not the same – not the same, at all. I'm not a well man; sicker in fact than I ever let on to your Mama. Doc Hahn tells me that my heart's enlarged. Comes of all those years of

260

asthma, so he says, straining for breath, and the heavy labour of the meat trade.'

Ed said: 'I never guessed.'

'Well no – your Ma is such a worrier. She'd have me wrapped in cotton-wool. That's why I'm in a hurry, boy. I want to see you and Georgie settled, your sister and Jon provided for. Life is hard for a woman on her own.'

'It won't never come to that. Whatever's burned, then we can build it up again. You'll live for years, yet. We can make it better – bigger – put in more machinery, take on more labour.'

They came down to the wharfside where only last night had stood stockpens and warehouses, packing sheds and workshops. The area, for as far as they could see, was a wasteland of charred timbers, still smouldering in places, with here and there lengths of metal, twisted by heat and rearing up into bizarre shapes.

Ed poked among the debris. He found the hog-hoist, the wooden spokes of its wheel burned away, the iron rim distorted. He recalled his horror of the wheel in those first weeks when he had come to this place to learn slaughtering and packing. He felt an exhultation at the sight of its destruction. He looked to his father's face and knew that George had read his mind.

'You never really took to it, did you, Ed?'

'It's a part of the job, Pa.'

'But you like the work in the shop a whole lot better, don't you?'

'Guess I do at that.'

George said: 'I have a proposition for you. It's been in my mind these weeks past. This fire has made room for changes.' He peered at Ed through the deepening twilight. 'Are you hungry?'

'Now you come to mention it –'

'So am I! Tell you what, there is a restaurant on La Salle Street that keeps open all hours. Your Mama won't expect us home for a couple of hours yet. I've got plans. Things I want to talk over with you.'

George smiled for the first time that day.

'State I'm in, they wouldn't normally allow me through their

261

front door. But a burned jacket lately is a badge of courage in these parts.'

They began to walk away towards the bright lights of the business section.

In the far distance the clanging of a firebell sounded. George sighed. 'Somebody else's turn tonight.'

The restaurant had crystal chandeliers, thick carpets, and separate white-clothed tables set with silver and flowers. Ed blinked in the blaze of so much light. He hung back.

'Hey Pa! Do you really think we should?' He looked down at his grimed hands. 'I look like a chimney-sweeper.'

George gave him a push in the direction of the men's room.

'Don't worry so much, boy. They all know me here. Nobody cares overmuch about a man's appearance. You can't wear anything finer in Chicago than a fistful of greenbacks! Go get washed-up and I'll order for us both.' He grinned. 'Reckon that a dish of roast pork would be appropriate in our circumstances.'

No word passed between them until the meal was eaten. Ed laid down his knife and fork; he studied his father. He said: 'I expected you to be more downcast, Papa.'

George said: 'I was prepared in my mind. We're not alone in our loss. They're saying that last night's conflagration destroyed eight hundred thousand dollars worth of real estate. But we're insured with a British insurance company. They have the reputation of paying-up promptly, and in full. Which brings me to my plans for you. How does the job of meat-market manager appeal? How would you like to take the full running of the shop into your own hands?'

Ed said: 'I'd like that real fine, I surely would.' He hesitated. 'But what about Georgie?'

'Georgie stays with me. He'll be fourteen come January. He's a bright boy; he'll make a good butcher, a good packer. But he's a handful, Ed. He needs discipline and guidance.'

They talked on, about sites for the new packing house, the number of men to be employed.

Their table was placed in the furthest corner of the long

room. George sat faced away from the rest of the diners. He continued to talk while dessert was served. Only Ed could observe how one by one, and then hastily, people rose, abandoning half-eaten meals.

He said: 'Pa, there's something happening outside. There's hardly anybody left in here.'

George clipped the end of his cigar; he lit it, savouring the smoke with obvious pleasure. 'Probably a knifing or a shooting in some saloon. Things get pretty rough about this time of night.' He called a passing waiter.

'Say, what goes on out there?'

The man seemed nervous and yet curiously excited.

'Fire, sir. They're saying it's the big one this time!'

'But we had a big fire last night. It burned down four blocks over on the West Side. I should know. I lost half my business!'

'Couldn't have been nothing like the size of this one, sir.'

George paid the bill. He and Ed began to move, without haste, among the empty tables. They came out on to the street into light that was almost as bright as midday. There was a roaring sound, like that of a great wind; even as they stood, a rain of cinders began to fall. Ed's thick black hair began to smoulder; he shook his head, dislodging several glowing embers as he combed his fingers through it.

George said softly:

'Oh my dear Lord. That fellow had the right of it.'

He clutched Ed's sleeve.

'We've got to get back as fast as we can to your Mama and the children.'

He turned back into the restaurant doorway, where stood the nervous waiter.

'When did it start?'

'I don't know, sir. But they're saying it's jumped the river. It's everywhere at once. Chicago's doomed! It's said to have crossed at Adams Street . . .'

'But that's where the Gasworks stand – come on, Ed! If we get into Washington Street or even into Randolph, we can cross at the bridge and get back to the West Side.'

They began to walk. Ed wanted to run, but measured his steps to fit his father's slower pace. He became aware of the people around them. Young women, many of them clad only in night-attire, their faces grimed from smoke, ran along the sidewalks, a baby or small child on one arm, some prized item of furniture or clothing dragged behind them. There were older women pulling handcarts piled with household goods. Some struggled to save carpets that already smouldered; one hauled to safety a parrot in a cage, another held a china teapot in one hand, an iron kettle in the other.

Men pulled trunks along the street. Ed saw a well-dressed, elderly man, an oaken bureau still stuffed with business papers, pushed before him on a baby-carriage. As they came closer to Washington Street, the tolling of the Courthouse bell could be heard above the roar of flames and crash of falling buildings; and here the people had ceased to run. They stood, several hundreds deep, all around the Square, oblivious to the rain of cinders, enthralled by the easy destruction of Athenian marble and cream-coloured stone which melted and fell before the flames.

George said: 'I can go no further.'

Ed looked at the pallor of his father's face, saw how his chest heaved to gain each breath in the hot and smoke-filled air.

'We'll rest here, for just a minute, Pa.'

They stood among the silent crowd, and there was an awful grandeur in the scene that made them unconscious of the danger. All around them elaborate façades crumbled and were lost. The Chamber of Commerce building, which housed the Board of Trade, folded inwards upon itself with a sound like sighing.

George said: 'I can't believe this is happening. They told us that this block was fireproof.'

The bell in the Courthouse cupola continued to toll; spontaneous fire seemed to seize the building, smoke appeared at every window. The flames took hold with amazing speed. All at once the front doors of the Courthouse burst wide open, and from them came a great crowd of men, who howled like animals as they ran through the square.

264

George said: 'They've released the prisoners from the jail.'

Ed said: 'They're smashing in that jeweller's window, much good may it do them.'

The bell continued to clang as the cupola caved inwards, ceasing only when it hit the ground. New people came into the Square. Some said that Crosby's Opera House was gone, and the St James Hotel. Others said that the Sherman House was going, that all the river bridges were on fire; that the fire was leaping back and forth from the North Side to the South Side of the city. That the Army planned to use explosives to create a fire-break; that firemen, exhausted from their efforts at last night's blaze on the West Side, had collapsed beside their hoses, allowing flames to run unchecked. Lengths of burning packing-wood, borne on the strong south-west wind, began to whirl above the square and came to land among the crowds. People screamed and began to run, hair and clothes ablaze.

Ed gripped his father's shoulder. 'Papa – we mustn't stay here any longer! We must try to make it to a bridge.'

They began to move, carried forward involuntarily by the mass. They came into Clark Street to find the bridge approach choked with waggons, merchandise, and the livestock chosen to be rescued by their owners. Ed saw an aged woman, a brown hen tucked underneath each arm. A young girl pulled a goat on a frayed rope.

George said: 'This is no good, Ed! We've allowed this crowd to bring us in the wrong direction. It's at Lake Street or Randolph that we need to cross the river.'

They went back, picking their way slowly across heaped-up treasures, abandoned by owners whose sole aim in the end had been to achieve the relative safety of the West Side. Ed stumbled over a pile of leather-bound volumes which lay neatly on top of a silver-framed mirror. A violin and bow spilled from a case, across a yard-high oil painting of two horses. Ed paused before a ragged child who lay, face downwards on the smoking pavement, two ropes of gleaming pearls still twined around his fingers.

265

George said: 'The looters come in all shapes and ages.' He bent to touch the boy's head and saw the great wound in the forehead.

They passed the garden of a burning mansion, where two gentlemen dressed in velvet smoking-jackets dragged a grand piano towards the hole they had dug for it among the flower beds. The carriages of the wealthy, laden with silver and valuable papers, continued to roll westward towards the many bridges; only to be seized on by drunken mobs who were making full use of abandoned liquor stores and deserted saloons.

They came at last into Lake Street, and here the fires burned so fiercely that the break of day had come unnoticed. George stumbled many times and would have fallen but for Ed's supporting arm. 'We must make it over this bridge, Pa! This is our only chance. The wind keeps changing. It takes the blaze in all directions.'

The rails of the bridge had broken away on both sides. Boats, laden with goods and people continued to pass beneath it on their way downstream. Ed saw how those who were forced to the far sides of the bridge fell frequently into the water; only to be ignored by the passing vessels, their cries for help unheard in the din of explosions and tumbling masonry.

They entered the great press of bodies; he placed George before him, both hands clamped hard upon his father's shoulders. Ed was careful to position them well away from the dangerous edges; they shuffled forward. Beside them ran dogs grown vicious from fear. A bolting horse broke free from its tethers and charged the throng of moving people. Two men seized the halter and jerked sharply on it. Ed heard the snap of the creature's neck as it fell down. Children, separated from their parents, ran to and fro among the crowds. A little girl, red hair streaming out behind her, was pushed to the edge of the bridge and fell shrieking to the water. He felt the slackening of his father's body, the faltering footsteps. 'Hold on, Pa,' he shouted. 'A few yards more and we shall have made it!'

Ed grabbed his father, both arms wrapped about his chest.

266

Slowly, kept upright only by the tight-packed bodies of those around them, George and Eddie gained the safety of the West Side.

They were to halt and rest many times on that long walk back to Green Street. The streets of the West Side were in confusion, filled with those who had survived the night. Ed sought a cab but there was no conveyance to be had. People were kind; women came from their houses to offer cake and coffee. They crossed over Jefferson Street and then Des Plaines, and here were the familiar landmarks, the reassurance of whole blocks quite untouched by flame.

The day was Monday, the skies above them overcast; a strong wind was still blowing from the south-west. They came to a high place from which a view might be had of the far side of the river. At two of the afternoon the flames still marched like a determined army on Van Buren Street and the fine residences that stood along the Lake shore.

They came limping into Green Street. George paused on the corner beside the church. He said: 'It's all here, Ed. Twice threatened, but still standing.' He gazed at the strange pale-blue house with its crenellations, fancy carvings and tiny turret.

'Your Mama was right, you know,' he said quietly, 'she said this place was a safe haven. If we had done as I wished and moved to a more . . .'

George was overtaken by a fit of coughing more severe than any Ed had yet witnessed.

'Don't think about things like that, Pa! Hold on to me. There's but a few more yards to go. Look now. Here's Georgie and Ma coming out to meet us! And it's raining. Oh thank God, it's raining!'

★

Tuesday, October 10, 1871
The fire is out and Chicago burned, but my loved ones, our home and business all *intakt*. Can only think that our dear Saviour saw fit to spare us for a purpose, since fire no

respector of a man's worth, and many good and honest folk burned out of house and home, so many lives lost.

Can scarcely bring myself to pen the agony of past hours when we knew not what had befallen dear George and Ed, or if they still lived. Had expected them home about ten on Sunday evening, but around that hour I was summoned by Mr Sangren, our German neighbour, who informed me that fire had broken out again and was visible from the top windows of his house. Georgie went over to the Sangren house many times. On being told that George and Ed were at the wharfside, Mr Sangren invited Georgie to his attic window, from which my boy observed events, and came back each hour to bring me news. Kept vigil all night long, but no sign of my dear ones.

Cannot deskribe my *feelings* when light breaks on Monday morning and still no sign or word. We take turns at keeping watch from our windows that face the street. It is not until three of the afternoon that two blackened ragged men come stumbling past the church, and Rosa cries out: 'Oh Ma, here come Pa and Eddie!'

Had tried to qwiet my fears by keeping all in readiness against their return. Broth simmered on the stove, fresh bread was in the crock. Had heated water in the wash-copper and bid Georgie bring the hip bath into the kitchen. Clean clothing hung ready, airing on the fireguard. My forethought well rewarded upon sighting the two, who were in *parlous state*.

Poor Eddie's beautiful hair much singed, and many small burns about his face and person. George in likewise condition, but in his case a more seerius state; my husband's breathing very bad and his face of a waxen aspekt what much alarms me. Send Georgie for Dr Hahn, but am told that the doctor is down by the Randolph Street bridge tending badly-burned children. Must needs use my own skills and judgement. George needing urjent attenshun, is helped by Ed and me to bathe his scorched and weary body, and get into clean linen. Administer the linctus what helps his asthma, but much smoke on his lungs, and he much agitated. Will not go to his bed but sits up, with pillows,

268

by the open kitchen door, so as to catch the fresher breeze brought by the rain.

Eddie, once bathed and in clean nightshirt, is hungry and recovered. I tend his burns, and in my agitashun I clip short his scorched curls with my best sewing shears, what are now ruined, probably. But never mind! Am so glad to have my dear ones safe I near drive them wild with my fussing and clucking. Ed goes to his bed and there remains, he being qwite exhausted.

I sit with George. His breathing eases enough for him to take a little broth.

He says: 'Ah Rhoda, the sights I have seen this night. It was like looking down into the depths of Hell and all its demons. I had not dreamed that one man could show such inhumanity towards another.'

I cannot bear the angwish of his eyes and face. I stroke his hand. I say: 'Try to put it from your mind, George! You and Ed are safely home. We are together again. It is more than I had hoped for.'

He say: 'That boy, Rhoda – he saved my life you know. Many times he all but carried my full weight. He could have left me and saved himself. He urged me on. He made me walk when I would have given up the ghost.'

I say, through tears: 'He is devoted to you. After all, you are his only true parent.'

'He loves you too.'

'I know it. But it is not the same. The tie of Blood cannot be gainsaid.'

October 12
Walked out this morning to view the ruins of Chicago!

George still sick. He bides at home with Jon. In the company of Eddie, Georgie and Rosa I at last tread those streets where I have so feared to go before the fire.

The devastashun is awful to behold. All is gone of the great hotels and stores. The manshuns of the rich are destroyed. The houses of ill-repute and the saloons are no more to be seen, but

269

many churches also consumed. It is hard to understand. Ed says that lumberyards, railroad depots, elevators filled with grain, all are perished in the blaze. I look and look, and as far as the eye can see in all directions there are heaps of blackened stone, deep ash, shards of glass and lengths of metal twisted into strange shapes by the heat.

I say to Ed: 'I know not how you and Papa came live thru' all of this.'

His face takes a strange look. He says: 'It was not yet our time to go, Mama.'

The bravery of people is very great. It would seem that, even as the final flames were qwenched by rain, the small tradesmen of the city, who had lost everything, were once more about their business, and with such humour and cheerfulness that puts to shame us fortunate ones who lost but little. As the embers cool we see the owners of banks and jewellery stores digging down into the ruins to find vaults and safes wherein lie their fortunes. Small handcarts appear on street corners, with apples and tobacco for sale. The streets are filled with people. Men say to one another: 'Cheer up! We shall raise up a better city.'

There is, of course, much evil to be seen. Looting still goes on from warehouses and half-burned stores. Was much reashurred to see the mass of bluecoats and their shiny muskets on all the main streets.

We are told that the military were brought in last night by General Sheridan who telegrafed Fort Leavenworth for help against the vagabonds and cut-throats what haunt the streets.

October 13

George still indisposed. Dr Hahn says *rest*; that so much smoke upon the lungs will take time to clear, and that George is much run-down due to hard work and worry.

Ed and Georgie open up the shop. No fresh meat to be had, but plenty of pickled pork and beef, smoked hams and sausage in store, for which our customers are grateful. The boys bring news. The homeless are being housed in schools and churches. Food and clothing comes hourly from distant cities. There have

270

been many shootings of looters by the military. They also bring broadsheets. The Board of Trade now have their rooms at 51 and 53 Canal Street. They are holding meetings. I expect George to grow restless at this news, but he says nothing. All important new locations are printed in the broadsheets. Our church is to be used as the US Custom House, Depository and Marshall's Court, an honour no doubt, but it is to be hoped that some small corner will be left clear by these gentlemen for the faithful to *praise God* on Sunday.

October 17

One week since the Fire. George not much improved. You will feel better, I tell him, when the weather cools and the air is fresher. I have an extra washday. So many things begrimed with smoke from our Saturday evening fire here on the West Side. I look at the suits worn by George and Eddie in those dreadful hours, and find them full of holes, and qwite beyond repair. I hold up the shirt of pleated white silk what is likewise damaged.

'There is nothing to be done with it,' say I, 'although in parts it is still good.'

George sits by the open kitchen door, in the wicker armchair, and propped-up by pillows. His breathing still bad, he will not bide abed, but likes to watch me as I work.

'It does not matter,' he says. Later on he asks: 'Do you see me as a vain man, Rhoda?'

I smile. He is sick and so I am careful with my answer.

'Of the two of us,' I say, 'you are the one with the brightest plummage, and I am the little brown-feathered wife who stays close to the nest.'

'You are more than that. You are my anchor, the steady one.' He halts for breath.

'It grieves me to see you working at the wash-tub. How many times have I offered you a servant?'

'I had a servant once,' I remind him. 'They are more trouble than worth! As soon as they are trained-up properly – they go off and get married. And in any case, what should I occupy myself with in all the long hours you are absent?'

'You are not content with me, are you?'

'I am as content as most women.'

'That is not what I meant, Rhoda.'

I sqweeze the blue-bag in the rinsing water; I plunge the boiled linen into it. I am in a sudden fury. The words I *dare not* utter boil up in my mind like sheets and pillowslips in soapsuds. I gaze at him in silence, while my thoughts run unchecked. So what *do* you mean, George, when you ask if I am content? You have posed me that same qwestion once before, and I have said then that I never think about contentment. Well, I am thinking of it now, George. I thought of it as I looked upon Chicago's ruins; as I threw what is left of your silk shirt into my rag-bag. Like that shirt, our marriage remains good in parts. You are a kind man, you do not mean to hurt me. But I was never first with you, was I? You call me the steady one, your anchor. I am the keeper of your hearthstone, the mother of your children. I am Rhoda, who wears dark gowns trimmed with a touch of white, who parts her brown hair in the middle of her forehead, and keeps your account books.

I have a secret, George. I do not at all times *want* to be your anchor. Sometimes I *long* to be unsteady. To be indulged and petted and protected. To be feckless and a little giddy! Oh, it shames me. On Christmas Eve I shall be forty-one years old. It is too late for romance, for light-heartedness, for laughter, but I *still* want those things.

I mix starch up in a bowl. I catch him looking at me. I begin to sort my washing. Sheets and pillowslips for starching, white shirts and collars, tablecloths and antimacassars. I turn my face away. I compose my features.

I say: 'We have much to be thankful for.'

I dip the linen in the starchbowl. Starch stiffens the fibres. An item so treated will have a new appearance and wear longer without soiling. I have heard myself, since in this country, referred to as 'that starchy little Englishwoman'.

George observes me; something he has not done for a very long time. 'I guess you were frightened when the fire threatened?'

272

'I was afeared. Left as I was, with full charge of the children and the house, it was to be expected!'

'I do not criticise you, Rhoda. I was surprised and pleased that you showed no panic, that you were cool and well-prepared for ought what came.'

'Then you do not know me!' I burst out. 'You judge me by my *actshuns*. You *always* do that. You have no notion of what goes on inside. Oh yes, I can do what must be done, but within me I am all a-tremble.' I hold out my wet hands. 'Look, George, I tremble still!'

He is silent for some moments and I fear that this time I have gone too far. He says at last: 'I am not clever about women. I am what is called a man's man. I cannot know what you are feeling unless you tell me.'

I pause, a bunch of his shirt collars held aloft in the washtongs. I say: 'Perhaps if we had spent more time together,' I try to smile, 'after all these years I should no longer be a mystery to you.'

'My *professhun* does not allow women – but you don't mean butchering, do you?'

I thrust the collars through the starch. 'No,' say I, 'on a *farm* we could have worked *together*, as do my sisters and their husbands, as did your parents and mine.'

He grows angry. 'I am tired of hearing you sing that song, Rhoda! Your mother died early and so did mine. I have given you a better life. I may not be a ladies' man but this at least I managed. You have never needed to stack hay or milk cows.'

His breath grows ragged.

I am ashamed. I say: 'You are right, of course. I have never needed to stack hay or to milk cows.'

I begin to fold wet sheets. I put them to the rollers and turn the wringer handle. Water pours down into the tub. My white wash emerges, flat and clean, and good as new. My nerves begin to steady. It is the Fire, and fearing George and Eddie lost, that has upset me.

George says: 'When you are finished with the washing there is the Insurance Claim to be filled in. We must make an inventory of our losses.'

He holds out both hands towards me, and I go to him.

He says: 'Always remember this – no matter what happens, I love you very dearly, I could not go on without you.'

October 18

Eddie brings the broadsheets put out by the *Chicago Tribune*. There is a paragraf what strikes terror in me. They say that a great *forest fire* destroyed much of Northeastern Wisconsin, on the selfsame night that Chicago was burned down. The loss of life was far heavier than here in the city. News is still scarce due to the telegraf being burned out.

I must write at once to Elizabeth and Robert.

Chapter Nineteen

Girls noticed Eddie. On Green Street, where the population was made up largely of stocky fair-haired Scandinavians and Germans, his height, his English colouring and aloof air, attracted attention. The aloof air was due to shyness, and the shyness had lately become a challenge to the neighbourhood's young females. Love-notes, that smelt faintly of cashous, were delivered to Ed by a smirking Georgie. But the name Ed sought was never signed across these tender missives. He had never really thought it might be.

The dry-goods store stood at the corner of Green and Halstead, opposite the church. Mama dealt with Mr Ziegenmeyer because he sold English tea, was known not to water down his milk, and had wire screens fitted to his doors and windows to keep out flies. Ed stood each night beside the polished counter and inhaled the smells of sauerkraut and pickled herring, smoked cheese and garlic sausage. He gazed at the shelves where stood rows of paper collars, bottles of stomach-bitters and other medicaments guaranteed to cure anything from ague to snakebite. Sometimes he purchased a candy bar for Jon or a love-cookie for Rosa, hesitating over his selection, dragging out the moments until he placed his few coins in the girl's hand. On Friday nights, Ed collected Mama's weekly grocery order from Mr Ziegenmeyer, even though the grocer had offered to deliver. This transaction, he had discovered, could be spun out to quite amazing lengths, while he checked each item in the box, and studied carefully the bill she had prepared.

Annaliese Ziegenmeyer was tall and slender; her fair curling hair was caught up in a ribbon at the nape of her neck; she had delicate features and eyes that were sometimes blue, and sometimes grey. She was known to be studying the violincello. By day, she attended the Academy of Music on Peoria Street. In the evenings she worked in her father's store.

Ed had known her since his first days in Chicago. At that time, when Mama had refused to leave the house, he and Georgie had shopped daily at Ziegenmeyer's. But he had been a child then; now he was seventeen years old and as tall as his Papa. It was last winter, when skating at the little lake in Jefferson Park, that he had looked at her with recognition. On the crowded ice they had collided; to steady themselves, they had been obliged to join hands and skate a few yards close together. It had all been quite proper, but Ed had never ceased since then to dream about that moment. In the days that followed, Papa had talked to him about girls. Abrupt and awkward exchanges had been uttered, in which Ed, blushing deeply, had assured Papa that he had never even dreamed of doing those things which Papa now said he must not do with girls. In the ensuing months, he reflected bitterly on his father's words. What with his own shyness, her frequent glances towards her father, and the width of the oaken counter between them, chance, thought Ed, would be a fine thing!

In the end it was the Fire that allowed them a private conversation; in a burst of largesse Ed selected a toffee-stick, a fortune-cookie, and an apple. Annaliese wrapped each item separately and slowly. Her father, engaged with a drummer at the far end of the shop, was discussing the current shortages and inflated prices.

She said, eyes downcast, 'Are you quite recovered from your burns, Mr Salter? We heard how you were trapped on La Salle Street. I think it was very brave of you to carry your poor father to safety.'

Ed touched the bandage which Mama insisted he must still wear on his left hand.

He said: 'Well – well thank you, Miss Ziegenmeyer. But I wasn't all that brave you know. Anybody would have done it.'

She looked up at him then. He gazed for the first time full into her eyes.

'No,' she murmured, 'you really are too modest. Your Mama told us how at one point your hair caught a-fire! How she had to trim the singed bits with her dress-making shears!'

She regarded him, her head a little to one side.

'But no real harm done, I think, Mr Salter. The shorter style seems to suit you very well. It makes you look more manly.'

He picked up the packages and laid a dollar bill down on the counter. In a dream he moved towards the door. As it closed behind him she called out:

'Your change, Mr Salter. You've forgotten to pick up your change!'

Ed drifted down Green Street. The November night was clear and frosty, the sky set thick with stars. He whispered her name. *Anna-liese-Ziegen-meyer*. It sounded like music. If the frost held, there would be skating in Jefferson Park on Saturday evening. Perhaps they would collide again? He began to run, his long legs flying over the uneven boardwalks. She had called him Mr Salter. She had liked his shorter haircut.

He let out a wild and joyous shout of 'Yippee!' Why – anything could happen, he told himself, from this night onwards. Why goshdarn it! He might even be called upon to heed his Papa's warnings?

So long had Georgie been hemmed in by his elders and betters that, when it came, he did not straightaway recognise release. Bonds had been eased on the night of the Fire when he was allowed to view the blaze from Mr Sangren's attic window. Mama, who kept herself to herself, had wept on Mrs Sangren's shoulder when she believed Papa and Ed were dead. Nowadays, in spite of a lifetime of drinking English tea, his mother took 'kaffee and kuchen' in Mrs Sangren's parlour, even though that lady came from Prussia, spoke a heavily-accented English, and worshipped at the Lutheran Church. Georgie, himself a gregarious soul, approved of these late signs of normality in his reserved little mother. Come Christmas, and Mama might even be persuaded to throw a party that was not made up exclusively of Episcopalians and Congregationalists!

277

Papa and Ed had also slackened their keen observation of Georgie's every move. Since the Fire, Pa had been a changed man. He no longer dined with businessmen in the city, but sat at home nights. As for Ed, with the management of the meat-market resting on his shoulders and a sick father to contend with, he had no time to upbraid Georgie. Anyway, Ed was in love above both ears with Annaliese Ziegenmeyer, and so hardly expected to be in his right mind.

A new delivery-boy had been taken on. The straps of the second basket were shortened to fit the bony shoulders of twelve-year-old Shamus Feany. The boy had been spoken to by Papa and Ma. Shamus confessed himself a devout Roman Catholic; his family, who lived in Conley's Patch, had lost all in the Fire. He and an older sister were now, so he said, the sole support of their widowed mother.

Georgie had studied the thin white features, the water-slicked red hair. Shamus had light-blue eyes that swivelled constantly between sandy lashes; he told lies with an ease that astounded Georgie, who knew for a fact that Shamus had a father, and lived in a cottage at the rear of Randolph Street. The innocence of Papa and Ma was an embarrassment to him; he felt ashamed of their gullibility, and at the same time protective of them. Ed was no better. Even he, long familiar with the street-urchins of Chicago, failed to recognise chicanery when he saw it. Georgie could have set them all to rights – but who had ever listened to his opinion of anything?

With Papa out-of-sorts and Eddie moonstruck, and his own fourteenth birthday but a few weeks away, the future for Georgie had broadened in the most delightful fashion. Ed made it clear that he depended on his younger brother. Papa now treated him like a proper business partner. The first wise move his father had made since the Fire was to put the training of Shamus Feany entirely into the hands of his second son. Shamus and Georgie made the long delivery-round together each morning. Sometimes the route would take them into burned-out streets.

In those first days after the disaster, Georgie had gone alone into the ruined business district. Ed had needed to know the new locations of certain offices and people: Such as, if and where fresh-slaughtered beef and hogmeat could be obtained? and where had Papa's insurance company set up their office of enquiry? It had been scarey by himself in that wasteland of charred brick and stone, those ankle-deep ashes. He stood on the corner of Randolph and Halstead and remembered it as it had been just a week ago, before the Fire; the streetcars and the sweating horses, the sidewalks crammed with strolling people, the vendors of doughnuts and hot coffee, one of whom had once demanded to know if he and Ed were set on burning down Chicago?

All his life Georgie Salter would remember the way it had been, the excitement of it. But now, in the company of Shamus, he was to witness the rise of a new, even more prestigous city.

★

December 12

I have looked every day for a letter from Wisconsin. Now it is come with news both good and bad. I withhold Elizabeth's letter until Sunday evening, when we are all together in the parlour. As soon as our Bible reading is over I say I have news from Suamico, Brown County. I see that I have the full attenshun of my family. I begin to read.

Dear sister Rhoda, and brother George Salter,
Your welcome letter to hand which brought us the first word of the Chicago Fire; our Telegraf being burned out early in September so little news has reached us from the outside world. Was much releeved to know that you are all safe and your house and shop still standing. Trust that poor George and Eddie now recovered and again in business. Have thought many times, dear sister, in these past weeks that the end of the world was nigh! But we have been spared and must thank God for it!
We are all sound in wind and limb, save for my feet what were badly blistered when the barn took alight. My left heel mends only slowly

279

and I must rest it in the afternoons, so therefore you may find this letter somewhat longer than usual. It already looks to be a severe winter, and the plight of many people here is pitiful to see. Very little help has reached us so far, all eyes being on Chicago and her troubles. You have written oftentimes, dear sister, of the good people of your Church. If this letter of mine could be passed among them, the more affluent of them might find it in their hearts to spare a few blankets and cast-off clothing for the destitute people of these districts. Those of us whose losses were light have already stripped our cupboards bare to help our less fortunate neighbours, but it is still not enough. Four hundred farms are burnt-out and over a thousand people dead. The number of homeless is not yet counted, and this breaks my heart to see, for these homes were hard to come by, and many farmers too old and sick now to start over. Like Robert and I, they had come to the great woods with but a cart, a pair of oxen, an axe and the will to work. Fifteen or twenty years on, and the cabin of logs that was their first home had become a stable for the horses. Like us they had built a good frame house with a proper staircase. We have all had our failed crops in these northern climes, but drouth had never touched us until this year of 1871; nor had we dreamed of a blaze that would march for a full one hundred and fifty miles, altho' with the benefit of hindsight there were certain omens. The first sign was a winter as mild as ours in England. The sledges stayed within the shed, we visited with neighbours in December and January. People said that we should have a wet spring, that June and July would bring a deluge. It never happened. By August we were short of water. The swamps were so dry we could walk across them from one side to the other, something quite unknown even among the Menominee Tribe who have lived here for generations.

By the beginning of September we were all very anxious. Our closest neighbour, Captain James Black (veteran of the Civil War, officer and gentlemen) was advising us to be prepared for trouble. As foreman-logger for Mr Martin Tremble at the Mill, Jim Black was often in the deepest forests. He spoke to us of seeing isolated burnings; a great oak or cedar that had stood for generations would leap to sudden flame before his eyes, the whole tree consumed in a space of seconds. He leaned to the opinion that the fire was spreading underground thru' dried-up swamp, helped on by fallen leaves and underbrush, and this being so we could be but vigilant about our homes, and pray to God!

On September twenty-first the fires came very close. Three railroad camps were wiped out, and the telegraf all destroyed between us and the city of Green Bay. Robert and our oldest son, Johnny, were obliged to make the usual monthly trip to Green Bay to sell our produce, since spoiled crops had left us short of cash. They returned to report thick smoke for many miles and great losses among farmers. They brought with them several copies of the Green Bay Advocate dated October fifth, and passed them out among our neighbours. We read of steamers on Green Bay having to navigate by compass and blow their foghorns, the shoreline being invisible due to smoke. Thousands of birds driven from their roost now flew about and found no place to settle. Flakes of white ash fell like snow over all the countryside. We read the newspaper report of our own most recent burning. 'On the Big Suamico a large lot of logs in the bed of the river, amounting to over 130,000 feet have been burned. They belonged to Lamb, Watson & Co, and Mr Martin Tremble.'

Well, we continued to pray for rain but no rain fell. Our fences burned down, many stands of hardwood perished. Our ox-team of four, in the charge of our youngest son and returning from a long day's ploughing, stumbled on the edge of dried-up swampland and was consumed by flames that Willum said leaped up from nowhere, leaving him, thank God, with no more than scorched hair and eyebrows and otherwise unharmed, still sitting on the cart.

On Thursday October fifth our friend Captain Black set out for the town of Peshtigo, where he had business with the manager of the great woodenware-mill situated in that place. Robert spoke out against this journey, but Jim is of Scottish blood, and his mind never to be altered once it is made-up. Robert warned him that most of the corduroy and plank roads leading north had been burned-out; that it would be wiser to wait for the onset of winter before setting out on such a trip. We watched Jim go with deep misgiving, and oh how right we were to fear!

On the night of Saturday, October seventh, a tornado of fire struck the area in which Jim travelled. The town of Peshtigo was all

281

destroyed, not a stick nor stone of it remained. It is said that one thousand, five hundred people perished within one hour. The loss of life and property being far greater than that of the Chicago fire, which, you will not need me to remind you, dear Rhoda, occurred on the selfsame night.

On Sunday morning it began to rain. The smoke was blown away by fresh winds. We were left with blackened fields and burnt-out clearings but we were alive, our house and barn still standing. Jim did not return. We mourned him for a month, and then, as the first snows came, a horse and rider came down past the house. Johnny ran in from the milkingshed. 'It's Cap'n Black,' he shouted. We went out, all of us, into the bitter night, lacking shawl or jacket and quite unawares of cold. We ran to the Black Farm, and there was Jim collapsed in the arms of his brother, Matthew, both hands bandaged and no more than a stubble of black hair left on his head.

Robert cried: 'Oh my dear Lord – oh Jim, what has happened to you?' Jim looked at us as if we were strangers. 'I've witnessed Hell on earth,' he said. 'In four years of war I never saw such horrors as took place that night in Peshtigo.'

That is all he said, dear sister. From that hour no word of what he suffered has ever passed his lips. He was never a talkative man but now he has grown too silent for his own good. It is as if the fire has seared his very soul.

I lay down the pages of my sister's letter. I look to George, who does not look at me. I think back on his sickness of soul of these past weeks. Can it be that some men have more sensitivity of feeling than we women grant them credit? I recall my vain efforts to galvanise him to some interest in life, and suspect that I may have failed him in his hour of need. I turn to him to ask his pardon, but my apology is never to be uttered.

He says, like a man who awakens from an awful dream: 'I have had enough of this country of America! There is nothing left for me here. I shall write to my brother John with a view to the purchase of a butcher's business. We shall go home to England, Rhoda, in the new year!'

★

It was possible, Georgie now discovered, by means of a stated devotion to his profession, to spend the maximum of time away from home and his Mama. So firmly did his mother believe in honest toil and self-reliance, that her words might have been stolen from the sermons that were thundered from the pulpit on a Sunday morning; and in fact, with his changed status of instructor to Shamus Feany, had come a creeping satisfaction. He no longer wished to change the sign above the meat-market, but took pride in that final gold-leaf letter *S* which made him a part of *George Hodder Salter and Sons*. Since the fire his route had extended well beyond the environs of Madison and West Halstead. Word had spread among the wealthy dispossessed that good fresh meat was to be obtained from an English butcher, and Georgie learned by a process of osmosis that to be born of English parents carried with it a certain 'cachet'. In the past few weeks, and inevitably, he had felt demeaned by the wearing of the delivery basket. He had said as much to Ed, who grinned and remarked that Papa might be persuaded to purchase a small handcart, if approached in the proper manner.

'I had more in mind a pony and trap. We could have our name painted on the trap's side. It'd look more fitting, Ed! Have a word with Papa for me?'

But his father was not to be persuaded.

'Pride,' he told Georgie, 'goes before a Fall. Now just you heed my words, boy! He who would ride horseback should first buy himself a saddle!'

His father's talk of 'going home to England', Georgie discounted as being an old man's fancy. Pa was sick; he no longer walked with them to West Halstead Street. It was Ed who shook Georgie awake at five every morning; who poured hot milk onto crumbled bread, and pushed the bowl of brown sugar across the table; Ed who held the keys of shopdoor and cold-room. These days their Pa came down to the store at around mid-morning. Shamus and Georgie, returning from the first round of deliveries, would observe his slow progress, his laboured breathing.

While Ed repacked the delivery baskets they would rest-up in the back room. Twenty minutes of huddling beside the glowing stove, eating bread and cheese and drinking scalding cocoa, and they were back on the street, frozen feet and fingers only partially thawed. This second delivery of the morning was made to the kitchens of the wealthy who dined late in the evening; and this was the route that took them into burned-out districts, where the occasional large house and mansion had miraculously survived. There was a residence on Chicago Avenue that stood unscathed among scorched ruins, its fragile conservatory of glass without a single broken pane, the trailing leaves of exotic plants still showing green in that extraordinary landscape.

Business was carried on in every grand house that had been spared by the capricious fire; the lower rooms now being in the occupation of insurance brokers and bankers, real estate agents and merchants of every kind. Trading was brisk on the ground and first floors of these buildings, while the families of the owners retreated ever further into top bedrooms and attics. It was to these exiled and bewildered ladies that Georgie and Shamus brought pork loins and crown roasts. They no longer delivered at the servants' entrance but entered by handsome front doors which stood wide-open to the street, and bore crudely painted signs which declared this house to be the new premises of Field and Leiter & Co, or the Bank of Chicago.

On Monroe and Randolph, on Madison and Lake Streets, temporary structures of new pine, knocked together in haste, served as trading posts for the less fortunate merchants. In these first months of the year of 1872, Georgie Salter witnessed at first hand the rebuilding of this city that he loved. Their deliveries made, he loitered in the company of Shamus. They looked down into the open cellars of last year's great houses where wooden shanties now gave shelter to the homeless. He lingered beside the former warehouses and wholesale stores where iron stoves and implements welded by heat into one intractable mass, were being drilled apart and blasted by an army of workmen. Every day saw a clearance of the tons of rubble. In the severest winter known for many years, three thousand bricklayers and masons had come into the city. In temperatures

284

that had formerly made the wielding of a trowel, the spreading of mortar, an impossible task, they lit bonfires all around the rising walls. A small fire burned on every bricklayer's mortar-board. Georgie warmed his hands before the blaze and reflected that fire, which had burned Chicago down, was now helping to rebuild it.

It was said in the district that Annaliese Ziegenmeyer was 'a fine girl'. Even Mama, who was hard to please and hopelessly biased in favour of all things English, had been heard to remark that the German storekeeper's daughter was 'every inch a lady and bound to go far in her chosen profession of violincellist'.

Ed was happy. These grey days of February and March were sweeter than any springtime he had ever known. But his delight was of the secret kind; he withdrew into his own heart intent upon preserving the fragility of love, and protecting the secret places of his soul from the invasive Georgie. Ed thought about his younger brother. Georgie was all exuberance and vitality; he had no secret places, held back on nothing. His broad grin and quick tongue terrified Mama, but there was no trace of wickedness in him; only an energy for living that Ed sometimes envied, and that at times was more than their quiet household could contain.

Love had made Ed resourceful and inventive. He contrived to be in those places where Annaliese might be seen at times when his brother was in the far-flung limits of the delivery round, or safe at home eating supper. There were hours in the day when Ed was also free to walk the winter streets. He waited impatiently each morning for Papa's arrival. Calls needed to be made daily on stockyard commission men; since they now lacked a slaughter-house, dressed-meat had to be ordered. A small detour was made in his route to these gentlemen that brought him through Peoria Street at around the noon hour. Students of the Academy of Music took their lunch at twelve sharp. Careful pacing, Ed had found, would bring him level with a certain streetside maple at the exact moment when Annaliese Ziegen-meyer came swinging through the tall gates. He would loiter beneath the huge tree, close his eyes and open them again as if he could never quite believe in the glory of her. He thought he would never, in all his life, become accustomed to this first sighting from afar. Annaliese walked with the free and swinging stride that caused Chicago's winter gales to whip the blue cloak tight about her slender figure. His Mama, he suspected, would find Annaliese's style faintly improper; Ed found it more tantalising than any poster that depicted can-can dancers. Her pace would slow as she approached him; the cloak settle into less inflammatory folds, the innocence of her features shaming his secret thoughts. She had lately progressed to calling him Eddie. He shortened her name to the diminutive Liese. After the shy, initial greeting he walked with her to a spot that fell just short of the windows of Ziegenmeyer's store. He carried the case that contained her sheet-music. As he handed it back to her, as her fingers curled around the carrying handle, he always succeeded in touching her gloved hand. The contact sustained him until evening, when he would face her across her father's counter. If Mr Ziegenmeyer should be present Ed was forced to buy tobacco, which he did not smoke, or bon-bons for Rosa and Jon. But more often lately, the storekeeper and his wife would be at their supper, and Liese, white-aproned, the braids of flaxen hair a halo in the lamplight, would bestow on him the full magic of her blue gaze. With the iron stove hissing orange flame in a distant corner, standing among the herring barrels and the sacked rice and flour, Eddie Salter confessed to Liese Ziegenmeyer the story of his life, and his deep feelings for her.

Summer for Georgie meant warm feet and fingers; restored circulation healed his chapped hands and chilblains. He had, so said Mama, grown another three inches over winter. New cuffs were added, lengthening his jacket sleeves and trousers. Soon he would be as tall as Ed. He had never paid much attention to talk of distant relatives, of whom his family possessed an incredible number. On those Sunday evenings after Bible-reading when Mama produced the most recent missive, Georgie would close his mind to the interminable reading and subsequent discussion of it. He had more exciting projects to think about. Shamus Feany had offered to teach him how to play poker and gin-rummy.

Just lately however the envelopes which bore stamps depicting Queen Victoria came not from his mother's dull censorious kin, but from Papa's brothers in Winchester, Old England. It seemed that Papa, in spite of his lethargy and low spirits, had meant what he said about going home. Enquiries had clearly been made of uncles. And now, no one listened more attentively than Georgie when Mama began to read. Even Eddie had taken up his pen and written to the Uncle John he so fondly remembered. The reply to this particular letter was more worrying for Georgie than any that had gone before.

My dear Nephew, Eddie,
We was all mighty pleased to hear from you and to hear that you was all well, and getting on so well. I consider that both you and Georgie have now got a good start in life. We was all so glad to hear of our dear little Niece's success on the piano and sewing machine. She must be a great comfort to her Mama. I assure you it would give me great pleasure to see you all. We often talk of you and all what occurred when I was living with you at Charlotte. Just fancy what a change in our settlements since then! I am back in England, and you have left the State of New York for Chicago! I hope that none of us will ever have any occasion to repent of these changes and that we shall all prosper to our satisfaction.

From what you say, dear Nephew, I should think you must now be the tallest of all the Salters. You say that you and Georgie look very like your Papa, and he was always an English beauty with his dark curling hair, blue eyes, and fresh complexion. I do hope that the poor man enjoys better health nowadays. I often think what severe attacks he used to have when I lived with you all.

We have all said, dear Eddie, that when you and your brother arrive at manhood, we shall full expect to see you and Georgie in England for a visit, if nothing more! I assure you, one and all, please come whenever you will, and you will have a good hearty welcome from us.

I was very glad to hear that your father was back in business after the Fire. My dear Brother George has written to me to know my advice about your all returning to England to go into Business. I can only say that things are not too good here. It is not so easy to get along these days. To give you an idea, the following was on my Books at New Year.

Household furniture. Good-will. Stock on hand. Horse and cart. premises.

Total value £2,050 Pounds Sterling.

So you will see that it takes a good Three Thousand Pounds to keep one's Head above Water in England these days!

In conclusion, dear Nephew, our kindest love to you and your dear family.

I do remain your most affectionate Uncle

It was true then! They really meant it. Even Ed had gone behind his back. Georgie waited until the candle was doused and the house settled down to sleep.

'Hey Ed?'

'I'm asleep.'

'No, you ain't, then. If you are – I'll come over there and pummel you until you wake up!' Georgie's tone was pained. 'Why'd you write to Uncle in Winchester, huh? Why'd you have to go that far?'

'I knew him when I was little, when he lived with us in Charlotte. He's a grand sort of fellah. I just wanted to keep in touch.'

'No, you didn't, then! You're as bad as Pa. You got it in mind to go over the Atlantic ocean. What would you want to go there for? Who needs England? What's wrong with America?'

'Pa's homesick, Georgie.'

'So will I be homesick if we have to leave Chicago.'

'You're just a dumb kid.'

'I'm fourteen goin' on fifteen. I'm near as tall as you are. I'm one of the *sons* on that old signboard. I should have *some* say in what goes on!'

Ed sighed. 'You just don't have any understanding, do you? You're so American, so goshdarned *Yankee*.'

'Well, I was born here, for goodness sakes! What do you expect me to be? An English milksop? You were born here too, Ed. You better not forget that!'

'That'll be enough of that sort of talk, *boy*. Every drop of your blood is pure English; don't you ever think on that?'

'No, I don't, and I don't mean to! Anyways – Pa don't have three thousand pounds – why that's – let me see now – that's around twelve thousand dollars!'

'He'll be getting the insurance money. Then there's the meat-market premises and good-will. His seat on the Board of Trade is worth at least five thousand dollars.'

Georgie struggled unsuccessfully to hold back tears.

'What,' he asked, 'what about you an' Liese Ziegenmeyer?'

'None of your business.'

'It is too!' Ed's betrayal made him reckless. 'I saw you hanging around in Peoria Street, waiting for her.'

'She'll most likely come to England with us.'

'Ole man Ziegenmeyer 'ud have a conniption fit if you so much as mentioned such a thing! But say, Ed, she sure is pretty.' His envy was sincere, his admiration genuine.

Ed said: 'We'd get married first.'

'You're too young. Both of you!'

Ed's voice sounded dreamy. 'It'ud be just exactly like my mother and father, only in reverse. We'd make a new life together. I'd take good care that *she* never got homesick.'

Georgie said, surprised: 'You really fancy England. I mean, really *fancy* it, like as if it was some good place to live in. Well tell me this, Ed. If it's so darned wonderful, then what made our parents leave it in the first place?'

'It's not that I really want to go to England. But I think we should do what Papa wants. He came here with a whole parcel of dreams. He feels now that he's a failure. He's pretty sick, Georgie. I kinda guess, although he never says so, that he'd like to die in England.'

'But he can build a new packing-house. He's got you and me to set up another packing-business. It's all he's ever talked about, for heaven's sakes!'

289

Ed said: 'The heart's gone out of him. You need only look at him to see that.'

'I won't come with you. I'll never leave Chicago.'

Georgie had, until now, never touched a pack of playing cards; described as they were by Mama as the 'devil's playthings', he had seen them only in shop windows. On the day that followed his night-talk with Ed, he sat in a burned-out lot on Randolph Street with Shamus Feany, and was made privy to the mysteries of gin-rummy and strip-poker.

It was August. The maple trees on Green Street were white with dust, a hot wind blew straight off the prairie; people said that life in this month was kinda tasteless, and wouldn't they just be mighty glad when fall came.

Ziegenmeyer's store was empty on that Monday evening. Ed gazed at Annaliese; he thought she had never looked so beautiful. The sleeves of her blue gown were puffed-out just above her elbows. Her forearms were bare; the sight of their creamy skin, her long fingers, the pearl-like fingernails, made his heart turn over and his voice unsteady.

He said: 'That colour suits you. You should wear it always.' He hesitated. 'There's a secret, I never told before to anybody.' He watched her blue eyes turn to solemn grey and knew that he could trust her. He pulled a scrap of worn silk from his jacket pocket. He said: 'This here's a piece of the gown my real mother wore when I was a baby.' He laid the silk down on the counter. She reached out a finger and touched it gently. He said 'It's kinda childish to keep it I guess. It's a habit I've got into.'

She said, tears in her voice: 'Why, Ed, that sure is the sweetest thing I ever heard. I don't wonder that you love the colour blue. Did your real mother have fair hair?'

He nodded, too moved to speak.

They gazed deep into each other's eyes. With one accord they leaned inwards and across the counter. Their lips met, gently at first and then with shy, sure passion.

He said: 'I might be going away, soon.'

She said: 'I'll be with you always, Ed. Wherever you go, I'll go!'

★

August 17

Weather hot and sultry, but many thunderstorms and with such a deluge as to keep all fear of fire at bay. This year we have a new disaster. Typhoid has broken out in many districts. It is the young and the old and sick who are falling victim to it. It is a sickness from which very few recover. Why, even Prince Albert, the Consort to our Dear Qween, could not be saved from it. They blamed the drains in Windsor Castle for the poor man's death, what could not ever have been worse than the drains here in Chicago!

I go to see our Dr Hahn.

'You are not,' I tell him, 'being altogether honest with me, sir! I want your true opinion of my husband's state. He is set on going back to England, but I think he does not have the strength.'

The doctor pats my shoulder.

'Then let George have his head in this case, Mrs Salter. I will not lie to you. He is unwell, and acting only out of instinct. He longs for England. Many business men who suffered losses in the Fire are experiencing a lowness of the spirits. Combined with asthma, and the smoke that he inhaled – why don't you help him in this matter? There is little else you can do.'

I say: 'There is another worry on my mind. Typhoid is raging in the Tenth Ward. There have already been three deaths on Green Street.'

The doctor smiles. 'In a household as spic and span as yours, my dear lady, you have little to fear. The disease is borne in dirty milk, it is floated on dust, it is rampant in homes where there is a lack of simple hygiene. Be especially careful in the case of Jon, who is susceptible to all infectshun. Watch out for George. His system is weakened by his illness. As for the rest of you – why you are all as strong as street-car horses! Boil every

291

drop of milk and water. Keep doors and windows shut against flies and dust – and pray to God, Mrs Salter.'

August 21

The epidemic grows worse. Newspaper articles are critical; I read in the *Tribune* that it is the task of the Board of Health to control disease. Thirty-four Board members are expected to oversee the condition of a population which exceeds three hundred thousand. For each Ward of the city only one Inspector of Sanitation has been assigned; these are conscienshus men, but they are too few.

The Fire has destroyed many thousands of insanitary dwellings, but the programme of rebuilding now brings in an army of unskilled workers and their large families. Flimsy rear-lot shacks are being thrown up, without foundations or essentshul plumbing. The poorest of these people live in cellars and barn lofts; children sleep in pantries and clothes-closets. Rickets is commonplace; epidemics are increasing, says the *Tribune*. There is much cholera and smallpox. In this summer of 1872, of every hundred deaths that occur in Chicago, sixty are of children below the age of five years; and against Board of Health regulations, every Ward still has its garbage-strewn alleys, its filthy vault-privvies. Black smoke pours from stockyard chimneys, and from soap and glue, and fertilizer factories. Over all, says the *Tribune*, hangs the stink of the polluted Chicago River.

September 1

Have thought *long* and *hard* on the words of the newspaper article and Dr Hahn. Make-up my mind that if it is England George desires – then England he shall have!

It is the *duty* of a wife to submit to the wishes of her husband. We talk over all aspekts of such a move. George says we can be back in Somerset within three months. Think this to be on the optimistic side of Hope, but manage not to say so. We decide to acqwaint the children with our *joint* decishun. I make a speshul little supper-party for them, to celebrate the good news. To my astonishment it is Eddie who pushes back his filled plate, and asks to be excused from table! Have never known him moody in his life. Can his little friendship with the Ziegenmeyer girl be more serious than I imagined?'

September 3
Keep a keen eye on Jon and George tho' they appear as well as they can ever be. Ed has taken hard our news of the return to England. He is mopey and silent such as I have never seen him. Georgie says that Ed is lovesick. Think he may, for once, be right.

I warn them all of tainted milk and water. Do not, say I, ever eat or drink away from home. George says that another four of his customers are dead of the fever. I no longer take Jon from the safety of our house and garden. Of us all he the one at greatest risk.

September 4
Ed complains of headache; he does not sleep well. I hear him stirring in the night. I go downstairs to find him sitting in the kitchen. I say: 'What is it?'

He is very pale. 'I cannot seem to rest,' says he, 'and yet I am so tired.'

'Well, is it any wonder?' I ask him. 'When you are roaming the house at two of the morning?' I sit down beside him. 'Are you upset at our plans to leave Chicago? Is it,' I say gently, 'the thought of leaving your new friend that has distressed you?'

He does not answer. I take his hand, and it is burning! I touch his forehead, and in spite of his pallor my poor boy is afire!

'Come back to bed,' I say. 'You have taken a little chill. You will feel better in the morning.'

I make my voice sound unconcerned, but in my heart I am afraid. Ed's lack of appetite, his mopey silence of recent days was not as I had thought to do with our return to England. It was the onset of a sickness!

*

Georgie hardly ever talked to Rosa; he saw no good reason

293

why he should. He had Ed. He could never understand why Ed was so patient and nice with their little sister. Truth to tell, he was faintly resentful of the time Ed wasted; the way he sat with her some evenings and listened to her piano-playing. The grave attention he gave to her endless prattle. The compliments he paid her when she pirouetted for him in some silly frock she had stitched on the sewing-machine. Why, Ed even boasted about Rosa in the letter he had sent to Uncle John in England! Men, thought Georgie, were unwise to encourage forwardness and vanity in the female members of their family. He had lately preceived the insidious power of women; their ability to influence a man against his better judgement, to sweet-talk him into folly. Rosa practised on Georgie a brand of charming reasonableness that drove him wild; in the ensuing arguments he was always the loser. Silence, he found, was the most effective weapon he possessed against her. Several months had gone by since a single word has passed between them. He could, if he really tried, forget her presence in the house altogether. The shock of her words was therefore very great when she barred his entrance to the house on that Monday evening.

He attempted to push past her. He looked down on to her neat dark curls, her flounced and ribboned tidiness, and was, as always, uncomfortably aware of his own dishevelment, the grubbiness of the day that had accrued on his clothes and person.

She said: 'Eddie's awful sick. Mama says you're to wash first, and then go eat your supper, but you're not to go upstairs.'

'Don't lie! Ed's *never* sick, and I'll go upstairs any time I please. Since when did you start giving orders around here, Rosa Salter?'

She laid her clean hand on his sleeve. Surprised into closer observation of her, he could see she had been crying. He felt a contraction in his stomach muscles and did not recognise the pain as fear. Rosa clutched his arm and shook it.

'Well, he is *so* sick then, Georgie! I would never lie about a thing like that. Dr Hahn was here. Ma's soaked a sheet in disinfectant and hung it over Eddie's bedroom doorway.'

294

'Ed had a doctor come?' He sat down on the top step of the stoop. He said in a dull voice 'What happened? Did the cleaver slip and cut him? Did his hands get damaged? He'll never work again without his hands.'

'It's nothing like that. If only it were.' She sat down beside him all heedless of her white starched skirt and petticoats; he watched the tears slip down her cheeks, the sickness of horror mounting in him He wanted both to comfort her and shake her; he said instead: 'Tell me what happened,' and was astonished at the adult tone of his own voice.

'Ed had a nose-bleed. A real bad un.'

'A nose-bleed ain't – isn't nuthin' to be feared of. You don't need a doc' for a little nose-bleeder!'

'It's more than that, Georgie. Ed's temperature's way up. He's wandering in his mind. Dr Hahn says – he's of the opinion – that Eddie's took the fever.'

'What fever?' His shout echoed far out into quiet Green Street. Rosa said: 'Hush up! Do you want him to hear you!' She paused. 'Ed's got the typhoid, Georgie.'

Illness in the house was not a new experience. Pa was always ailing. The convulsions of Jon were regular in summer. Some folks, Georgie thought, were born to frailty and sickness. But not Ed. Never Ed.

In a household where cleanliness was akin to, if not superior to, Godliness, the intensified regime of hygiene, the bathing and disinfecting, all but drove him crazy. He was glad when morning came, when he could shoulder the delivery basket and step out into the crisp fall air, Shamus Feany at his side.

Shamus knew all about typhoid fever.

'If you live past the twenty-first day of it,' he told Georgie, 'then you can bet your boots that you'll get through it. It mostly kills little kids and old folks.'

'Ed's stronger'n any of us. I never knew him sick a single day.' Georgie paused. 'Mind you, he's in a bad way at the moment. There's a woman who lives near us. She hires herself out to care for ill folks. Pa's paying her to come in and help

295

with Ed. He don't seem able to rest easy. He keeps getting out of bed, all restless-like and yet he's so blessed weak he can scarce stand on his feet.'

Shamus nodded. 'That's how it takes 'em,' he said gravely. 'My Uncle Declan had it once. He had this rose-red rash, and his tongue was all brown.'

'Did he get over it?'

'Sure he did.'

'Ed's got that rash, and the tongue like what you said.'

'You've seen him then?'

'Ma won't let us near him. She talks to my sister, and Rosa tells me all.'

Rosa was excused school so that she might tend to Jon. Ed's bed was manhandled down the stairs by Dr Hahn and Papa, and set up in the front parlour, to make the task of nursing easier for Mama. Pa was forced to employ an assistant butcher. Until Eddie was absent from the meat-market, they had none of them appreciated how much of the work was done by the young man.

The September days were warm and sunny, the nights cold. Georgie lay awake.

He heard the faint sounds of movement and voices in the room below him. He counted the weeks; the crucial twenty-first day, as specified by Shamus, must he thought be already long past. He was drifting towards sleep when Papa shook him gently: 'Come downstairs, George. I think you'd better come.'

The significance of the spoken name appalled him. Papa never called him George; no one ever had. He stumbled from bed, the long white flannel nightshirt clutched about his skinny frame. A wave of rage and fear mounted to his head and then receded, leaving him weak and close to tears. He wanted to knuckle his eyes, to snivel like a baby. He wanted always to be spoken to as the second son of the family; to be Georgie, the little brother.

He hardly recognised the parlour; the brocaded chairs and

sofas ranged all around the walls, the photograph-laden table thrust hastily away. All his mother's treasures beating retreat, cowering in fear before the lamplit sickbed. He felt a kinship with the gold brocade, the bewhiskered faces in their silver frames. The once-elegant room had a jangled, bizarre appearance. He longed to run into a shadowy corner, to turn his face into the wall, like Jon did at the onset of a convulsion.

Papa's hand was on his shoulder, urging him forward. He looked everywhere but at the bed. Rosa sat on a low stool, her hair tumbled anyhow around her shoulders, her face puffy from crying. Mama sat upright on a kitchen chair, the kind that would not allow a Vigil-keeper to nod-off. She beckoned him to her. He went on trembling legs, head still averted. She held Ed's hand in both of hers.

She said: 'Dr Hahn's just left us. Ed's taken a complication. Pneumonia's set in. It won't be long now.'

The words, spoken in his mother's sweet, prim voice made no sense at all. He wanted to fly at her, pummel her to some awareness of his consternation. Words screamed inside his head. Don't say such things out loud! If you speak it, you make it come true! If you walk on the black cracks in the sidewalk your father will die before nightfall! A howling dog means a death to the house! But they had no dog, and Papa who was always ailing stood alive and upright at his side.

But for the head and face upon the pillows, the bed might have been empty. It was Ed, and yet it was not Ed. His hair had grown long again, the dark curls clustered around a head and forehead made strange and noble by pain. His brother, thought Georgie, now looked like a figure in a stained-glass church window. The Eddie he knew, the grinning good-natured disciplinarian of his childhood, the young man who stole kisses across old man Ziegenmeyer's counter; who carried a scrap of blue silk in his pocket and thought it was a secret; that Ed was long gone.

He attempted speech but no words came. Georgie tried again, croaking from a dry throat.

'Can I go now?'

'No,' his mother said. 'We must stay together. We are his family.'

He looked closely at her then, recognised her agony, different from his own, sharper and more poignant. He had once heard her tell Papa that Ed had been entrusted to her.

He said: 'You shouldn't talk like that. You mustn't say it won't be long now. He'll hear you. He'll be scared. I know that I'd be, if I were him.'

Papa said: 'Ed can't hear us, George. He's deep in coma. He's gone from us in every way that counts.'

It was then that his tears came. He hated the ugly sound of his weeping, the indecency of it.

Mama said: 'We should have prepared him. You know what he's like, George. I said he'd take it hard.'

Georgie clutched at the only stick with which he might beat them. 'You never tell me anything,' he sobbed. 'You're always treated me like I'm a stoopid little kid!' He moved close to the bed, looked down at the strangely beatified features, the closed lids.

'Ed's *mine*,' he said. 'He belongs to me more'n any of you. He talked to me, we told things to each other.'

The realisation that he had slipped into the use of the past tense tore a loud cry from him.

He wrenched away from his father's hand. 'Whatever will I do without him! I want him back, you hear me!

He gazed from one face to another. Papa looked older and greyer than ever; Mama, who, no matter what happened, never seemed to look any different, had a dazed appearance now; her jade-coloured eyes like deep holes in her white face. They surveyed him with the kind of helplessness that promised no future comfort. He sank to his knees beside the bed. He began to tremble, his teeth chattering together.

It was Rosa who came to him, who put her arms around him and held him tight until the shaking eased. He clung to her, grateful for the warmth.

He felt a stab of shame at his unmanly conduct; he tried to edge from her embrace, but again felt hysteria creep upon him. Rosa held him for a long time.

October 8, 1872

This day we laid to rest our eldest son, William Edwin Salter. Had he lived but a few weeks longer he would have seen his eighteenth birthday. He suffered much in those last days, and we could not have wished to see him linger. I am weary to the very bone, yet I cannot sleep. I come to this Journal as to an only friend, to whom the events of the day must be told.

The cemetary is called Rosehill. It lies a long way from the city. The hearse is drawn by four coal-black horses with plumed heads. Three following carriages hold the mourners. There is our Minister and his wife, Dr Hahn and his wife, and the Sangren family. As we move off from Green Street I close the curtains at our carriage windows. Georgie cries out that he cannot bear to go in darkness, so I am forced to part them and witness a bright autumn morning, with fit young men going about their business as if it is any ordinary day.

Jon sits qwiet in his father's arms, as he is used to doing when faced with what is beyond his understanding. Georgie and Rosa sit close together, hand-in-hand. I cannot comfort them. I know not how.

It is a far way up to Rosehill. Dr Hahn informs us that the cemetary is but twelve years established. We go in through wide gates. The graves are set out between broad pathways and underneath sapling trees. It comforts me to see that Eddie will lie beside a young, straight maple, the leaves of which are all aflame.

Jon walks hand-in-hand with Georgie and Rosa. George carries our wreath of white lilies tied with purple ribbons. I hear the prayers, the children's weeping. George bends to scatter earth upon the coffin. I recall the recent days and nights; the way we fought to save him. I feel as though my very soul has left me. I turn and start to walk away, and see among a stand of beech trees a tall, fair-haired girl dressed all in blue. Her head is bowed, her features shadowed by the bonnet-brim. But she cannot deceive me. I would have known her anywhere.

299

I run out towards the trees.

George follows me, he grabs my arm.

'What is it?' he cries.

I point to the girl, the long pale curls falling to her waist. The scrap of blue and white silk trailing from her fingers.

'Surely you,' I say, 'of all people on this earth should recognise Susanna when you see her!' I turn upon him. 'She has come to blame me. It is my fault that typhoid came into the house; and the pestilence did not take *my* child, did it? Oh, I had thought her left behind in Charlotte, but, towards the end, whenever Eddie looked at me it was with his mother's eyes. It was always so. I am twice to blame, George. First I failed Susanna, and now I have let die the child that she entrusted to me!'

My legs begin to tremble so that they will scarcely hold me.

It is the shock in George's face that brings me back at last into my right mind. He lays his hands upon my shoulders in none too gentle fashun. He shakes me hard so that my head rocks back and forth.

'Look again,' he shouts. 'It is but Ziegenmeyer's daughter. The girl has trailed us up here in her father's buggy. You must know that she and Ed were sweet with one another?'

He stares long into my face.

'Oh, my dear,' he says, 'it's not your fault that Ed got sick. The blame is all at my door. Young, strong men like Ed very rarely die of fever; because of me his strength was undermined. I took him into that awful Fire. Because of my afflictshun he was bound to work the clock round. I took so much for granted. It is I who should lie with lilies at my head; never my poor boy . . .'

We cling to one another underneath the trees.

We weep, our hearts nigh to breaking. We go back to join the funeral party. We drive home in silence to Green Street. I serve a cold repast to our dear friends, who try to give us comfort.

It comes to my mind that from this day on we shall sit only five around this table.

Chapter Twenty

October 12

Rosa helps me put the parlour back together, but no matter how nicely we arrange things it does not look the same.

Georgie says he cannot stand to have Ed's things around him. I empty Ed's wardrobe and the highboy. In the top drawer, I find his treasures. There is a rusty penknife, fought over long ago by the two brothers. There is the prayer-book that was once his mother's, with her name written on the fly-leaf. Wrapped carefully in paper I find the little wooden horse, given to him by his uncle, John Salter, on Ed's second birthday. Set apart, there is a length of blue silk ribbon what is brand-new, and a single glove of matching blue, that has the look of sweetheart's mementoes.

I place these things in a small box, and put it with my family treasures. It seems so little to save; but then he had lived for such a short time.

December 5

A letter from Elizabeth in Suamico what is full of sympathy at our great loss. She menshuns at the very end that the Lord has heard her prayers at last.

At the age of forty, when she had given up all hope, she finds herself again with child.

★

The first days of 1873 brought Georgie's fifteenth birthday. The true bite of winter was felt in January; ships froze fast in the

301

river basin. He trod the icy delivery route with Shamus Feany, and reported to Papa the completion of the new Chamber of Commerce on La Salle Street. A new County Jail, finer than the old one, was under construction on Hubbard and Dearborn. On Washington Street Georgie watched the rise of the 'Reaper Block', the property of Cyrus McCormick. On every street of the devastated district rose new hotels and great stores, offices of government and banks; and this time the city was built not with wood, but with brick and stone, and Athenian marble. The completion of each new permanent structure was like a signal to him, a confirmation that he should never leave Chicago.

He longed to talk about his feelings, the fears that had lately come to haunt him. He suffered a few months of frustrated silence; in the end he made do with Rosa. She was all he had. He was forced to feign an interest in her music, in her complicated stitching of what she assured him were fashionable garments. While Rosa toiled at handsewn hems, Georgie threaded needles for her with appropriately coloured thread, and they talked to one another; shyly at first and then with trust. Sometimes they forgot, and spoke of Eddie as if he were still with them. Whenever this happened the guilty one would halt, gape-mouthed, and colour fiercely, as if some indecent act had been performed in public. They would recall the grave beneath the maple tree and say the same things to each other, like 'That's a long ways up to Rosehill,' and 'I sure hope he don't get too lonely.'

Jon no longer searched the house for his lost brother. They envied him such quick forgetfulness. They tried to emulate him by talking about other things. They sat each evening at the far end of the long kitchen, where the sewing-machine stood close beside a glowing stove. Georgie sat on a straight-backed chair, his long legs stretched out towards the warmth, his feet bare.

Rosa said: 'You'll get chilblains sitting that way.'

'So I'll get chilblains.' He never argued nowadays with Rosa. This policy of appeasement was due partly to his need for her company and understanding; it also assuaged the guilt he felt about past misdemeanors. Georgie knew, had known since that awful night of Ed's death, that he alone was to blame. The Lord punished sinners by taking away the object they most loved, and Georgie had done wrong in so many ways. He had once used his church-collection money to buy playing-cards, so that he might at least stand equal alongside Shamus Feany. He had learned to play poker; had on one terrible occasion gambled and lost his work-jacket and then lied to Papa about the loss. He had noticed that when one member of a family died, another often followed. The mystery of Ed's death, the way that he alone contracted fever while the rest of them stayed healthy, was always on his mind.

Rosa said: 'Typhoid comes from dirty food and water. But we all ate and drank the same things. Remember how Mama kept warning us? Eddie always heeded Mama.'

Georgie thought about last summer, the heat and flies, the familiar stench that was Chicago; the street-corner lemonade sellers, the Italian ice-cream vendors.

'No,' he said slowly, 'there was one time at least when Ed paid no mind to Mama's warnings.'

★

April 10

Went out this evening into my poor garden what is much neglected. I find the lilac brought from Charlotte. I recall how Eddie skinned his fingers in the planting of it. New shoots are pushing hard and strong from the cold earth.

George comes to stand beside me.

He says: 'Mama, I have just remembered something. I know how Ed got sick.'

I look into his troubled face. I wait.

'The only thing he ate away from home was ice-cream. He bought some most hot days from Marcinellos.'

'And you?' I ask him. 'Did you not also buy some?'

'Can't stand the stuff,' says he, 'I never eat it. It gives me head-aches.'

303

May 20

Have deep-scrubbed my house in the past weeks. Smallpox is raging, so George tells me, in the Sixth and Seventh Wards. We are again into hot and heavy weather. For all the fine new buildings, all the bragging and boasting of our politicians, pestilence and death walks tall among Chicago's streets.

George speaks often of England. He longs to be in Dorset, to walk again beside the River Frome. He has grown so frail and fine-drawn lately. When he talks of home his very speech is altered, he goes back to the tongue we both knew in childhood.

'Canst thou bear this place a few months longer?' he asks.

'Yea,' say I. 'I can bear it, George.'

'Thou hast borne much on my account. I have not deserved thee.' He looks long into my face. 'Should I ever go under – if thou'rt left alone – remember my words. Seek out a good man for to be a husband to thee; and a father to our children, and remember kindly George Hodder Salter.'

June 1

A letter from Elizabeth. She gave birth in March to a fine and healthy son, his name to be Robert. Her letter is joyful. This late-born child, says she, has made her happiness complete. I lay her letter safe away. I look to my own preshus children. Georgie is downcast. He is, it seems, devoted to this brash and evil city. His tendency to argue does him little credit. He says he will remain here in America; find himself lodgings and work with a neighbourhood butcher.

George says to him that when we go to England, we sail all five of us together, *or not at all.*

July 29

Word comes from the Salter family in England. They will be glad to see us on our return, they will help us to get a fresh start. George takes heart from his brother's words. The Seat on the Board of Trade is now offered up for sale, likewise our meat-market, its goodwill and fittings; our furniture is also to be sold. Once again we are to move a great distance, with no more than our clothing and personal treashurs.

August 18
All is sold. We sail for England on September twenty-eighth on the steamship *Brittania.*

George cannot make up his mind where we shall settle. He speaks of Dorchester and Taunton. We are to go first to Winchester, where the Salters have a thriving butcher's business. On the letters that come from them there stands a crest that states them to be *Purveyors of Meat to Her Majesty the Queen.*

'Do you,' I ask George, 'ever feel regret that you came to this country?'

He shows me such a strange look.

'I have come to believe,' says he, 'that our lives are pre-destined. That there is only one road for us to tread, no matter how we try to change it. Be it corduroy or smooth plank.'

His words disturb me. I cannot put them from my mind.

September 21
All is done what can be done. Five steamship tickets lie before me. Our trunks are mostly packed and standing in the front hall and still I have this sense of moving ever forward, and yet remaining on the same spot. In all my days I have never gone in for muddled thinking and premonitions, and yet I cannot seem to see a future. One thing I know for such; George is sick. Oh, but he is mortal ill.

On September 23, 1873, my dear husband, George Hodder Salter, passed peacefully away in sleep.

The ship bound for England will sail without us, just as I had known it must do. There is after all only one road for us to tread, be it corduroy or smooth plank.

Chapter Twenty-One

The road up to Rosehill seemed shorter this time. She did not touch the carriage blinds. She could see how, on West Halstead Street, the stores had put up their shutters and ceased trading for a few hours, as a mark of respect for the English butcher. As they passed through the business district many private carriages, trimmed with black crepe, joined the cortege. It must, said Dr Hahn, be very gratifying for her to see how well-regarded George had been.

In her mind reality and dream had fused. Susanna had come to claim back her own. She had never really let them go. Rhoda looked down at the black dress, worn for one year already, and thought it could not have another twelve months of decent wear left in it.

The day was cold. The sun shone from a clear sky. The wind, that in Chicago never ceased to blow, whipped up red and yellow leaves and drove them briskly down the broad streets. In England the autumns had come gently, with mists and golden mornings; evenings blue with woodsmoke. Fall was an abrupt word, it spoke of shock and sudden partings. Inconsequential thoughts saw her through the journey; they rode in through Rosehill's wide gates, as they had done twelve months before. The sapling maple tree had grown; its hospitable branches spread a little wider. Last year she had cried: 'But he was only eighteen.' This year, she thought: 'But he was only forty-six.' Did the span of acceptable years always lengthen to fit circumstances?

Chief mourners stood in privileged positions close around the graveside. She gazed from one face to another and found them disturbingly familiar. The prayers were the same; the sheaf of lilies tied with purple ribbon. A slow conviction grew within her that the intervening year had never happened; that she was doomed forever to attend the same funeral, in the same style, until all her dear ones had been taken from her. She grappled with hysteria. There was no George to grab her shoulders this time, to shake her back into her right mind. As the handful of ritual earth rattled down upon the coffin she closed her eyes.

Gentle hands led her away towards the carriage; behind the thick dark veil her eyes were dry. On that journey back to Green Street she faced-up for the first time to her position. What remained of her strength and purpose must be hoarded like miser's gold. The time for grief, for weeping and remembering, must come later.

Georgie had moved in less than a year from the comfortable niche of second son to the pinnacle of oldest male member of the Salter family. Like a prince thrust upwards into unexpected kingship, he doubted his ability to fulfil all expectations. Folks said it was his duty to be a comfort and stay to his widowed mother, his sorrowing sister and little brother. No one took account of Georgie's feelings.

Not that anything had really changed. Where he was concerned, Mama had always been, still was, the bossman. Her new ploy of consulting with him, of inviting his opinions, was no more than a clever method of coercion. But what was he to do?

On the day that followed Papa's funeral they sat like shipwrecked mariners among the roped-down trunks and boxes.

Mama said: 'You know we can't stay here, don't you George?'

He nodded.

'The new tenants have been most forbearing, but they have bought out furniture and fittings, and paid a month's rent. By the end of this week we must be gone.'

His mother paused. She held her head a little to one side. She said, in a meek tone, 'Where do you think we ought to go, George?'

Rosa, whose opinion had not been asked, said: 'But surely we

shall go to England? It's all arranged for us to stay with Uncle
. . .'

'No,' Mama interrupted. 'We cannot impose upon your
father's family.'

'But we wouldn't be imposing! You have thousands of
dollars! Oh, I had quite made up my mind to go to England.
The English are so classy and elegant, and they're your own
people, Mama. Surely, at a time like this, you want to be with
them?'

'There is no one in England who would wish to take on a
widow-woman and her three children. Those thousands of dollars,
Rosa, would go nowhere once converted into sterling pounds.
No.' Mama spoke thoughtfully. 'There is only one thing for us
to do, one place where we are sure of welcome . . .'

Georgie, who had never interrupted his mother's speech in all
his life cried out, 'I thought it was *my* opinion you wanted? But
you're absolutely right, Ma; there is only one thing for us to do.
We stay right here in good old Chicago!'

His mother shook her head. 'No,' she said. 'I'm afraid that
won't do either, George.'

She held up the five unused steamship tickets that should
have taken them to England.

'Mr Sangren is quite sure that in the circumstances the
shipping-line will pay a refund. I propose that we sail west
instead of east. The lake-steamer *Superior* leaves Chicago on
Friday, bound for Green Bay. I intend to telegraph your aunt
Elizabeth, and warn her of our arrival in Brown County,
Wisconsin.'

They sat in the parlour, the place where Ed had died, where
Papa's coffin had stood on trestles for those three days before
the funeral. For Georgie even to raise his voice in this room
would be sacriligious but the words burst from him.

'But we're city folks,' he cried. 'Whatever would we do all
day, living among the wild men and the loggers in the backwoods!'

Rosa said: 'What about my singing lessons? It was Papa who
wanted me to get my voice trained.'

311

The silence lasted long enough to be intimidating.

'If,' Mama said, 'you two are taking as your models-in-life the false and sinful populace of Chicago – then I should say that the pioneer families of Suamico will compare very favourably with them.' She paused, and looked from one face to the other. 'My mind is made up. I have to do what is best for all of us.' Her gaze went to Jon who sat quietly beside her. 'You two are strong and whole. A change of situation will not harm you. Jon cannot fend for himself; never will. I need to take him to a safe place.'

Georgie crossed the room; he stood beside the heaped-up luggage.

'Two trunks at least,' he said, 'are full of Papa's things. Would you like me to go through them for you? I – well – I'd like to keep one or two mementoes, I guess you and Rosa would feel likewise. As for the rest, well I could take it down to the Mission for the Homeless on Walnut Street? There's no sense in carrying tuxedos and butcher's aprons to the pineries of North Wisconsin.'

'Why, that's thoughtful of you, George. I had quite forgotten that the clothes were packed before your father . . .' She turned away, her voice unsteady. 'Rosa can help you. Keep anything you wish. Just do as you think best. But please, please don't let me see you do it.'

He selected for his own a matching cummerbund and cravat in blue silk; a waistcoat of crimson brocade. Rosa took a white silk scarf; she laid aside her father's prayer-book, brought from England. 'For Mama,' she said, 'but not yet. Not until we reach Brown County.'

'Brown County,' he said. 'Guess it even sounds kinda dull and slow, like nothing ever happens in it.' He laid his forehead on the trunk's edge. 'I wanted so bad to stay here in Chicago, Rosie!'

'I know,' she said, 'but we have to think of Jon and Mama.' She laid her hand on his. 'It might'n be all that bad. There's three cousins that we've never seen, and Aunt Elizabeth and

312

Uncle Robert. Life's different in the country, Georgie. We'll just have to get used to it, is all!'

Georgie walked down to the Mission for the Homeless. The clothes, he said, firmly, were to be collected straight away from 96A Green Street. The curate who ran the Mission called him 'Sir'. It was, Georgie thought, not so hard after all to be a man.

Leaving Green Street did not bring Rhoda the relief that she expected. Their luggage had been taken by carrier to Pier 23; Dr Hahn was to drive them to the wharfside. Her farewells to friends and neighbours had been said on the previous evening. She looked up for the last time at the strange old house with its faded paint and gingerbread additions. The memories it held were close and painful. She remembered the day of their arrival. Eddie saying by way of comfort: 'Well, at least it's bigger than our old place.' George carrying in the baggage, while the children explored the upper rooms. Her own conviction that here was a place of safety; which had not been altogether false. The house stood safe while neighbouring streets had burned to ashes. George and Ed had come home to her on that night of awful fire. If tears were to overwhelm her, then this was the moment and the place. She gripped her hands tight together and willed the ache to pass.

The ride to the wharfside restored her calm. It was here, on these choked and noisy streets, that she recalled her thousand reasons for leaving this city. She held Jon close to her, feeling his tension, his bewildered agitation. Rosa sat calmly beside her older brother. It was only Georgie who gazed longingly from side-to-side, as if he would imprint Chicago forever on his vision. He spoke but once. He said: 'I shall come back, Mama. No matter how long it takes, or how old I get, I shall come back here.'

Pier 23 was crowded with passengers and their luggage. The Captain, said Dr Hahn, would wish to sail with full holds and as many persons as he could cabin at this late time of the year. Rhoda wore her cloak of long-tailed sable and the mourning bonnet, bought for Eddie. The children wore black armbands

313

over thick woollen jackets; they stood very close together, hands linked.

The SS *Superior* loomed tall above The Levee; she was painted overall in white, with a crimson smoke-stack. The boarding ramp went down, and people moved towards it.

She turned to Dr Hahn. She said: 'I don't have words enough to thank you . . .'

He said: 'No thanks are called for, Mrs Salter. It's been a privilege to know you and George, and your little family.'

He laid a gentle hand on Jon's head.

'You've made the right decision. He'll do fine upcountry. Write me when you have the time.'

Their cabins stood adjacent with a connecting door between them. He was to bunk with Jon, Rosa with her mother. Georgie had seen Mama's confusion, her physical withdrawal, as they boarded ship, from the boisterous types who were Milwaukee-bound. On reaching the cabins she ordered Georgie to lock both doors.

'You are not,' she said to Rosa, 'to move one single step unless I am with you!'

To him she said: 'Now, George, it will be up to you to protect us on this voyage! You are full six feet tall, and although you are not yet sixteen you have a very ready tongue. I shall expect you to acquaint yourself with the whereabouts of the dining room and the observation platform. You might also, when you see one standing idle, enquire of an officer how long it will be before we reach Green Bay.'

The orders had been issued in all of Mama's old fiery style, but he had caught the tremor in her voice, observed the pallor of her face.

He turned to Rosa. 'You can start unpacking. 'I'll fetch Mama a tray of tea, and she can put her feet up.' He rumpled Jon's smooth brown hair. 'And you can stand on this stool and look out of the porthole. See there! You can watch all the big ships coming up to the wharfside!'

Within that day he became familiar with the passenger deck

and its elegant appointments. He visited the dining-rooms and salons, walked slowly over thick red carpet, sat on velvet sofas and admired the cut-glass chandeliers, the embossed paper on the walls, the little gilt chairs and white-clothed tables. At every turn, in tall gilded mirrors, he came face to face with his own image.

Until now, what with all the hustle and excitement of leaving Chicago, and his elevation to protector of his family, he had managed almost to forget the actual reason for their travel. It was with a sense of superstitious shock that he first met his own full-length likeness, walking towards him through a looking-glass across the crimson carpet.

Just for a moment he almost cried out: 'Hey – Eddie! How'd you get here?' Then he remembered the maple tree at Rosehill that sheltered both his father and brother. He thought, with a flash of adult insight: however can Mama bear to look at me? I must be a living reminder of them, every minute of the day.

He went up to the observation deck and stood for a long time watching the wake of the ship upon Lake Michigan's blue waters. His thoughts were confused, his feelings muddled, Chicago lay out of sight; Brown County was just a name, a place where folks cut down timber and lived in log-cabins. He looked down at his new suit of grey, well-cut worsted. He thought about Mama in her sable cloak and silk gowns; and then there was Jon who did not really understand what had come to pass. Who still asked at intervals: 'Where Eddie gone? Where Papa?'

For all of Mama's talk of her farming childhood in Old England, the present Salter family was city-bred. Five significant years of growing-up in Chicago had left its imprint. Even Mama, in recent times had abandoned her old-fashioned gowns, and now wore the more stylish creations stitched for her by Rosa. As for his young sister, well she was elegant to her fingertips; she had all the refinements of a proper lady. But who, in the backwoods, would call on Rosa to sing or play Mozart on the piano. Who would even recognise or appreciate that their mode of dressing was in the very latest fashion? As for himself, and although not quite sixteen, he was, he considered,

315

pretty wise in all the ways of a big town. He knew how to speak and act, was at ease and confident in restaurants and cafés. He remembered, with anguish, the times he and Ed had been taken by Papa to the famous eating-houses on La Salle and Clark Streets. He had been told, by a drummer who knew Brown County and its environs, that the people there drank moonshine liquor all the time, and ate raw venison and black squirrel with their fingers.

This mad journey north, made in haste by his Mama, and with no account taken of her children's feelings, was bound to end in trouble. He would, he thought, have found preferable even damp and dreary England. Decisions, Papa had always said, should be made at leisure and with great forethought.

At the thought of Eddie and Papa, left so far behind him in Chicago, Georgie leaned his head against the observation window, and wept.

The upper deck was enclosed with glass and heated by wood-burning stoves. By the time they reached the port of Milwaukee, to sit on a leather bench and view the passing scene had become Jon's favourite occupation. He sat beside her on that October morning, absorbed by the loading and unloading, the dis-embarkation of immigrants from the steerage compartment, the taking on board of coal and provisions.

Rhoda studied his small thin body in the knickerbocker suit of dark-grey, the armband of black crepe around his sleeve. His pale and gentle features expressed neither sadness nor animation. She wondered what went on in his mind; had accepted long since that Jon would remain forever childlike. But what was a slowness, capable of concealment at the age of seven, was bound to be remarked upon and jeered at as he grew older. She could never forget that filed away in some archive in Chicago was a Census document which declared that Jon had been categorised as 'Idiotic'. Yet there were times when he confounded all her fears. Only yesterday he had asked: 'Papa carry Jon on big ship? Eddie go with Jon on railroad?' She had failed at first to catch his meaning, then it came to her that what he spoke of was that

316

journey made five years ago, from Charlotte to Chicago. By some miracle his damaged mind retained a memory of it.

She said, wonderingly, 'So you recall that do you? But you were only two, going on three.' She took him on her knee. She said for the hundredth time: 'Now you remember what I told you. Papa couldn't come with us on this trip, and Ed stayed behind to keep him company.' She smiled, forcing reassurance. 'But we've still got Georgie. He'll carry you when you get tired. Your Papa got weary too. But he's safe now, all his suffering is ended.'

Repetition of this tale, first told for the sake of Jon, had sustained her through the days and nights since George's passing. At each time of telling the vision became clearer. Susanna and George; Eddie and the baby brother, who had lived for but a year. All of them, together. Reunited in Heaven. Her habits of simplicity and neatness, her need for order and reason made this conclusion bearable. She had known, since those first days in Charlotte that George and Ed were only loaned to her. The day of reckoning had come in Chicago. The time for borrowing love was over. Grief made channels in the mind. Old sorrows merged with new ones. The first days aboard had passed in a maze of weariness and melancholy. Between Chicago and Milwaukee she had hardly slept, eaten little, and spoken even less. For the space of this journey all responsibility had been taken from her. There were no meals to be prepared, or rooms to scour. No decisions were required. Her corner of the observation deck was respected by other passengers; people noticed but avoided the thin pale lady, so obviously just-widowed, and the small silent child who was always at her side.

The weather was growing wintry; since leaving Milwaukee temperatures had fallen. Huge stoves maintained the warmth in the passenger cabins and salons, but most other parts of the ship remained unheated. There was a rumour that 'flu had broken out among the immigrant families who travelled in steerage. Rhoda unpacked the trunk that contained her children's warmest clothing; laid between crocheted shawls and comforters

317

she found the green leather covers of her Journal. Later, when the children slept, she turned back the pages. She began to read that first entry which told of her move away from Patchwood and her father; the account of her first sighting of George Hodder Salter, the emotion she had not dared to show towards him.

She read, on, past midnight and through the early morning hours; and there it was, set down in her own hand, complete and bitter-sweet, that love which had always been tentative on her part, always seeking to possess but never quite succeeding.

Some entries made her smile. How sure are the young and untried; how foolish then had been her certainties. Life, it might be said, had dealt harshly with her. There was much sadness in between the lines of those tight-written pages. She closed the covers, laid the Journal down and locked it. She rose and walked towards the long mirror on the cabin wall. The black mourning gown did not become her; it hung loosely on her thin frame. Her face was very pale, the green eyes set far back beyond the high cheekbones, the brown hair scraped hard away from its centre-parting.

She began to think for the first time about Elizabeth towards whom she was steaming with all haste. Elizabeth, the busy farmwife, with her family of grown sons and brand-new baby. Eighteen years had passed since their last meeting, and now, almost a stranger, would come Rhoda with her three children, her haggard face, her sorrows, into her sister's busy life.

Rhoda put on her sable cloak, looked in on her sleeping children, extinguished the lamp and left the cabins, locking both doors behind her. She went up to the observation deck. In the east a pale moon hung in the lightening sky. She turned to find the ship's Captain at her side.

He nodded towards the distant shoreline.

'Manitowoc,' he said briefly. 'We shall be putting in there by mid-morning.'

Rhoda said: 'How long before we get to Green Bay?'

'Well, that depends, ma'am. On the state of the weather. On how long the turn-around takes in each port of call. I guess you're kinda keen to get there?'

She said, with that touch of asperity, the lift of the head that would always mark her out as English: 'My son enquired of your officers as to the length of this trip, but was given no satisfactory answer.'

He grinned. 'You've never been any further north than Chicago?'

'I have not.'

'Then let me explain a few matters to you. It's like this, ma'am. Come November, a mass of polar air begins to move south. It slides down over Canada and across Lake Superior. From there it hits the Lakes of Michigan, Huron, Ontario and Erie. Winter comes sudden and bitter in these parts, a first freeze can bite without any warning. Why, you'll wake up one morning to find harbours turned overnight into a sheet of ice; bays that are locked in and piled up with ice floes. What I'm saying, ma'am, this one'll be our last trip. We need to move fast enough to get back to our home port before the cold comes. On the other hand, with a winter laid up in port, we can't afford to miss out on any business on the way.'

'So we shall get to Green Bay before the harbour closes?'

'I surely trust so, ma'am.'

'Tell me, Captain, what kind of city is it? Are there good hotels there?'

'Well, there must be one, I reckon.' He looked doubtfully at her. 'That's a pretty wild place, Green Bay. Not fit for a widow-lady travelling with children.'

'I have my son.'

'He's but a boy, ma'am.'

'That boy will have to suffice, Captain. He is all I have, now.'

The Captain went away. Rhoda stayed beside the window. She watched the sun come up, rising red out of the blue lake. Georgie had told her that schooners were built at Manitowoc. As they came closer to the dockside she saw a fleet putting out, their masts full of white canvas, lifting to the wind. Life, she thought, in these northern latitudes, would demand a different sort of courage. That mass of polar air might even now be

319

moving south across Canada and towards the Great Lakes. By the time she arrived in Green Bay her emotions must be in order, her plans formulated.

She allowed herself, very tentatively, to think about Eddie and George. The agony, she discovered, had subsided now into an ache. She acknowledged how rash had been her flight from Chicago, how reckless at this time of the year. She considered her sleeping children; their dependence upon her. No more, she told herself, could her burdens be laid upon other shoulders.

For the first time in many weeks she took breakfast that morning.

They steamed into Green Bay on a Sunday morning in late October.

The air was cold. Sunlight, that held a peculiar quality of brilliance, lay across the landscape. The waters of the bay, Georgie noted, really were green. He walked to the ship's rail and leaned across it. As the chill struck into him, his long thin body shuddered. He viewed the approaching township without enthusiasm.

Last night, when he was on an errand for Mama, Captain Hansen had spoken to him.

'You can tell Mrs Salter that we shall be docking about ten tomorrow morning. Your mother was asking me about hotels. I made a few enquiries. The Altona is about the most civilised – or so they tell me. Don't expect anything too fancy, though. This is Green Bay, not Chicago!'

Georgie said 'Well thanks, Captain.' He straightened his shoulders, deepened the tone of his voice. 'My Ma kinda frets about having hot water and proper locks on the doors. For myself you understand – well I'm not so all-fired fussy. But it'll surely ease her mind if I say that the Altona comes recommended by the Captain.'

'How old are you, young man?'

'I'll be sixteen in just two months.'

'What exactly are you planning on doing in Green Bay? Seems an unlikely spot for a lady like your mother?'

'Mama has this sister who lives up in the pineries. Nothing else would do but we must take ship for North Wisconsin.'

'Are you to be met by your relatives?'

'I guess not. Ma telegraphed to my Aunt Elizabeth to say we were leaving Chicago, and on our way up here. Reckon we'll have to telegraph them again when we get to Green Bay.'

The Captain looked concerned. 'In that case you could be stuck in town for a week or more. That's a real rough city that you're going into. Best stay put in your hotel. Don't you or your family ever go out wandering the streets!'

Georgie laughed. 'I don't mean any disrespect, Captain – but remember where I come from? Chicago's not exactly the most peaceful city in the world!'

'That's true, boy. But you at least got some kinda law in Chicago. Green Bay is a wide-open town. For a population of ten thousand they've got more than one hundred saloons, not to count the gin-mills and the whiskey-holes. Nobody's ever counted the bawdy-houses. It's reckoned to be a real fun-city for lumberjacks and sawyers. Come winter, and every sailor who's laid-up in dock will be whooping it up in Green Bay!'

Georgie said: 'We should be out on my uncle's farm long before the harbour freezes in.'

'Just you make sure you are, young man!' The Captain paused. 'That's a real fine lady, your Mama. The kind you don't meet with all that often. Guess that takes a special kinda nerve for a woman to set out by herself on this sort of expedition.' He shot a thoughtful glance at Georgie. 'Women – especially ladies – are in real short supply up here in the north woods. You could find yourself with a step-papa, in a couple more years.'

'My mother's not by herself. She's got me alongside her. As for remarrying – why she's deep in grief – or hadn't you noticed?' Georgie's voice, which still hovered embarrassingly on the brink of manhood, had risen to its most childish pitch. 'So you just keep your eyes on your navigating, you hear me, Cap'n Hansen!'

'Open up the trunk, George,' Mama said, 'and hand me your father's butchering tools.'

He handled the leather apprentice-case with reverential care. It was to be his own now; his Papa's special bequest. He watched as his mother slipped the catches and threw back the lid. From beneath her pillows she drew the sharp, shining cleaver and the knife used for skinning. She passed them to him without a word, and he fitted them back into their appropriate slots.

'I suppose,' he said bitterly, 'you'll be wanting these again when we reach Green Bay?'

'But, of course, George.' She had nearly smiled. 'You surely didn't think that I was altogether unaware of the perils around us?'

'And here was I, thinking that I was your protector.'

'But so you are! We also have Rosa to look out for – and I am carrying money with me. Your Papa's knives provide us with a little extra insurance, that's all.'

Georgie grinned. 'Guess I can quit worrying about the wild state of Wisconsin, then, eh Mama?'

'Wisconsin,' she said stiffly, 'is to be your home.' There was a new note in her voice that caught all his attention. 'In my life I have moved great distances, and always for the sake of those I loved.' She paused, and it seemed to Georgie that she was fearful to trust him with her private thoughts. He felt a great pity for her; it welled up inside him, blurred his vision.

He said: 'You've had a bad time, lately.' His words seemed to ease her hesitancy.

'I came to this land,' she continued, 'for the sake of Eddie and your father.' She smiled. 'And for my own sake, too, if I am truthful. I loved your Papa from the moment I first saw him. But I have never done the things *I* wanted, nothing was ever of *my own* choosing. I remember landing in New York and sailing up the Hudson River. All the tidy, prosperous farmsteads; the herds of dairy cattle, the orchards.'

He said, fearfully, 'But I'm to be a butcher, Mama!'

She said, as if she had not heard his words: 'I shall look to buy a farm in Suamico, George. It's what I've always wanted.'

PART FOUR

Chapter Twenty-two

Sometimes in north Wisconsin there comes a rare week in late autumn that is mild and windless, brilliant with witch-hazel blossoms, and the shedding leaves of oak and cottonwood and sugar-maple. On days like these it is possible to think that winter might hold off forever.

Elizabeth had watched the road for almost a month, starting up at every sound of a turning wheel, even though she knew that it was too soon, that the journey from Chicago could not yet be accomplished by Rhoda and her children. She prayed that they might come before the snows and blizzards of November could rob Suamico of light and colour. That there could be a few mild days when they might walk together. Elizabeth deep-scrubbed her whole house; she washed the lace window-panels and the quilted bedcovers. She picked bunches of wild asters and placed them on window-sills and tables. She baked welcoming cakes which were promptly eaten up by her grateful sons.

It was on the last day of October, on a golden evening of that week of Indian Summer, that she saw Alwin Hunter's stagecoach driving slowly down the track to halt before her gate. Robert, who was catching the last of the light to mend a corn-crib, went running down towards the stage. Elizabeth put a hand up to her hair, she ripped off her apron and threw it in a corner; for a moment she stood on the top step of the porch. Eighteen years! When last together she and Rhoda had been young in Buckland St Mary! She began to move slowly down the path of stepping-stones that led from house to gate. This was the meeting she had dreamed of in the lonely time of her first years in the northwoods; the sister she had longed for in the agonising hours of her last confinement. They stood face to face, and the years of separation fell away. They wept and clung together. They said: 'You haven't changed a bit – I'd have known you among thousands,' even though the words were not quite true. They walked towards the house, their arms about each other, as they had once walked so long ago on the snowy slope of Dommett Hill.

★

November 6, 1873

It is less than a week since our arrival, but already it seems a familiar place, so sweet is the company, my family so dear and loving.

Of our arrival in Green Bay there is nothing good to be said. In the *best* hotel recommended by our ship's Captain we find bed-bugs and assorted vermin, and in conseqwence sit up in chairs the night thru'. Make haste the next morning to find a reliable stage bound for Suamico. We are brought here at last by a decent coachman name of Alwin Hunter. Our main luggage to be sent on in the next days.

So much to set down, I scarce know where I shall begin.

There is Suamico, what is an Indian name meaning 'yellow sands'. It reminds me in many ways of Buckland St Mary and the Blackdowns, except that here the farmsteads are scattered, not between dark hills, but among forests the size and majesty of which I had never even dreamed. For the last part of our journey here, and in spite of darkness falling, I sit up on top with the driver of our stage, the better to witness what manner of country I have chosen to bring my children in to.

A killing frost, says Mr Hunter, has taken the leaves from the hackberry trees and several others. But suffishent foliage still holds to take away the breath in wonder. The air is pure. I smell pine instead of stockyards. The roads are narrow; in places but no more than Indian trails and overhung with branches. But they are empty! We meet hardly a soul on the way from Green Bay. The feeling comes over me that I have chosen aright.

When I reach my sister I know this to be true. Such a welcome from them all, so many tears, so much true understanding.

November 15

I am but two weeks here but already my mind is made up. Suamico is to be our home. Jon is abed. Rosa and George are to a husking-bee with their three cousins. This evening I talk long and earnestly with Robert and Elizabeth. There is a vacant farm that lies but one-quarter mile along the road from here. I am wishful to buy it. Robert says that since this steading reaches up to the land owned by his friends, it will be as well that we talk the qwestshun over, all of us together.

Jim and Matthew Black are brothers, batchelors and Canadian-born of Scottish parents. Their single state is not to be doubted. They have not two shirt-buttons that they may fasten, between the pair of them. They are also unkempt about the head and mustash. The younger one, known as Matt, has a sickly look, what comes, Elizabeth says, from near-mortal wounding in the Civil War. The one called Jim is a fine figure of a man, as are most men of Scots' blood. He is very dark and fierce, until he smiles. My sister and her husband, I soon see, put great belief in this man. The brothers are most courteous towards me. They are gentlemen born, never mind their wild appearance.

Elizabeth makes coffee, and we five sit down together. Mr Jim Black enqwires what do I know of farming?

'A considerable amount,' I inform him, 'since I am from farming generations in old England, and was skilled in dairy work by the age of ten years!'

He shows surprise.

I say, somewhat put out at his raised eyebrows, 'Pay no heed to my looks, sir. I am lacking inches, as the good Lord made me. But my sister here will vouch for the strength of my arm, and my capacity for hard labour.'

The man smiles. 'I guess,' says he, 'that your tongue is also kinda powerful too, ma'am.'

I say in a qwieter tone: 'I do not like to be misunderstood,

327

Mr Black. But have no fear. I am as capable as any man and more determined than most.'

We settle down to talk of the 53A farm.

I enqwire as to state and type of soil, condishuns of drainage and *why* the place has been vacated.

Jim Black has the goodness to look impressed. He says more respectfully: 'The last owner died of old age; he batched it on his own, and got into a pretty sad condishun.'

I look meaningfully at the buttonless shirts, and the shaggy heads of both men, but they are unabashed. He goes on to tell me of the state and nature of the Section, and I am best pleased with what I hear.

'It sounds,' say I, 'as if I might do something with it.'

'It also,' says Robert, 'is close enough for you and Elizabeth to visit daily with each other. She could not bear to be parted from you now.'

'Nor I from her.' I feel the tears start to my eyes. 'I had not known how lonely I truly was until I came here.'

Mr Jim Black says: 'But how will you manage? We shall all pitch-in, of course, to get you started. That is our way, here! But what about day-to-day chores? With great respect, Mrs Salter, ma'am, there are jobs that a woman cannot tackle.'

'I have,' say I, 'a tall strong son of almost sixteen years. He is trained for a butcher and slaughterer, but there are no stockyards in the district I am relieved to see! It is high time my Georgie put away his fancy suiting and his satin waistcoats. Oh I shall make a farmer of my boy. Have no doubts on that score, Mr Black!'

November 17

A cold dry day of cloud and high wind. Walk out by myself this forenoon to look at the Lutz farm. The trees stand well upon the land, what is proof that it is in good heart. I go into the empty fields and know that here, come April, will grow good grass and clover. Close to the house I find a spring of cold clear water. On my father's farm in England was such a spring. Around it he built a little house through which the water was

328

channelled in wooden troughs. By this means, in the very hottest weather, we kept cool and fresh our butter. Such a spring, to a dairy farmer, is worth more than gold. I look over the outbuildings. There is a cow-horse barn, a chicken and a hog-house. There are several corncribs and a granary. There is no garden, but an orchard of some six acres. All fences broken, much repairing to be done, but nothing that willing hands cannot put to rights.

★

Rosa woke early in the strange house. A bed for her had been made up in the parlour. She lay still and listened to the early morning sounds that were so different from those of Green Street, Chicago. Mama and Jon slept in a small room on the far side of the kitchen. Georgie had gone, uncertainly, to bunk with his three Vickery cousins. She began to think about Papa and Ed as she always did in the moments of waking. At home in Green Street, and even on the steamer, she had managed to pretend that they were still close by, that death had never happened to them. For the space of those brief minutes she felt secure and warm, the events of the past year but a bad dream. Realisation always came, of course; the ache of loss settling deep inside her chest, the desire to weep having to be overcome. On these first mornings in Suamico, Wisconsin, the good feeling did not come. Papa and Ed seemed to know that there was no place for them here. She was not surprised. Rosa herself had the very same feelings.

On the ship she had managed to keep Chicago with her; needed only to close her eyes to see Ed and Papa, dark and tall in their white butchers' aprons, busy in the meat-market on West Halstead. Sometimes she imagined herself walking hand-in-hand with them on crowded Adams Street, with the street-cars clanging, the newsvendors shouting, the smell of fresh coffee and doughnuts in the air. People had looked twice at the Salters as they walked by; she and Georgie, Ed and Papa.

She left her bed and moved silently across the rug towards

329

the window. She pulled back the drapes, lifted the lace panel and looked out on to the greyness of November dawn. From the kitchen came the small and careful din of men determined to be quiet. A teacup clattered in a saucer, a boot dropped; wood sparked and crackled in the stove. A door closed quietly. Four figures moved slowly down the path and on to the track that led towards the village. So had Ed and Pa and Georgie gone through Green Street in the early mornings. Now there was only Georgie, who had no place to go. Rosa shivered; she pulled the quilt from the bed and wrapped it close around her. She went back to the window, sat on a stool and watched the sky flush rose and pearl; and that was something new, never witnessed in Chicago, where smoke from the stockyards had blotted out the dawn. She thought that Eddie and Papa must be somewhere up there, walking together in that pink light.

Georgie also woke early; partly from habit, but mostly due to his lazy days combined with the early bedtime hours kept by the Vickery family. He would hear his cousins creep from their beds: Willum who had bunked beneath him, and Chas and Johnnie who slept just an arm's reach away in the tiny room. They blundered about in the darkness, fumbling for shirts and britches, neckerchiefs and socks; noisy in their efforts to be considerately quiet. His envy of them was fierce and bitter, and almost to the pitch of hatred. So had he and Ed blundered and stubbed toes on chilly fall mornings. So had he and Ed gone downstairs to a firelit kitchen, where Papa had set out bowls of bread and hot milk on the table. The departure of his cousins to their work in the lumbermill was the very worst time of Georgie's whole day.

He had managed on the ship to control his tears but here, in this unbroken Vickery family, the unmanly habit had begun again. He, like Rosa, pulled the quilt from his bed and draped it around his shoulders. He padded down the narrow staircase, steeper than any he had ever seen. He found Rosa wakeful by the parlour window. By the time full light had come, the redness would have left his eyes.

They sat together for a long time without speaking. He said at last, his voice as scornful and nonchalant, as he could make it. 'We shan't be staying here, you know. Mama is way too smart to be happy in the backwoods. She's somewhat under par right now – well, that's to be expected. All that sickbed nursing and stuff, and then the selling-up! But just you wait till she's recovered, she'll want to get right back into business. Why, she was always the figuring brain in George Hodder Salter and Sons. Papa sure did depend on her. She kept store with Aunt Elizabeth when she was a young girl in England. They talked all about it last night over supper. Oh yes,' said Georgie, 'our Ma is a business woman. She'll soon get tired of this hick town.'

Rosa said: 'I don't think so.'

★

November 20

The maker of decishuns I now see, must tread a hard road. I sit the children down and tell them that we are to stay right here in Suamico. That I am to purchase the old Lutz farm.

Georgie takes this news badly. He is upset. Much worse than when we left Chicago. Have I, he asks, thought properly about all this? Have I considered my age, the weakness of Jon; that Rosa is not cut out to be a farmer's daughter? That Georgie himself has no knowledge of agriculture or country matters; and, what is more, not a scrap of interest in them! He speaks up like a man, though his top lip trembles, More and more each day I see his father in him, he is rash yet loving, and such a dreamer.

I say, as gently as I can: 'I have thought much about it, Georgie. I am trying to be wise on all counts. In this place we are safe, we have family here. A widow of means is in a dangerous posishun. I need to have my kin beside me. As to Jon, well here is clean air and freedom for him. Your concern for your sister does you credit, but Rosa is young enough to learn new ways. As to yourself,' say I, 'well you are not qwite sixteen years. Given the chance you will also come to love the

331

farm-life. In any case,' I ask him, 'what alternative is there? Suamico is a small place. It could not support a meat-market.'

He pounces on my words. 'Exactly!' he cries, 'but Green Bay could! With a population of 10,000 we could have an up-and-coming business in Green Bay. Real estate is the surest way of money-making. We could buy a slaughter-house which I would manage. Rosa and you, Mama, could run the meat-market . . .'

I halt him. 'George,' I say, 'I have brought us here to get away from cities. You will have to forget your Chicago notions.'

★

Daughters stayed close to their mothers; sometimes they stayed so close as to stifle independent thought. In their years in Chicago, Rosa had been Mama's confidante, her constant companion, her only solace. Rosa wanted to love Wisconsin because her mother loved it.

She did not understand Mama's great haste; this race against snow and ice to buy property and land; to be settled in their own place before Christmas. All her sympathy, now, was for her brother George.

Mama had gone to Green Bay with Uncle Robert. She returned with the Indenture that proved her the owner of a 53A Farm. Aunt Elizabeth made a celebration of it. These people of the northwoods caught at every small excuse to make a party. Farmers and their wives and children had rolled up by the waggon-load to sit around the huge pinewood table and eat pork-and-dumplings and drink home-brewed cider. A lady farmer was something new in their experience. They had come to look-over the Salter family, said Georgie. To size-up these dudes from Chicago City, who fancied themselves as pioneers!

Mama had been angry with him. Hard work, she had cried, was to be the family watchword from now on! He would see before too long that farming was no daylight task, no speedy means of making money, but rather a way of life that held dignity and meaning.

The brothers Jim and Matthew Black had spoken kindly to Georgie, as if he were, in fact, already a man. They had offered help, had said that they would put him in the way of mending walls and replacing shingles on the Lutz house. Georgie had been ungracious to Matthew to the point of rudeness, which had further angered their Mama.

When the party guests had gone, she had cornered Georgie in the kitchen.

'I have set my hand to the plough,' she said, 'and there is no turning back now! Surely once in a lifetime a woman may do something what is for her own sake, without all this opposition from her menfolk?'

The first snow came, but gently. A silent drifting whiteness that clung to the blistered paint of the farmhouse, and hid the ramshackle state of barn and sheds. It also covered the broken fences and unploughed fields, which said Robert Vickery, was a very good thing, since the ground was now iron-hard, and no outside labour possible before next springtime.

Their urgent task, said Mama, was to put the house to rights. She had every intention of celebrating Christmas in her own place; of returning the hospitality that had been shown to her. Rosa wondered at the wisdom of the scrubbing and polishing; her mother still had a delicate, too-thin appearance. Sometimes, in the night, Rosa woke to hear Rhoda's muffled sobs, and knew that she still grieved for Ed and Papa.

Rosa thought the farmhouse would be the nicest home they had ever known. She loved the great hickory and maple trees that stood close by it; there was a deep and shady porch that would be delightful in the summertime. In the living room stood a fireplace of hand-hewn stone that reached the height and breadth of one whole wall, and was topped-off by a mantelshelf of black oak. The kitchen was large enough to hold a table that would seat twenty men. There was no convenient pump above the sink. All water would have to be carried from the yard. But this was Suamico and not Chicago.

In a pair of old boots borrowed from her aunt, swathed in a

burlap apron, and with her curls tied up in a duster, Rosa toiled beside her mother to clean the accumulated grease and dirt of years from walls and floors. Tubs of lye soap were used, and a whole sack of soda crystals. Their most urgent need was for boiling water, every drop of which must be heated on the cook-stove, or the open fireplace.

Georgie viewed the snow-covered woodpile with deep disfavour. He recalled how logs had come ready-split to their Chicago home. Mama had complained of the extra cost this entailed, but Papa had believed, and wisely, that he and his sons had more valuable ways of spending time than in splitting firewood. Georgie hefted the weighty wood-axe in both hands and thought of the size of the cookstove's firebox, and the vast maw of that pioneer fireplace. He began, halfheartedly, to brush snow from the woodpile and drag logs towards the chopping-block. He shivered in the aching cold and started, inexpertly, to swing the axe. Within ten minutes Georgie had removed his jacket. An hour later and his hands were blistered, his shoulders ached, and the heap of dry hickory wood beside him still vanished into the house faster than he could split logs.

Georgie gazed out across the cold and silent fields, and beyond to the forests of white pine which, he believed, must stretch to the world's end. He remembered Chicago on a winter's morning: setting off with Shamus Feany, the delivery basket heavy on the outward journey, light on their return. He could almost smell the good rich cooking odours that came from the German restaurants on Halstead Street; the fragrance of coffee from the vendors' stands, the spiced delight of cinnamon doughnuts. There had been people, hundreds of them, pushing and thrusting along the sidewalks. Men in loud checkered suits, and brown boots and derbys; women with delicately rouged lips and flounced gowns, the kind Mama described as 'flighty'. There had been boys of his own age, sharp and cunning fellows, ever ready to turn a dishonest dollar or pick a pocket. With these he had felt assured, knowing their ways, convinced that he could outsmart them; unlike his Vickery

334

cousins, amongst whom, after one month spent in their home, he still felt inadequate and put-down. It was nothing they had said; in fact their very taciturnity unnerved him. In their company he heard in himself a tendency to talk too much, to boast, to sound-off like a Chicago City wise-guy. He studied his blistered palms, touched the cut across his cheekbone where a chip of flying hickory had struck him. He dreaded the confrontation at the supper table, when they sat opposite him; three pairs of brown eyes, three wind-burned, unsmiling faces, three tolerant expressions bent above their piled-up plates. There was no way he could match them, let alone outdo them. He had thought himself a hearty eater, but now knew himself for a finicky fussy town-boy, when set against his trencherman cousins. Breakfast at the Vickerys' alone was sufficient to satisfy Georgie for the whole day. He watched in wonder as the Vickery men, father and sons, devoured platters of home-cured ham and fried eggs, dishes of hashbrowns, hot toast soaked in yellow butter, and stacks of pancakes drenched in maple syrup. There were other areas of deep shame. His dressing and undressing was performed in darkness; country folk it seemed did not believe in wasting candles. But the Friday-night bath, taken before the kitchen fire, had the benefit of lamplight. On the first occasion his cousins had, considerately, since he was a guest, allowed him to use the water first.

'And anyhow,' Chas had observed, 'you're a darned sight cleaner than we are!'

Georgie had removed his shirt and trousers beneath the interested gaze of the three young men. He stood for so long in his long woollen underwear that Johnnie had complained, 'Well, git a move-on, George; that water takes a might of heating-up! It'll be stone-cold when it comes to Willum's turn.'

He had whipped off his undershirt, and drawers in double-quick time and leaped into the water. But they had noted his long and skinny frame, the pathetic whiteness of his skin. He saw them gazing, pityingly, at one another. As he dried himself before the fire, he watched surreptitiously as each suntanned muscular Vickery boy stripped-off and soaped his enviable torso

335

in the cooling water. Georgie had lain awake that night, more than ever convinced that, like his Papa, he, with his physique and his superior intellect, had never been intended to be wasted on a farming way of life.

His thoughts returned to the task before him. Since provision of firewood was to be in his sole charge, some means must be found to protect his hands.

It was at lunchtime, when even Mama was forced to halt and catch her breath, that Georgie crept back to the Vickery farmhouse. He opened up the trunk that held his souvenirs of Papa. Underneath the waistcoats and cravats lay a pair of chamois gloves, soft and supple and bright yellow in colour. He wadded a clean white handkerchief in each palm and pulled on the gloves. With both hands pushed into the pockets of his mackinaw he went back to do his afternoon stint beside the woodpile.

When work on the house was finished for that day, Georgie held out his raw and bleeding palms, expecting sympathy at least. But Mama, weary from hours spent scouring and waxing said briefly: 'Bathe them in salt water. When the blisters are healed rub alum on your hands to harden the skin. You'll need a few callouses, George, before we get into the Haysel and harvesting.'

It was Rosa who wept on to his ruined palms, who smoothed on salve and bound him up with clean rags; who said how unkind it was of Mama to expect him to split logs all day long. At the supper-table the Vickery family maintained a diplomatic silence over his clumsy handling of spoon and fork. But he could read the thoughts of Chas and Willum, and the poker-featured Johnnie. Their hands, he noted, were broad and red-brown, with broken fingernails, and seamed with old scars. Rosa had said that George's hands were just like Papa's; strong and long-fingered, but delicate and skilful, meant to handle a skinning-knife, never a wood-axe.

The ground floor rooms had been the first to know the Salters' scrubbing-brush and floor-wax. Old Mr Lutz had lived and

336

slept, and probably, thought Rosa, also died in the spacious farm kitchen. Mama now ventured up the dusty staircase and threw open doors on to second-storey rooms long unused. Beneath the cobwebs and grime of thirty years accumulation stood handsome walnut highboys and clothes closets. With the help of Aunt Elizabeth, and a few neighbouring farm wives, who were intrigued by the newcomer's courage and zeal, the rotting drapes were torn down from the windows and burned, along with ancient mattresses and bedclothes. When the final floor was waxed, the last windowpane polished, Rosa had to admit, and so did Georgie, that what emerged was a comfortable and pleasant home. The old Lutz furniture, once cleaned, fitted nicely with the new things brought by Mama from Green Bay. They no longer boasted the elegance of yellow brocade, but must settle for a dimity-and-gingham style of homespun fashion. But as Mama said, this was to be a working farmhouse.

Moving-in day found Georgie grim-faced and silent, and wielding the axe beside the wood-stack; the yellow chamois gloves still on his hands. His blisters were healing but his pride still smarted. Every day spent in Suamico found out some lack in him, yet further tasks to which he was ill-suited. It was time to cut down the community Christmas tree. At Mama's insistence he had gone with his cousins into deep woods. They had taken the Vickery sleigh; Willum had pointed out to him the spoor of rabbit and wolf and black bear. Several sons of neighbouring farmers had come with them; they were a merry crew, joshing and laughing as they went from tree to tree, seeking the finest and best-shaped.

It was when they had found the branchiest tree that the trouble started. The village boys had grinned at one another. A smiling blond giant name of Christian Olsen had suggested that the newcomer amongst them should be allowed the honour of the 'first cut'. Georgie looked around the watching circle. He took up the axe with bare hands and got set to swing it. But long before axe could connect with fir trunk Christian Olsen said

'Hey, George boy! Ain't you missin' something? There's

word goin' about as how you can't do a single hand's-turn, without you're kitted up in them fancy yellow gloves?'

Georgie felt his colour rise. He delivered one mighty swipe at the tree, only to find the axe too deeply embedded for his retrieval of it. It was Willum and Chas who came to his aid. Chas, with one pull, released the axe. Willum growled to Christian: 'Leave him be, you hear me, Olsen! He's but lately come out of Chicago. You can't expect much of him, yet.'

Christmas in Suamico was a time of celebration, when the hardworked community set aside their anxieties and came together, in the school-room, and in one another's homes. The Salters did not, in the end, give the party they had planned for. Mama, all worn out from her efforts in the Lutz house, was happy, after all, to accept her sister's invitation that Vickerys and Salters should stay together until New Year.

The trouble with farming, Georgie thought, was the way a man could never quite catch up. Long before one skill had been mastered, some ox or cow, some freak of weather, would call for abilities he did not have. A house-cow had been purchased. A golden opportunity, Mama had said, since Bertha was a docile creature, for Georgie to learn the dairy side of farming. But the cow, until now accustomed only to women's fingers, took affront at Georgie's handling of her. A score of times he sat down on the milking stool, only to land, bucket on his head, in a far corner of the byre. In the end it was Rosa's sensitive and long 'piano fingers' which coaxed milk from the prejudiced Bertha.

Georgie tried not to argue with his mother; she looked so pale and fine-drawn, seemed never to let-up on planning for the future. This restlessness, said Rosa, was all to do with losing Ed and Papa. Widowhood, his sister told him, affected women in various ways, and took an awful lot of getting-over. Well, he too missed Papa and Ed. Without them he felt exposed and raw, as if a vital limb had been torn from him. The leaving of Chicago, the lake-trip to Green Bay, had diverted him from

338

grief; but here in this place of endless snows and terrifying forests, denied the occupation at which he was already skilled, he would sometimes when alone still break down and weep, only to find that, in Suamico, even warm tears froze upon his face.

The days of winter passed for Georgie in a misery of aching muscles and failed endeavours. He simply could not get the hang of farmwork. Shingles, nailed by him on to leaking roofs, slithered earthwards when the next storm hit. Tools had a way of turning awkward in his grasp. Creatures, without exception, viewed him with distrust; almost, giggled Rosa, as if they knew that by profession he was a slaughterman and butcher.

Life in the northwoods was ruled by the seasons. Every month brought its own harvest, and every harvest called for celebration. In March the sap began to run in the sugar-maple trees. The grove of maples stood north-west of the village. Georgie rode there with his uncle and cousins in the Vickery bob-sleigh. This territory, tapped each year by the Vickery family and Matthew Black, was extended now to include the Salters. Georgie learned how to bore a hole, using a T-handled auger; with the help of Matthew he fitted the staghorn sumac spouts into the holes, set up his buckets, and watched the slow drip of the sap. There was, Matthew told him, only two-inches depth of sapwood on a maple tree. Sap would not run in mild weather. The best time for sugaring was when the nights froze hard, and the thaw came in the daytime; when the snow still lay deep upon the ground, and the wind blew from the west.

The maple groves covered many acres; a score of families came to tap adjacent trees and build the fires over which the pans of sap were boiled down into syrup. This was the time when the young folk came together. Rosa found this first trip into the woods a picturesque and exciting occasion. She had come with the Peterson family and their seven daughters.

Signa Peterson, at the age of sixteen, found the girl from Chicago stylish and fascinating; as for Georgie, she thought him the most elegantly handsome boy ever to set foot in the State of Wisconsin. She confessed as much to Rosa.

339

Rosa watched her brother plod from trees to fire, the heavy sap buckets yoked across his shoulders. She saw the grim set of his face and guessed at his determination to show no sign of flagging before the other men.

The best part of sugaring was the time of testing. A measure of boiling syrup was poured on to fresh snow. If it hardened right away into a sheet of candy it was considered ready. Signa stood with Rosa and George for the first sampling of the Vickerys' syrup; she broke off a piece of the brittle taffy and handed it to George. It was, had he but known it, a gesture which held, between girls and boys, a certain romantic declaration.

Signa waited while George crunched and tasted. At last he smiled at her.

'Now that,' he said, 'is real good candy. Best I ever tasted.'

Jon sang the tuneless little song which meant that he was happy.

The snows had gone, the sun shone in a blue sky. He liked the house and farm, where every day brought new delights. He wished that Ed and Pa would come to join them, but Chicago was harder to remember with every week that passed. Jon knew that he was not like other boys. The children on Green Street had pelted him with stones and called him 'dummy'. Ed and Georgie were always getting into fights on Jon's account. Here, in the new place, people spoke directly to him, instead of muttering to Mama above his head. They said: 'Well hi-ya, Jon boy! How're ya doin' then? Why, you sure are gettin' to be a real smart farmer!'

It was true. In some way, which nobody could comprehend, Jon was a whole lot smarter in the country. He never forgot to close gates or fasten shed doors. For the first time in his life he was trusted by Mama to do chores that were all his own. He had not suffered a single 'falling-down-spell' since their arrival in Suamico. There was still a heap of things he did not understand, but no one got impatient with him. Uncle Robert had made him a box-on-wheels so that he could haul split logs into the fire-box. Matthew had brought a huge black bearskin to set before the fireplace. Jon loved to lie on the soft fur and watch the sparks from the hickory wood fly up the chimney. It was Matthew who showed him how to lift the baby chickens so as not to hurt them, and how best to tilt the bucket when he fed the calves. His cousin Willum had shown him how to carry eggs in safety; had put a twist of hay into Jon's woolly cap and laid the eggs inside it. The hens and their chicks were now his especial chore.

Strange feelings stirred in Jon at the sight of the flowers and the green grass. He no longer felt 'different'. He was, so Mama said, much brighter when it came to farm-chores than his brother Georgie.

Rhoda walked in her fields on a morning in late April; she paused where the thin sweet clover blades pushed green and strong from damp earth. Together she and Georgie had ploughed and harrowed, and seeded a meadow. She had taught him about oxen; how to walk on the left side, the whip in his right hand. Since the mouths of oxen were too narrow to take bit or reins the only method of control was by shouted orders. '*Gee*,' called for a right turn, '*Haw*,' for a left. The whip, she told Georgie, was to be used only as a touch upon the neck, since a thrashed ox became stubborn and inclined to bolt. They were patient creatures, slow but very strong; it was, she reflected, that slowness and patience which angered Georgie. Her son's temperament, all his inclination, was towards the swift deal in business, the fast-turning of a dollar. To wait for the ripening of crops, the growth of a meadow, simply was not in him.

She turned to look back towards the house in which she fitted as if it were some familiar place to which she had now returned. She would stand sometimes before the great stone fireplace and recall the inglenook at Patchwood. When needing reassurance her hand would seek the grain of wood; she stroked the hand-hewn beams and lintels which supported the corners of the house and remembered William, her father.

On this April morning Rhoda stood beside the growing clover and thought of the fields still lying fallow, the work that

341

needed a strong man's arm. She offered up a prayer that George, her son, might have sufficient Greypaull blood to keep him at her side and farming. A further ninety acres lay adjacent to her own land, only waiting to be taken up. A parcel of ground, the Indentures made out to the name of George Hodder Salter, might be the incentive to stay which Georgie needed.

Nine years had passed since that day in Tennessee when Jim Black had picked up his severance pay, had the order of release stamped in his Army Paybook, and begun the long trek north-wards. They had been quiet years. He and Matt had bought more land and tilled it. Jim believed himself content with the way his life had fallen out – until the arrival in Suamico of Rhoda Salter and her children.

Their coming had coincided with his departure for the pineries which lay beyond the banks of the Fox river. The introductions had been brief but he carried with him the memory of a small, delicately-featured woman, her demeanor that of sorrow, staunchly borne. In the short days and long nights lived in the lumbering camp, Jim caught himself thinking often about Rhoda. He had heard her story from Elizabeth. How sharply she had called him to order when his speech did not suit her. He grinned at the recollection. Well, he liked a woman with a touch of salt on her tongue. He could not see her as a farmer. It would take more than her stiff-necked English pride and cussedness to set right the years of old man Lutz's neglect; and yet he could not put her from his mind.

The supper invitation came soon after his return from the logging-camp.

'Guess we'd better spruce-up a bit,' said Matt. 'I reckon Mrs Salter is used to men of some refinement. Her husband must have been some dapper dresser if young George is anything to judge by.'

Matt dragged a rusty flat-iron from a cupboard. He put a knife crease in their Sunday trousers, and pressed the only two checkered shirts that still held a full set of buttons. They took turns at clipping short each other's hair and beard. They cleaned the soil from their fingernails and boots and walked the short stretch of road which brought them to the Lutz place.

Matt had mentioned changes, but his vague hints had not prepared Jim for the wide-board polished floors, the charm of flower-sprigged drapes and cushions, the rose-shaded oil-lamps. A shelf of coloured-glass and silver trinkets reflected the fire's glow; a Wall of Honour held family portraits, and a coloured engravement of Queen Victoria of England and her Consort, with their nine children. His time with the Army and in logging-camps, his years of batching-it with his brother, had accustomed Jim to the use of tin-plates and mugs. The finest of Suamico's housewives could not better the display of linen cloth, dainty china, and polished cutlery on Mrs Salter's table. There was even a centrepiece-vase of wildflowers. Odours drifted from the kitchen. He identified fresh bread, roast beef and spiced apples.

When the meal was ended he said: 'Why, Mrs Salter, ma'am, I never had such a fine feast since I left my mother's table.'

His hostess smiled: 'A compliment indeed, Captain Black!'

The table was cleared and the company gathered at the fireside. Jim and Matthew requested permission to smoke and had it granted. Jim relaxed against the rare luxury of cushions. He drew deep on his cigar, his mood became expansive.

'Must congratulate you, Mrs Salter, ma'am, on the way you've done-up this old house. Why, I guess it never looked this good when Mrs Lutz first came in here as a bride.'

He paused.

'Don't do for a newcomer to make too many changes though. It's all right to straighten-up a house; well, after all, that's women's business. I was taking a look at your fields just yesterday. I see you've put a whole thirty acres down to clover.' He leaned forward, the half-smoked cigar a pointer in his hand. 'Now why?' he asked. 'Why ever would you want to do a thing like that?'

'Because,' said Rhoda quietly, 'clover is what cows like best, Captain Black. What is more, it ensures a high yield of milk.'

'But now surely – that's a powerful lot of grass for one old house-cow?'

'But not for a herd, sir! Thirty acres will go nowhere for a herd. I already have an option on an adjacent ninety acres which I shall also seed to pasture.' Her tone remained soft but even as she spoke Rhoda's spine grew stiff, her colour heightened.

Jim Black, unused to talking business with a woman, failed to observe the danger signals. 'But, ma'am,' he continued, 'this is grain-growing country. Most folks round abouts put down corn and barley, oats and rye.'

'And when your crops fail?'

'Well – well, we tighten our belts a notch or two, that's what we do!'

'I have no intention of tightening my belt, Captain! As a girl I was skilled in cheese and buttermaking. The county of Somerset is the dairyland of Old England, and dairywork is the proper province of a woman.'

Matt said: 'Reckon she's got you beat with that, Jim.'

Jim stared at his brother. 'You too, huh? Well, I never thought to hear you speak up in favour of cows.' He turned back to Rhoda. 'Our Pa was a grain-man. The cornfields in Ontario stretch for hundreds of miles. Cows is a long-term proposition. Takes years before you see a decent profit from 'em.'

'Oh, I have time, sir. I don't go in much for your Yankee hustle. You see,' said Rhoda, 'since the day I set foot in this land of America my ambition has been to own a good herd. I have already waited eighteen years.'

'A herd you say?' Jim abandoned his cigar-butt to the heart of the fire. 'How big do you reckon a herd is in Old England?'

'Twenty cows, with followers, of course. I already have six calves. My Holsteins will be up here in a few more days.'

'*Holsteins?*' Jim was on his feet and pacing. 'Have you seen the size of them creatures? That's the biggest and heaviest breed of cow in all creation!'

'And exceptional milkers, Captain.' Rhoda smiled sweetly at him. 'Oh, they are large and tall, I grant you that. They are also late-maturing. When their useful dairy-life is over I shall still be left with a valuable animal suitable for slaughter. Let me tell

344

you about Holsteins, sir. The very first herd in the USA was kept by a man called Winthrop Chenery of Massachusetts. In 1852 he purchased a cow that had come from Holland on a Dutch ship. This cow had provided fresh milk for the sailors. Mr Chenery knew a good thing when he saw it!'

Jim returned to his chair. A silence fell and lengthened. Georgie grinned and ate an apple. Rosa clutched at her embroidery and looked apprehensive.

Matthew sent warning glances to his brother. He said: 'You just should have been here, Jim, when Mrs Salter started in on the ploughing of them thirty acres. Why, them old oxen fair done anything she wanted of 'em.' He turned to Georgie. 'And George here, he done real fine at handling the ploughshare. Worked from sun-up to twilight they did! I never saw a better team.'

Georgie said: 'You helped us, Matt. You and Uncle Robert. Times we got stuck in that mud, we'd be in there yet if you hadn't come to free us.'

Jim breathed deeply. He said, 'Now, you see, ma'am. It's like this. Ladies and cows just don't go together. There's a side to dairying what's not nice for the eyes of a womanly woman,' he paused, 'and you, ma'am, if I may say so, are of the female gender.'

Rhoda stood, abruptly. 'That,' she said, 'is the only true remark you have made all evening, and as a person of the female gender I will bid you good-night, Captain Black. This supper was intended for a thank you to your brother for all his great help. I am sorry that my plans are not to your taste. I hope that your arguing will not give you indigestion.'

★

May 15, 1875

The time has come for proper Ledger-keeping. I make a list of all moneys spent in the purchase and fitting-up of the Salter farmstead. Think I may have been ambishus in my figure of twenty dairy cows. Have decided that eight will do to be going-on with. Went this day with Robert to Flintville, to view the herd of Mr Oswald Lundgren, what is very fine. Took note of the cowbarn, its style and fitments. Asked him many qwestions about the Holstein breed and was much pleased at all the answers. Settled on a figure agreeable to us both. Eight first-year milkers to be brought to me by Mr Lundgren and his son on May twenty-eighth.

Walked last evening in my fields. Matthew comes to join me. I decide that the four acres of long grass will go down to hay, tho' it is not of a qwality to give good fodder. All my land much neglected, but must needs do the best I can with what lies to hand. Talk with Matthew about Haysel, and learn that the word in Wisconsin is rather Haying. Other matters also explained to me by him what I find less easy to digest.

'You must understand,' says he, 'that my brother was an officer with Abe Lincoln's Army. He was used to giving commands and having them obeyed. He is also foreman-lumberman for Mr Tremble at the Mill. Jim has upwards of a hundred men under his control each winter, and most of them lumberjack boys is mighty wilful.'

Matthew gives me a sidelong glance.

'Jim don't mean you any disrespect when he speaks up kinda sharp. It's just his way. Why, he's full of good words for you! Said he never saw such a brave little woman in all his days!'

'Indeed!' say I. 'Now thank you, Matthew, for explaining matters to me. I can see how your brother has fallen into habits of command. But,' I speak softly because he is a gentle soul, 'I am not in Captain Black's platoon, neither am I a lumberjack. I am but a widow who is doing the best she can for her fatherless children. I also know my own mind. It may be as well if you explain *that* to your brother.'

May 18
My oats and barley showing well, tho' Robert did advise me to put down more grain. Must hope now for a heavy crop and a dry August, lest the menfolk roundabouts have the laugh of me!

May 20

Elizabeth and I visit every day with one another. Already we
are grown closer than in our young years in England. I talk to
her of the times in Charlotte when I first came to this land. We
speak of Susanna, and I venture to tell her that I feel George and
Eddie to be now in Heaven, reunited with our dear cousin and
the baby who died young of fever. They are, say I, a family
again, all together, and happy. Elizabeth does not find my
thought a strange one tho' she observes that I am a generous
soul. I say, not generous; I still have my three children, and the
farm I always longed for. I may live for many years yet; it is as
well if I am contented.

Truth to tell, my frame of mind grows more tranquil lately,
and tho' the sorrows of past years never altogether fade, hard
work is a powerful pacifier for an ankshus nature such as mine.
I now sleep long and deep, and only Jon's cry in the night can
rouse me. Sometimes I dream of George and wake with tears
upon my face. Such dreams come unbidden, and there is
nothing I can do about it. I see him young and eager, his colour
fresh, the curls blue-black upon his forehead. In the dream I
look to him for approval of all I am doing. I tell him it is for
the good that we are here; that farming is the business I know
best, that I will not be profligate with his hard-won dollars. He
will know that I am with my dearest Elizabeth, and good kind
Robert. Surely George will remember how I could never bear
to be too long alone?

May 25

The girls come around to look for Georgie on these warm May
evenings. They come, three and four together; they say it is
Rosa whom they seek, but their glances are all for my handsome
boy! There is a blonde-haired, pink-cheeked one name of Signa.
She manages to sit beside him on the front-porch. Seeing them
together, tho' they are but children, I am reminded of Eddie
and his Annaliese, and how cruelly short was his young life.

Matthew comes most evenings. I make junket for him and
milky puddings, what is soothing to his damaged stomach. I

347

suspect that his use of the frying-pan is as much to blame for the state of his health as are the Confederate bullets. Elizabeth jokes that the care of delicate men seems to be my espeshul talent.

May 27
Matthew has a way of instructing Georgie in farming matters that does not hurt the pride of my city-bred son. Today we have made all ready for the Holsteins, and agreed on our separate labours. Rosa and I are to do the milking, and dairy work. Georgie will attend to the feeding, and the cleaning of the barn. It is better that Matthew should put him in the way of things. Such orders do not pass comfortable between mother and son.

Was down to look at the clover-field late this evening. Met Captain Black, whose cornfield stands adjacent. How different in every way are these two brothers. Matthew has the grey-streaked hair and tired face of one who suffers pain. He is thin and walks with a stooped gait. Jim Black is a fine, well-set-up figure of a man, with straight black hair brushed back from his forehead. He is ruddy-complected and strong of feature. The only sign of softness in him is the twinkle in his brown eyes, what is reserved totally for Jon.

He views my clover with a long look but says nothing. I suspect he is no judge of meadowland.

'So tomorrow is the big day, eh, ma'am?'

He is jocular, but I am not.

'If you speak of my Holsteins, Captain, then you are right.'

He grins. 'Matt tells me only eight of the Dutch ladies are expected. I had thought you talked about a herd of twenty?'

I say, as if the mistake is all on his part, 'Oh no, sir! Be reasonable now! However could a frail woman and two city-raised children manage properly a herd of twenty? In time,' say I, 'twenty is the number I should hope for. But that will mean taking on a hired man, and hired men expect their food and wages!'

'Ah,' he says. 'Well, I am glad to see you are not as headstrong as you first seemed. You may in time come to see the folly of putting good grain land down to meadow.'

I stand four-square before him. My anger well-nigh chokes me.

'Captain Black,' I say, 'go home and shave that nasty beard off! It truly does not suit you!'

May 28
My Holsteins are come!

If what I have been told of them is true, then I have chosen wisely. They are said to be a breed of vigorous constitushun, their milk being suitable for both cheese and butter-making; that butter standing-up well against the heat, and so good for long-keeping.

Cannot bring myself to qwit the barn this evening, but stand looking long at my purchase. The journey here has not upset them; they feed contented in the stalls. Spoke at length with Mr Lundgren who says the herd is well-broke in to grazing grass, and so may be turned out each day with no ill-effects.

My dairy scrubbed and ready for the morning's work; the furnishings left by Mr Lutz, once scoured and polished, being qwite suitable for my use. I set out skimmers and quart-pans, scoops and pails. I reflect that dairy work is much the same the whole world over. I close my eyes and smell the sweet warmth of the barn, there is the rustle of straw beneath the cows' hooves, and I am full of a contentment I cannot explain. I lay ready two clean burlap aprons, and put a pile of udder-cloths beside them. These actshuns bring Susanna back so clear into my mind that I can see her as she was on that long-ago evening in the barn at Dommett, when we resolved to leave my father's rooftree. I ponder for a long time on the conseqwences of that evening talk. How that first brave move led us on to make others. It could, I think, be said that on that night was made the first step which brought us to this country of America. I go back into the house. I find the trunk shipped long ago from England; in it is the elmwood milking-stool with the letter R writ upon it. I take the stool and place it in the barn beside the hay-forks; it looks to be at home, as if, like me, it had waited long to be in this cow-barn, in Suamico, Wisconsin.

349

June 28

Our few acres of poor old grass, laid down years ago, is hardly worth the mowing, and soon put-up inside the barn. Now our turn is come to pay back our neighbours for all their help. We three go every day, after milking, to other homesteads. My children now learn what it is to labour long underneath the sun. I expect complaints, but instead I see them romp and laugh with the Petersen girls and Erdmans' boys. They are weary at the day's end, but each farm wife provides a feast for all the helpers. We make many new friends.

July 14

A few qwiet weeks before the start of harvest. I have but fifteen acres down to corn and oats. Six weeks are passed since the arrival of my Holsteins. On our Haying visits to other farms I learn much about the butter market. Had already heard from Elizabeth how butter here is classed as being either 'gilt-edged' or 'grease', the latter selling at only a few cents per pound. I am at work in the dairy when Jim Black comes across to beg the services of Georgie for an hour or two, since Matthew is suffering much stomach pain and cannot leave the house.

'You will find my son in the clover meadow,' say I. 'He is setting up fresh salt-licks for the herd.'

'Ah yes, ma'am, and how are the Dutch ladies settling in?'

I am skimming cream and need a steady hand. I say, 'Very well,' and pretend not to notice the wide grin on his face. 'And now,' I continue, 'I have much to do, so if you will excuse me?'

He pays me no mind, but stands in the doorway. 'Whatever,' he asks, 'are you aiming to do with all that butter? The storekeeper won't pay you in hard cash, he'll take what you bring him in exchange for groceries, and tell you he's only being accommodating – which he is! He'll be lucky if the travelling butter-buyer pays him six cents on the pound-weight. Summer butter in these parts is mostly only grease, and the agent don't expect it to be otherwise.'

I lay down the skimmer the better to outface him.

'Captain Black,' I say, 'do I look to you like a woman who is fool enough to invest in a farm, spend good dollars on a valuable herd, lay most of her arable land down to grazing – and then sell her butter at six cents on the pound, or in exchange for groceries? I am fortunate to have a deep well on my land, and a fresh cold spring of water. I have placed an order with Mr Erdman, the cooper, for one hundred firkins, and warned him not to make them out of basswood, which, I am told, gives off a strong scent, so ruining the butter. My product will be of the gilt-edged sort. I intend to sell at thirty cents the pound. Hard cash. In Green Bay.'

He stares at me as if I have grown an extra head.

He says at last: 'Well, is that a fact now?'

He leaves without a word of farewell. I see him walk slowly out towards the clover meadow where my Holsteins graze in sweet contentment. He pauses once to fill his tobacco-pipe and light it. I have given Captain Black a lot to think upon!

August 12

The weather fine and hot. We are in to harvest-time, and, oh, how good it is to see those words writ on this page. My crops are first to be cut. Captain Black and Matthew come to help us. The Captain mows well, he cuts a wide swathe and never wearies. My place is to come behind him, gathering up the sheaves and binding them. I suspect he deliberately sets up a fast rate so as to outpace me. By milking-time my back is aching fit to break, but all my oats and corn sheaved and stooked.

August 18

The weather holds. Today, with the help of Robert and Elizabeth we carry in my sheaves and stack them in the barn.

It is a very big barn what makes my stack look all the smaller. I see now that I have miscalculated. I admit as much to Robert. 'I should have heeded your words. It will not be enough to see us through the winter.'

Robert says: 'It's a heavy crop. It'll thresh well. But you may have to buy in feed if the winter is a long one. Another ten acres put down to corn would have made all the difference.'

351

'Oh, I know it. Next spring I'll be guided by you. Ah well,' I say, 'my mistake will serve to amuse your military friend. He waits every day to see me bankrupt.'

Robert sends me a long look, so that I am almost discomfited.

He says: 'I think you misjudge him, Rhoda. He is concerned about you. I guess he's not always over-diplomatic in his way of speaking, but you must remember that Jim's always lived in a man's world. He's just not used to womenfolk's ways.'

'Espeshully,' I say, 'to a woman like me who is farming in her own right, and seeds clover instead of corn?'

The corners of Robert's lips begin to twitch. 'And one who speaks up on a subject where only men do the deciding. Oh, my goodness, Rhoda! You've surely got poor Jim Black all confused.'

Robert goes away in a good humour.

I begin the evening milking qwite out of temper. 'I am,' I say to Rosa, 'growing weary of hearing the men in this place praise that know-it-all Captain Black, and make excuses for him!'

September 14

I need pigs! I menshun as much to Robert who says that Jim Black is to go to a Hog-Fair on Friday, and why don't I go with him? Since my need is urjent I have but small choice.

September 19

Am this day to a Hog-Fair with Captain Black. Leave my Georgie in sole charge of all things, give him many instructshuns, and offer up a prayer! The Captain is to take me to a farm in Flintville. We set off straight after milking, riding on a shabby cart what has no springing. He has put on a clean shirt, and trimmed his beard. He looks tolerably tidy. His first words are:

'Why hogs, ma'am?'

Well, what else do I expect of this man?

I say slowly, as I would to Georgie or Rosa:

'You may know, sir, that in the making of butter there is a liqwid left over. It is called buttermilk.'

352

He glowers at me. 'Why of course I know that! My Ma made butter for the house on our spread in Kingston.'

'I have a surplus of buttermilk, and, because I cannot abide waste, I intend to use it up on fattening weaners.'

His silence lasts for at least a mile. Then he says: 'Cows milking-down well, then?'

'Very well.'

He flicks-up the reins although we are going at a fast pace.

'Guess I have to say thank you for that butter you sent over. Best I ever tasted in my whole life. I'd kinda got used to that axle-grease what Matt churns up.'

He turns to me and smiles.

'Reckon you're spoiling us old batchelors, ma'am.'

He is not a smiling man, leastways never in *my* presence. I am disarmed so far as to say: 'Then Matthew need churn no more. It would please me to keep you going in butter. After all, it is small enough return for all you do for me.'

I glance sideways from beneath my bonnet-brim, and am astonished to see a red colour creep underneath his sunburn. A few soft words have done what my sharp ones never could! He keeps his gaze fixed straight ahead.

As we come into Flintville he says: 'Could well be that you and me got off on the wrong foot, Mrs Salter. But you must understand that I never before met up with a – a lady farmer. 'Specially one what talks nice English, and then goes and takes her turn a-walking behind the plough and stooking sheaves.'

He shakes his head and continues complaining. 'I got used to your sister a long time ago. But Elizabeth ain't the farmer in that family; Robert is the boss-man. Now you, ma'am, you got me fair puzzled. I never met a woman like you. I fear you'll hear a deal of strong language at this Pig-Fair.'

He is still grumbling as we come into Flintville.

The sale is held on what seems to be a fairground. There are the waggons of the patent-medicine sellers, the hawkers of baskets and pots and pans. There are a few Indians with their squaws, who have lace for sale and leather belts and bootlaces. There is a stand where doughnuts and coffee may be bought,

353

and I am reminded of Chicago. The memory halts me. I stand qwiet in all the uproar of shouting farmers, and it is as if George stood beside me. I recall the disaster to our fortunes suffered through hogs, long ago in Charlotte. I seem to hear George say: 'Be advised, Rhoda. Let this good man guide you in your purchase!' I turn, half-believing my husband to be standing at my shoulder, but it is Jim Black, bearing coffee for us both.

We walk between the rows of farmcarts in which litters of small pigs are netted-down. We go around the pens what hold boars and sows of qweer breeds and strange looks, such as I have never seen. I look up at Captain Black. I say: 'It is very confusing. I am at home among cows, but pigs were in the charge of my brothers, in my home in Old England. I will have to rely on your choice, I am afraid, sir.'

He is only too happy to oblige me.

We find a farmer who stands beside a pen of ten healthy looking creatures. The Captain enqwires (from behind his hand, and softly) if the male pigs have been 'cut'. The owner whispers back, after one glance in my direction, 'Yes.' I speak up loud and clear. I say: 'There is no need to mutter, gentlemen. I am qwite familiar with the term. In England we call it castration. As a matter of fact, I was about to make the same enqwiry myself.'

The deal, after some haggling on my part, is settled to the satisfactshun of us all. My hogs are loaded-up, and we are home in time for evening milking.

October 12
Two weeks of sadness, when all my thoughts begin – this time last year I lost George – two years since and Eddie left us. I relive those days and nights of sorrow, and there is no help for it. Grief must be gone through. Georgie and Rosa also re-member. On those speshul days we pray together. Oh, how glad I am to be here with Elizabeth and Robert.

It is autumn, but this time a fall of such beauty as I have never witnessed. People say the frosts are late this year. The trees hold all their leaves still, and look to be aflame. Wisconsin

354

is so beautiful. It catches at the heart and brings a lump into the throat. There is such a purity of light, the air like wine, the earth so rich. It is almost a year since we arrived here.

I count my blessings. Jon stayed well, even in the summer. He suffered no more than three seizures, and them only short ones. He learns new words. He favours the company of Captain Black who is very *good* with Jon.

Am forced to sell my butter to the travelling agent who pays me twenty-five cents on the pound-weight, tho' I know it is worth thirty cents, and more! He declares each firkin to be a gilt-edged product, and the finest he has tasted. He views the arrangement of my dairy and spring house. He asks why do I not join the Wisconsin Dairyman's Associashun what is lately started-up.

I say: 'They might not want a woman in their ranks.'

He says that dairying is on the increase in Wisconsin and my place a model for any man to follow.

Am gratified tho' still feel cheated by him. Would have done better in the Green Bay market, I suspect, but all the men now into winter ploughing and no time to spare for jaunts into the City.

Have seen nothing of Captain Black since our purchase of my weaners. Matthew agrees with me that my cows all safe in-calf, and hogs fattening well towards the Christmas market.

November 20
The winter is upon us. Our first snow fell this morning and it is pretty as a picture; tho' I shall doubtless change my mind on this before the week is out.

Matthew very sick. He cannot leave his bed for weakness. Captain Black shows much tenderness in the way he nurses his brother. He has put off leaving for the pineries, and cannot say when, or if he will go at all. He consults with me daily upon Matthew's condishun. I cook all food for both men. The Captain follows my advice in the care of our paishunt. In fact, he agrees wholeheartedly with me in all that is to do with Matthew's health and care; what is just as well since we are at odds with one another on most other matters.

355

November 27

Snow falls each day and we are hard put to keep open the road between Elizabeth and us. Captain Black hauls up a cord of firewood, and George kept busy, sawing and chopping. I congratulate my boy on the toughness of his hands and muscles. He grows skilled about the yard and barn work. In past months he has learned to pitch hay and sheaves, to plough a straight furrow, to swing the flail. Rosa helps me with milking and about the dairy. She is turning out to be a fine little cook. Jon does his chores among the chickens in the most *faithful* fashun. Captain Black set several clutches of eggs, and now Jon raises ducklings and goslings, what makes him very *pleased*.

Oh, how proud I am of my three good children!

December 1

I make soup and take it in a jar to Matthew, along with milky pudding in a large dish, and some boiled chicken. Rosa comes with me to the Black farm. We find our poor friend much improved. He is out of bed and sat by the fire, wrapped in a red blanket. Captain Black is working in his barn, but at sight of us he leaves his chores and comes into the house. He bids us sit beside the fire while he makes tea. Rosa talks with Matthew. I straighten Matthew's bed and tidy around. When the tea is brewed we all sit down together.

The doctor, we hear, is pleased with our paishunt, but says great care is needed now so that he does not take a chill in his weak state. Captain Black says that he will not leave Matt on his own until the warmer weather, what I am very glad to hear! We fall to talking about spring-time, what brings us to the old vexed subject of crops, versus cows.

'What,' asks the Captain, 'do you think is the advantage of dairying over grain-raising? If indeed there is any gain to be had, ma'am?'

'If you speak of a margin of profit,' say I, 'then in dollars they will both foot-up more or less the same, any difference coming out in favour of the dairy. But think about the climate of this land! There is bitter cold, and long drought in some years. Then there are wet springs, and great storms. I have spoken with Robert on this matter. He says on average his crops fail once in every four years. Did you ever,' I enqwire 'hear of the failure of a clover-meadow? Grass will still grow, sir, no matter how low the temperature.'

He makes me no answer.

'Then,' I go on, 'there is the glutting of the markets, when grain will sell for less than it has cost to grow. Cows keep their value. The price of cheese and butter varies but little be it of good qwality; and those two items are always in demand.'

'But cows,' says Captain Black, 'are a great tie. There's milking, morning and evening, not to menshun feeding and cleaning of 'em. Then there's the dairywork. Now that surely is the *only* task in farming what keeps a man housebound every day in the year?'

I say: 'But of course, sir! But then – I never knew a dairyman to be footloose or restless!'

The man looks troubled. He asks my permishun to smoke a pipeful of tobacco, and I grant it. I see that I have the advantage of him.

I say: 'There is something else, and it is a qwestion that you American farmers would do well to ponder upon. Soon you will reach a day when your good soil is exhausted. For years you have taken-out and put nothing back. When you next step across to my place, Captain Black, cast your eye over my manure-heap! It grows bigger by the hour, as my Georgie, who cleans the cowbarn, will bear witness. We shall be busy, come April, fertilising our poor fields. The job is known as dung-spreading in Old England.'

He looks at me in an annoying fashun. He says in a laughing way: 'I reckon, Mrs Salter, that our two farms would work better if we joined forces. I'll raise the crops – and you make the butter!'

He leans forward, knocks his pipe out on the stove.

'What say you to a partnership between us?'

I am dumbstruck.

I begin to hunt about me for my shawl and purse. I feel the

heat rising in my face; it drains away and I am white with anger.

I say: 'You and I could never work together. We disagree on every subject.'

He stands up and takes a step towards me. I look up into his face, and all at once I know that we are no longer speaking about corn or cows, or a partnership of business. Now I remember the touch of his hand upon my arm as he guided me thru' the Pig-Fair; the way he helped me down from the waggon, his freqwent visits to my house. I gaze into his eyes and see what I should have known these many months past. Captain James Kerr Black has been courting me in the fashun of this land!

Chapter Twenty-three

December 7

The first blizzard of the winter strikes and we are isolated. Overnight, great drifts pile up around the house, covering the lower windows. I say to the children: 'We are on our own now. It is up to us to show that we can manage.'

They all speak up bravely, but I see that they are ankshus. Rosa brings all our thickest clothes into the kitchen. Georgie has had the forethought to bring shovels into the house so that we are eqwipped to dig our way out and to the cow barn.

I say to Jon: 'Better you bide in the warm kitchen. George will see to your chores.' But he runs to the place where his boots are kept. He pulls them on, and looks for his cap and mackinaw. His little face is streaked with tears.

'Jon come too,' he cries. 'Jon's chickens all dead!'

I see that there is nothing for it but to take him with us.

We are a long time shovelling our way out to the barn. By the time we reach them my poor Holsteins are in great discomfort. Rosa and I set to about the milking, while Jon contents himself that his preshus flock has survived the night. George feeds the hogs. He builds a fire, fills pans with snow and melts it so that we have water for the stock and dairy. He cleans the sheds, puts down fresh straw, cuts hay, chops wood and carries it back into the house. I say to Rosa: 'One year ago and he could hardly swing the axe. I am so proud of him, the way he buckles down just lately.'

She says: 'He is trying to show you something, Mama.'

'Show me what?'

'That *he* is all the man you will ever need about this farm.'

My girl bends her head towards the pan of milk; her hand is not qwite steady as she skims the cream.

'Why Rosa,' I cry, 'whatever do you mean?'

Her cheeks are flushed. 'Oh nothing! I just thought – perhaps Uncle Robert or Johnnie or Willum won't be able to get through to us.'

It is not what she meant and we both know it. I turn to find Georgie standing at my shoulder. He sets down two pails of water. He says: 'Have no fear, Mama! I guess your brave Captain friend will be shovelling his way over before the day is out, even if the drifts should stand at twenty feet.'

I wheel qwickly to outface him, but Georgie shows me such a sweet smile that there is nothing I can say.

December 9

Snow now lying four feet deep on level ground. Robert and his boys break through to us this forenoon, they being ankshus as to our situashun in this, our first taste of a farming winter in the northwoods. They are pleased to find us all safe and cheerful, our stock fed and watered and all in order. Robert says: 'You have a good son in George. It can't have been easy for him this past year, growing-up like he did in the city, knowing nothing about farm life.'

'Oh yes,' say I, 'I qwite rely on him these days. Whatever should I do without him!'

My brother-in-law looks me foursquare in the eyes. 'Maybe,' says he, 'you should not always be so dependent on your boy for help about the place. From what he says to Chas, young George would like to go on with his butchering apprenticeship. After all, it was what his poor father wanted for him.'

For no reason that comes to mind I feel a blush upon my face.

I say in some haste: 'I shall never hold him here if he is set on leaving! As you say, the butchering is his proper trade. I might hire a man to do the heavy chores.' We are standing on the stoop, the Vickery one-horse sleigh (which I am told is called a cutter hereabouts) stands waiting on the cleared path. Robert looks across to where a plume of smoke curls up from the chimney of the Black Farm.

'Now there,' says he, 'lives one of the finest men in this whole territory. A real good guy if ever I saw one! He sure does hold you in high regard, Rhoda!'

I am all at once nervous. I pull my shawl close about me. I have such a wish to change the subject of his thoughts.

I say in a high tone: 'Why Robert, how American your speech is become!'

He goes on as if I had not spoken. 'This blizzard is but the start of a hard long winter. You'd do well to think about your future, Rhoda! A woman alone has a tough life in these parts!'

He climbs into the cutter, his two sons beside him. They wave, and I wave back, my head in such confushon! I stand until the sound of sleigh bells fades away. I call out, too late: 'But I am not alone here, Robert,' and my cry is lost upon the wind. I turn back into the house. In the kitchen the children make ready to go out again into the bitter weather. They laugh and joke together, but there are dark marks about the eyes of Rosa and Georgie; I feel the droop of weariness in my own shoulders.

Jon says: 'How long snow stay, Mama?'

'Until April,' I tell him. As I speak a great loneliness comes upon me. Jim Black has not come thru' the drifts to see us. I recall our last meeting and am not too surprised!

December 20

Johnnie Vickery brings his mother over to us in the cutter. Never was the sound of sleigh-bells sweeter or more welcome. Elizabeth and I have much catching up to do. It is three whole weeks since last we were together. She remarks that I look weary, what is small wonder! She offers to send Willum to me to help out.

'It is such a kind thought,' say I, 'but my Georgie is so set on proving himself. He would be mortally hurt if Willum came here. He is touchy at present over any outside aid.'

Elizabeth looks troubled. She begins to talk of the three Englishmen who lately came to Suamico. Their house and barn, she says, was finished just before the deep snows fell, what is fortunate for them. 'Altho,' says my sister, 'there can be very little homeliness and comfort in a place where three men "bach" together. Mr Goodman,' she adds, 'is a poor-looking specimen and never likely to get wed. Mr Sutton, on the other hand, is qwite presentable while Mr Hopkins is downright handsome, having all his own teeth, and a full head of hair even tho' he is middle-aged.'

'Perhaps,' I say, 'they do not wish to get wed. In fact, it is my belief that if a man is still unmarried at the age of forty then he is a lost cause and best left by himself. Such men become set in their bachelor ways, they grow selfish and self-opiniated.'

Elizabeth gives me a keen look and begins to speak of other matters.

For some time past it would seem that Suamico folk have wished to build a church where the Episcopalians might worship in comfort. The women of the congregation have formed a society to raise money. Jim Black is their Treasurer. He himself, says Elizabeth, has already made a contribushun of five hundred dollars.

'He does not,' say I, 'give the impreshun of being so well-off.'

'Oh,' says Elizabeth, 'Jim is not the man for outside show. But remember, Rhoda, he is a foreman-logger. Such men command high wages in the lumber camps. When the season ends, Jim never goes on a drinking spree with the other "jacks" into Green Bay. He comes home straightaway to his farm, and saves his money.' She nods. 'Yes, yes! Jim Black is prudent. He is probably among the best-off of all the farmers hereabouts.'

'It is easy,' I say, 'for a non-drinking bachelor to hoard his gold. How else should he spend it? He certainly wastes little on clothing and home comforts!'

Elizabeth smiles. 'Perhaps he has never had the chance – yet? Perhaps he is longing to spoil some lucky woman?'

I make no answer.

My sister asks how long it is since I have done any qwilting. Not for some time, I tell her. She says what a pity, since I am qwick and skilful at the task.

'We had hoped,' she says, 'to hold a Qwilting Bee. A fine patchwork qwilt will fetch as much as fifty dollars. It would help a good deal towards the funds for our new church. But in weather such as this it will be months before a group of us can meet together. I hesitate to ask when you are so hard-pressed in the yard and dairy . . .?'

'But I would love to make a qwilt!' say I. 'It is a soothing occupashun on a winter's evening.' I point out our tablecloth and cushions. 'These are all the work of Rosa. As you know, I learned plain qwilting in England. But Rosa is very skilled in the American fashun of patchwork.'

My sister says: 'I have a customer in mind, Rhoda. One who will pay a good price for a fine qwilt.'

I laugh. 'Do not tell me who it is. The Suamico ladies are such skilled needlewomen. To know her name would make me nervous.'

Rosa comes into the room and we tell her of the project. She runs to find our scraps bag. We spend a happy hour sorting thru' the pieces.

December 22

The dairy work is long and hard in these low temperatures, but a log barn cosier than I would have once believed. How interested my father would have been in this American way of building. My Holsteins seem content; they still milk-down at a good rate. Our butter is as sweet and rich as any I have ever tasted, and no trouble as to storage of it in this bitter cold. In fact, Georgie and I need to set up a small stove in the dairy. since the cream will not rise in frosty air.

Smoke flies every morning from the chimney of the Black Farm. The fields that lie between my house and his are deep in snow, tho' the main trails now opened up. He could visit me if he so wished.

December 23

Elizabeth comes with news that the doctor is calling once again at the Black Farm. Jim Black, she says, now has his hands full, what with caring for his sick brother, and all the chores of house and yard. 'It would,' she says, 'be a Christian act on your part, Rhoda, to go across and see them.'

When evening comes, I fill a satchel with jars of my preserves, and some cakes fresh-baked by Rosa. I bid Georgie to take them to Matthew Black. On his return, my son's report causes me to worry. Matt has developed a deep and wracking cough and is most unwell. Furthermore, snow begins to fall as Georgie makes his way home. I am wakeful in the small hours. From my window I see that a lamp burns night-long over at the Black Farm. The wind gets up and I am fearful of a blizzard.

December 24

It is my birthday! I am forty-four years old, but no time to ponder on it! Once again we awaken to drifted snow and blocked trails. We are obliged to dig our way out towards the cow barn. We go about our tasks with heavy hearts. There is no doubt that we are once more qwite cut-off from all our dear ones. The storm rages round the house and barn, the path being blocked almost as fast as we can clear it. By evening we are all worn-out, even Jon, who is beside himself with worry for his feathered flock, and so must come with us where 'ere we go! As I pen these words my little boy falls fast to sleep across the bearskin rug before the fireplace. Georgie carries him to bed.

Christmas Day 1874

The storm is over. We awaken to clear skies and starshine, tho' the frost still deep. We gather in the kitchen where Georgie has already fired the stove and has coffee boiling. He has a glum look. 'First time,' he says, 'that I was ever sent out to work on a Christmas Day!'

'Well I'm sorry, Georgie,' I tell him, 'but unfortunately our Holsteins take no heed of the Season.'

Rosa is also low in spirit.

'I was so looking forward to dinner at Aunt Elizabeth's. It's so much nicer being with them. They're still a proper family.' She sends me an apologetic look. 'Well, you know what I mean, Mama. They still have a father.'

Oh yes, I do indeed know what she means. At this time of year, more than any other, I remember George and our first years together, when Eddie was a small boy, and all our lives seemed to stretch out before us. I recall my dear husband's premonition that his would be a short span; and poor Ed, cut down in the flower of his young manhood. Tears come to my eyes. The children see this and are contrite. Georgie begins to help Jon put on his many layers of warm clothes. Rosa clears away the breakfast dishes. She says in a bright voice: 'I know what we can do! We'll begin to make that qwilt, Mama! We'll start this very evening!'

We say a short prayer together before setting out upon our chores.

The path between house and barn has stayed clear overnight. But the half-mile of trail between us and Elizabeth, and to James Black, is still blocked by deep drifts.

The thought of the qwilt qwite lifts our spirits. We talk it over thru' the milking. I say: 'Better I think if we stick to the sort of sewing I know best.'

'Oh no,' she cries, 'this customer will want bright colours and a bold pattern. After all, Mama, if a person is willing to pay fifty dollars into the church fund, then we must come up with something more romantic than your plain qwilting.'

'I had never,' say I, 'thought of qwilts and romance both together.'

'In American families,' my girl tells me, 'a qwilt is so much more than a warm covering in winter. It is a symbol. There are engagement qwilts and bridal qwilts, and each has its own speshul pattern.'

'You seem to know a lot about it.'

'Oh, indeed I do, Mama! You recall when we first came to this house and I made throws and cushions? It was Aunt Elizabeth's friends who showed me how to piece the patterns, and each one has its own name. There's Grandmother's Flower Garden and Courthouse Steps, Barn Raising and Log Cabin, Drunkards Path and Cathedral Window, and, oh, a whole heap more! Some of the designs,' says Rosa, 'have *hidden meanings*.'

365

We finish the milking and go to the dairy. Georgie comes into the barn. He is ready to clean up and put down fresh straw. He hears our talk. He says: 'There's an old qwilting-frame up in the attic. I'll get it down for you when we're all through with chores.'

We almost forget that it is Christmas Day, and that we are isolated by the snow. The work goes with a will! After supper is done with, Georgie brings to us the frame. Rosa cleans it with a damp cloth. It is in perfect order. Already, Jon has sorted out our scraps bag. He makes heaps of each separate colour, but Rosa says we are far short of what is needed. We go each one to our highboy drawers and cupboards, and find odd garments, rarely worn. I have a few bolts of plain calico, bought in Green Bay when we first came here. All together, says my girl, it should be suffishent!

We sit around the kitchen table, the frame beside us. Now comes the great decishun. What pattern should we follow?

'I am in your hands,' I say to Rosa. 'It is you who knows all about this American fashun of patchwork.'

'Well,' says she, 'there is a *most romantic qwilt*, always in demand. It's not the easiest to make, but oh, it looks so fine when finished!'

Georgie sends his sister a very *hard* look, and I think he is about to speak, but then he would seem to bite back on the words. Rosa's cheeks are flushed, her eyes a-sparkle, her dark curls shining in the lamplight. I see how pretty she has grown.

'Since we don't know,' she goes on, 'who our customer will be, it may be safer to choose a tradishunal qwilt. The one I have in mind is called Double Wedding Ring. It's a repitishun of linked circles made of patterned fabrics against a plain background. Oh, Mama, it looks so elegant, do say that we can do it!'

I am doubtful, but do not wish to spoil her pleashur. I say: 'If you are sure about this?'

She turns to face her brother. 'You'll help us, won't you, George? The Vickery boys help Aunt Elizabeth with *her* qwilts on winter evenings, and it's all in a *good cause*.'

December 27

More snow falls. We turn to our new evening occupashun, thankful for the interest. I pay Jon two bits for one night's needle-threading. He is kept busy with three of us to thread for. Georgie, after some small struggle, takes up a needle. He is slow but neat. We decide, in the end, on a background of lilac-coloured calico, with the rings of the pattern worked in pieces of flowered and checkered cotton. To my surprise I find this American patchwork a most calming occupashun.

January 1

Robert and Elizabeth get through to us this forenoon! They are concerned that we spent Christmas by ourselves but I tell them we were not too low in spirit. Rosa shows them our qwilt and they are full of praise. We spend two happy hours together. They say that, as they came, a party of neighbours were clearing the trail up to the Black Farm.

January 4

No more snow. The cleared trails stay open. My conshunce troubles me on behalf of Matthew, tho' truth to tell we could not have reached him until now.

Our morning chores once done, I say to Rosa: 'We *must* go over to the Black Farm.' I pack a basket. We take soup and cakes, and a batch of my fresh muffins, with a crock of our new butter to be melted on them. George bides to home with Jon.

The door of the loghouse is opened to us by Captain Black. I am shocked at his appearance. He has grown so gaunt in these past weeks. More still am I alarmed at Matthew. I go into the rear room to find that he has taken to his bed again and looks mortal sick. I say to Jim Black: 'Whatever happened? I thought your brother to be almost recovered when I last came here. He was sitting out and on the mend.'

Captain Black is very low, has quite lost his old style of command and is so humbled in his spirit that I am driven to comfort him.

'I am sure it was not your fault that he had a set-back. Your care of him is so devoted. But he does not seem at all well.'

367

'It was the blizzard, Mrs Salter. Matt said that he was better. He would come out to help me with the yard work tho' I said he shouldn't.'

Even as we speak, a bout of coughing wracks poor Matthew. We rush to help him.

I say to Captain Black: 'This is bronchitis! We need to get moisture into the air to ease his breathing! You *must* keep a kettle boiling on the stove at all times.'

I look around me. The little house is in a sad state, the sink piled-up with unwashed dishes, the floors unswept, and Matthew's bed all rumpled-up and needing clean sheets.

'Bring me fresh linen,' I say, 'and lift your brother for a moment while I put it beneath him.' I remake the poor man's bed, for which he thanks me. As I do so, I notice the poorness of his blankets, which are heavy but give little warmth. 'It is a qwilt you really need,' I tell him.

'Our mother made qwilts when we were children back in Kingston,' says Matthew. 'Oh my, but they were nice and cosy.'

Jim Black grins at his brother. 'And you shall have a qwilt again right soon! Elizabeth tells me that Mrs Salter here has gotten started on my order.'

He turns to me. 'I shall pay my fifty dollars to the church fund just as soon as you have put the last stitch in, ma'am!'

By this time I am toasting muffins at the fire. A burning colour floods my face, what I pray he will put down to my occupashun.

I am too mortified to answer. I recall the qwilt design of the Double Wedding Ring. Such patterns, my daughter says, are meant to carry hidden meanings. It is an American tradishun. Well the message of *my* qwilt cannot possibly be clearer, can it? For a widow to stitch such a pattern for a batchelor's bed surely is unheard of?

I say in a faint voice: 'My sister said she had a customer waiting. I did not guess that it was you, sir.' My anger drives me to be busy. I set about me with broom and duster. I wash up dishes while Rosa feeds Matt from a tray of soup and buttered muffins.

I say to Jim Black: 'Better that you go outside and chop-up wood, sir! You are such a *large* man. You all but fill this little cabin.'

January 6
Our work on the qwilt now has an urjent feel about it. What is very silly, since only yesterday I took three of my own plain old qwilts across to the Black Farm for Matthew's use.

It is Jim Black who harps on about the new one I am making. He has, so he says, a superstitious feel about it. That it alone will see the turning-point for Matthew.

'What nonsense!' say I. 'It is good medicine your poor brother needs!' I pick up the doctor's bottle of red-coloured liquid, and sniff at it.

'This is of little use to a man in Matt's condishun. It will only serve to irritate his damaged stomach. Now I have a remedy, Captain Black, what will sooth his cough, and put new life back in him.' (Truth to tell, I needs must turn the conversashun since talk of qwilts now sends the colour burning to my face.)

'What we really need,' I go on, 'is a number of lemons. Since we have none then a quart of Elizabeth's apple-cider will do just as well. To the cider you add glycerine and honey in the qwantities that I will show you. This mixture to be used as needed, one or two teaspoons at a time. The honey has life-giving qwalities and will not harm Matt's stomach.'

I see by his baffled look that the cabin holds neither glycerine nor honey.

'Oh, never mind,' I cry. 'I will make the linctus for you, and send Georgie over with it!'

January 8
Was again today over to the Black Farm. Matt takes his new medicine; he says it tastes much nicer than the old one, tho' his cough not yet much improved. I fear the bronchitis will turn to pleurisy. I say to Jim Black: 'We shall need to take sterner meashurs if we are to cure your brother.'

'Anything!' says he. 'We are in your capable hands, ma'am.'

369

The concern shows in his face, and I am moved to see it. Perhaps I have somewhat misjudged him? On reflectshun, it might even be that I have been at fault? I have sometimes, I know, goaded him to argument on farming matters; but in normal times he has such a big and *commanding* presence, that I am driven to take issue with him.

I say: 'There is another remedy, long known of in my family. It reqwires a chamois vest and a qwantity of black tar, but I have neither.'

Jim Black smiles. 'But we have tar, ma'am! A whole barrelful out in the barn. We have a piece of chamois too.'

'Then,' say I, 'there is yet hope for Matthew.'

It turns out to be a slow and pungent operashun. The smell of warm tar fills the cabin, bringing tears to all our eyes. I spread the stuff on Matthew's chest and back, then sew the vest of chamois on him tightly, so that he is all encased from neck to waist. It takes some time, and all the while Jim must needs support his brother, so weak has Matt become. As we labour around our paishunt, Jim's fingers touch my own, but it is accidental. He says, when we are finished, and Matthew resting qwietly:

'Ah, Rhoda, whatever should Matthew and I do without you!'

January 10

Jim comes across each morning to help me with the milking and churning, while Rosa goes over to minister to Matthew and give him breakfast. There is no doubt that a man's strong arm makes all the difference on a farmstead. Find myself less tired by evening, and so able to work longer on our qwilt.

Jim turns out to be a first rate dairyman. I was not sure at first if we could work together, but so far all is harmonious between us. He points out that I am running short of winter fodder, but forbears to menshun that this lack is due to my own wilful wish to grow clover rather than corn. He loads up his cutter with sacks of flour and grain, grown in his own fields, suffishent to see me thru' until harvest comes around again.

★

Private conversation was difficult to come by. Georgie longed to talk to Rosa but Mama was ever present. They had become a family which worked and ate together, and even when their outside chores were done they gathered close around the quilting frame each evening. Opportunity came on Sunday afternoon when Mama, having sent her daughter on an errand to the Vickery farmstead, grew alarmed at darkening skies and begged George to go at once and bring his sister home.

The track which lay between the farmsteads was narrowed by snow heaped-up on either side. Small flakes, soft as feathers, began to fall from a yellow sky. Rosa started to walk faster, but he deliberately slowed his pace.

She said: 'Don't dawdle, Georgie', but in an abstracted way as if her thoughts were elsewhere. He looked down at the untroubled face underneath her bonnet brim. He studied the neatness of her, the precise way in which she placed one foot before the other on the uneven ground. He fell behind a further half-dozen paces. Her composure angered him, so that the question he had intended should be subtle burst from him in a great roar.

'What's going on between Mama and Jim Black?'

Rosa turned very slowly round to face him. He moved towards her, looked down on her from his superior height.

She said in the high and careful voice that sounded so exactly like the English tones of their Mama: 'Why – whatever can you mean, George?'

He should have been warned by the clipped consonants and short vowels, but the fire in his brain, held so long in check, now flared up, consuming all discretion.

'Don't pretend with me, Rosa Salter! Don't treat me like I'm stupid or something!'

She came so close that he could see the glints in her blue eyes. Two small, gloved fingers tapped the thickness of his jacket.

'You are *so* stupid, Georgie Salter. The whole trouble is that *nothing's* going on between them.'

Shock held him fast so that he could neither speak nor move. The sweet voice went on, without emphasis or passion: 'Mama's

371

in love with Captain Black. Pity is that she's the only one who doesn't know it.'

His voice seemed to come from a great distance. He heard himself say: 'Well I didn't know it!'

'Oh you! You never see what's underneath your long nose. Why, Signa Peterson's been mad about you ever since the sugaring-off. Now tell me that you haven't noticed her!'

'He said: 'I haven't noticed her.'

Rosa said: 'What *do* you think about, George? You look so keen and smart, but I often wonder what goes on inside your head.'

He considered.

'I think about Chicago. Often. I remember Ed and me, and all the plans we had. We never did manage to get that pony. I think about Papa, and all the dreams he had. He did so want us to be George Hodder Salter and Sons, Meat-Packers of Chicago.'

Rosa took his gloved hand and patted it. 'You could still do that, George.'

'How could I? My apprenticeship is only half-through. Looks like I'm doomed to be a farmer all my life.'

They began to walk again, but very slowly.

He said: 'I don't want another father. I want things to stay the way they are.'

'Do you really, Georgie?' Her voice was soft in the way he most distrusted. 'Think about it, why don't you? If things stay as they are, you'll never get back to Chicago, will you? You'll never finish your apprenticeship. You said it yourself. Looks like you're doomed to be a farmer all your life. Now if we had the Captain for a father then you'd be free to do whatever you choose.'

'I thought,' he burst out, 'I thought you loved our Pa the same as I did!'

'But I do, George. I miss him all the time, and so does Mama. But she's lonesome, too. All the burden falls on her now, and there's always Jon. He'll never be able to manage on his own.

Mama never could bear to be alone, not in all her life. She needs a husband.'

They walked on together through the thickening snow. She gazed anxiously up into his face.

'Promise me,' she said, 'that you will at least think on what I've said. You were meant for a businessman, George – it's what Papa wanted for you.'

January 15
Today my George is seventeen years old. We make the house festive with paper-chains and green boughs. After all, we have missed Christmas! Between the morning and evening milking I take an hour or two to look at my appearance. My gown of crimson silk with the narrow bodice and deep-frilled skirt, still lies in tissue-paper. Rosa irons it for me while I wash my hair. She is critical lately.

She says: 'Why must you always dress your hair so severely, Mama? It would wave so nicely if only you would not scrape it back behind your ears.' She seizes the comb and begins to braid, but loosely, She coils the braid and pins it high upon my head. I look in the mirror. It is not a fashun I am used to, but the result is not displeasing. The hair indeed waves softly round my face giving me a *younger* look. Even Jon has noticed. When I am dressed in the crimson silk he says: 'You look real pretty, Mama!'

The road is open between the three farmsteads. The whole Vickery family come over, even little Robert who soon falls to sleep, and is laid in Rosa's bed. Poor Matthew, tho' still too weak to leave his bed, *incists* that Jim shall join us. We are a merry party! We drink my boy's health in apple-cider. Our table groans beneath the food set out upon it. I look around the dear faces of my relatives and friends, and know that life is *good*.

'Another toast!' I cry. 'Let us drink to this great land of America, and especially to the State of Wisconsin where we have all found such a welcome, and a good home.'

My eyes are drawn often towards Jim, who is looking

uncommon fine. He wears trousers of a tight cut in dark-green plaid, with a short jacket of black velvet trimmed with silver buttons. His shirt is of silk with a frilled and lace-edged jabot. His shoes black-patent with silver buckles. I whisper to Elizabeth: 'What is that outfit?'

She says: 'It is the tradishunal Scottish. He wears it only on very *speshul occashuns*.'

We sit long at table. The men ask if they may smoke. Cigars are lit and there is the rich smell of good tobacco. The talk winds around to the time when we older folk were also seventeen.

Georgie says: 'And what were you doing, Captain, when you were my age?'

'Why,' says Jim. 'That's just the age when I left the home farm and started lumbering. My father died when Matt and I were children. Years later, when Mother passed away there was nothing to hold us – we just lit out with our few belongings – Matt and me.' He grinned. 'That's when we came to America and met up with you folks.'

Robert says: 'That must have been a hard life.'

'I was a young man in a young country. At the age of eighteen I was riding the log-rafts down the Ottowa River.'

Georgie leans forward in his chair, his interest caught: 'I've heard about life in the logging-camps. Is it really as tough as it's made out?'

'It's a mite more civilised in these days, but I guess it's not all that different. Being snow-locked is the worse thing, when mail and extra supplies can't get through. That's when a foreman needs to be real strict.'

'How,' I ask, 'does a man come to be a logger?'

'Well it's not always voluntary. It's like this – the company agents mostly set up shop in a saloon. When recruiting starts there's a brisk flow of free whisky. There's many a youngster who comes in looking for his buddy, or just to warm himself before the fire – and he wakes up hours later in a sleigh on the backroads to the pineries – and with a thundering headache!'

Rosa says: 'Did that happen to you?'

'No. I went of my own free will. I'd watched the men who ride the log-jams in the spring. It looked to me like a fine adventure. But such men are part of a skilled crew. I had first of all to learn to be a logger, before I could be a white-water man.' Jim grinned at Georgie. 'The camp life is pretty dull. You get up in darkness, and you come back in darkness. There's no home comforts. Fifty, maybe sixty, men to every bunkhouse, a couple of box stoves with wet socks and other garments hung on lines above 'em. There's always a card game going on, but never for money. Gambling stirs up hard feelings in the men, likewise alcohol makes 'em slow and stupid. There's always one who can play the flute or the harmonica, so we sometimes have a sing-song. Sundays is for letter-writing and mending ripped clothes. Nobody shaves. Most men sleep all Sunday through, only waking up when the cookhouse gong sounds.'

I say: 'What kind of food is served in such condishuns?'

He smiles at me. 'Why nothing so excellent, ma'am, as the meal you've given us this evening. But the camp food is good and a decent cook is worth gold. There's always salt pork and beef, potatoes and baked beans. Pies and cake are favourite – washed down with strong tea. Sometimes the cook will barter sugar with the Indians for a few pails of blueberries or cranberries.'

Georgie says: 'Tell us more about the log-drive.'

'That's the most dangerous time of all,' says Jim. 'First of all you have to get your logs down to the river. I send a couple of men out overnight to sprinkle water on the track, so that the sleighs will pull well on the icy surface. We calk the horses shoes – ah but that's a fearsome sight, to see the great horse-drawn sleighs loaded up with timber! Then we wait for warmer weather. When the snow melts the river level rises. The stacked-up logs are rolled down to the water, and that's a risky job too. A log-jam is the worst of all. There's many a young man lost his life working to free a jam.'

'How long,' I ask, 'does it take to get the logs down to the mills?'

'Why, several weeks, ma'am. The cookshack goes with us.

375

We sleep in tents along the river-bank as we move downstream. Those nights are awful cold, and a man gets pretty well soaked through working on the river. I've known mornings in the early spring when my clothes were frozen solid to my body. There's no time to stop and dry things. Just got to keep moving every day.'

I say: 'It's a wonder you're still here to tell your story!'

'It's a job for strong men,' says he, 'who are not afraid of hard work.'

'What happens,' asks George, 'when the drive is over?'

Jim draws on his cigar. His dark eyes twinkle. 'You've been hearing talk, I don't doubt, about the binges that occur when the lumbermen hit Green Bay and Escanaba, with six-months pay burning in their pockets? Well, I'll tell you. The most of them stories are true! Oh I won't mislead you folks. Matt and I went on a binge or two when we were young blades. But I've been Mr Tremble's foreman for a good few years now, and I've learned some sense along the way. Put it down to my Presbyterian upbringing, or that I come from Scottish stock – but I'm real careful with my dollars these days!'

He looks at me across the table. He says: 'Guess I'm as respectable and qwiet a man as any gently-brought-up lady could ever want?'

The colour rises in my face so that my cheeks match the crimson of my gown. They are all watching me. I say, to change the subject, and because it is the first thing that comes into my head: 'Perhaps you would like to see the qwilt, sir? It is more than half-way finished.'

He says in a most *seerious* tone: 'Show it to me, Rhoda, when you have it all done.'

February 10
No entry made since George's birthday. We work every evening on the qwilt. I go to visit Matthew most days. He improves, but slowly. George now talks admiringly of Jim, as does Rosa. Indeed, I also see him in a different light since learning more about him. To know is to understand. Allowance can be made

376

for the roughness of a man's appearance when the cause is hard work and condishuns. How I regret my high words about his beard when he came back from last spring's log-drive! It was after all, a very fine beard, black and curling. Jim is altogether a most imposing figure of a man, and qwite the strongest I have ever known. Watching him when he helps out around my yard and cowbarn I am *amazed* at the ease with which he lifts bales and sacks. The work goes twice as fast with Jim's help. The little I can do for Matthew seems small return for so much kindness. I must go now to take my place at the qwilting-frame. Rosa is already sewing. Georgie grows speedy with the qwilting needle, and Jon kept busy threading for us all.

My Double Wedding Ring qwilt is almost finished.

February 17
Elizabeth comes over in the cutter, bringing little Robert with her. Jon and he play well together. My sister, being skilled at the American patchwork, helps to put the final touches to our qwilt. We spread it out across the kitchen table. The linked rings are in shades of blue with here and there a touch of red and yellow, flowered and striped patches, matched carefully by Rosa who is the *artist* among us. The rings show up fine and bold against the lilac-coloured background. Elizabeth looks at me with meaning. She says:

'Oh my, but Jim will surely love this qwilt!'

I say: 'It is meant to bring good health to Matthew. Jim has this fanciful noshun about it. That it will be for a turning-point.'

Elizabeth smiles in that secretive way of hers that tells me she has *prior* knowledge. 'Oh I don't doubt but it'll be a turning-point for somebody!' says she.

I begin to talk fast about my butter. 'When the weather eases,' I tell her, 'I intend to sell my whole stock in the Green Bay butter market where the price is better.'

My sister lays her hand upon my forearm; she pats the finished qwilt. 'You were ever good at hiding your true feelings,

Rhoda; but do be wary of hiding them too well! The men of this country are simple and direct. Without encouragement of some kind a suitor might well become faint-hearted and give up the chase. Espeshully if he should be a bachelor of mature years, and not used to women's ways.'

I gather up the tea-cups. I say: 'How nice it is for Jon to have your little boy to play with. I fear he is too much with us older folk.'

Elizabeth shakes her head, gathers up her child, and drives away.

February 19

It is in these candle-hours that I am lonesome. The wind roars tonight about the house, the children are long a-bed, and here sit I, my accounting Ledgers spread out upon the kitchen table. But I have no heart for adding figures. I am lower in spirit than I have been since we left Chicago.

Jim comes over to help George put new roofing shingles on the hog-house. When he is all done he comes into the kitchen. I show him the completed qwilt.

I say: 'Well, here it is – and I hope it is what you wanted.'

I can see he is impressed. He stands back a pace. 'Mag-nif-icent,' he cries.

I wait, but it seems that the one word is all that is to pass his lips. I say, in a *desperate* fashun: 'It is the Double Wedding Ring design. It is not easy to do.' I try to make the words sound offhand, as if the whole matter means nothing to me. After all I still have some pride left.

'It is a Bridal Qwilt,' I say. I think he must surely take heart from all of this, but he stands tall and broad and mute.

The silence between us is *awful*. I cannot bear it. I begin to bundle the qwilt fast together. I push it into his hands.

I say, rather coldly, 'Well, I hope it looks well on Matthew's bed.'

Jim turns and walks away.

As he goes I cry out: 'Now, don't forget, will you? You owe the sum of fifty dollars to our church building fund!'

February 22

Meetings between myself and Captain Black grow more awkward by the day. He loses all his former boldness and is now as tongue-tied as my George gets when Rosa's friends come calling. It is very *vexashus* since *I* am now more than a little fond of *him*.

February 23

I know that he wants me. It is in his voice, his look, whether or not he will *admit* it. He just cannot seem to broach the subject. Oh, whatever shall I do? It is up to me to bring him to the *point*. But how best to do it without loss of face, or seeming *forward*?

February 28

Trails are now open between all farmsteads, altho' snow still lying deep in fields and on the backroads. The raising of funds for our new Episcopal church is becoming urjent. Young couples who have planned to wed at Eastertide must go all the way to Green Bay if they would marry in their family faith. A 'Basket Soshul' is to be held by the ladies of our congregashun. This is a very pleasant and *romantic* American means of raising funds for a good cause. The habit is for the ladies and girls to each one decorate a box or basket and fill it with refreshments for *two*. On a certain evening the community assembles in the school room, and each box or basket is auctshuned-off with the men and boys bidding on them. Of course, no one is allowed to know the owner of these lovely boxes, since they are all carried in great secrecy in a Brown Paper Bag.

I say at first that I will not have time for all of this. Truth to tell I am downhearted and lack inclinashun. But Rosa will not let the matter rest. 'You cannot,' she cries, 'be the only woman in the congregashun who has no luncheon box to auctshun!'

I think long and deep about the matter. There is a qwantity of lilac calico left over from the qwilt, and several pretty patches. I begin to sew. I make the Double Wedding Ring pattern. When a suffishent length is put together I cover my basket with it. When the evening of the auctshun comes, I fill the basket to the brim with the cakes and cookies that *he* fancies most. I go with my children to the school room, and place my *brown paper bag* among fifty or so others. When the people are assembled the paper bags are taken off, and the baskets and boxes lined up upon a trestle-table. Mine looks most *distinctive*.

If James Black does not recognise my message this time, then he is not worthy of my feelings for him!

Oh brave words, Rhoda!

When the moment comes and the bidding begins I am as ankshus and fluttery as any schoolgirl. Suppose he should bid for someone else's basket? I think I could not *bear* it.

When my effort is put-up a silence falls. The bidding starts. It comes from the far side of the room. I recognise the voices of Matthew and Jim. They call for some long time, one against the other. Cheering breaks out among the company as the competishun grows fierce. When the figure called by Jim reaches twenty-five dollars, Matthew cries: 'Enough! I can't match that!'

Everybody starts to laughing. There is much good-natured teasing. It is clear to all that the contest was *arranged* between them.

The custom is that the winner of a basket should sit together with the maker of it, and eat the lunch provided. As the young men claim the makers of their prize, I see how many a romance is begun in this way. The winner of my particular prize comes striding towards me. His face is flushed and he is smiling *broadly*. We retire to a secluded corner and sit down together.

He says: 'I shall treashur this basket all my life, Rhoda! I recognised your pattern straight away.'

He looks deep into my eyes, he takes my hand.

He says: 'Will you not share a double wedding ring of gold with me?'

Chapter Twenty-four

March 1

Captain James Kerr Black has proposed marriage to me, and I have accepted. The date has been set for April first, the ceremony to be held in Green Bay. Elizabeth and Robert are overjoyed. Likewise my three children. As for myself, well, my heart was decided upon Jim these many months past; it just takes a little longer for my mind to follow.

March 4

Elizabeth comes over. She finds me churning in the dairy. She says: 'You look pale, Rhoda.'

'I had but an hour of sleep last night,' say I. 'There is much to think over.'

My sister looks troubled. 'I hope you do not feel that we have manoeuvred you towards this marriage?' Her voice is wistful. 'But, oh my dear, it does seem so *right* that you and Jim should be together.'

I smile. 'I do have my own mind, and usually I know it. But in this case, there are the children to think about.' I pause. The heavy actshun of the churn-blades tells me that my butter has at last 'come'. I lean heavily across the handle.

I say: 'This marriage will also mean that I never see Somerset again.'

She says: 'We are Americans now, likewise our children.'

'In his last days,' I tell her, 'poor George spoke often about England. He had always seemed so American in all his ways of thinking, yet, at the very end, it was Dorset that he yearned for.'

'I think,' says Elizabeth, 'that it is better for us women to

381

keep our minds fixed on hearth and home, and family. No good can come of longing for what we can never have. As for your children and their feelings, you must know that they are devoted to Jim and Matthew.'

I nod, finding it difficult to speak the next words. I say at last, 'Do you not perhaps think that this remarriage is a little *soon*?'

Elizabeth smiles. 'I wondered how long it would take you to get around to that point. You still think like an Englishwoman. This is pioneer land, Rhoda! For practical reasons it does not do to live alone. Why, I have seen a widowed man remarry within *weeks*. Jim's courtship of you has been lengthy by local standards.'

'I did not,' I point out, 'realise at first that I was being courted.'

I turn to face her. 'What do you suppose that George is thinking of me? I know that he is with Susanna, but it is only eighteen months . . .'

'Did you never talk about the matter?'

'Yes,' I say slowly, and even as I speak the memory returns. George, saying in those last, sad days: 'Thou hast borne much on my account. I have not deserved thee. Should I ever go under – if thou'rt left alone – remember my words. Seek out a good man to be a husband to thee, and a father to our children.'

I straighten my shoulders. I go back to the churn and lift out the butter.

'You are right,' I tell my sister. 'George would want me to be happy.'

March 10
For the first time in many weeks the temperature goes up! Jim says it is above the freezing point. There is a softness in the air and a south wind rising. I am drawn from the house by the sounds of a slow thaw; water trickles everywhere, snow slides and thuds from roofs. I walk alone to the edge of my meadowland and stand for a while beside the fence. The depth of the lying snow grows less even as I watch. If I listen hard, I can hear my clover growing.

Elizabeth comes over, bringing a dress-length of silk she 'just happened' to have by her. It is of a deep gold colour, and very handsome. 'You cannot,' she says, 'wear any of your old gowns to get married.'

She and Rosa begin to cut and stitch.

'Keep it simple,' I say, 'remember that I am no blushing girl, but a woman of forty-four years!'

March 20

There is much to talk over. Jim comes every evening. He is shy but loving, and tho' the time is short he is set upon a proper courtship of me. He brings me little gifts: a tiny gold-and-amethyst brooch that was his mother's; a handful of pussy-willows. On Sunday afternoon we drive out, just the two of us; the snow is almost gone and there is colour in the land. We follow the course of the Suamico River to the place where it runs into the Bay. Jim points out Willer Island and the Tail Point Lighthouse. We gaze on the cold green waters of the Bay. A steamship passes, and I look back, inland, to where winter wheat and rye is showing in the fields. From this spot I can view the tidy farmsteads of our good friends. There is the Valentine house, and that of Peter Krause. The Sensiba place, and that of Al Fraker which runs down I see to the very shore-line.

I say to Jim: 'I hadn't realised that Suamico stood so close upon the Bay.'

He says: 'How happy are you, Rhoda? Does the sight of a ship set you hankering for England?'

I choose my words with care. 'For twenty years I have moved from one place to another, and none of them a settled home.' I take his hands in both of mine. 'I will always be an Englishwoman. You will have to bear with me in that.'

He grins. 'It's no hard thing. That bit of starchiness is what first drew me to you.' He pulls me closer. He murmurs above my head: 'Guess I still can't qwite believe that you agreed to have me.'

I gaze up into his face. 'I was beginning to fear that you would never ask.'

We fall to laughing, and I marvel at the easy way we have with one another. 'I am happy, Jim,' I whisper. He halts my words with a long kiss. I say at last: 'We must go back. There is the milking to be done.'

'Ah, yes. There is always *that* confounded chore!' His words are cross but his mouth is smiling, and this time it is I who seeks the long kiss.

We drive back at last thru' the cold spring twilight and to the sound of birdsong, what comes, says Jim, from the vesper-sparrows and the killdeers down in the marshlands. We drive into Suamico, and between the budding trees we see lamplight shine out from kitchen windows. I have a sense of peace such as I have never known in all my life.

March 29

Have only now considered how two extra men in our household is bound to make a difference. Jim and Matthew drive over in a waggon loaded high with fishing-gear and shotguns, heavy boots and clothes, and trunks filled with 'treashurs' which they haul up to my attic-room.

Matthew is a new man since Jim and I became promised. He says it is the prospekt of a proper home at last that has so cheered him up. By his own reqwest he is to have the small room what opens off the kitchen. It is warm in the winter, and he makes it cosy with the help of Rosa. He hands back to me the Double Wedding Ring qwilt.

He says: 'This rightly belongs on your bed now, ma'am.' He grins. 'Well, it surely will in just a few days.'

I see that he knows about the hidden meaning. I take it from him, blushing. I say: 'It has served its purpose.'

March 31

We are to start very early in the morning for Green Bay. Elizabeth and Robert will come with us to be our witness. Jim *insists* that we two bide-over an extra day or two. He has waited, he says, much longer than most men for a 'honeymoon holiday'. He will make the most of it now! I point out that the

Green Bay hotels crawl with bed-bugs. He says that he knows of clean lodgings kept by a decent Canadian couple. I say, but what about my Holsteins? What about Jon?

He grows stern. He says that Matthew will be already moved into the house to oversee things. That Robert and Elizabeth will come across each day. He asks: 'Can't you *trust* George and Rosa to be responsible for once? Must you always be checking on them? As for Jon, well they would never see him come to any harm!'

He is right. I bow my head.

So all has now been done that can be done to make our absence easy on the family. A large batch of baking, loaves and pies, cake and puddings, stand in the pantry. Jim has cut a qwantity of hay bales, and brought grain and feed to lighten Georgie's labour. Jon has been promised a present from Green Bay. My children are so excited at the prospekt of my absence, that I still wonder if I am *wise* to go! Rosa asks what should they call Captain Black after I am married to him? She and Georgie have talked about this. They can never bear, says she, to call him Papa. I say that Jim and I would not expect this. That they must find for themselves a name that suits them all.

My butter is packed ready for the Green Bay market. If the price is good then the profit should purchase two, maybe three more Holsteins for my herd.

The gold silk gown, stitched by my dear Elizabeth, hangs ready for tomorrow. I shall wear my cameo brooch, and keep my hair dressed in its new style.

Jim has bought *two* wedding rings, one for each of us, so that the meaning of the qwilt shall be fulfilled.

Chapter Twenty-five

April 7
The first writing I have done since my marriage to Captain Black. I begin on a new page to set down this rekord of my changed life. I had never thought it possible to be so happy.

We have started out for Green Bay at five of the morning, Alwin Hunter's stage being specially cleaned for the occasion, and fur rugs and foot-warmers provided at no extra cost. Jim and Robert fear that because of the thaw our trip might see us axle-deep in mud, but on the eve of our departshur an iron frost sets in, and so we go safely.

I wear my fur cloak and see a darkening of Jim's brow at sight of the sables. I fear that Elizabeth might have menshuned that the cloak was bought for me by George in our time of plenty. I make a great fuss about the safe stowing of my butter firkins so as to distract his mind. But I take heed of his hard looks; it is not easy in marriage to take another's place, as I know only too well, having once trodden that stony path myself. Before we are five miles gone from Suamico I begin to fret about Jon, about the morning milking, whether Georgie can manage, whether Matthew will stay fit and well until we return. Elizabeth shakes her head at me across the carriage. I nod understanding. She says: 'Now, you're not to come rushing back home as soon as you're wed! Take this as a new beginning, Rhoda! You'll have Jim's broad shoulder to lean upon in the future!'

I feel his fingers tighten round my own hand, warm and strong.

I say: 'We shall not come home until Jim is good and ready.'

On reaching Green Bay we go first to the butter market. My

386

butter is tested and pronounced to be 'gilt-edged'. The sale is made and a high price given. The Bill is made out in the name of Rhoda Salter; it is my last little triumph as a widow.

Jim takes us to an inn that is tolerably clean and not too noisy. He says that in a few more weeks the lumberjacks will hit this city, their pockets full of dollars.

He says, after we have eaten: 'We shall just have time before the ceremony to buy your wedding gift.'

I say: 'There is no need for presents.'

'*I* think there is, Rhoda. I want to do things *right*. Remember, this is *my* first and *only* wedding.' His black brows draw together. 'I don't care overmuch for that cloak you're wearing. Never did like sables. For a start they're too dark for a wedding day!'

I say: 'I have no other cloak, and the wind comes bitter off the Bay.'

He bids Elizabeth and Robert stay snug inside the inn while he and I go shopping. He rushes me along across ice-rutted streets and broken boardwalks. We come to a store wherein furs are hung all around the walls and doorway. The owner is a Frenchman. Jim speaks to him in the man's own language, and is shown several coats and cloaks what he dismisses out-of-hand. At last he spies a cape hanging high up; I think it must be the most expensive pelt in the fur trader's store. 'That one?' he asks. 'How much is the mink?'

The man reaches down the most beautiful cape I have ever seen. It is of finger-tip length and of a creamy beige shade. Jim settles it upon my shoulders. There is a strip of cracked looking-glass propped up against a wall. He pushes me towards it, and I gaze at my reflectshun. Jim stands behind me. 'Oh, but you look beautiful,' says he.

I am transformed! The mink, worn over the gold silk of my dress, is so elegant that I could *weep* for joy. Jim halts, his head a little to one side, considering.

He says to the Frenchman, so that I can understand: 'Is there a mink hat to go with it?' I remove my own dark and heavy bonnet, and a hat is brought to me. It is of the style known as pill-box (and perches rather than fits upon my head) being fastened with ribbons underneath my chin. Jim ties these ribbons in a neat bow. He steps back a ways. 'Well, that's better! That's a *whole heap* better.' He pays the Frenchman.

I turn away, the tears pricking at my eyelids. No man, in all my life, has ever before paid attenshun to my dress or even remarked upon it. No man has ever told me that I was pretty or even passable in looks. But this man has called me beautiful, he has himself picked out a cape and hat worthy of a Princess, and shown no shyness in so doing. I begin to look at him with new eyes. Just when I think that I know *all* about him, that is when he can surprise me. We take my sable cloak and leave it in our lodging. Elizabeth and Robert admire my cape and bonnet.

We are married at three of the afternoon in a tiny church near St James Park. It is a simple service. Jim speaks up loud and clear that he will take me to wife. Robert and Elizabeth depart before dark falls; our parting from them is a tender moment. Jim and I take an early supper, and go back to our room.

I remarked elsewhere in this Journal (but when I was much younger) that I have been most happy in my life when I did not recognize the feeling. Well, this much have I learned since: that happiness is a rare thing in this Vale of Tears, and so to be savoured. I say this to Jim when I lie safe in his arms in the small hours of the morning.

I whisper: 'I had never dared to hope that I might love again.'

'You must,' says he, 'have cared pretty deeply for George Salter to leave home and country for him?'

'It was the love of a young girl. He was the first to offer for me.' (I recall the Curate, but think him not worth the menshun.)

'But yes,' I go on, 'I loved George very much, tho' I must confess we did not always see eye-to-eye on business matters.'

Jim laughs. 'That I can believe!' He asks in a different tone: 'You were married to him for a good span of years. By his photograph, and your children's looks he must have been real handsome? Young Georgie is just like him, I guess, and not only in appearance?'

'Georgie is very like his father. He is qwick and strong in his feelings, he has great dreams of doing well in business. He has worked so hard on the farm, but only for my sake. His heart is not in farming. He never wanted us to leave Chicago.'

Jim says: 'I will try to be a good father to them, Rhoda, tho' I know I can never take the place of George Salter; not in their hearts, nor in yours.'

Moonlight slants in at our window. It allows me to see his face, his ankshus eyes. In all my life I have never counted my words as carefully as I do now. So much depends upon my answer. Twenty years since, and I stood in the selfsame situashon where Jim now finds himself. The difference is that he has spoken all his doubts out loud, and not hugged them to him in secret, as did I. I put my arms around him and hold him close.

I say, in a smiling way: 'I had not thought to be talking over such things on my wedding night, Jim! But our courtship was so short. All we spoke about was qwilts and Basket Soshuls, and which room should be Matthew's. Perhaps it is as well that we talk earnestly now, while we are far from home and by our two selves.'

He is still and silent, and I pray that I might find the right words.

'I do know something of what you are feeling. When I came to America, twenty years ago, it was to be George Hodder Salter's second wife, and to care for the child of his first marriage. I had loved him long before he wed Susanna, but I wanted to be first in his heart, as he was first in mine. Such circumstances can't be changed, though. We have to learn to fit ourselves around them. If we are lucky, another chance may come our way. With you I am a first wife, the one and only Mrs James Kerr Black.' I pause. 'There is something else I'd have you know. You are not the stamp of man I have ever felt myself drawn towards, except for your looks, and I always had a weakness for a handsome face. But I am not used to such masterful ways as yours, nor to a man who has the knack of always being right in his predictshuns. Already, I have learned a little meakness from you, James Black, and that's no bad thing.'

I look at his face and he is smiling in the moonlight. I touch my fingers to his lips. I say: 'I learned something else. That it is possible to love again, and not as a young girl loves, but like a woman grown. Truth to tell, there has scarcely been chance for us to know one another, but with every day that passes my feeling for you deepens and you must never doubt that.'

I try to make my tone light now, but this is hard to do.

I say: 'You are forty-six years old, and a fine set-up figure of a man. You can hardly expect me to believe that I am *your* first love?'

He is so long in answering that I grow ankshus.

He says at last: 'Well, I've lived no monk's life, Rhoda. Got to be honest with you there. There was a girl, down in Nashville, Tennesee. One or two others in various places. Nothing that counted. Not a single girl I felt keen enough about for marriage. I'd begun to see myself as a bachelor born until you came along.'

I turn away from him. I feel a jealus pang, what is very foolish of me. I already know from his sure ways of loving that there have been others before me. More than one or two.

I bide qwiet while my rush of envy passes.

I say at last: 'I think for both our sakes we must agree on something. We should never talk like this again: not I of George, nor you of your old sweethearts. It does not do to come trailing old sad memories into a new life.'

He gathers me back into his arms.

He says: 'You are all I ever looked for in a woman. Just can't believe my own luck. No, sir! Not even with double wedding rings to prove it! I agree. From this day forward we talk of nothing but the future,' his arms grow tight around me, 'and it will be good. I make this promise to you. It will be all you ever wanted.'

★

These days and nights lived with Jim in Green Bay were the most perfect she had ever known. For almost a week she put worry from her mind, and wherever she was timid he persuaded her towards adventure. On sunny afternoons they watched the horse-trotting races in St James Park. He took her to the very edge of the notorious district known as 'Muscrat City', so that she might at least boast in her old age of having seen the whisky-holes and gin-mills. He showered her with small gifts: lace shawls and panels, fine as cobwebs, made by Menominee sqwaws; a pair of smart button-sided boots, which, the owner of the trading-post assured her, were the latest fashion in Chicago; and to go with them a pair of silken stockings at which she laughed and grew shy, and said that she would never dare to put them on.

Rhoda also searched the city stores for presents. She found a fine silk shirt for Georgie, a dress length of velvet for Rosa in her favourite blue. For Jon she bought a tiny game of checkers, carved in ivory by some deep-sea sailor. To Jim she gave a set of tobacco pipes, one for each day of the week.

The thaw returned, and this time spring fulfilled its promise. They rode home in Alwin Hunter's stage over roads and trails made treacherous by mud, but with bud and blossom showing in the deep woods. The Suamico River lay silver in the moonlight; from the marshlands a whipporwill sang his sad song. On the Black Farm, lamps of welcome shone in every window.

★

June 1

Today Jim and I are two months married.

The candle-hours are no longer lonesome for me, but are instead preshus times when he and I can be alone together. He is so loving and attentive. I had known one or two small doubts; but Jim has settled down to be a husband and a father as if to the manner-born.

Once again we sit six around the table. We are what Rosa considers a 'proper' family. The children, after much talking

391

over, have resolved to call Jim 'Father Black', what I think is thoughtful and shows a nice respect on their part.

There is much to be decided regarding our two farmsteads, and all must be settled before we are into haying and harvest. The evenings draw-out, and it is still light when we are done with milking. Jim and I walk across to view his old house. We go through the apple orchard. A few pink and white blossoms still show in the top boughs, but in the deep grass we find lilacs and the dark-blue wild lupins. Wild roses climb thick along an old fence what is leaning. I say to Jim: 'That fence must be replaced, and soon!'

'But not,' says he, 'before the roses have done blooming.'

He has this way of gentle-speaking, what puts me in my place; but nicely. We agree that his old house will make a good dry barn.

June 8

Our Holstein herd now numbers fifteen. We have also six followers and eight calves. Jim goes over to the gristmill in Flintville. On his way home he meets up with the three Englishmen who farm on the far side of the Suamico river. They tell him of sickness in their cows, what are scouring and growing thin. They ask if *I* would visit with them. Jim says that they are brusque men, who keep very much 'to themselves'; but they have heard that Mrs Salter is good with cattle. I say: 'They are countrymen of mine. I must go over.'

We find Mr Hopkins in his cowbarn. Of the other two there is no sign. By his accent I would say he is from Yorkshire. His speech is short and to the point. When I have viewed his ailing herd he snaps: 'Well then, missus! Dost tha' think there's owt to be done about 'em?'

'How long,' I ask, 'has this gone on?'

'Two weeks,' says he, 'or mebbee a bit longer.'

I touch the flank of one poor creature, and find the bone coming almost thru' the skin.

'Why?' I shout. 'Why have you let them get in this state? You have tongues in your heads! Surely one of you could ask

392

for help. All your neighbours are experienced farmers. Mr Rabinchan would have told you what to do, likewise La Fortunes or Aschenberners. Mr Parmentier also has a fine herd. My brother-in-law, Mr Robert Vickery, would have advised you.'

'We don't mix much with them furriners roundabout. As for Vickery – well we took him for a Yankee by his speech.'

I tremble from rage.

'You are,' I say, 'the most ignorant man I have ever met! It grieves me to say so of one of my countrymen, but it is high time that you were told! These "foreigners", as you choose to call them are your fellow Americans. They would help you gladly. As it is, your stiff-necked pride could lose you your whole herd.'

The man looks chastened. 'Happen I should have spoke-up sooner.' He sends me a fierce look. 'Well then – dost tha' mean to help or not?'

I say: 'When did you turn them out on to grass?'

'End of April.'

'And with what did you "bait" them?'

'I don't understand you.'

'Cows need to be prepared for a diet of fresh green grass. Mr Hopkins. By turning them out as you did, suddenly and wholly upon grass, you have caused them to scour and grow weak. Any change of diet should always be gradual. My husband and I,' I look fondly at Jim, 'we feed mangolds or turnips, a little early-cut hay, before turning our herd out to orchard-grass. This "baiting", with small amounts of green food saves a whole heap of trouble. I am surprised you didn't know this?'

'We're Dalesmen. Sheepmen. Had nowt to do with cows before we settled here. Anyway, we were running short on foddering. We were glad enough to turn 'em out to pasture.'

I feel a twinge of sympathy for him. I, too, have made my small mistakes.

I say, kindly: 'Now don't despair, Mr Hopkins. All is not lost yet.'

I look to Jim, and he nods his head. 'We will send my son

393

Georgie over with some hay and a few sacks of dry meal. Feed them small amounts, but often until the diarrhoea abates. Then turn them *gradually* back on to grass, and don't forget to give them salt-licks. Perhaps,' I say, but not looking at Jim while I say it, 'perhaps you should look to your crops, Mr Hopkins. It is not good practice, you know, to set too much land down to timothy-grass and clover. You would do well to grow more grain, along with extra root-crops. In that way you will be able to "bait" your herd next springtime and so avoid all this trouble.'

The man looks much relieved. He shakes us by the hand.

He says: 'I'm much obliged to you, Mrs Salter. How can I repay thee?'

I smile. 'Mrs Black, since April,' I correct him. 'As for payment – well we are thinking of buying in a few Merino sheep, and since we neither of us know much about the creatures . . .?'

'Gladly,' he cries, 'any help tha' needs. Just call on me!'

We drive home. Jim says: 'I was real proud of you there, Rhoda! You managed in almost one single breath to give the Englishman a lesson in citizenship, in pioneering-ways, and in dairying.' He glances down at me: 'With a lecture on good crop-raising practice thrown in at the end.'

I look up warily at him. But there is not even the ghost of a smile on his dear face.

Tonight I must write letters to the Salter family in England. I hope they will not think ill of me that I have remarried in such a short time. I must also pen a few lines to my sisters Mary and Joan. There is a letter owed to my brother James, who must also be told of my altered state.

August 29
Three months past since I took up this pen. My fingers have grown more used to the hay-fork and the skillet-handle lately. We were no sooner done with Haying than Harvest was upon us. The last of our Indian corn brought in last night, and in fine shape. Now we have a pause before the roots are ready.

394

Matthew, now much recovered from last winter's sickness, was a grand help to us.

A letter comes from Winchester, England. The Salter family answer to my letter with much kindness and understanding. My brother-in-law writes:

My Dear Sister,

I assure you I was delighted to get such a nice long letter from you about a Fortnight ago and to hear that you and your Dear Children are quite well and also to hear you have such a good Husband, which affords me much pleasure for it is a very great comfort to me to think my Dear Brother's wife and Children will be taken care of. Not that I wish to flatter you but you are deserving a good husband for I had proof of that the time I lived with you, and I have always spoken of you as such. And I am proud to congratulate you on getting a good Second Husband and you may depend on it I shall always have the same respect and love for you as if my Dear Brother George was still alive and if your Dear Husband ever came to England I shall only be too pleased to see him or your Dear Self or Dear Children. I should very much like to get the Black likeness. In my last letter I told you we was going to have ourselves and the Dear Little Ones taken, we have not yet, but we hope to soon, and I will be sure then to send you a copy. I am pleased to tell you that we have 4 Dear Little affectionate children as ever lived. Pollie and Eva the two Eldest are learning the piano. Now, my Dear Sister, I hope you don't think that I am inquisitive when I ask you respecting the money that was left you by your Father, as just after your Father's death your Brother James was at Lymme and told my Sister Selina that there was 500 Pounds left to you and 500 Pounds for Dear Little Eddie when he got to be 21 years of age, but that you was to come home for it. Now I will enclose three different paragraphs from Pulman's paper, which I am sorry to say is about your Brother and money that he has in trust. I hope it is not the money that is left for you, but I thought it best to send it to you and I know you will tell me all particulars as far as you know, and if there is any money coming to you from here I will with your permission try and get it for you. Now my Dear Sister let me beg of you to write me a good long letter and tell me how far you are from Chicago.

395

I lay the letter down. Tears come to my eyes when I remember John Salter, and those first years in Charlotte when we were all young together. I take up the first page and read over again where he says I am deserving of a good husband. As I do this the newspaper clippings from *Pulman's Paper* fall out upon the table. I regard them as I would a deadly snake. I fear to read about my brother and the trouble over Father's money. Jim comes into the kitchen.

He says: 'Why Rhoda, what is it?'

'A letter from England, from my brother-in-law Salter. He is very pleased to know that we are married.' I point to the newspaper clippings. 'He has also sent me news about my Father's Will what makes him sorry. Oh, Jim, I cannot face to read it.'

He studies the newsprint. 'Two of these clippings are advertisements for the whereabouts of a Mark Greypaull and a William Greypaull?'

'My brothers – somewhere here in America – or so I believe.'

'The other is a Notice served on a James Paul Greypaull of Buckland St Mary, Somerset, to pay over certain monies owed to his sister Mary Crabbe.'

I sit down. 'So it is still going on, then! Oh how can my poor Father rest easy in Heaven while his children still fight over his money and possessions?'

Jim says: 'I think you had better tell me all about it, my dear.'

So I tell him all.

Jim takes me in his arms. He holds me close. He says: 'Put it from your mind, dear love! You have no need of Greypaull money. England is a long ways off – and I won't see you dragged into any legal wrangling!'

He crumples the newsprint and throws it into the log-box.

'Now,' he grins, 'what do you want me to do with that bottom field when we've gathered in the squashes and pumpkins?'

Later on, when Jim has gone to call the cows home for milking, I go back to the log-box and pick up the crumpled cuttings. I smooth them out and put them in my apron pocket.

When supper is done with, I shall go over to the Vickery farm and show all to Elizabeth and Robert.

October 10
My half-year accounts all done with. We are *more* than solvent. The agent, once again, has declared our butter to be gilt-edged, and worth *thirty cents* the pound. We have hay standing in the yard and barn, corn in the bins, roots stored against the frost, cows milking-down and hens laying. We are all fit and well, even Jon and Matthew. It would seem that my good time has come at last.

★

The newspaper clippings lay for a long time on the Vickery parlour table, set carefully down by Elizabeth beside the big black Bible, as if proximity to the Good Book could somehow sanctify, and lessen their potential for ill-will. The scraps of paper became yellow with age and thin from handling, but still she could not bring herself to move or destroy them; they were dusted when she cleaned the parlour, along with ornaments and photographs. When visitors called, the clippings made a subject for conversation of which the Suamico ladies never tired. This story of the inheritance in England, already denied for ten years to Elizabeth and Rhoda by their Barrister brother, was better than any romantic tale printed in the *Tribune*'s page for Ladies. The presence of two English heiressess among their number was a matter of pride among the population. There was talk in the harness-repair shop and at sewing-bees; heads nodded wisely at mention of affidavits and lawsuits. The consensus being that 'it was high time something was done about it all'. People waited to see the departure of Mrs Rhoda Black for England, or at least to an Attorney down in Oshkosh. They waited a long time, and still no move was made by the dispossessed sisters. Two winters were endured, and two more harvests gathered in. In the fall of the year 1877 came a letter, so disturbing that Rhoda and Elizabeth were bound to take notice of it.

397

October 27 1877

Elizabeth comes over. She finds me in the dairy, scouring pans.

'A letter from our sister Mary,' she says, 'and it is full of trouble. Mary is bankrupt.'

We go into the kitchen, I pour coffee for us both. We sit down at the table, Elizabeth unfolds two pages of scrawled and blotted writing. She begins to read:

Dear Sister Elizabeth,

Six years have passed since I took up my pen to write to America. Daniel and I have been out of business for the past two years. The farm was taken from us, and we forced to rent a cottage from Mr Thomas at one shilling a week. Times are bad here, dear sister. Nothing to be done if a man gets out of business. There is no chance of getting in again. I have a large family. It costs me a great deal to keep them. We are in dire straits since our ground was taken from us.

Brother James intends to keep all Father's properties for himself. He will not sell any of it, nor give us a fair price for it. If we allow James to go on in this way we shall none of us have nothing. He should never have been made Trustee, but Father once said to Joan and me that we could trust James. If we stick to him, all of us together, we can make him sell at once.

Joan and I went up to the house last summer, to see him. I asked him where he thought it right to go on in this way. He offered to read Father's Will to us, and I told him I did not want to hear it. When he offered me one pound and ten shillings as my share of two years rents, I falled-out with him. I said I would not allow this to go on! He said he would make me allow it.

If James would only let me have my part of the inheritance then Daniel and me, and our children, could come out to America, to be with you and Rhoda. So please tell me that this would be a good move for us to make, and that you and Rhoda will join forces with Joan and me, against Brother James.

398

I have told you all what is going on here. Give my best to Robert and the dear children.

Your loving sister, Mary

Elizabeth lays the letter down.

'What can *we* do about it,' I ask, 'from a distance of four thousand miles?'

'We could put it into the hands of an Attorney?'

'Oh,' I burst out, 'how I do detest all this wrangling and bitterness! It is an awful thing that we should go to Law, against our own brother.'

'It would be for Mary's sake, mostly. Imagine, Rhoda! All nine of her family are living now in Mr Thomas' cottage. As I recall, it had but three rooms.'

'While James,' I say slowly, 'lives in solitary splendour in the big house and Dommett Farm is rented out to strangers. Then there is the blacksmith's shop and house, and all the cottages . . .' I turn to Elizabeth. 'Perhaps we should have made some move before this? We can't stand by and see Mary and her family go under!'

Elizabeth pulls from her apron pocket the newspaper clippings from *Pulman's Weekly*. 'I wonder,' says she, 'if our brothers Mark and Will were ever traced? It will need the signatures of us *all* if we are to make a move to claim what is rightfully ours.'

When Jim comes in I aqwaint him with all what has come to pass. He grows thoughtful, and after supper he goes across to talk to Robert.

November 24

Snow comes down on a strong north wind. I do not expect to see Elizabeth until the blizzard eases. In the hour before the snow starts, Georgie takes me in the cutter to the dry-goods store. On our way home we call in on Mr Toussant Teller to collect our mail.

'Seems like one of your long-lost brothers has turned up, Mrs Black,' says our postman. 'He rode into Vickery's last night just in time for supper.'

399

George is excited. 'I can take you to him right now!' he offers.

I hesitate. I say: 'It will be your Uncle Mark. I feel it in my bones. I shall need to talk to Father Black before I see my brother.'

My son lifts one eyebrow at me, a touching little habit that was once his father's. He is puzzled at my words. 'Your Uncle,' I tell him, 'is a trouble-raiser. He and I have not met since we lived in Charlotte.'

November 25
The storm has passed, leaving drifts all around the yard. We set-to, all six of us on clearing pathways, what makes us late for chores and milking. It is past one of the clock when we gather at the table for our midday meal. Father Black is saying the Grace, when the kitchen door flies open, and there stands Mark!

He is all smiles and bluff good-humour.

'Well, howdy little sister!' he cries. 'It sure is good to see you.' He looks to Jim. 'I'm glad to make your aqwaintance, sir. Elizabeth told me all about you.'

He turns back to me. 'My oh my, Rhoda,' he grins, 'you never lost your eye for a handsome fella, did you?'

I qwell him with one look. I say: 'Have you eaten, Mark? If not, you may join us at table.'

He stamps snow from his boots, pulls off his mackinaw, and seats himself. His eye now lights on Georgie and Rosa. He acts astonished.

'Well, aren't you two the living image of your Pa!' He turns to me. 'You have a pair of good-looking children, Rhoda. Salters through and through!' He begins to spoon soup into his mouth.

'They are indeed,' I say sharply, 'and every day I thank God for it.' I go on, in a very *pointed* manner. 'This gentleman, here, is my very dear brother-in-law Matthew Black, and this is our beloved Jon, who *also* repays notice.'

But there is no shaming him; he grins around at all of us. 'Well now, ain't this nice. Just like old times, eh, Rhoda?'

I say: 'How long to you expect to stay here?'

'Just long enough to settle one or two important matters.' He has a mean look when he is no longer smiling. I am all at once afeared. I look to Jim, who says: 'We're pretty busy folk right now, Mr Greypaull. We never talk serious before the evening time.'

'Oh that's fine by me, Jim. I'll just stick around until you're both good and ready to *parlez*. I guess you already know why I'm here. If you're the good man of business that Robert says you are, then you'll bend an ear to what I have to say.'

He 'sticks around' just as I expected. I see him deep in talk with George; as my boy splits logs and carries feed into the cow barn, Mark stays close at his side. Later on, he goes to Rosa in the dairy. I glimpse him being gallant, lifting pans and buckets for her. He is up to mischief. I am certain of it.

My brother has not yet spoken one single word to Matthew or Jon.

I prepare the evening meal in a most uneasy frame of mind.

I say to Jim: 'I could wish that Robert and Elizabeth were here, when that rogue states his business with us.'

Jim says: 'My thoughts exactly! I'll ride across before the light goes.'

The minute I am on my own, Mark joins me in the kitchen. He straddles a chair, and waves a hand what takes in the whole house.

'Smart move, Rhoda,' says he, 'best you ever made, eh? In one fast stroke you found a father for your children, two unpaid cowmen, a fella to warm your feet on, come winter nights – and, best of all, you doubled-up your farmlands.'

I am so angry I come nigh to choking.

But I know of old that words are wasted on him. I say: 'Age has not improved you, Mark.'

'Ah, come on!' he cries, 'I'm a fine figure of a man, still!'

I study him. He is as slim and upright as I remember; his hair still thick and curling yellow to his shoulders. His face has the reddish tint that goes with too much gin, but his eyes are sharp and overbright.

I warn him: 'Do not meddle with my children. I saw you talking to them.'

'I *am* their Uncle, dammit!'

'We do not allow profanity in this house.'

He sighs. '*You* never change, that's for sure and certain.'

I put the qwestion I have not yet dared to ask. 'What news of brother Will? He never writes to any of us.'

'I guess he's dead. Leastways, I've never come across him in my travels. There've been advertisements for him in lots of newspapers. He's either dead, or lying doggoe for some reason.'

He grins. 'Now, brother James, on the other hand, shows no sign of handing in *his* dinner-pail. He's put on thirty pounds of flesh since you last saw him.'

'How do you know that?'

'Because, dear sister, I spent all summer in dear old England; in Buckland St Mary for much of the time. Oh, I have such a tale to tell you!'

Elizabeth and all her family come over. Little Robert, who is already sleeping, is wrapped in a blanket.

'I had not thought,' say I, 'that our talk was to be all that important?'

I look to where the young Vickerys are deep in conversation with Georgie and Rosa, and I see what I should have long since realised. That none of them are any longer children. Johnnie Vickery is twenty-two years old, and stands head and shoulders taller than his father. Chas and Willum make up a trio of earnest, God-fearing young men. I look to my own two. In the faces of all five cousins there is a stamp of determination what is new.

We sit down, all eleven of us around the table. I have a small speech prepared, but before I can say a single word, my brother is on his feet and speaking.

'Since I am the most senior member of the Greypaull family present here this night, it is up to me to explain matters properly to *all* interested parties, and to see that you are treated fairly.'

I interrupt him in a voice as dry as I can make it. 'Your worry on our behalf does you credit, Mark, tho' it is somewhat unexpected. How much, I ask myself, is your brotherly concern liable to cost us in dollars?'

He grins at me.

'My sister was ever hard and unbelieving of my motives.'

He pauses. 'But I have come here to bring you good news. There is money tied up in England – a lot of money, and it is rightfully yours if you wish to claim it.'

Elizabeth says: 'But we know all about that. Father made our brother James the sole Trustee. It was a legal Will. We could never break it.'

'You are wrong, dear sister. We can do plenty. I've spoken to solicitors in England. Father's Will can be contested – it can go to the Parliament if necessary – to the very House of Lords – for a fair judgement.'

'But that,' I cry, 'will cost more money in litigation than the Estate is worth!'

'Not if we win, Rhoda. Then James will have to pay the Court fees. We shall see him twice defeated!'

'And if we lose?'

'We shall not lose. We have a cast-iron case against him. We can all of us bear witness that we are in need of that money. Some of us are in *dire* need!'

Elizabeth says: 'It is not what Father would have wanted. All his children arguing and fighting, taking to the Law, qwarrelling about his money.' She is close to tears.

Mark changes course. He speaks gently to her.

'Father was hoodwinked by brother James. Who better than a Barrister to draw up a Family Will and slant it all in his own favour? Father was sick at the time. In his right mind – without the convulsions – he would never have agreed to give James power over us all.'

Mark turns to me.

'What say you, Rhoda?'

'I say we can none of us afford to go to Law.'

'But we *must* afford it! You haven't seen poor Mary's plight, they are nigh on destitute, and James has lifted not one finger to help that family. Then there is Joan, widowed and alone in Taunton, making dresses for complaining women who are never satisfied!'

His face has a self-rightshus look now. 'As for me – well I have already made one trip home on *your* behalf. Worked my passage on a cattle-boat, but I'm not complaining.' He pulls out the linings of his jacket pockets. 'It's left me without a dime –'

'What about Ann?' I interrupt him.

'Ann is not well-off either! Her husband, Robbins, has remained a Curate. They have one daughter, and live in genteel poverty. It broke my heart to see my poor blind sister. Father meant Ann to have servants and a carriage.'

I grow thoughtful. 'You are right, Mark. I have a letter written by Father wherein he states that he has made provision for her.'

'But James controls all monies, Rhoda. These past five years we have not one of us received a penny of Interest from the Estate. He still talks about repairs to buildings, plastering and thatching; the rise in Income Tax, and so forth! Oh you should just have seen him! he has grown very stout and pompous. He rides around Buckland as if he owns the village. He has a lady-friend these days – a spinster of 'mature years'. He tells me that she is an heiress, that he himself had drawn up several local Wills that are in her favour. He has given her our mother's ruby ring. I felt tempted to rip it off her finger!'

Elizabeth says: 'I had no idea of all of this. He writes me such very friendly letters.'

'Of course he does,' Mark cries. 'It suits him well to have you and Rhoda four thousand miles away, and never asking for your share.'

Mark speaks directly to my son. 'And now you, George Hodder Salter. You have a right to speak. What say you to all of this, and you, John Vickery, what is your opinion on it?'

I say: 'Leave them be, this does not concern them.'

To my surprise, my son gets slowly to his feet. He stands very tall, a look of fright upon his face. He says: 'Begging your pardon, Mama, but I think it does concern us. I know that we're not in great need of money – well, none of us is blind or bankrupt. But Grandfather meant for Uncle James to help us – and he never has yet.'

He hesitates.

I say: 'Go on then, George, let's hear it all.'

'Well – it's this way, Mama. I'm coming up for twenty in a few weeks. You and Father Black are good to me, but I have a need to be my own man. Papa meant for me and Ed to carry on his business. If I don't soon get back to the butchering proffeshun it'll be too late.' His voice grows bitter. 'I'm never known as George Hodder Salter in this place. They refer to me only as "Mrs Black's boy"; but for me to go into business on my own will cost you money. Money that you don't have.'

George sits down, and up stands Johnnie. His face is flushed and nervous. He says: 'My Pa needs more land, and he needs it badly. Time is coming up when we three oldest boys'll have to leave the home farm, just because it can't support so many grown men.'

I say to Mark: 'These are your words they are speaking. They were all of them content until you came here.'

'Were they, Rhoda?' It is my husband talking. 'Seems to me that your brother has only brought certain matters to a head.'

'Oh, he was ever good at that,' say I. 'You will think differently when he asks you to finance him in this risky venture.'

Robert speaks for the first time. 'I'll stake the man a trip to England, if Jim is willing to go half. This business had dragged on ten years already.'

Jim nods. He says to Mark: 'We'll pay your passage and give you living-money enough to last six months. But we expect results – and qwickly!'

'You'll get them, gentlemen! That I can promise.' Mark smiles on Elizabeth and me. 'I shall need your affidavits, so that I can collect what is rightfully yours. Within one year from now you two will be wealthy women.'

December 1

Mark returns whence he came, which I now find out is Oshkosh, where he has friends. He says he will return to us when we have raised the money for his passage to England. I am all against this. 'No,' I tell him. '*We* will come to Oshkosh. *We* will purchase your ticket to sail.'

He is unconcerned. 'Very well, if that's how you want it. Might do you a power of good to travel a bit more, Rhoda. You're getting very narrow-minded since you settled in these backwoods. There are English families living in Oshkosh. You remember the Pomeroys and the Gillinghams? I'll introduce you to them.'

Chapter Twenty-Six

Early January, in the Fox River Valley country of Wisconsin, was not the best of times to undertake a journey. From the window of the railroad car Rosa gazed at the wind-sculpted snowdrifts with only a red-painted barn or a sagging fence to break their whiteness. The reason for the trip to Oshkosh was not quite clear in her mind. Rosa had not expected to be included on this rare jaunt; for all three women folk to be absent from their home and dairy duties was extreme, but Mama when happy was easy to persuade.

'After all,' she had said, 'it's the men who have made it necessary for us to go to Oshkosh. Why should Rosa have to bide at home and tend them? Let them manage for a week or so! They'll appreciate us the more, Elizabeth, when we get back! Come to think of it – why shouldn't we stay there for a whole week?'

And Mama *was* happy these days, in a way that she had never been in all of Rosa's eighteen years of life. When the moment had come for them to part with Father Black that morning, her mother had clung to him as tearful as any young bride. Rosa thought how strange it was that such old, old people could still act and feel in such a way. She began to think about her own great romance; how would it happen, and with whom? In April she would see her nineteenth birthday; already she had stitched a dozen quilts, her Hope Chest overflowed with embroidered pillow-slips and crocheted lace-mats. But Suamico, with its farming population of first and second-generation Germans and Frenchmen, its Scandinavian and Polish families, could not give her what she sought. Rosa loved and venerated all things English. If she could not find an Englishman to marry, why then – she would die a maiden-lady!

The township of Oshkosh stood on the banks of Lake Winnebago and at the mouth of the Fox River; and down that river rolled the logs of clear white pine, of ash and hickory, of maple and elm. The coming of the railroads had brought in a different kind of migrant. To Oshkosh came blacksmiths and mechanics, carriage and waggon-makers, manufacturers of furniture, of kegs and barrels. The constant supply of timber saw the setting up of factories and wood mills to supply the new farmsteads which were opening up the land as far north as Escanaba.

By this year of 1878, Oshkosh was counted among the most important saw-mill centres in all the nation. Many young Englishmen, having heard of the fortunes to be made in the New World, had brought their skills across three thousand miles of ocean. James Gillingham, maker of carriages and waggons, wheelwright and blacksmith, had left Old England in the year of 1857. With his wife and young son Thomas, he had settled finally in Oshkosh. His business at number 99, Marion Street, was thriving, his home a popular meeting-place for the expatriate English of the district. Mark Greypaull had spent many pleasant hours in the Gillingham household; he had told the story of his withheld inheritance, and how, with help from his sisters, he intended to claim what was rightfully his.

When Rhoda and Elizabeth arrived in Oshkosh they were taken, with Rosa, to a small hotel. An attentive, smiling Mark saw them comfortably settled-in. The appointment with an Attorney had been made, he told them, for the following morning.

'And then,' he said, 'we have a tea-and supper invitation that I think you ladies will enjoy. You are to meet the Gillingham family who come from Dorchester, Old England.'

The business with the Attorney was lengthy and complicated. Mama and Aunt Elizabeth put their signatures to a document which was then handed up to Uncle Mark. Over lunch, he assured them that he would do his very best for his sisters, at all times.

It was mid-afternoon when they drove into Marion Street. An impressive signboard swung high above a group of timber buildings: it announced the business to be that of 'Gillingham and Son, Manufacturers of Carriages, Waggons and Sleighs.' In smaller letters were printed the words '*Lumbermen's Supplies. Boat and Mill Blacksmiths.*'

The house was a pretty frame construction painted pale green; it stood to one side of a busy yard which held stacks of lumber and piles of iron ingots. The house door opened, and they were welcomed in by Mrs Gillingham. They were given English tea and thin bread and butter, and the talk turned at once to Buckland St Mary and Dorchester, England.

Rosa listened for a time, but at last she moved away towards a window, which overlooked the yard. Between the rows of piled planks a young man in a neat grey suit walked up and down, a notepad in his hand.

Mr Gillingham, noticing her interest, said: 'That's my boy Thomas. You'll be meeting him at supper.'

After four days of shopping, three visits to the Gillingham family, and one slithering walk along the frozen shores of Lake Winnebago, Mama and Aunt Elizabeth abandoned their rebellion, and began to hanker for Suamico and home. Only Rosa was reluctant to leave. She said as much to Mrs Gillingham.

'But you must come back and stay with us! Come in the fall, my dear. Thomas has a boat. You could go fishing on the Lake, isn't that so, Tom?'

He had nodded in that earnest, half-smiling way of his that was so very English. Even his shyness, thought Rosa, was refined and good-mannered, and quite different from the tongue-tied awe shown by Suamico boys when in her presence.

'Take Miss Salter over to your office,' his mother had insisted. 'Show her your new Filing System and your Business Diploma.'

The office of Gillingham and Son turned out to be a small brick building.

'It needs to be absolutely fireproof you see, Miss Salter,' explained Thomas, 'since it holds the Safe and all our Business Records.'

She had admired the cabinet of small drawers, the illustrated catalogues of Sleighs and Waggons; the Account Books entered up in his tidy sloping script.

She looked at the single desk and chair, so obviously his.

'So where does your Papa sit, Mr Gillingham, to do his figuring?'

'Oh, Pa handles all the practical side of things. He detests paper-work of any sort. He sent me to Business College here in Oshkosh. In fact,' Thomas blushed, 'in fact I won a Scholarship to the Commercial Department, that was worth all of forty dollars towards my tuition. I finished the Course last year. Since then I've taken over all the accounting and so forth. Pa made me a full partner with him on my twenty-first birthday.'

Rosa managed to gaze up at him although they were of almost equal height. 'Oh,' she breathed, 'I think that's so wonderful – so enterprising of you! But then, like me, you're English, aren't you? It makes us just that little bit special, don't you feel? My Papa was a businessman too, he had a Seat on the Board of Trade in the city of Chicago.'

Thomas had seemed puzzled. 'English?' he said. 'I'm not English. I'm an American, I was born here – so were you.'

'But by blood,' she said, 'through our parents, you and I come from pure English stock – you can't deny that!'

'I've never even thought about it.' He dismissed his heritage of a thousand years with a wave of the hand. 'Now tell me all about your father, and Chicago, and what he did there.'

The train took them slowly but safely home through the winter landscape. They passed through Neenah and Menasha, Kaukauna and De Pere, and Rosa dreamed of Thomas Gillingham, who, by blood, was one hundred per cent English, and already a little in love with her.

*

March 14

In a letter from Mrs Gillingham I learn that my brother left Oshkosh for England one week since. Our new school is finished. It looks very fine, has two doors by which the children enter, one for boys and one for girls. It is to be known as the *White Pine School*.

September 27
It is high time that my muddled head was set into some kind of order. I have lately aqwired a knack of saying the wrong words at the wrong time, and so upsetting my two older children. There are days in a woman's life when to be a mother is a doubtful pleasure.

Perhaps it is because of Jon that I am in such confushun. No matter how tall and broad he grows, in his mind he stays but five years old; what makes it hard sometimes for me to see that George and Rosa are in *every way* full-grown.

It all begins with my brother Mark, and that night of family talk, when my George stood before us all and declared his independence. Hard on that shock comes our trip to Oshkosh and Rosa's meeting with young Thomas Gillingham. So now, as I say to Jim, we have on our hands a restless youth and a lovesick maiden, and only Jon content to bide alongside us on the farm, and feed his poultry flock. At this very minute Rosa is away on a two-week trip to Oshkosh, while Georgie has gone with Jim to meet a butcher in De Pere, who is willing to complete my boy's apprenticeship for him.

Matthew says that I should be pleased and proud that I have such strong and independent children. It is, says he, only natural at their age to wish to 'fly the nest'. But not yet, I argue. It is all too soon. Jim also says in a sly voice: 'Didn't I hear some story someplace about a parcel of young women back in England who set up keeping store, and all against their Papa's wishes? Went off and lived all by themselves, goshdarn it! Then two of these girls sailed off to America and never saw their Pa again. Be careful, Rhoda! By tying them to your apron-strings, you could yet lose them altogether!'

October 19
It is all settled with Georgie. He is to go to De Pere in the New Year and live-in with the butcher and his wife until his

411

apprenticeship is complete. Jim reports that this is an elderly couple who will retire in a few years, and so need to sell their business. It was hinted, says Jim, that should George prove satisfactory in his work they would be prepared to turn over the house and butchery to him at a most *favourable* price.

Rosa comes back from Oshkosh all a-glow and happy. We hear how she has walked and walked with Thomas, how they have sailed and fished on Lake Winnebago. She brings with her a letter for me from Mrs Gillingham, who congratulates me on my charming daughter, and hopes that Jim and I will see our way clear to allowing a friendship between her son and Rosa, and a regular correspondence between them. My girl has hardly unpacked her trunk before she is penning a letter to Oshkosh. Later on, I find her with Jon sorting thru' the scraps-bag.

'I thought,' says she, 'that I would start on another qwilt, Mama.'

She looks meaningly at Jim, who smiles back at her.

'I have a notion to repeat the Double Wedding Ring design. Is that a good idea, Father Black?'

Jim say: 'Why not? Every girl should have a Bridal Qwilt all ready and waiting. Just see what happened with your Ma, here! For the want of a Wedding Ring qwilt she all but lost me! Why, them patches were pieced together so fast it's a wonder that they hold together.'

There is much laughter around the table, as there always is when Jim is present. But later on, when he and I are working in the cowbarn I warn him to be careful.

'We shall have the expense of George and his meat-market in a few years. It is what his poor dear Father would have wanted for him. He is not, and never will be a farmer. But it will cost us dear to set him up. We shall not be able to afford a wedding for some years to come.'

'What is there to afford?' asks Jim.

It is clear that he has no notion of bridal matters.

'Well first of all there is the linen. A girl should have at least a dozen of everything, with the monogram embroidered on them. Then there is her trousseau. Most important of all there is her Dowry.'

'Seems to me,' says he, 'like a whole lot of fussing about nothing.'

'The Gillinghams,' say I, 'are a well-to-do English family. They are people of my own class. They will know what is proper in such matters. In any case, Rosa is my only daughter. She will marry with a Dowry, or else bide single.'

Jim says: 'She's mightily impressed with this young Thomas.'

'I know. She is in love, and I am happy for her. But we must not encourage it too much. It will be several years before we can *afford* to launch her.'

January 1, 1879

This New Year begins with partings. Jim drives Georgie to De Pere in the cutter. I set my boy up with new long woollen underwear and several butcher's aprons. I cannot hide a tear as we say farewell. I recall that winter's morning in Buckland St Mary, when his father rode up on a black mare, and bringing the green leather case what held the tools of his proffeshun. My Georgie carries with him now that same case into his new life. He looks so like his father. He has so many dreams and high hopes that I am fearful for him.

Jim sees my distress. He says: 'You must let him go, Rhoda. He needs to be his own man.'

I say, surprised, because I have never seen the truth till now, 'He has never been qwite the same since Eddie died. They looked like twins, as if they were two halves of the same person. He so relied on Ed.'

'All the more reason,' says Jim, 'for George to strike out on his own.'

I know this to be true, oh but it hurts me just the same.

Elizabeth comes over to give me comfort. She is very worried about Johnnie and Chas, who by Georgie's example, are also ankshus to try their wings. They talk all the time of moving to the Far West. They have a fancy to go ranching in Texas or Wyoming.

413

'If we had the money due to us under Father's Will,' says my sister, 'then we could buy more land, and my sons would never need to leave me.'

February 4

Was over to the Church this evening. Jim takes a cord of wood to fuel the stove, and I sweep the floor and clean the alter brasses. As we are leaving we meet up with Toussant Teller, who cries out: 'Hey there! Mrs Black, ma'am! You folks got mail from England! Two letters come together this very day. Guess it's good news from your brother, eh? Though, come to think of it, he never paid postage on either of them letters. I had seventy-five cents to collect from Mrs Vickery on account of his forgetfullness!'

I say to Jim. 'It must be word from Mark.' Even as I speak there is a sound of sleighbells thru' the darkness. It is Robert and Elizabeth on their way to visit with us.

We go into the house, all four of us together. The kitchen is warm, Jim puts coffee on to boil. Jon brings the cookie-jar. Matthew hands around tobacco to Jim and Robert. When we are settled round the table, Elizabeth lays down two letters, both of them unopened.

'I just couldn't touch them,' says she, and pushes them towards me. I study the postmarks. The first one has been long underway, the last is dated but a month ago. I open the letter dated August 22, 1878. I begin to read out loud.

Dear Sister Elizabeth and Robert Vickery, Sister Rhoda and James Black,

I arrived in England in good shape and made my way at once to Somerset, stopping first in Taunton to see our sister Joan, who is often sick with severe pains in her forehead, and as a result has had a falling-off in her dress-making business. She sends you her regards and says that she is much in need of Father's money.

I came next to Buckland St Mary, where I found Mary and Daniel in very poor cirumstances, and altogether dependent on the charity of the Parish, and their children who are working. Daniel is very sick

414

and Mary disturbed in her mind due to worry over money, and the hard-heartedness of our brother James. They also very keen to prosecute him.

Ann is still living at Rook's Farm. The Curate Robbins is a weak reed. She cannot lean on him for help. They have a pretty daughter who does her best for her parents. Father made provision for Ann, but James was to be her administrator. Ann says James pays scant notice to her affairs.

William is here. He is lodging with our cousin Henry, and refuses to say a single word about his long silence or what has come to pass as regards his wife and children. But I have his affidavit to go against James Paul, since brother Will has only the clothes to his back and the charity of Henry.

Much has happened in the past year. Father's wife is dead and her children left the village. The house has been bought by the spinster I spoke of, the lady from Crewkerne name of Henrietta Martin. She is wealthy in her own right, owns a Bank and lands, and is a very shrewd woman. Now I must give you the most surprising news of all. Our brother James Paul is to marry this lady-friend, and he is at present a lodger in her house, the place that was once our Father's home. The two of them of course being chaperoned by servants, but I can tell you that this state of affairs is causing great gossip around Buckland.

I have taken a room at the Lamb and Flag Inn. On Monday next I am to see Solicitor Reeves of Ilminster, and will put all before him for his good advice.

I lay the pages down and open the second letter. It is dated just a month ago. Mark begins:

Solicitor Reeves says that we have a good case. He will prepare forthwith a Petition on behalf of all of us, that Father's Trust property be sold and the proceeds divided between us. This Petition to be presented in the County Court, but it will take some time before it is heard. In the meantime I am very low on funds, and shall be obliged if you can see your way clear to sending me fifty dollars.

I will write again as soon as I have news.

Your loving brother Mark

415

We gaze at one another. Jim is the first to break our silence.

'Your brother has us over a barrel where money is concerned. Seems like we shall have to dig deeper in our pockets if we mean to see this business through.'

Roberts says: 'We're in too far now to turn back. He's the man on the spot. He knows the truth of what's going on in Buckland. Who else can we trust?'

Elizabeth says: 'Well some progress has been made. Solicitor Reeves is to take our case to the County Court.'

I have nothing to say that will be of comfort, so I bide qwiet.

Easter Day, 1879

Georgie comes to spend two days with us, and Thomas Gillingham arrives from Oshkosh. We are a full and happy household. Oh, how I do love it when we are all together! My boy and girl are cheerful, Rosa is moonstruck over Thomas and shows him off around the district. George has changed much in these few months. Like Jim says, we sent a boy away to De Pere, and he has come back to us a full-fledged man. Jon is beside himself with joy to have Georgie home. He pulls his brother straightway to the hen-house to see the broods of new chicks. There is much work to be done in dairy and kitchen, but Matt is an ever-present rock for us to lean on. Dear Matthew. Whatever should we do without him.

We go all together to Church on this sacred Day of our Saviour's resurrectshun; our Church is filled to the doors with the faithful Episcopalians of Suamico. I look around me. Six pews are taken up by Vickerys and Salters, and their kin. It comes to me then that America is now my true home, and Suamico the place where I have been most happy in all the world.

April 20

The wettest spring in living memory. It rains for a month, so that Jim and Matthew have time to build a little mud-room on to the kitchen where boots and wet clothes may be left to dry. This work being done on days when our spring corn should have been planted.

416

We are now five weeks behind with all our field work. Our Holsteins still housed within the cowbarn, since all tracks and meadows too waterlogged to bear their great weight.

June 18

All crops now planted, but too late says Jim to give a first-rate harvest. What we do have in abundance is timothy-grass and red clover. All hands will be needed this year when we get into haying. We shall miss Georgie sorely, as will Robert feel the loss of Johnnie and Chas, who departed a few weeks ago, on their way to Wyoming.

September 19

It must be faced, our crops this year are very poor, giving only half the yield that is needed by our cattle. Jim and I talk this over after supper. We shall need, says he, to buy-in grain, and that will come expensive. He does not say what is in both our minds, that much ready cash has been outlayed on sending George to De Pere, not to menshun our share of the cost of sending Mark back to England. Only Jon, with his well-tended flocks of chickens, geese and turkeys, and his eggs, sold in the dry-goods store, looks likely to make a profit this year.

It is while we are talking all this over that Matthew comes back from the fields where he has been shepherding the stock. He says that five of our in-calf heifers have gone missing. We go out at once and begin to search. We find them in a far corner, underneath a hickory tree. All five, in a distressed condishun, stand around the lifeless bodies of their new-born calves.

'It is too soon,' I say. 'They were not due until the end of November.'

Jim asks: 'What could have caused this?'

'Many things,' say I. 'There is a disease among cows that will cause aborshun. On the other hand, this field stands close beside the railroad track. They could have taken fright – or a dog might have chased them.'

'How soon shall we know?'

'We have four more in-calf cows. If they manage to hold on to their calves then we shall know that this was due to accident and not disease.'

September 29
I complete my Half-Year Ledger reckoning. Our state in terms of cash is very bad. No more cows have yet aborted, but even so we shall have to sell a horse or two and maybe more if we are to come safety thru' the coming winter. Rosa returns from a week in Oshkosh. She and Thomas wish to be betrowthed. Only, say I, if you are content to have a *long* engagement to him. Another letter comes from Mark in which he states that our Case is to be heard on October second in the County Court. He reqwests a further fifty dollars for expenses.

Jim calls us all together. There is no help for it, he tells us, but that he must go back to the logging. It seems that Mr Tremble has approached him and offered his old job as foreman, with a bonus added on.

'No,' I cry. 'I cannot bear that you should go away for six months. It is such hard labour. You might take a fever, or some accident befall! There must be some other way?'

He comes and puts an arm about my shoulders. 'There is no other way, Rhoda, and you won't be on your lonesome. You'll have Matt and Rosa, and our champion poultry-farmer Jon right here beside you!'

He grins. 'You could always stitch another qwilt to pass the time. Six months at the logging could foot-up to a great many dollars for us.'

I know that he is right, but I have such a *bad feeling* about this whole venture.

October 5
This day Jim leaves for the Pineries that stand beyond De Pere, and close to the Fox River. It is his responsibility to get a team of horses together, also skilled teamsters, axemen, good cooks and their helpers. He must purchase provishuns to see them thru' the winter, also medicaments in case of accident or sickness.

Once again I get ready warm underwear and clothes, and bid farewell to another of my menfolk. It is true that we need the money, but, oh, it is so hard to see him go!

I write letters to our Salter kin in England, and to my sisters Joan and Mary. I catch-up on sewing and darning. When these tasks are all done with I bid Matt bring down the qwilting-frame from the attic.

'If Jon will thread needles for us, Matthew,' I say, 'then I will instruct you in the ways of American Patchwork.'

Christmas Eve
The children have made the house festive with paper chains and berried boughs. Our Christmas tree stands in a corner of the parlour. The greatest time for celebration in this country is in November when they have Thanksgiving Day, but for us who are English by birth, Christmas will always be our time of most joy.

Georgie arrived but an hour ago, bearing gifts for all of us from De Pere. He says he had trouble getting to us, that snow lies deep around De Pere. The lumber-camps, says George, have been snow-locked for several weeks now.

Well, I had not expected to see Jim, but still I hoped for a miracle, but it is not to be. This separation from him is so hard to bear. He cannot possibly get home before the first of May at least.

It is my birthday.

January 1, 1880
A new Year. A new Decade.
I must needs count my blessings on this day, for I am very low in spirits. Without Jim and George the work is heavy in cowbarn and dairy. Matthew grows frailer with the years. He offers me his Savings from his Disability Pension, since he knows I am worried about money. I thank him from my heart, but say that we will be all right when my inheritance comes thru' from England.

Our cows have calved-down at the time expected, so no

danger of contajus abortshun in the herd. An engagement has been agreed on between Thomas and Rosa. The ring to be given on April twenty-second – her twenty-first birthday. Georgie is content in his employment, and talks of taking on the business when his employer retires. Jon's convulshuns are few and far between.

As for myself, well I have the best, most loving husband in the world. I have my dear Elizabeth and Robert always close-by, and many good friends of our little Church.

Therefore, I have *no right* or *reason* to be worried or down-hearted.

February 20

The corn-bins are empty as we had known they must be after the poor harvest. I am forced to buy-in grain at a high price. It is either that, or let my cows go. We are now very short of hard cash. Elizabeth and Robert in similar state. Robert takes work in the saw-mill to help out, as does Willum. This de-presshun in business is most hard on the younger people, and those with many children. I read in the newspaper of farmers who go out to their barns and hang themselves or put a shotgun to their heads. Only last week a young woman in Outagamie County was found frozen to death on the river bank. It is thought that she wished to end her life since she had been deserted by her husband, and there was no food in the house for her seven children. Many cases of drunkenness and arson are reported. But it is mostly these hard times what turn a good man towards gin and whisky, and envy will cause a destitute man or woman to fire a neighbour's barn or house.

Matthew finds me close to tears this evening and takes the *Tribune* pages from me. We have worries enough of our own, he scolds. It's terrible what's happening to good folk, but there's little we can do about so many tragedies.

April 2

A note from Jim, very short, to say that all is well and he will be home in early May. The camp now opened up, he says, and the log-run soon to start down-river. My *releef* so great on hearing from him that I am overcome by faintness, thus alarming Matt and Rosa who *incist* that they will manage evening milking by themselves.

So here I sit, cossetted and shamefaced, a shawl around my shoulders and my feet upon a stool. Elizabeth comes over.

'Look at me,' I say, 'they will make an old woman of me.'

'Let them!' laughs my sister. 'You have worked the clock around since Jim went to the pineries. A lazy day will do you no harm.'

The trouble with lazy days is that there is too much time for thinking.

This year will see my fiftieth birthday. When my children were babies I worried about croup and fevers. Now I am *ankshus* for Georgie, who wants so bad to be in business like his father and Salter Uncles. I fear to lose my only daughter who is deep in love with Thomas Gillingham of Oshkosh. I pray each night that I may be spared to care for Jon. Whatever would he do without me? Even as I think about him, he comes into the kitchen, a basket of eggs carried carefully in both hands. He is coming fourteen years old. I have told no one in the Old Country of my son's *afflictshun*, have said only in letters that Jon is not strong. He is safe here in Suamico, known to all and treated gently.

Jim's note is in my apron pocket; I shall sleep well tonight with his dear words underneath my pillow.

April 15
The Gillinghams are to come North for Rosa and Thomas's engagement party. We spring-clean the whole house. Our *qwilt* is now abandoned in favour of dressmaking. Rosa's new gown is of stiff silk in her favourite blue. It must, she says, have a bustle, what seems to me a silly style, but I guess it is the *fashun*!

April 26
The Gillingham family take their leave of us this morning. Robert drives them to the railroad depot. We are sad to see

421

them go, the days of their visit having been so pleasant and homely, the only sorrow being Jim's absence, the need for which they qwite understood. Rosa weeps, on and off, for the rest of the day. Her ring is a pretty thing of rubies and pearls, what is an heirloom and once belonged to Mrs Gillingham's mother. Rosa says she cannot bear it, that she is in Suamico and Thomas down to Oshkosh. She will not take off the ring, but wears it all thru' milking and churning, looking at it every other minute and breaking down in fresh tears.

I am obliged to be stern with her at the last.

'You agreed,' say I, 'that if Father Black and I allowed your betrowthal to Thomas, that you would be content with a long engagement. You know how money-matters stand with us. We are in no posishun to afford a Dowry, let alone a wedding. There is also your brother to consider. When his employer retires we must do our best to set George up in that meat-market in De Pere.'

'But Mama,' she wails, 'it all sounds so far into the future, and I love him so, with all my heart!'

'It is just as hard for Thomas,' say I.

I soften my tone, for my sympathies are with her, after all. 'Take off your lovely ring,' I say, 'and put it in its velvet box. It will only get damaged if you wear it around the dairy. The time will soon pass. There will be letters and visits for you and Tom, and all the plans to make for your life together.'

May 1
Our little nephew Robert Vickery starts this day to school. I walk up to the road to see him go. He is kitted-out in new tweed knickerbockers and a white shirt. Elizabeth goes with him on this first morning, but he keeps a pace or two ahead of her, his little lunch-pail in one hand, a bunch of windflowers for the teacher clutched in the other. To see the youngest member of our family on his way to the new White Pine School (for the building of which we all worked so hard), is very satisfying. I walk back to the dairy through the lovely morning. Our fields are green, all the orchard trees in blossom. A letter from

Thomas has set my Rosa singing as she churns the butter. If only Jim would come – but it cannot be long now. He will be pleased to find that Matt and I, with a little help from Robert, have finished the spring planting.

May 14

It is evening when he comes. I hear the sound of hoof-beats and run out to the front porch, and there he is riding down towards the house. I go out to meet him. He dismounts awkwardly, as if in pain, but when I ask what ails him, he laughs and says that it is nothing. The meeting between us is sweet after such long parting. We go into the house and I see by the light of the lamp that all is not well. There is a pallor to his skin, and lines of pain come to his face when'ere he moves. His beard has grown again, still black and curling, but grizzled silver this time at its edges. I busy myself at cook-stove and table. I say of the beard: 'Do not even think to shave it off, it truly suits you. That touch of grey makes you look so distingwished.'

Matt and Rosa come in, and there is yet another glad reunion. Jon, who must always see his poultry flock safe-housed is ever the last to come for supper. His joy at Jim's return touches me to tears.

May 16

Jim talks of everything except the trouble in his leg and right arm. After seven months of camp-life he is grateful for sheets and pillowcases, proper cutlery and china. He is also happy to be with me, once again.

'Not a day went by,' says he, 'but what I didn't miss you.'

'And I you,' I tell him. 'I shall never let you go away again.'

The dollars he has brought, with the bonus added, will ease our situashun for some time to come, but I fear that a high price has been paid in the earning of them.

'You might as well tell me,' I say at last. 'I know you are in pain. Did you have some mishap?'

'It's just some stiffness in my arm and leg. It's an old problem. If I pay it no mind then it goes away.'

June 10

We are early into Haying. Elizabeth and Robert come across to help us, also Willum. It is clear to all who see him that Jim is not his old self. He is slow about his work. He mows for but ten minutes, and then must needs lay down the scythe.

'Talk to him,' I say to Robert. 'Tell him this can't go on. It breaks my heart to see him suffer so!'

Even as we speak, Jim picks up the scythe and starts to mow. Two minutes of swinging the heavy blade and he faints clear away.

We carry him back into the house. Willum goes to fetch the doctor, who is visiting close by at Toussant Teller's house. When he comes, Doctor seems not at all surprised to find Jim in trouble.

'What did I tell you?' His look and tone is stern. 'Go back to the logging I said, and you could lose the use of that arm and leg altogether. Why, you stubborn Scotchman, you never heeded a single word I said!'

He hands me a dark green bottle labelled *Embrocation*.

'Rub this on him, it might help some. What he really needs is rest.' He turns back to Jim. 'Have you tried yet for that Disability Penshun?'

'No,' says Jim, 'I've managed just fine these past fifteen years. I won't go begging now.'

'And I've treated you these fifteen years for damage you suffered while on active service for your country. You've paid a mint of money out to me in treatments. Now you've come to the end of your rope, Jim Black. You'll never go back to the lumbering again; you may not even work your own lands for much longer. Don't be such a fool, man! You're a Veteran. The US Government owes you that Penshun. Make application for it!'

June 16

Our hay all cut. We move across to Robert's fields, but *not* with Jim.

He is in much pain. He is also very angry, and will not listen

424

to my words. But he does not know *me* when my mind is fixed upon a thing. I bide my time. It is after a good supper, when we sit on the porch in the evening cool that I am brave enough to broach the subject. 'From what Matthew tells me, you were qwite a hero in the Civil War.'

He moves uneasily in his chair, but says nothing.

'I would like very much to hear about it, Jim.'

'Every man who fought in that War was a hero. It took guts just to stay and see it through.'

'Matthew says you were injured while rescuing a comrade. That on another scouting-misshun your horse took fright and threw you, and you were dragged a qwarter-mile over rough terrain, your foot caught in the stirrup.'

'My brother is the one who took real damage. He got bullets in the stomach.'

'But you,' I say, 'you are also sick now from damage in that War.' I reach out to touch his hand. 'It must have been a bad time, Jim.'

He is silent. I recall what Elizabeth has said of him, when I first came here. How he is a man what hugs hurt and sorrow to himself, who cannot share his fears and heartaches. How he had suffered in that great Fire at Peshtigo, but had refused to speak one word about it. I study him thru' the fading light. All around us there is peace and plenty. Whipporwills call from the long grass, down in the marshes. The lindens are coming into flower in Teller's garden. The cut hay smells just the same as it once did in England. I say, in a way what is sure to fire him up: 'Well, of course, I don't blame you for wanting to forget that War. A lot of good men died for Abraham Lincoln's cause, and to very little purpose that I could see. I've heard it said that most negroes didn't know what to do with their freedom when it was granted to them! That Johnny Reb was not such a bad guy, after all!'

He frowns at me then, his thick black eyebrows like two straight lines. 'That's the kinda talk of folks who were never there. You should have been inside the Libby Prison for Officers! I spent the worst time of my whole life in that place.'

'Libby?' I ask. 'Isn't he a big name in business?'

Jim stirs in his chair. 'It was in one of his old warehouses that we officers were held. It became one of the most notorious hell-holes of the whole Civil War.'

All at once he sits upright, his hands gripped tight together. It is almost dark now.

'You want to hear what happened, do you? Well then, I'll tell you! It was August-time, real hot and sticky weather, with the midges biting like to drive us crazy. We were scouting along the banks of the Rapidon River. I was Acting Office of the Picket Guard that night. They snuck-up on us in their hundreds, we never stood a chance. I ended up in Richmond, Virginia. I'll never forget my first sighting of that Prison. It was an old building, three storeys high in front, and four in rear. There were six big rooms. Before the War it had been used to store tobacco. Twelve hundred men were locked up in those rooms at any one time, mostly Federal Officers of all ranks, from lieutenants up to colonels. Many of us who were in that Second Battle of Bull Run ended up in Libby.'

Jim eases back against the cushions of the rocker, and now he speaks more to himself than to me.

'I don't know how many hundreds of good officers died there. The place was cold and damp. We were issued rations of sour bread, turnips and cabbage. We were supposed to cook our own food, but hardly ever given sufficient fuel to do so. The prison hospital was grossly overcrowded, and no wonder! There was one water closet to each of the six rooms, a primitive old privvy, that fouled the air. There was a lot of fever. Worst of all were the cells of solitary confinement, where they kept the men who were awaiting trial. Officers who went healthy into Libby came out broken men in mind and body.'

'And you?' I ask softly. 'What was your state, Jim?'

'I had taken damage to my shoulder and my right side long before I was captured. The injuries got worse in Libby, as did those of us all. As to my mind, well I went to Worship with the rest of them at seven every morning. Come evening, and I said my own prayers. I thought about my boyhood home back in

426

Alberta, and about Matthew. I worried a whole lot over Matt. I promised God that if I ever got out of that place that I'd live a good life from there onwards. Maybe help to build a Church up to His glory.'

He turns towards me. 'We tried to keep occupied. We started up a newsheet, called it the *Libby Chronicle*. Well, in the end a whole bunch of us were exchanged for a number of the Greycoats' top brass. I found myself down in Nashville, Tennessee, working at a desk job. In the spring of '65 I came back to Suamico.'

'You should have told me about your injuries.'

'Elizabeth had mentioned how your husband George had been a sick man for many years. I figured that if you thought I was less than A1 fit, you might not want to take me on.'

'Oh Jim!' I am near to tears by this time. 'How could you have so misunderstood me?' I go to kneel beside him. I take his hands in mine. 'There's to be no more pretence between us. You kept your promise to God. He brought you safe out of the Libby Prison, and you have helped build up our little Church here to His glory. Now is the time to think about your ownself. The doctor says you'll never go lumbering again. That in time you may not even manage work about the farm; the day could come when we really need that Disability Pension.'

He looks uneasy at my words. 'I don't know, Rhoda. It means going before an Attorney, swearing depositions and so forth. I've heard that it takes years . . .'

'You were ankshus enough to send my brother off to England to dispute my father's Will. You have even invested dollars in that uncertain outcome.'

All at once a broad grin comes to his dear face.

'You're right,' says he, 'I guess this country owes me something, after all. We'll see an Attorney just as soon as I'm in a state fit enough to travel!'

June 20
A letter comes this day from Mark. Nine months have passed without a word from England. I say to Elizabeth: 'It will be yet another story of how he must have more dollars for expenses.'

We sit on my sister's front porch in the cool of evening. Jim and Robert smoke pipes of fragrant tobacco what gives off a thick smoke, and so keeps away the June bugs. Elizabeth and I drink tea. The envelope unstamped as ever, lies unopened between us.

'Oh well,' I say at last. 'Might as well see how much he wants from us this time.'
I begin to read.

Dear Sisters Elizabeth and Rhoda, dear Robert and Jim.
You will be wondering at my long silence, but the first news was not good, and I thought not to worry you with it. Our Case against James, when heard in the County Court, was decided in his favour. I at once instructed Solicitor Reeve to put in an Appeal to the High Court of Justice in the City of London. This was done on November tenth 1879. Our brother James was told that before the Case could be heard, a sum of twenty pound must be paid to the Court, in advance, against expenses and costs. This money to come from the Trust held by James for his brothers and sisters. James informed the Court, and me, that no such sum lay in the Trust Fund.

Therefore, our case could not be heard. The only way left to us now to gain our inheritance from Father, is to carry our Plea to the highest Court in England. The House of Lords. I am told that from them will come a final decision.

Brother James is very angry at this outcome. He thought to foil us by not paying out that twenty pounds, and he did not think I would dare to push matters up so far as the House of Lords.

I hope and trust that you all approve of my efforts on your behalf. I shall not need any further money from you, since I am lodging with Joan in Taunton, and supporting myself by means of cattle-dealing.
Your loving brother, Mark

We can only look at one another.
Robert says at last: 'He's done very well by us. I never thought he had it in him.'
I say: 'Well, at best he's working for his living. That must at least be good news for us. As to the final outcome of all this – we are now in the hands of the Law Lords, and some of them

are liable to be cronies of Barrister James Paul Wyatt.' I take up the letter and study it again. 'He says nothing of when our Case is to be heard.'

Elizabeth says: 'I shall be glad when this is all over.'

Can only agree with her, heart and soul.

October 5

No time for writing all thru' harvest. Such hard work this year with Jim still suffering pain, espeshully in his arm and shoulder. He feels awful bad about it all, but rest, says our Doctor, is Jim's only hope. All crops safe gathered-in. Rosa and I get busy with pickling and preserving. Thomas comes up from Oshkosh and bides two weeks with us. George rides over from De Pere and stays a week-end. The young folks are so merry and light hearted together. George tells us all about the township of De Pere. Thomas says he is to bid for a plot of ground close by his father's business, where he and Rhoda can build their house. Jon suffers only two convulshuns all thru' summer.

October 14

Yesterday we took a trip to Green Bay, to sell my butter in the Market. Took with us ten cheeses to sell for Elizabeth, and several jars of honey for Mrs Valentine, she having had a surplus this year. A keen price obtained by me for all goods.

We had set out in sunshine, no wind, a perfect fall day. Jim remarked on the wealth of berries to be seen along the way, what is said to foretell a bitter winter. As the day wore on a strong wind rose from off the Bay. As we drove home, great blue black clouds built up behind us. We rose this morning to a powdering of snow what is *very* early, even for these parts. The men bring in a cord of wood. I clean the stove what is used in the dairy in cold weather. We do jobs what are ushally left until November. I recall the story of the steamboat Captain who told of the mass of polar air what sometimes slides down over Canada and Lake Superior. A first freeze, he said, can come without warning. Harbours can turn overnight into a sheet of ice.

429

Rosa has gone with Thomas back to Oshkosh.

October 16
We are struck by a blizzard such as no living person ever witnessed in the fall of the year. That powdering of snow was but a warning. We are roused in the night by a wild wind what bears thick sleet and snow. Jim and Matt are fearful for our barns and sheds, it being so early in the season our buildings have not yet been given their years-end overhaul. We light lamps and peer from upper windows. We hear a crashing and rending of wood, but can see nothing save a spinning whiteness. When daylight comes we are releeved to find the big cowbarn left in good shape, save for a few missing shingles. It is the smaller sheds what have suffered damage. Some of the poultry flock have perished. Jon's angwish is pitiful to witness. He is beside himself, and will not be comforted. I fear a convulshun.

Come mid-morning, and deliverance arrives in the shape of Willum, who has struggled thru' deep drifts to see how we have fared the night. He straightway sets-to about the mending of Jon's sheds, my poor boy helping where he can, what calms his agitatshun. This help from Willum a great blessing to us, since neither Jim nor Matthew in a good state of health to do heavy labour in freezing weather.

October 20
No more snow, tho' temperatures very low for the time of year. Jim and Matthew go to the harness-shop this morning, and to the dry-goods store, where they hear dreadful tales of what befell on our night of storm. The winds, they report, reached one hundred and twenty-five miles per hour across the Bay. Since navigation had not yet closed down, many ships caught unprepared and so were lost. The great steamer *Alpena* is qwite vanished with all on board her.

I pen a note to Rosa in Oshkosh, that she should come home with all haste, lest condishuns worsen. I pack a parcel of warm wollen clothing for my Georgie in De Pere; the work in a slaughter-house and meat-market being chilly, even in mild weather.

November 2

Rosa home from Oshkosh. Land, so she tells us, has been purchased for the building of a house for her and Thomas. The cost of a wedding and Dowry begins a total-up again inside my head. It is such a worry that I must needs qwickly push it from my mind. As I say to Jim when we are on our own, all our wealth these days is on-the-hoof, or stored in corn-bins, and this winter looks set to promise the worse condishuns we have ever known.

November 23

The mail, held-up for weeks by storm, brings news from England. A letter from Mark. We foregather this time in Elizabeth's house, since little Robbie has slight fever, and cannot be left. I pick up the envelope, and my first remark is that Mark has paid the postage on it! I begin to read.

Dear Sisters and your Husbands,
At last I have good news to report. Our case was heard in the House of Lords on September twenty-eighth, and a decision given in our favour. Brother James was stripped of his position as Sole Trustee of Father's Estate, and also ordered to pay all costs.

A Sale is to be held on November twenty-fourth at the Lamb and Flag Inn, at Buckland St Mary. Offered up for auction are the cottages and house, gardens and orchards, the meadowland and field enclosures, being situated at Dommett, Dommett's Cross and Pomeroy's. I enclose the Bill of Sale knowing it to be of interest to you.

Our brother James now seems to be a broken man. His lady friend, Miss Henrietta Martin, is likely to be the highest bidder at the Sale. There is no longer talk of a marriage between them – leastways not on her part. Mary and Joan send their warm regards and will be writing to you. Your share of the auction money will be sent to you by James.
Your loving brother, Mark

I draw out the folded Bill of Sale and lay it on the table.

Jim says: 'More than thirteen years this business has dragged on! May the Lord be thanked that it is over.'

'It must,' say I, 'have been mortifying for James to have the Law Lords find against him. He was always such a proud man.'

431

November 24

A strange day, qwite unlike any other Wednesday I have ever lived thru'.

I go about my work, make breakfast for my menfolk. Rosa and I are finished in the dairy in good time. I find the bread crock almost empty. It is time that we were baking. Rosa sees my state of mind. 'Go across and visit with Aunt Elizabeth. Leave the kitchen chores to me, Mama.'

She is right. I am so far away in my mind that I am like to use salt instead of sugar. Jim says that he will drive me in the cutter. I say that I would sooner walk, tho' there is snow hard-packed underfoot, I have a need to be by my own self.

I put on all my warmest clothes. In my pocket I carry the Notice of Sale sent to me by Mark. I go the long way round to the Vickery farm, taking the narrow trail that goes close to my orchard and snowbound fields, and up thru' woodlands. It is very qwiet in the great forest. Until now I have ventured-in only at maple-sugaring time, and in the company of many people.

The sky is blue and qwite without cloud, the sunlight keen enough to hurt the eyes. The cold is severe. Every branch and twig of pine, claret-oak and soft-maple stands thick with hoar frost. The tracks of fox and rabbit run crisscross to the under-brush. I note a wider spoor and think it must be that of wolves. A snow-bunting sits alone in the black alder bushes. From the village comes the tinkling of sleighbells, a sound what carries far in this kind of weather.

In England the day will be much softer. I remember late November in Dommett Wood, the smell of old leaves under-foot, the damp and misty air. The gypsies will be making ready to move closer into Tauton for the picking of Christmas holly and mistletoe around Norton Fitzwarren. At the Lamb and Flag Inn people will be gathering this day for the Sale of my father's land and houses. Brother James will be there, shamed before the populace, that he has lost the Court case in the House of Lords, and must now share with his brothers and sisters what is rightfully theirs. Mark will also be present, watchful

432

for our interests. It would seem that I may have misjudged *him*. I can picture them all, those Buckland farmers, cigars in one hand, cider tankards in the other, coming to silent attentshun as the auctioneer's gavel falls first on one Lot and then another. I remember my wise and kindly father who could never have meant that things should fall out in this sad and contenshus way between his children.

I begin to move down towards Elizabeth's house. From my kitchen chimney smoke is rising. Rosa bakes bread this day without help from me. In fact, my daughter seemed over-ankshus to have me gone, to be mistress of the baking-board, if only for a day. It is time that she was married, with her own place. If all goes well this day in Buckland St Mary many dreams could yet come true.

December 28
A very qwiet Christmas. George wrote to us early in December that his employer was sick of the gout, and in conseqwence my boy would be needed in De Pere all thru' the festive Season. Rosa also absent, she having been invited to spend the holiday in Oshkosh. On Christmas Day we stand only four around the tree.

Jim, seeing my low spirits, says: 'It can't be helped, my dear. They have their own lives now.'

He is qwite right of course.

We go to a party given by Elizabeth for the sake of young Robbie. Her heart is also heavy. Letters come from Texas, Wyoming, Dakota. Johnnie and Chas say that they are still footloose and enjoying life, and that she is not to worry about them. She and I shed a private tear together. We try to comfort one another.

I say: 'You were lucky to have a late-born child. Robbie will never leave you and Robert.'

'And Jon will always be with you and Jim,' says my sister.

February 14, 1881
We are already six weeks into this New Year. No change in the

weather. It is colder than even the oldest chief of the Menominee Tribe can remember; so says the Indian Agent who was talking to Jim in the dry-goods store. Jim orders two more wood-stoves for my dairy, since cream will not rise in these low temperatures.

March 2

A blizzard, predicted in the news-sheets these many days past, has finally hit us. Snow began this forenoon, brought in on a wind so powerful that Rosa and I were hard-put to keep our balance between house and cowbarn, and must needs cling to one another. The herd, altho' snug and warm and well-fed, seems to sense the storm and are restless in their stalls. This evening's milking took a long time, and we are all weary. Jim and Matt, forewarned of blizzard, have brought firewood into the mud-room. Rosa and I check thru' our stores and find them short of nothing.

March 3

Am so weary my eyes will not bide open, but I must put down on paper some account of this terrible and strange day. We woke to darkness as is normal at this time of year. Jim rises first and lights the stoves so that Rosa and I might come down to a warm kitchen. Matthew brews tea and heats the porridge favoured by himself and Jim. We eat a qwick repast, enough to see us thru' till breakfast, and don our heavy boots and clothing. Jim opens the kitchen door to find his exit blocked by a *wall of snow*. We run to all the windows holding lamps up to the glass. We see a glistening whiteness what tells us that the house is covered-in, most likely to the roof top. I am caught by panic. Matt sees my fear. He laughs and says: 'It's just the drifting, Rhoda. Happened often in our young days, up in Alberta. We just tunnel our way out, is all.'

He makes it sound so everyday ordinary that I am reashurred. We five all set-to with shovels and buckets and a way is soon broke thru'. We walk over level snow only to find the cowbarn in the same state as the house.

All this day we must needs work with lanterns since all windows blocked in house and sheds. The storm does not let-up even for a minute. Rosa says that all the snow in all the world must be falling on Wisconsin. Am thankful for the extra wood-stoves in the dairy. We must keep up our butter output. Who knows how much this winter will have cost us by the time spring comes at last?

April 2
Snow still lying deep. Gangs of men and boys work with shovels and ox-teams to clear the roads. Surface snow melts in daytime sunshine, then freezes overnight forming a crust so hard and thick that a sleigh and team can go across it. New trails are formed across-country in this way, sometimes over the tops of trees. School has been closed these many weeks. We have scant news of our neighbours. No mail, no news-sheets. We are cut-off in this white world where the wild birds are dying in their thousands, and even our own supplies are running low.

But there are compensashuns. We get early to our chores, often fighting a fresh way out and to the barn and sheds. The hours between morning and evening milking are spent in the kitchen by a roaring stove. Rosa and I sew and bake. Jim and Matt bring in tools what need repair, many jobs are done around the house, things are mended that I have never thought to see fixed. In the evenings we gather round the stove. Jon brings a dish of apples up from the cellar. We tell old stories from our childhood. Jim and Matt talk of Alberta, I speak of Somerset, of Buckland and Taunton.

I worry about George in De Pere, and wonder how he is faring in this bitter cold.

May 12
Snow still lies in patches on high ground, but all trails open now tho' deep in mud. Jim and Matthew go over to the grist-mill. On the road they meet with Toussant Teller who reports the first mail coming thru'. Find myself in two minds about this news. There was a certain peacefulness about our recent isolashun.

435

May 15

As sweet a morning as I have ever known. I hear Jon singing his
funny little song what means that all must be well with the
new-hatched chickens. I walk down, after morning-milking, to
the clover meadows. There is good heat in the sun, our fields
will soon be dry enough to take the weight of grazing Holsteins.
I dawdle a moment or two. On higher ground Mr Rabinshaw
has put a set of drags to work on his big field. It is good to see
dark earth again, and green grass. There are fewer birds this
springtime, but I hear a killdear and a whipporwill. Across at
Vickery's the hillside is all blue with the hepaticas. In Elizabeth's
orchard the plum and apple blossoms are out at last. The lilac
bush by my kitchen door is in full bud.

I found a few strands of grey in my hair this morning.

It is while I am lingering in this blessed sunshine that I see Mr
Teller driving down towards the house. I begin to hurry home.
It will be the first mail we have seen these many weeks.

I pay no heed to the letters stamped from England but tear open
the one in my George's hand. All is well. He has come healthy
thru' the bitter winter. His employer's gout has taken a turn for
the worse, and the butcher has decided on a swift retirement.

Jim comes in and I hand him George's letter. Before opening
the Buckland mail I take the precaushun of seating myself. One
letter is in Mary's hand what is difficult to read, one is from
Mark and another from James.

I say to Jim: 'Put the kettle on for tea, there's a love! We shall
both need reviving when we have made-out my sister's news.'

I speak truer than I know. Another envelope has lain hidden
beneath others. Now I see that it is black-edged. I push it to one
side. I open first the letter in James' hand. It is ill-written and
not his regular 'Barrister's' script. The message is brief and
attached to a money-order. *'Enclosed, your share of Father's
Estate, plus that of our dead nephew Eddie. The House of Lords
decreed that this eighth share should also come to you since you had the
care and raising of him.'* The total figure, written out in pounds
sterling, has no real meaning for me. I hand the Order across to
Jim. I say in a faint voice: 'How much is that in dollars?'

He answers in a shocked way.

'Why – why that foots-up to round about two thousand four hundred, Rhoda!'

I turn to the letter in my brother Mark's hand. It has a December date and speaks only of the Sale of Father's lands and houses. He says nothing of his plans, or if he will come back to Oshkosh. I pick up Mary's letter. It is postmarked February. I do not touch the black-edged missive. My oldest sister writes of her releef that the Court cases are over. The whole County, says she, has been afire with talk at the Greypaull Will being brought before the highest judgement in the land. She is also jubilant that we have lost not one penny thru' the long litiga-shun, the Law Lords having made our oldest brother pay up all costs, which decishun, says Mary, has like to bankrupted James. This outcome being all his own fault since he could have settled with the family at any time in all these thirteen years. She adds that Joan and Ann are both very well, and that Mark stays close these days to Buckland St Mary.

I look up to find Jim watching me across the table. He picks up the mourning envelope. He says:

'Shall I read it for you?'

'Oh please,' I say. I have such a bad feeling about it.

Jim begins to read Mary's second letter. It is very recent, dated April tenth 1881.

Dear Sisters and your husbands,
You will be shocked to hear that our brother James is dead. He was found lying on the floor of his study by his housekeeper Jane Coterill, who was with him when he breathed his last. James had grown very stout in recent years and had caught the brandy habit. Doctor Masters is of the opinion that our brother probably suffered heart failure. Death occurred on April fourth. The funeral took place on April ninth.

There was no Will to be read out. Our dear brother, tho' a Barrister, chose to die Intestate. Our Father's house of course has been for some time the property of Miss Henrietta Martin. James lived there as her lodger. But all his books and valuable possessions are still in that house, likewise his clothing and the Family Bible. I was up to

437

the house several times, but Miss Martin barred my way and would not let me in. She is a very nasty woman. It is said in the village that since James's death our brother Mark has taken James's place as Miss Martin's lodger tho' of this scandalous state of affairs I have no proof.

Will keep you informed of all what comes to pass.

Your loving sister, Mary.

'We must go across at once to Vickery's', I whisper. 'Elizabeth and Robert must be told.'

I begin to weep. I say: 'Oh Jim, I thought it was at an end, all the bickering and feuding. Now James has died without a Will it will all start up again. Already there is trouble over his possesh-uns!'

Jim takes me in his arms. He strokes my hair. He says: 'You are thousands of miles from all that ill-will. Put it from your mind. You have the money that was rightfully yours. Just forget about the rest of it.'

I look towards the pages scattered over the table.

'It is the letters,' I tell him, 'I dread the coming of those awful letters.'

Chapter Twenty-Seven

Sept 18
Our corn is golden in the husk, the moon is in the Harvest Quarter, our baskets are repaired and ready to be filled with the heavy ears. This year Jim allows Jon to drive the horse and waggon between the rows. My boy laughs and claps his hands each time a loaded basket is emptied into the cart. I am fearful at first lest he should suffer a convulshon and so fall beneath wheels or hooves. But Jim watches out for signs of trouble, as do we all. The work goes well, Jon comes to no harm, and how could I take away his pleasure? He is *so proud* to take the reins and work alongside us.

September 30
We are solvent *in our own right*. Even with a bitter winter, still it has been a good year overall, a heavy harvest. I take no accounting of the English Money. That is something *separate*, to be used for my children, and their children when the time comes. I believe it is what Father would have wanted. Jim is in full agreement with me. Elizabeth and Robert feel the same. When good land falls vacant they will buy for the sake of their sons, and the generations yet to come.

October 18
Jim and I go to De Pere. Papers are signed and money paid over, what makes the house and meat-market the sole property of George Hodder Salter the Second. This is a very proud moment. It is a good piece of real estate in a busy trading posishun. Oh, how proud his father would have been to see this day! The house is a large one. George will live alone there. Jim

and Matt, who know only too well the discomforts of 'baching', advise my boy to make an early marriage. We examine the meat-market and the slaughter-house and find all to be in good order.

De Pere is a tidy little township, fast growing into a busy factory centre. There are many flour-mills and iron-furnaces. It is served by the Milwaukee and Northern Railroad Company. My boy could not possibly have chosen a better place in which to settle for his line of business.

We travel home, well pleased with this day's work.

Christmas Eve

My poor old birthday almost forgotten in all the excitement of this year's celebrashun. Georgie will come late tonight from De Pere. Thomas is already here from Oshkosh. Rosa makes the house look pretty with greenery and garlands. Jon goes to the woods with Willum to choose our tree and fell it. The house is full of the smell of pine boughs, and plum puddings boiling in the copper. How it takes me back to my young days. Christmas Eve in Dommett, and my mother giving me a ribbon for my hair to mark my birthday, lest it go unnoticed.

Elizabeth comes over. She brings me the gift of a shawl in my favourite shade of lilac. It is crocheted in a pattern of tiny shells and has taken her many hours of paishunt work.

I say:

'Can you recall the Christmas times at home? Before our mother died, when we were all merry together?'

She says sadly:

'Was there ever such a time?'

January 21, 1882

Rosa and Thomas are to be married on April twenty-second, her twenty-third birthday. Already, we have almost daily mail from stores in Green Bay and Oshkosh. The parlour is taken up with dressmaking patterns, swatches of silk, pictures of wedding veils and gloves, and fancy shoes. We cast about us for a young female relative who might act as bride's attendant, and find that we have none. It is settled that Jim shall give the bride away. Georgie to act as Best Man to Thomas.

The Dowry, agreed to by Jim, is a generous one, what is only fair since a good sum given to Georgie to settle him in De Pere.

Another hard and bitter winter, but we make lighter of it this year. We have so much to plan for. Jim suffers much pain in his leg and shoulder, but will not see the doctor.

April 25
Cannot help but feel thankful that I have only the *one* daughter. Am qwite worn-out, 'tho it was a lovely wedding, a perfect spring day, and all went like clockwork. Rosa made a most pretty bride. In fact they are a very *handsome* couple.

My girl has been gone from us but a couple of days, and already I miss her sorely. Am now in Elizabeth's sad state of being the only female in the household. We have bought, by means of Mortgage, another one hundred and forty-one acres of good meadow land.

July 19
Haying all over with, and I am weary. A heavy crop from our new fields, but needed to *employ* men this year what mops up a percentage of the profits. Have also been obliged to take on a dairy maid, a flirtashus young woman, what has to be watched when around the hired help. But cheerful letters come from Oshkosh and De Pere. My children are happy and settled, and that is *all* that matters!

October 14
All crops safely gathered in. Jim and Matthew go to a Pig-Fair. I have a new girl in the dairy, hard working and reliable, name of Ellen. It is while she and I are scouring and scalding cream-pans that Jon comes in, our mail in his hand. One qwick look tells me it is from Buckland, Old England, the handwriting that of Mary. Some fifteen months have passed since we last heard from my family. It is never good news. Even when the money

441

came it was followed straight away by the death of Brother James. This envelope is big and heavy. I tell Jon to put it on the kitchen table. I have not the heart to open it while I am all alone. I send Ellen across to Vickery's with a message for my sister.

It is late evening when we all come together. Elizabeth gives me a long look.

She says: 'I will read it this time, if you would rather.'

I hand over the pages, and she begins in her low, sweet voice.

Dear Sisters,

My dear Husband is ill and will never be well again. With so much trouble I could not be collected in my thoughts to write to you as soon as I would have wished. Much has happened here since I last put pen to paper. Our brother Mark was wed to Miss Henrietta Martin only four months after we had buried poor James. Mark had told us not a word about his wedding, but behaved as bad as he could. They rode to Church in a fine carriage and pair, the only guests were friends of Miss Martin, down from London. I was not good enough to even look at them.

Since our brother James died Intestate, there has been much trouble over his Estate. Mark and I were appointed by the Court to be Administrators. Mark said that he held the affidavits of both his sisters in America, and would put all monies due to them into the Taunton Bank when the Case was settled.

A Sale of James's effects was held at our Father's house (tho' it is now of course in the ownership of Mark and his new wife). On the evening before the Sale I went up to the House with my oldest son Samuel, to see my dead brother's effects, as it was my Duty to do as an Administrator.

Mark would not open the door to us for a long time, but abused me from inside the hallway in a most shameful manner.

I told him I had come to see the whole of James's property, as it was my Duty to do before the Sale.

He said that it was nothing to do with him. That all of it was being done in the name of his wife, Mrs Henrietta Greypaull.

442

I said, that in such case it was all the more important *that I should have everything done in an* honest *and* truthful *manner.*

At this point Mark opened the door. He ordered me and Samuel off the doorstep! When we made no move to go he pushed us! He called us all the names he could!

I looked him straight in the face. I said, 'There is something wrong here. Do you intend to deal truthfully with Rhoda and Elizabeth?' He said that he did, and again pushed us from the place. I said: 'Goodbye, Mark. Shake hands with me.' He said: 'I won't shake hands with you.' (I believe all this was done to please Mark's wife. She has a very nasty temper, and is a crafty woman.)

The Sale was held, dear sisters. There was James's wallet and books, his clothing and furniture. When all was reckoned up and costs deducted there remained a sum of Fifty Pounds to be paid to each of us. I was paid my money by the Court, as was Joan, Ann and William. But I have lately found out from Solicitor Reeve that my sisters in America have not yet received their share.

I am sorry to tell you both that Mark took your Affidavits to the Treasury Office in London, he drew the one hundred pounds that was rightfully yours and has disappeared. It is many months since he was seen around Buckland or Taunton, but is known to have stayed recently in London. It is my belief that he has cheated you, dear sisters. Solicitor Reeve says that Mark is a thief and should be hauled back and sent to Prison. He should never have married Miss Henrietta Martin. She is fifty-eight years old. It can hardly have been a love match.

Dear sisters, you must do as you see fit in this matter. I enclose a Pamphlet from Solicitor Reeve on the Law of Intestacy. Study it well, if you mean to seek the Law against Mark and his wife.

Write soon and tell me all I ought to know conserning this matter. Your loving sister,

Mary

Elizabeth says: 'I have a feeling that Mary is still fond of Mark. That she blames this new wife of his for what has happened.'

I say: 'It's no more than I expected from him.'

I look up into Jim's face. He is wearing the black scowl that I seldom see.

'Six months in a logging-camp would be good medicine for Mr Mark Greypaull. He'd soon learn the ways of honesty among two hundred lumberjacks!'

Robert nods agreement. 'We trusted the man. What sort of blackguard is it that'll cheat his own sisters?'

Elizabeth says: 'Well what are we to do?'

'We are upset now,' say I. 'Let it lay awhile until our judgement is sounder.'

October 29

George spends some days with us. He now has a middle-aged assistant butcher and a young apprentice in his employ, so is able to leave his business in safe hands before the weather closes in. It is so good to have him home. He walks with us to church on Sunday, and my heart is fit to burst with *pride*. He is every inch the business man. He looks so like his father. He is also good at 'keeping his own counsel'.

My boy is at home only *two* days when the pretty mail begins to come. Pale pink envelopes, with a touch of perfume on them, and written in a small and tidy hand. One letter *per day*, and not one word of explanashun! Father Black is much inclined to tease. 'Why, George boy!' says he. 'Your assistant sure makes out his reports on some fancy letter paper?' But Georgie only smiles and puts the mail into his pocket.

January 1, 1883

Snow lies hip-deep since December. We spend a qwiet Christmas, as do Elizabeth and Robert. They get mail from Johnnie and Chas in North Dakota. We hear from Rosa in Oshkosh, and Georgie in De Pere. But it is not the same.

I look at my Ledgers. As to stock and hard cash, we have never been so well off. But, oh, how I do miss my dear children.

★

The years had seen some changes in George. He had attained his full and considerable height, his shoulders had broadened. He now wore his hair a little longer and cultivated a fine black moustache. He carried himself proudly, assured in his good looks.

Leaving home had not been easy. Away from the safety of Mama and Rosa, George discovered in himself an unsuspected shyness, a hint of the English reserve that until now he had thought to be a fault shown only by his mother. He did not readily find friends when set down in strange territory.

His employers were a childless couple, second-generation French, and devout Roman Catholics. They grew fond of George and saw him as a surrogate son. The single drawback of the household was the alien faith; and since the social life of De Pere depended on membership of a church or chapel, he had been lonely in those first years. He had gone from one religious meeting house to yet another; had sat through the services of Lutherans and Wesleyans, Presbyterians and Baptists, and failed to find a single kindred spirit.

It was on a cool fall evening of his third year in De Pere that George entered the little Methodist church, drawn in by the exceptional singing of the congregation. The hall was full; he stood in shadow close beside the door, intending to slip away when the service was over. But these Methodists, mainly first and second generation Welsh and native New Yorkers, were so friendly towards him that to leave at once would have been churlish. His hand was shaken by a score of men; he was introduced to the Pastor and the Choirmaster. George spoke of the fine music and singing which had called him inside their doors. Within the hour he was sitting down to supper at the Choirmaster's table, made welcome by James Addison Annas, his wife Esther, and their large family.

The return of George to the Methodist church on the follow-ing Sunday had nothing to do with his appreciation of its music. Among the eight young people seated around the Annas supper table had been one whom he could not put from his mind. A brown-haired, blue-eyed girl, name of Sarah Ann, who had never even glanced in his direction.

445

It had been a very slow and proper courtship, conducted in full view of her family and the entire congregation of the Methodist church of De Pere. Sarah Ann Annas, only sixteen years old when first seen by George Hodder Salter, was guarded closely by her parents. It was not until her seventeenth birthday that the Choirmaster would permit George to walk his daughter to and from the evening service, and even then only when in the distant company of other worshippers. On Sundays, wet and fine, through snow and golden sunsets, George trod the half mile road between the church and the Annas house, Sarah Ann beside him. He had brought the art of walking slowly to a near perfection; had learned to measure the pace of his long stride to match her shorter footsteps. She barely reached up to his shoulder. His most familiar view of her in these first months of courtship was the crown of her dark bonnet, the shining coil of hair at the nape of her neck, and a rare and dazzling upward glance from her blue eyes. But it was in these minutes of near privacy that George first learned the quality of Sarah Ann. His family history, his present situation, had long since been revealed to James and Esther Annas across the Sunday supper table. It was the future plans of the young butcher that most interested their daughter, and George, believing that he had at last found a sympathetic ear, was only too eager to tell her all that was in his heart.

It was on a mild and rainy night, underneath a broad umbrella, that George began to talk of Eddie and Papa. He spoke of the ambitions of his English father, and how, because of sickness and ill-fortune, those plans had never quite matured.

'So you see, it's all up to me now, to carry on where Pa left off.'

'So that's how you see life, is it, George? Success in business is your only goal?'

Her question, unexpected and faintly critical, was one he could not answer.

'Well – I don't rightly know,' he floundered.

He halted, there in the rainy street, and looked down on her bonnet's silken crown. 'Guess that's what I am. Ambitious.'

She looked up at him then. In the light from the nearby church windows he could see clearly her softly rounded features, the creamy skin, the luminous shine of her wide eyes.

'Oh George,' she said, 'I'm so sorry to hear that. I shall miss you when you're gone off to Chicago.'

'But I want you to come with me!' he cried.

'No,' she said slowly, 'I could never leave my family. I could never leave De Pere. This is my home. In any case – I get real nervous when I'm around pushy people.'

A voice from the church steps bid them enter right away. George folded the umbrella.

'We must talk some more about this,' he whispered.

'There's no point,' she said. 'If you go to Chicago – then you go alone, George.'

People said of James Addison Annas that he was an original. He was in fact a man of many talents. A native New Yorker, he had attended Yale, and came west to Wisconsin in order to teach school. His great passion was music. He had for many years been Choirmaster at his church, and was himself an expert flautist. He was also inventive: had been working on a gramophone at the time when Edison revealed his finished product. He had fought bravely in the Civil War. Since settling in De Pere, he had worked as a cabinet maker, a profession in which he was also highly skilled.

Georgie learned about this quiet but happy man from Sarah Ann, and marvelled that one so talented could lack all drive and go! 'But your Pa could have done great things. He could have been a top-flight musician or a famous inventor! Instead of which he's a . . .'

'. . . a dearly loved husband and father,' she said. 'He's contented in his heart and mind. Not always straining and striving to get ahead. To be richer or more important than other people.'

It was a philosophy of life with which George was unfamiliar. He studied the slender and diminutive Sarah Ann, her calm and pretty features. He had already caught a hint of the iron will beneath the softness. There were times when her determination frightened him a little, so oddly did it come from one who was so sweet and pliant in appearance. The need to assert himself with her took up most of George's waking thoughts. It was, he at last decided, her name that was at fault; it had an intimidating ring about it. He would shorten those hyphenated syllables. He would invent a new word, shorter and more intimate, and his exclusively. He would call her 'Satie'.

To own a meat-market in De Pere had never been his aim, and yet when the offer to set him up came from Father Black and Mama, George had thanked them, and accepted.

Together, he and Satie explored the large old frame house. He had kissed her for the first time in the parlour which was now his own.

'Are you content?' he asked. 'Is it what you wanted? Will you marry me, Satie?'

'Oh yes, George,' she said, 'and I shall be coming eighteen years old on April twenty-second.' She blushed. 'You can speak then to Papa. You can offer for me – if that is what you truly want?'

★

April 15, 1883

A gentle morning, sweet air, and all growing things are early this year. The leaves are thick on the cottonwood trees, catkins hang from the birches. The wild sweet crabapple, in back of the house, is in full blossom. The sqwills are out all around the front porch, making a blue carpet.

I go down to my far fields. I am busy planting beans when my Georgie arrives riding horseback. It is a shock. He canters up to where I am bent double across the seedrow. He jumps down from the saddle to stand above me.

'Mama,' he cries. 'Where are the menfolk? You should not have to work alone here like a fieldhand.'

I rise from my kneeling posishun and brush soil from my

fingers. I wait for him to mention my 'advanced years', I can see how the words tremble on his tongue's edge.

'I am not yet in my dotage, George,' say I. 'You must understand that Father Black has been bedfast this past week. Three days of walking behind the seed drill and he can scarce move at all! Matthew is cleaning out the cowbarn. Jon is feeding stock.'

'Then you must employ help. You can afford it these days.' George looks to where our herd grazes in lush meadows. I see the consern for my welfare in his dear face, but he does not understand.

I say: 'When I was but a girl in Buckland St Mary, another young man came to chide me, and for the self-same reason. I was with my sister Joan in our vegetable garden. We were as brown as the gypsies that year, our skirts tucked up and our hair all untidy. He said I would not need to work like a labouring woman if I would but consent to be his wife. I told him that to handle the good earth gave me satisfaction. That without it I would be but half a woman.'

George still looks doubtful. I take hold of his forearm. I shake him, gently.

'This is the difference betwixt you and me. You need gold in your hand to know that you are wealthy. The soil beneath my feet tells me *I* am rich.'

I begin to move back towards the house.

'You have had a long ride,' say I. 'You must be hungry?'

He takes hold of the reins and follows just a pace behind me.

'Mama,' he says, 'you sure are the darndest lady I have ever known! I ride up here, out of a blue sky so to say! You never ask one word of what brings me back to Suamico, but start right in telling me some tale about your young days in Old England!'

I glance back at him across my shoulder. I smile behind my bonnet brim.

'George. You are to me like an open book. You have come to talk over your betrowthal to the young lady who writes perfumed letters.'

June 28

George writes that he would like to bring his future wife to see us. I write back that if he means to come then it should be very soon, since we are on the brink of Haying. They come on Sunday, starting very early out of De Pere in the cool of the morning. George hires a smart rig with a fast horse, they bring with them as chaperone an older brother of Sarah Ann, named Willard. A nice young man what spends all his time talking with Matthew about hunting wildfowl.

Since they will need to start back early for De Pere, our main meal is taken at midday. The day is hot. I put on several cold dishes, using my best table linen and china, and crystal glassware. I could wish that Rosa were here to do a centrepiece of flowers. Tell myself a dozen times that Georgie's young lady is to come and seek for *my* approval of *her*. Nonetheless, it is I and my domestic arrangements what feel to be *on trial*.

Sarah Ann is shy with us, at first. She sits between Georgie and her brother, and eats heartily of all I offer to her. I take this to be a favourable sign. I have small paitshunce with the kind of young woman who picks her way among good food, sending most of it to waste. The girl Ellen, what mostly goes home to her father on a Sunday, comes today to help me out with chores. I leave her to wash the dishes and straighten around. All the menfolk, saving George, take a walk down to the meadows to view the standing grass. My boy stays close when Sarah Ann and I go to sit in the parlour. I see that he is nervous lest his affianced and I do not get on together. He fidgets his way around from mantleshelf to china cabinet to piano, picking things up and putting them down in all the wrong places. His state of mind affects the poor young lady. She sits very still, her ankles crossed, her hands clasped tight together. I see no chance of any talk between us while George is there.

I say: 'For mercy's sake boy! Go you and join the others in the field, or ask Jon to show you his flock of goslings. You know how it pleases him when you show interest.'

He goes, but with an ankshus glance at Sarah Ann.

He says to her: 'I'll be close by, Satie, if you should need me.'

I settle back into my chair. I smile at her. I say: 'He is a good boy, but you already know that.'

She does not smile. 'George is a fine man, Mrs Black. I am devoted to him. But he does have a tendency to high-flown notions. He does a deal of dreaming about his future plans. But I guess that *you* must already know that much.'

I sit upright in my chair. I look more closely at her. I note the firm set on her lips, the small but strong chin. My boy does not need to hover for the sake of his betrowthed. She is more than able to speak up for herself when the time reqwires it.

I view her with new respect. I say:

'You have my George very well summed up, yet you are willing to marry him in spite of his tendency to dream?'

'There is a difference,' says she, 'between what a man may think he can do, and what he actually achieves. A little ambishun is no bad thing, kept within bounds. You know he talks of going to Chicago?'

'He has sung that old song since he was fifteen years old. I would sooner see him bide here in Wisconsin than go back to that wicked and dangerous city. It was that awful place what broke his father's heart, and killed him.'

Now, at last, she smiles.

'Oh, how it pleases me to hear you say that! You and I think alike, Mrs Black.' She leans forward in her chair. 'I have already told George that I will never leave De Pere. He says that he is content to stay there if I will wed him. But does he care for me enough to give up his plans of dealing in real estate, and buying a Seat on the Chicago Board of Trade?'

'Oh, he cares more than enough,' say I. I can see how she is comforted by my words. I move my chair closer to her chair. I say: 'You and I are going to get along real well together. We both love George and have his best interests at heart. Between us we shall guide him into wiser ways of thinking. He will settle down once you are married.'

We fall to talking about wedding plans, and find that we are

451

of one single mind on all points. When George returns he finds us laughing together. He looks much releeved.

I say: 'You have brought me a sweet girl. She will be as a second daughter to Father Black and me. The good Lord was at your elbow, Georgie, when you found Satie Annas!'

He raises an eyebrow and seems displeased at my use of *his* word for her.

'Oh, I know it's your special name,' say I. 'But Satie says that Father Black and I may also call her that – tho' no one else.' I smile at him. 'We would deem it a great favour.'

July 18

We are but three days into Haying when poor Jim faints clear away from the agony in his leg and shoulder. He looks real sick, so white and drawn in his features. I make up a bed for him in the parlour. Dr Jones comes across. Once again the subject of a Penshun comes up, and this time Jim agrees that he will try for it, at least.

Matthew makes enqwiries amongst our veteran neighbours. We learn that the politishuns, who banged on the drum and blew the bugles to send young men into battle, are somewhat shy and absent when it comes to the matter of paying out Penshuns to those same men when they grow old. It will need a visit to a Green Bay attorney, affidavits from surgeons, the sworn statements of officers and comrades who were at Jim's side when the mishap took place. We also learn that there is an organizashun in Washington that will, for a percentage, come to the aid of men such as Jim, and put their case to the right qwarters. I write off to Washington and state our situashon. Feel better at least, now that *firm steps* have been taken.

October 1

Harvest is all done with, and I am thankful for it. Jim on his feet again, and working but not as in the old days. Our winter wheat is in and already showing green. Oh, but I am weary. Have felt so done up all summer long but better now the cooler weather is upon us.

Jim goes with Robert to Green Bay to sell our surplus hay crop. He does very well at the auctshun. Comes home driving a spanking brown and yellow buggy, a *new* one with *springs*. A smoother ride to church on Sundays now, than with our old farmcart. Have retrimmed my bonnet to keep up with our fine transportashun.

★

Georgie had come painfully to manhood. Still mourning the loss of Eddie and Papa, he had taken on the task of being Rhoda's sole protector only because he could not bear to fail her. He remembered those first months in Suamico, the undiminished woodpile, his blistered hands; the conviction that he was never meant to be a farmer. He also recalled his mother's courage, her determination, the way she had scoured and bleached clean the old Lutz farmhouse and transformed it into a home. He recalled her persistence in teaching him to manage oxen, how she had tucked up her skirts and walked with him behind the team in that first spring ploughing of her fields. He had marvelled at her then, at the iron will that powered her slight small body. He would never forget her words, spoken on the steamship, in the hour before they were to dock in Green Bay. 'I have never done the things *I* wanted,' she had said then, 'nothing was ever of *my own* choosing.'

He had not, at the age of fifteen, understood her meaning. He understood it now.

People, thought Georgie, all too often got caught in traps that were not of their own making. Even Mama, who was strong and single minded, had been forced to wait until middle-age to achieve the farm that was her dream. Love, he saw now, had been his mother's hindrance. Because of love she had followed his father to New York and then Chicago. Georgie himself had been wiser in matters of the heart. He had carefully avoided entanglements with the farmers' daughters of Suamico and district. He had seen too often the captive son-in-law, obliged to walk behind another man's plough.

453

Georgie had left Chicago and came to the pineries for the sake of his Mama. Now it seemed that for love of Satie Annas he would be obliged to stay in Brown County.

August 2, 1884

George and Satie have set the wedding date for September third. Willum Vickery is also to be wed at that time.

Elizabeth and I sit sewing on her front porch. Our best gowns, worn to several hundreds of husking-bees and Basket-Soshuls, to money-raising suppers, baptisms and other folks's weddings, are too shabby to be seen at our own sons' nuptshuls. Elizabeth has chosen deep blue, trimmed with white. I have settled for a shade of dark rose, what I feared to be a little daring for my age. But have toned it down with cuffs and collars of ecru lace, and, in any case, Jim and Matthew say it suits me!

We have but little time for stitching, and so have started early on the gowns. Feeding the harvest gangs takes a deal out of the day, and we are neither of us blessed with daughters at home. Elizabeth agrees that kitchen help is nothing but a worry, the girls, even the plainest we can find, being so fresh and flirtashus around the hired men.

Rosa writes from Oshkosh. Her new gown for the wedding is to be in ivory grosgrain piped with burgundy velvet, what she says is considered very fashunable in the city. Are we, she enqwires, sewing *large enough bustles* into our skirts? Write back at once that we are not sewing *any* bustles in, since her aunt and I believe such peculiar fashun to be foolish on ladies of mature years.

August 20

The weather holds good. Our corn comes down in fine shape and is stacked to wait for husking. Everything is two weeks early this year.

My sewing machine breaks down. Jim says the working parts are red hot from so much wedding fever, but Matthew says that he can fix it. The men may laugh! They have gone to the

454

extravagance of ordering *store bought* suits for George's wedding!

Find myself getting more nervous as the day draws near. Elizabeth likewise. Willum reqwests that we all call him Will or William in future, what is his proper title. It don't feel right, says he, to be a bridegroom and still known by his old baby name. Elizabeth is sad to lose him, he is such a good son to them. But, like I say to her, she still has Robbie who is growing into a fine young man and such a help around the farm.

Laid awake last night and thought long about my Georgie.

September 2

We travel this afternoon to De Pere. We are to stay overnight with friends of the Annas family, and come home tomorrow evening. Robert and William are to see to our milking and chores. It is the first time we have all been absent from the farm at any one time since I came here. Feel myself all set to worry. Pumpkins and squashes are not yet in. The trees have begun to turn, the maples look like they are afire, the old locust tree beside the barn is dark red. Soon the leaves will be down and winter upon us. My gooseberries not yet gathered, what is a torment to me, since overripe fruit no use at all.

Jim sees my agitashun. He says: 'What is it? All this fussing about pumpkins and berries? One night and a day away from home won't make all that much difference! Or is it George?'

Dear Jim; we are grown so close that he knows my inmost thoughts and feelings. Oft times there is no need for words between us. Today, it helps to speak aloud.

I say:

'Satie is so very young. She is but nineteen. Georgie is twenty-six, she is deep in love with him, and he has his father's perswasive ways. He may yet talk her round to going off to that wicked Chicago. Then there is the wedding. We have not yet met the Annas family. Does my gown look homemade, Jim? Maybe I should have done like you and Matthew and ordered from the Catalogue? I wouldn't want George to feel ashamed of me. Then there is that great rambling Clemenceau house. That poor child will have her work cut out cleaning up those rooms. Eight bedrooms, never touched for years, and George and his assistant 'baching it' that long time, and only an old woman coming once a week to scrub out!'

Jim puts his arms around me, he folds me close. He says:

'Satie will manage George just the way you manage me. Your gown is fine, and you look lovely in it. As for the Clemenceau house – well that, my dear, is not your problem. Once Satie takes up residence there, it will be known as the Salter house, and if I'm any judge she'll have it scoured from roof to cellar.'

I know that he is right. I was never in this state before my Rosa's wedding. But the Gillingham's are Somerset folk. Almost, you might say, like own kin.

September 5

The loveliest wedding I have ever seen! A picture I shall carry always in my mind. Satie coming in on her father's arm in a gown of ruched white satin, a headdress of white flowers holding in place a long white veil, and a tiny Bible in her hands. She is followed by all five sisters. First comes Alma, then Alice and Hattie, and Mary and Eva. Such pretty girls, in daffodil yellow silk, what suits their brown hair and eyes. George had chosen Rosa's husband Thomas for to be his best man. I see my boy's face as Satie walks up the aisle towards him, and it is full of love and wonder.

Rosa very handsome in her ivory and burgundy, what sets off her fine figure. I also take careful note of Mrs Annas's gown, what is most elegant being of pale blue lace over dark blue satin, with matching bonnet. Content myself to see that Mrs Annas is not wearing even the *very smallest hint* of a bustle! Need not have worried about our meeting with James and Esther Annas. Like I said to Jim as we drove home, they are as nice a couple as ever stood in shoes! Esther confides in me that she much admires my gown and how the colour suits me. *She also* makes all her own dresses. Between them, she and her six daughters have sewed all the wedding outfits.

Can rest content now, knowing my George to be in good hands.

September 20
Well, I gathered in my gooseberries at last! I bake pies and boil-up jam, and take a basketful to Elizabeth, who has very few gooseberries this year. She makes a custard, and folds it when cold between the stewed fruit. I watch her at this task while I put the final stitches into the gown she will wear at Will's wedding.

'Surely,' say I, 'our mother made this dish for us when we were children?'

She smiles. 'Oh yes. Gooseberry Fool was her name for it. It was Will's special favourite,' and all at once I remember as if it were only yesterday. Will and I, picking in the hard green fruit, he with a basket, and I into my looped-up apron. He was taller and more skilled at all tasks. I recall that, when I wept because I picked so slowly, he emptied half the contents of his basket into my apron.

I sit in Elizabeth's kitchen; from her open doorway I can look clear across to the Black Farm. It is a satisfying prospect; the house, now painted pumpkin-yellow, has become a true home. I can see the stubble fields, the dark strip of furrows where the men have begun the winter ploughing. I can just make out our Holsteins coming at a good pace towards the cowbarn. Already, there is a nip of winter in the air and they are no longer disposed to linger late down in the meadows.

I say to Elizabeth: 'I must be going. The evening milking is waiting for me.'

As I walk back home a sudden mist begins to rise off the Suamico River. A whipporwill calls, and he is very close by. The sumac burns dark red all along the roadside. I halt and close my eyes for a moment, and I am young again, walking down the steep slope into Dommett, with a mist lying in the coombes

457

and hollows, and the crimson berries weighing down the haw-
thorne bushes. I seem to see my brother Will, his fair curls and
cheerful grin, and all at once the tears come to my eyes.

September 30
Recent days are full of romance and the happiness of our young
folk. Was in attendance at William's wedding to Grace Drew.
A fine celebrashun. Grace looking beautiful in white what
seems to be qwite the fashunable colour for brides just lately.
Elizabeth, by far the most handsome among the mature ladies
present, wears with *distinctshun* the dark blue gown trimmed
with white. I go in my deep-rose outfit.

As I say to Jim: 'I had better get my best wear out of it, while
I can. There will be no more weddings to attend in our little
family.'

He says: 'But there are bound to be baptisms, eh Rhoda?
You'll make a most fetching grandmother.' He twirls his mous-
taches. 'And I qwite fancy myself as Grandpa Black.'

Chapter Twenty-eight

She had taken her wedding gown and laid it away, as was the custom, in a trunk between the folds of an old, well-boiled, well-aired bed sheet. From the headdress and veil she could not bear to be parted. Satie kept them in a locked drawer of her dressing table, to be taken out and touched in moments of distress.

There were days, in this first winter of her new life as a married lady, when she needed to remind herself of the glory of that wedding day. Her parents' house was only a buggy ride away, but just too far for the reassurance of a daily visit home; she missed her family, especially her sisters. George was sweet and loving, and attentive. But he had a business to run. By November, the days had grown cold and short. In December, the snow lay deep and many roads were blocked. Between breakfast and supper she hardly saw George. In her parents' house she had never known a solitary moment.

The Clemenceaus had built in order to house a family of ten or twelve. In fact, no child had ever run through the spacious lower rooms, climbed the broad oaken staircase, romped and shouted in the many bedrooms. Satie, who had herself grown up in such a house, felt the sorrow of the unused spaces. It was not enough, she told George, to insist that this was now the 'Salter House'. It was up to them to show friends and neighbours that they were here to stay; that they would, henceforth, be known as the Salters of De Pere; and could she please fix up the house as a proof of their intentions?

George, in love for the first and only time in his life, had seen traces of tears on his young wife's face; he was aware of her loneliness and boredom. All he wanted for Satie was that she should be happy with him. Seated at his desk, estimating possible profits from Thanksgiving Day and Christmas orders, George failed to notice the warning signal in her large blue eyes. He felt no touch of permanence in the little hand that gripped his own. He reached for his wallet, drew out a sheaf of bills and gave them to her. Peace in the home, he thought, was cheaply bought for fifty dollars.

The mail order Catalogue had been used in the Annas household only as a guide to the fashions in gowns that were favoured by the ladies of Chicago. The December and January days were no longer dark for Satie; she studied all those pages of the great book that had, until now, remained unexplored. Fifty dollars, she discovered, was a tidy fortune when it came to the feathering of a nest.

Her father's wedding present had been their parlour furnishings; some very fine pieces made in his own workshop. There were two button-backed armchairs and a sofa upholstered in green leather; a tiny lady's bureau made of rosewood, and a glass fronted cabinet for the safe housing of her treasures. But these items filled only one corner of the spacious parlour. The Catalogue showed a handsome dining table with matching set of chairs. There were flowered china lamps, fringed rugs, elegant velvet-covered stools, whatnots and occasional tables.

Their own bedroom furnishings were complete and had been the gift of Father and Mother Black. A bed with beautifully carved head and foot boards, a pretty dressing table. A large wardrobe, and matching high- and low-boys for the storing of their linen. Satie roved through the house, the Catalogue clutched in her arms. She looked into each of the eight empty bedrooms papered and painted so long ago by the Clemenceaus, for the babies who had never come. She turned to the pages which showed wicker baby carriages and rocking cradles, high chairs with little iron wheels. It was a mite early to be dreaming; just a week or so, and she was far from certain. She looked again at the picture of the baby-waggon, the bodywork of which was painted in a dark shade, with an overall pattern of little white daisies. Oh, but it was pretty! She imagined the baby lying in it. A girl, she thought, with George's dark waving hair and her own blue eyes. Items ordered now, would be delivered in the springtime. By that time she would have good news for George. Satie planned for crisp white ruffles at her windows, drapes of striped brocade. A home so warm and pretty, so full of welcome, that George would never think more about moving to Chicago.

Georgie was happier than he had ever been. Satie filled the empty places in his heart. For the first time since Ed's dying and the loss of Papa, the shadow had lifted, and he was altogether his own man.

The meat-market was not far from the house. George halted on that February evening beside the deep-scrubbed shop counter. He reached out a hand towards the old green leather toolcase, brought from England all those years ago by his Papa. Just to touch it, lately, was enough to set him dreaming. Georgie still worked in the precise and careful style taught to him by his English father; retained the meticulous, almost finicky, care for the tools of his trade, the need for cleanliness and order in all things. Chicago had been his father's dream city. Georgie remembered the sign board, dark blue and gold, which declared that here traded *George Hodder Salter and Sons*.

Another year or two, and he and Satie would be Chicago-bound, perhaps with a small son to take with them. He walked towards the house. He could see Satie waiting for him on the front porch.

She began to run towards him.

'Oh George!' she cried. 'Such dreadful news. An accident on the Milwaukee Railroad. My father – my father's been hurt real bad! Eva came across to tell me. I'm to go home right away. Papa's not expected to live out this night!'

★

461

February 16, 1885

A letter from George, with news so awful that Jim and I can scarce take it in. Satie's father, James Annas, is dead. George writes in great sorrow and some agitashun. It seems that Satie is with child, but had not yet told George of her good news. The shock of her father's dying almost caused her to lose the preshus child. George writes how he has been beside himself with worry, but that all is now well, at least as far as Satie and the baby are concerned.

As to the poor Annas family, it is not hard for us to imagine their state of grief.

Jim says: 'A few months ago, and we were all dancing at Georgie's wedding. You danced with James, and I with Esther, Whoever would have thought . . .?'

Jim is overcome, and can say no more.

I try to brace-up for both our sakes. Matthew begs me to read aloud the newspaper clipping. I take a good grip on my feelings. It is better that we know the worst. The piece is dated February 14 1885, and states: *An accident which resulted in the death of one person, the serious injury of another, and minor bruises and scratches to several others, occurred about noon of this Monday on the Milwaukee and Northern Railroad, about one mile north of this place.*

As the morning freight train was proceeding north, it became stalled by the snow and a brakeman was sent back to put torpedoes on the track, and flag an engine with a snow plough and caboose, which had been passed at De Pere.

When it came, the snow plough ran into the caboose at the rear of the freight train, knocking off the rear trucks, and raising the rear end of the train and the caboose over the plough. In this caboose was James Addison Annas . . .'

Matthew says: 'Oh my dear Lord! He never stood a chance.'

I pick up the second newspaper clipping. It is an Obituary Notice. I read: *James Addison Annas died at his home in this city about midnight of Monday, from the injuries received the same day in the railroad accident of the Milwaukee and Northern Railroad. Mr Annas was born in Oneida County, New York State, and was fifty-five years old at the time of his death.*

462

'Mr Annas was a qwiet and inoffensive man and a good citizen. His wife and children have the sympathy of the community in their bereavement.'

Matthew is much moved by all this, he having spent some time in good conversation with poor Mr Annas when we were at the wedding party. He says: 'Guess I'll go check on the hogs, and see how Jon is faring with the turkeys. You two sit here awhiles. I'll get the milking started.'

I say to Jim: 'We must thank the Lord that Satie came to no harm from such shock, but, oh, poor Esther! She is left with young children still to rear. Little Jimmy is but eight years old, and Sam only fifteen. I know too well how that feels!'

All at once I am no longer in our cosy kitchen, with apple-logs crackling in the stove, and dear Jim sitting close-by. I am back in Chicago, on that dreadful day when George died. I relive that desolashun of the spirit. Jim sees how it is with me. He takes my hand in his.

He says: 'Esther Annas is more fortunate than you were. She has grown-up children too.'

I think about this, and take comfort from it.

Later on, when milking is done, supper eaten, and Matthew gone early to his bed, I say to Jim:

'I have been thinking about Esther Annas. I could never go thru' all of that agony again. In fact, I have decided that I will not! Widowhood, excepting perhaps the loss of a child, is the most terrible thing that can happen to a woman. If you should die first, then I shall follow you as soon as I am able. I shall have no more will to live if you are not beside me.'

Jim says:

'The same thought came to my mind while we were working together in the cowbarn. I don't know how I lived alone for all that long time?' Seems like I must have been waiting for you, Rhoda!'

He smiles.

'Don't worry any more about it. You and I are good for many years yet. Remember – there is a grandchild not yet born

463

in De Pere, and, please God, several more to come. When *our* day arrives to leave this world – then we shall go together.'

July 7

No diary entry for such a long time! All my writing is done lately on behalf of Jim, and the granting of his Penshun. It seems that the Army Surgeon's sworn affidavit is not suffishent proof that Jim was hurt so bad in the Civil War. Now we must furnish sworn statements from comrades who were at Jim's side when the mishap happened; and so the whole matter drags on!

Rosa is visiting with George and Satie in De Pere. She is to come to us on Sunday, and has promised to stay awhile, and help me with the cooking while we are about the Haying. She and Satie write regular to one another, and are firm friends.

July 28

Three weeks of real hard work, but a wonderful Hay crop. The last load comes down tonight, and we make a little celebrashun of it for Rosa's sake. Don't know what I should have done without her, this year. Jon affected much by this hot summer. He suffers many convulshuns and needs much care. Have not seen him so sickly since we left Chicago.

Rosa brings us all the news from De Pere. George is doing very well in business. He talks a great deal it seems about this new-fangled noshun called *refrigerashun*. Do not myself altogether understand what it is about, but *nod my head* as if I do.

Satie is blooming, says Rosa, and in fine health. The house is all fixed-up now and with such *good taste*. George makes a doting and generous husband. Satie's smallest wish is granted right away. He is hoping for a *son*, but will be happy with a little girl, if only all goes well.

As to the Annas family, well they are soljering bravely on thru' this bad time. Esther, who is a skilled seamstress and needlewoman, has set up a small workshop and already employs two women to assist her. She is also, says Rosa, to apply for a Penshun, thru' her late husband's Claim on the Navy for injuries he suffered in the Civil War. All she asks is her share of what he would have had, if he had lived. Can only hope that she is luckier than Jim in this matter of a Penshun, since she has two children still dependent on her, and only the work of her own hands to rely-on.

September 29

The Telegrafer's boy comes running up from the railroad depot. Am in the dairy, churning almost finished when Jim calls me into the house. My hands shake so much that I can scarce hold the paper. In the end it is Matthew who reads aloud the wonderful news.

Born Sept. 28. A daughter named Alma. Mother and baby both doing fine. I sit down in my rocker. I put my apron over my head and I weep in the most *foolish* fashun. Matthew scalds a pan of milk. He stands over me while I drink it down. I choke upon it.

'This is not all milk. There is brandy in it,' I complain.

'And why not?' he cries. 'It's not everyday you have a grand-child!'

'I am howling for releef,' I tell them. 'I have been so fearful. Poor little Satie – she is so young . . .'

Jim pours a small brandy and hands it to Matthew. He is reaching for his own glass when we hear the sound of buggy-wheels. It is Elizabeth and Robert.

Elizabeth is tearful, but Robert's smile the broadest I have ever seen.

'Fill two more glasses, if you please, Jim! We've just had news from Will – Grace has given birth to a fine little daugh-ter.'

He turns to me.

'Will says he means to name the baby for his favourite aunt. He wants you to be godmother to her.'

I burst out into fresh tears, what sets Elizabeth again to crying.

We cling to one another.

'Well, this is a fine to-do,' I sob, 'and me not even finished scrubbing-out the cream-pans!'

The men refill their brandy glasses.
'To Rhoda Vickery!' cries Robert.
'To Alma Salter!' cries Jim.

November 8

Weather still mild, the trees hold their leaves, it is an Indian Summer. Would so much have liked to go to De Pere to see George and Satie, and little Alma, but one thing follows on another, to keep me close to home.

Jim is troubled more and more by his old war injuries, and still no word from Washington about his Penshun; he needs help these days with dressing and undressing. Matthew also in poor shape at times. Have decided that we must take on a hired man, full-time, as well as the girl who helps me around the house and dairy.

Satie writes long letters to us. She says that her strength has all come back, and that baby is thriving. She also says that what with caring for Alma, and going almost daily to see her poor widowed mother, she sees little of George. Even on a Sunday, he is busy with his Ledgers, and reading pamphlets about refrigerashun.

I am *much tempted* to go pay a visit to De Pere.

November 12

A killing frost, and all the leaves are down. Within hours great clouds roll up from the north-east, and we have our first snow of this winter. From one day to another all is altered. I check my stock of dry goods. I bring down the winter qwilts and set them to air above the stove. Jim orders a cord of wood. The hired man, name of Wilbur, is worth his weight in gold. He goes with Jim and Matthew to the mill and does most of the loading and unloading.

Jon much improved with the onset of cold weather. No more convulshuns for the past six weeks. Without Jim and Matthew to help with Jon, I don't know what I should do!

April 1, 1886

Well, we came thru' that winter very well! My butter sales

should more than pay for the wages and keep of Wilbur. Jim is growing famous hereabouts for his fine herd of Holsteins. People come to *us* these days to buy calves, and ask advice.

Am uneasy in my mind about George and Satie. Something in her letters what is not qwite right. More what she does *not* say, that is disturbing. Jim says I am only content when I am worried about something. If I could but get across to De Pere, but it is out of the qwestshun. Tho' they would not admit it, Jim and Matthew need me more than ever these days; and there is always Jon.

July 20
The dryest spring and summer I can remember. Our Hay crop looks to be the heaviest we have ever known. The girl Mary is wanted home to help her father to Hay, just when I needed her the most. But, like I said to her: 'It is only right that your own kin should come first, when it comes to Haying.'

What with feeding the teams, and working all alone in the dairy, I am all tired out.

July 23
Have come to my bureau to record the payment of some Bills, but now that the pen is in my hand and, weary as I am, I find that I must set down what has come to pass, lest I should lie awake the whole night.

Satie came last evening. Matthew was down to the harness-shop picking up some tackle, when he spied her and baby coming from the railroad depot. He brought her into the kitchen just as I had set supper on the table.

I was so pleased to see them, my heart was near to bursting. I held out my arms, and Satie came to me, and at once began to weep, what set the baby crying.

'Oh, what is it?' said I. 'Has Georgie had some mishap? Is it your mother?'

'No, no! George thinks I am stopping over at my mother's house. But I need to talk to you so bad, Mother Black!'

467

We put the little one to bed. Satie is by this time much calmed down. I am not happy about her leaving De Pere without telling George but much releeved that she is come to *us*.

We sit out on the front porch in the evening cool, and Satie tells me all what is in her heart. First of all, she is again with child, the baby due early in the New Year. I calculate, and then remember. I say: 'The first three months are always the worst. It was ever so in my case. I grew upset at every little thing. Poor George tried all he knew to please me.'

I wait to see her smile at this. When she does not, I know that the trouble must go deeper. She sits, head bowed, her hands clasped tight together.

I say: 'Come now, Satie, whatever is it? What has my boy done to upset you so?'

She says: 'It's not so much what he does, as what he does not do. I hardly ever see him these days. Oh, I should not be saying this to you – you are his mother . . .'

'And you,' I say gently, 'are as a daughter to me. Father Black and I love you dearly, Satie. If George is in any way at fault, then he shall *hear* from *me*.'

She says: 'He still hankers to leave Brown County. He still longs for Chicago and the different life there. Business is not so good in De Pere. Several mills have closed down lately. Perhaps I should give way, and say that I will go . . .?'

I look at her, and see how young she is, how frail. With Alma only nine months old, and another baby coming, she would likely die of home-sickness if parted from her family. I remember Susanna, and the loneliness of a strange place, what broke her heart and cut short her young life.

I say: 'Now listen to me, Satie. You and Georgie are young. There are many years ahead of you, and Chicago has sat in Illinnois these several decades. It will still be there when Georgie is more established, when your children are older, when you are content to leave your mother and sisters. Why, Father Black and I have hardly glimpsed our granddaughter yet! If you moved to Chicago, then we should never see you more! As for my George, well you just leave him to his mother!'

468

July 31
Satie stayed with us until Sunday. I wanted awful bad to keep
her and Baby; it would have been so nice for her to see the last
of the hay come down. But I knew that Rosa would never
forgive her if she did not go to Oshkosh on her way back to De
Pere. In any case, it will do George *good* to be without her for a
few days more.

Baby is so wise and full of fun. Father Black and I could
hardly bear to be parted from her. Satie makes such a lovely
mother. My George should be the proudest man living, as I
wrote and told him. In fact, I wrote him a very stiff letter and
have worried ever since in case I have upset him. Find that
motherhood gets even more *ankshus* as the children grow older.

August 12
The barn is all full of Hay, and two loads on the threshing
floor. Also stacked outside is another twelve tons, all put up in
good shape. Oh, but it was hard work this year! The McInnes
family helped us stack, our team and Vickery's mowed and
drawed, while Almer Davies helped out. This week we have
stacked for McInnes, and for Elizabeth and Robert.

A letter comes from De Pere. Satie writes that George
received my letter, and was very qwiet for some days after.
(Can only guess that he was *thinking over* what I wrote.)

The good news is that all is now well between them. Satie
feeling better in her health, and business picking-up again for
George.

February 25, 1887
Another year, and I don't know where the time has gone. We
are grandparents again. A second daughter born to George and
Satie. They have named her Rosalind, but already little Alma,
who cannot say the long word, has shortened it to Lola, what
Jim and I think very 'cute and sweet.

Satie writes a cheerful letter. It seems that Lola was born at
her grandma Annas's house at about six o'clock in the evening.
After the first warning that the baby was coming, Satie went

469

into her mother's kitchen and *stirred-up a cake*. A thing that she says amused Doctor Kersten very much when he arrived.

Satie is such a good cook. She keeps a recipe book what qwite puts my plain English cooking in the shade. She is such a dear girl! She says that the new baby is dark-haired and not so fair-complected as Alma, who is the very image of George. It will be nice for Satie if Lola turns out to favour the Annas family in her looks.

May 16

Today we stand together in the tiny cemetery.

There are as yet but a few graves, this place being newly-settled, and the populace being mostly young folk. It is a sheltered spot, set away from habitashun. Our beloved Jon is the first of our family to be laid there. The sickness I had always feared took him mercifully qwick. A heavy cold, pneumonia, and within hours his span of one-and-twenty years was at an end.

I am supported on either hand by Elizabeth and Jim.

My sister says:

'He would not have lived so long and happy, had you stayed down in Chicago.'

Jim says:

'We will have a little stone laid, with his name and dates carved on it.'

I only know that from this day forth we shall sit three around the supper table.

I say:

'When we get home I beg you to go out straightway and take down the poultry houses. Give all geese and turkeys to any needy soul that wants them. There are some reminders that I cannot bear to live with.'

Chapter Twenty-Nine

May 12, 1888

This pen feels strange in my hand after such long absence. I have been sick for many months. Such a melancholy took me after Jon died. As if the mainspring of my life was gone, and no reason to wake up each morning. I have been such a great trial to Jim and Matthew tho' they will not have it!

'See what sickness you have nursed us thru',' they tell me. 'Let us take our turn to cosset you.'

It is one year ago today since we lost Jon. I have put off my black, my mourning bonnet. I owe a duty to the living. I walk to the cemetary in the sweet May morning, and look at the tree what Jim has planted, and the little carved stone with Jon's name writ on it. I feel better for the visit.

I come home, and there are letters from Rosa and Satie, long unanswered. The orchard trees are in full blossom. I stand with Jim in the blessed sunshine.

I say: 'I think I could take up my pen again now.'

He says: 'Perhaps we should have bees, this year. Young Ferguson makes first rate hives. How about that, eh Rhoda? You surely would like bees to talk with!'

September 21

Such a strange happening. Even now, I can scarce believe it.

We have brought in the last corn. Jim and Wilbur are havesting the pumpkins. Matthew is repairing the Hog-house. I am gathering gooseberries.

I see a man, a stranger, coming thru' the stubble field beside the railroad trestle. He is old, his shoulders bowed, his hair grey. I think he is one of those wandering men who ride the trains without benefit of ticket. We have often spied them, Jim and I ,

471

as they slide down from a freight car, when the engine slows before the depot.

I turn back to my task. I think how good the fruits have been this year. First the raspberries, then the blueberries. Red and black currants were abundant. A voice close beside me says:

'Good evening, Rhoda.'

It is an English voice. I set down my basket. I look close into the haggard features.

I say in a tone of disbelief: 'Mark? Can it be you, Mark?'

He smiles, and it is that old charming grin that tells me it is him.

I say, stupidly: 'Wherever have you come from? You always turn up unexpected!'

He gestures back towards the trestle. 'I stepped down from the train a mite early – I saw you picking fruit . . .'

He sways a little, and seems bound to fall among the bushes. I take his arm, and am upset and shocked to feel the pointy bones, the thinness of him.

October

Mark sleeps in Jon's old room. He eats, but sparingly and without pleashur. He is skin and bone, and that skin an awful yellow colour. He will not see the doctor. He says he saw doctors back in England. There is nothing to be done, so will I please let the matter lie! He is come to make his peace with Elizabeth and me. We cannot help but be touched at such a gesture. Our brother has come four thousand miles for our forgiveness and our understanding.

It takes a week of rest before he is strong enough for talk. When he speaks it is with regret. He tells us of the lawsuits; the final outcome when the House of Lords found in favour of the family. The swift decline in our oldest brother James when he was at last forced to share with his brothers and sisters. It is a sad, unedifying tale.

Mark comes at last to his own part in all this. He confesses to a kind of madness, once back in England. We wait to hear the story of Miss Henrietta Martin.

Mark has a shamed look. 'I had never,' he says, 'in all my life allowed a woman to dominate me. But Henrietta is unmanageable, like new-washed hair, or an unbroken stallion. As you all know, she was engaged to marry James. When he died – she turned to me. I could see she had marriage in mind. Well, she was fifty-eight years old and I must have looked like a last chance of matrimony. Oh my sisters! That is a powerfully persuasive female! Within three months of our brother's dying, the Banns went up in Buckland church. She is clever, too. I never understood the rights of her finanshul dealings, but she had poor old James tied up tighter than a pig for slaughter. She now owns outright the house that we grew up in. She claimed all Jame's belongings; his valuable Law Books, his leather Wallet, the busts and silver that Father left him. She even sold his shoes and clothing. She perswaded me that I must drive Joan and Mary from the door whenever they came calling.'

He pauses. 'I can't believe I did those things. We rode to our wedding in a fancy carriage. No family of mine had an invitashun. As we came to the church I saw sister Mary, standing by the lych-gate. I saw the hurt face of her, the tears, and I knew I had done wrong, but it was all too late. Within the week I was resolved to leave such a virago. Henrietta was impossible to live with.'

Elizabeth pours tea and takes it to Mark.

I say: 'But this was all of seven years ago!'

He says: 'Confesshun may be good for the immortal soul, Rhoda! But, like the Americans say, "That don't come easy." When I left Henrietta I set out for London. Well, I had been paid my share of Father's Estate, I was not exactly penniless. I did a bit of dealing here and there. I also had the hundred pounds from the Treasury Office – the money due to Elizabeth and you from Jame's Estate. As time went on, I was more and more ashamed to face you.'

He halts; he looks from Elizabeth to me. He says: 'I know how it must look to you – but I swear I had no intenshun of robbing either of you. It was always in my mind to come back here.' He grins. 'Guess I'm more of an American than an

473

Englishman, after all. Anyways, I've come back here to die, and that should tell you something!'

He looks so sick and frail that we can none of us argue with his words. In fact, I am surprised that he survived the long voyage out from England.

I say: 'You are welcome to stay here . . .'

Elizabeth says: 'You can come across to our place . . .'

'I think not.' Mark smiles. 'I have old friends down to Oshkosh. There's a cabin in the woods, close beside Lake Winnebago. I used to stay there years ago. The fishing's good. I have a fancy to be on my own.'

'But winter's coming on!'

'Don't fret yourself, Rhoda. I shan't see Christmas.'

He pulls from his pocket a wad of banknotes. He divides them into two halves, and hands one to Elizabeth and one to me.

He says: 'I can't make up for the trouble I have caused you, but this is something that I had to do.' He grins. 'Who knows? St Peter may look more favourably on me now when I reach the Pearly Gates?'

Elizabeth and I exchange a long look. We remember him as a boy, his refusal to cry when hurt, his bravado.

I say: 'I can't bear to think of you alone . . .'

Elizabeth says: 'Won't you be perswaded . . .?'

'I shall be on the morning train for Oshkosh,' says Mark, 'but I thank you, kindly sisters, for your offers.'

Elizabeth and Robert make their farewells, for they will not see him more. Jim and I drive him to the depot. It is a sad parting. We watch until the red caboose is out of sight. The train whistle has such a lonely note, what I had never noticed until now.

We ride slowly home thru' the sunshine of this late October.

December 12

Two letters come, one from Washington and one from De Pere. I hand the offishul-looking envelope to Jim. We start to read. We both begin to speak together.

'Well, what d'you know?' he shouts, 'they've granted me a

Penshun, back-dated it as well – it's way over twelve hundred dollars.'

'Satie says we're to be grandparents again – early next May, she thinks . . .'

We lay our letters down and beam at one another.

March 28, 1889
We come home from Sunday morning Service to find Georgie standing on the front porch looking at the sqwills, what are very early this year, and a real carpet of blue flowers. My first thought is how handsome he looks, and how much like his father. We go into the house. Georgie says that he came over on the train. There are lines of worry in his face.

He talks throughout the meal, but only about business matters.

Later on, when he and I sit together in the parlour, and Jim and Matthew are at the evening-milking, George says: 'You haven't asked me a single word about Satie and the children.'

'I am waiting,' I say gently, 'for you to tell me all, George. You are uneasy in your mind about something, and, from what you've said so far, you have no business problems.'

'It's Satie!' he bursts out. 'Oh, Mama, she's been real sick with this coming baby. Fainting-spells, and hardly keeping any food down and so weepy and depressed – why you'd hardly know her for the same girl I married.' He sighs. 'She was never like this with Alma and Lola. I just can't understand it.'

I begin to smile and nod my head.

'Nothing to fret over, George. This child is bound to be a boy – that's all that ails her. It's what we call 'a change of birth' back in Old England. A woman carries daughters without a mite of trouble – but sons – now that's a very different matter!'

★

It was the hour when Father Black and Wilbur cleaned the cowstalls and filled the mangers with fresh hay; when Mother Black and Mary churned butter and scalded cream-pans in the dairy. Alma was in the field with Matthew, helping him to plant potatoes.

Satie walked alone in the April morning.

Today, she was twenty-three years old. She was staying on Mother Black's farm, while she awaited the birth of her child. George had written her a most devoted letter. He had sent a card, the edges of which were threaded all around with pink satin ribbon, and in the middle was painted a picture of red roses. She carried the card in her skirt pocket, not bearing to be parted from it.

Leaving Lola had been the hardest thing; even more upsetting had been the little girl's willingness to go stay with her Grandma Annas. Satie recalled the unconcerned wave of the small hand as she and George had walked away. But it was, he had said, a fair division of favours that each doting grandmother should have a child to spoil.

Satie herself had been fussed over like any ailing child, and already the nausea which had plagued her in recent times was giving way to sharp hunger. Her nerves had steadied, the tension of months begun to slacken. She had even started to believe that the child she carried was the son George longed for.

She walked very slowly in these final days, so slowly that she took in every slightest change, each new blossoming and blooming. She looked from the deep pink of the currant bushes, to the paler shades of plum and apple blossom. It had rained in the early morning. Now the air was damp and heavy with a mixture of fragrance she could not define. The lilac bush beside the kitchen door was in full bloom. Bees came and went from the row of white-painted hives that stood beneath the cherry trees. Mother Black spoke of honey as a keen connoisseur might mention rare wines; she talked of basswood honey, linden and clover. Satie felt the weight of ancient wisdom contained in this one small Englishwoman; and yet there was such a youthfulness about her. Satie's heart had ached for Rhoda in that year of mourning which had followed Jon's death. When the suggestion had been made that this third baby should be born in the Suamico farmhouse, she had not been sure that it would be altogether fair on the hardworking farmers.

476

'But all her life,' said George, 'Mama has had somebody dependent on her. It's in her nature to care for people. Don't disappoint her, Satie.'

So she had come; into this place where the world turned according to the changing seasons, into this house where people had learned to live comfortably together. She heard, for the first time, the curious dialect English spoken only between Elizabeth and Rhoda. She saw the devotion of the sisters, each to the other. Their quality of Englishness was strong and yet not easy to define. There was always that reserve, that little stiffness of manner, thought by the unobservant to reveal the whole person. Yet, for those who took time to look deeper, there was merriment lurking, a dry brand of humour, and a kindness and compassion that had no need for spoken words.

From her bedroom window Satie saw the pale hay ripening in May sunshine; the corn standing straight and green, the great red-painted barn and the adjoining dairy. The square fields stretched away to meet forests of tall pine; beyond lay Michigan's green lake waters. Blue jays scolded in the woods; she could smell the heavy scent of lilacs.

She thought about George, who no longer spoke about Chicago, but still longed to go there. She considered, for the first time, the nature of the child so soon to be born; the child who would be half-American – half-English. It had never seemed to matter in the case of the girls; daughters grew up beneath their mother's wing. But a boy would be the concern of George; father and son would need to work together in the business. Perhaps he would have the Salter acumen and keenness when it came to doing business? Or maybe there would be some of Rhoda in him, that English love of land and livestock? He might be a musician, like her own father?

She began to move, away from the open window, and restlessly around the room. All had been made ready for her confinement. She smoothed a hand across the bedspread, quilted in a design called Grand-mother's Flower Garden. The sheets were lavender-scented, the pillow slips embroidered; on the

477

dressing table stood a bowl of pot pourri; on her bedside table a crock of her favourite cinnamon cookies lest she get hungry in the night hours.

Satie smiled at the thoughtfulness of Rhoda, the style of her; and all at once, she was seized by the first sharp pangs of birth.

★

May 19, 1889

Our grandson is born in the early morning of this day. He comes into the world to the sound of cowbells, and the peewees singing in the orchard trees.

I go down straightway and tell the good news to my bees.

Jim hastens to the railroad depot and waits while the message is tapped out, to be relayed to Georgie in De Pere.

My boy comes at sundown. He goes at once to Satie and there are tears in his eyes. He kisses her, and then lifts the baby from the cradle. He studies the tiny features.

'George Hodder Salter,' he whispers, 'for the third generation in this land.'

He touches his son's face. He speaks to the child in a voice so low that I must needs strain to hear him.

'We'll ride out together you and I, into the country. You shall become as fine a judge of beef on the hoof as was your grandfather from England. As soon as you're grown enough, you shall help me drive the cattle home for slaughter.

'Oh, I've got such plans for us, my son! I shall have a new sign painted, *George Hodder Salter and Son. Purveyors of The Finest Meat in De Pere, Brown County.*'

So now Georgie has another dream; and this time it is good and one which will not take him into danger. Each new generashun learns a little wisdom from those who have gone before.

I walk over to see Elizabeth in the cool of evening. She also rejoices. News has come to her this day of the birth of her first grandson.

'So,' I say, 'the names of Vickery and Salter are assured.'

Elizabeth smiles. 'I guess,' says she, 'that we can truly say now that we belong here.'

I walk home thru' the sweet May dimpsey-light, and watch the stars come out in the wide heavens of Wisconsin.

It was a dream that brought Robert Vickery out from Buckland St Mary. The same dream that called to my own dear George in Dorchester, Old England; and what is a man's life worth, in the end, if he has no star of hope to follow?.

AUTHOR'S
EPILOGUE
1989

One hundred years on, and Wisconsin in the fall is still a place of warm days and cold nights. The sun hangs low in the western heavens, it dapples the ground beneath the sugar-maples, seems to set alight the crimson sumac that grows at roadsides. There are scents of ripened apples, and here and there a wild plum tree can be found among the heavy musk of cut crops and turned earth. At night a red moon lights the stubble fields, finding out the pumpkins that are golden and heavy on the vine, still waiting to be gathered in.

The great forests of pine no longer stretch away to the horizon. The road that leads north is no more an Indian trail but a multi-laned highway. The traveller is offered hospitality these days at pull-ins called Dino's Diner and the Lunch Box, where may be sampled hickory-smoked sausage, and the best hot coffee and cinnamon scones in all Wisconsin.

When she is just minutes away from her destination, the seeker grows weary. The journey from England has been swift and easy. She has not, after all, come as Rhoda did, on a packet-ship under sail, nor endured a voyage of six weeks. Even so, she is jet-lagged. The only motel that she can find is luxurious, air-conditioned and expensive. From the window of her room she has a clear view of the green and gold colours of the Green Bay Packers' Football Stadium. Most of her fellow guests will be fans who have come up to Lambeau Field to cheer-on the game.

In the morning, when she is rested and her head no longer throbs, the motel manager directs her.

'Suamico, ma'am? Why you just turn left off Highway 41.

483

Take Exit B West. You'll see the signs from hereon in. Well worth a visit, ma'am, that is if your fancy is for history and old things.'

Her fancy is very much for history and old things.

She takes Exit B West, and knows in her bones that this must be the trail taken by those first English pioneers who came here to fell the pine, build their log-houses, and cultivate the land. She drives slowly, and here is the Suamico River running low between its banks after the dry summer. Here, still, are the great red barns, the neat and tidy farmsteads. New furrows are ploughed these days in the ancient cornfields. Ownership has passed into other hands. But the name of Vickery, she will discover, is still as much a part of Suamico as the old trees that shade the Town Square; and, in this Square known as Vickery Village, one lovingly restored building stands beside another. The little White Pine School is set close to the original Town Hall. The old Rooming House, once run by Albert Sensiba, has been brought from its marshy riverside site: seven layers of old paint have needed to be removed, in its refurbishing; but the scars made by lumberjacks' hobnailed boots are still to be seen in the floors of soft pine. The General Store, bought by the young Robbie Vickery, in 1905, is still a meeting place for the whole village.

There are faded photographs, old patchwork quilts. The frame farmhouses, once the pride of Elizabeth and Rhoda, are still charming residences. The little white Episcopal church, for the building of which so many basket-socials needed to be held, so many fund-raising suppers given, stands perfectly preserved on Riverside Drive.

The cemetery is small and neat, a place where Scot and German, Scandinavian and French, Polish and Irish, lie companionably together. Salters and Vickerys are side by side. The seeker from England is beginning to believe that, in this quiet village, the dead continue to hold tenure of all that was once theirs.

She makes notes and compares dates.

She finds Jon's marker and that of Matthew.

484

Elizabeth, Rhoda and Captain James Kerr Black have all lived on into great age.

Rhoda has survived Elizabeth by only three months.

Rhoda has survived her husband by only fourteen days.

Highway 41 leads directly back to Oshkosh. Here lives the grand-daughter of that handsome girl, Rosa Salter, who married young Thomas Gillingham, maker of Carriages and Sleighs.

A recent find of precious old family letters is shared. Copies of those letters are made to be carried back to England.

The fine adventuring spirit that brought the first George Hodder Salter out from Dorchester, England, still burns bright in his descendants. There are Salters to be found in many States of the Union, and all in honourable professions. They count among their number distinguished soldiers, professors and doctors, teachers and respected men of business.

It is in Waukesha, from a granddaughter of Satie and George, that the seeker learns the ending of the story. She is shown more photographs. She sees the sepia-tinted likeness of the young Sarah Ann Annas, that quiet unassuming lady, who bore ten living children, all of them remarkable and beautiful in their separate ways.

She hears how Georgie, the boy who had witnessed the Great Fire of Chicago, and who had so loved that city, returned there in his fifty-second year to become the man of business that had always been his dream.

It is possible to seek for truth in distant places and find that the lives of men and women, long dead, still hold more than a whisper of the glory they once possessed.

THE END